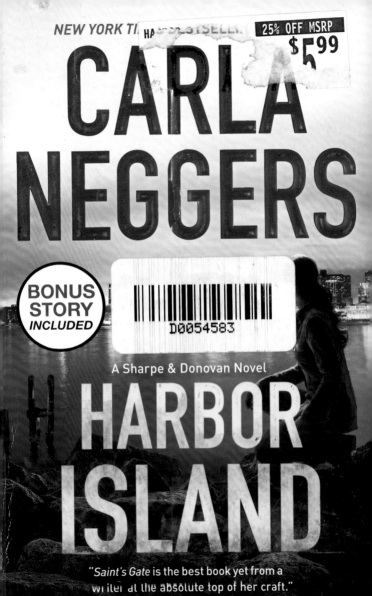

CARLA NEGGERS

D0054583

A Sharpe & Donovan Novel

HARBOR ISLAND

"*Saint's Gate* is the best book yet from a
writer at the absolute top of her craft."
—*Providence Journal*

ISBN-13: 978-0-7783-1779-1

MIRA®

www.MIRABooks.com

MCN0415IFC

Praise for Carla Neggers and her novels

"Neggers delivers another spellbinding, chilling, complex page-turner in this latest Sharpe & Donovan novel."

—*RT Book Reviews*, Top Pick

"Neggers' Sharpe & Donovan series has developed a wide following, and her books maintain a potent combination of suspense and romance."

—*Kirkus Reviews*

"Well-plotted, intriguing and set mostly in the lushly described Irish countryside, the novel is smart and satisfying, and the paths of three couples growing even more devoted to each other are deftly woven into the suspenseful story line."

—*Kirkus Reviews* on *Declan's Cross*

"Neggers' beautifully flowing and skillfully narrated novel is rich with dialogue that emphasizes the sights, sounds, culture and panoramic views of Ireland. Emma and Colin are as unforgettable as ever."

—*RT Book Reviews*, Top Pick, on *Declan's Cross*

"*Heron's Cove* gives romantic suspense fans what they want...complex mystery with a bit of romance. Neggers skillfully created a compelling puzzle, refusing to reveal all the pieces until the very end."

—*RT Book Reviews*, Top Pick

"*Saint's Gate* is the best book yet from a writer at the absolute top of her craft."

—*Providence Journal*

"With a great plot and excellent character development, Neggers' thriller *Saint's Gate*, the first in a new series, is a fast-paced, action-packed tale of romantic suspense that will appeal to fans of Lisa Jackson and Lisa Gardner."

—*Library Journal*

Also by Carla Neggers

Sharpe & Donovan Series

DECLAN'S CROSS
ROCK POINT (novella)
HERON'S COVE
SAINT'S GATE

Swift River Valley Series

ECHO LAKE
CHRISTMAS AT
   CARRIAGE HILL (novella)
CIDER BROOK
THAT NIGHT ON
   THISTLE LANE
SECRETS OF THE
   LOST SUMMER

BPD/FBI Series

THE WHISPER
THE MIST
THE ANGEL
THE WIDOW

Black Falls Series

COLD DAWN
COLD RIVER
COLD PURSUIT

Cold Ridge/U.S. Marshals Series

ABANDON
BREAKWATER
DARK SKY
THE RAPIDS
NIGHT'S LANDING
COLD RIDGE

Carriage House Series

THE HARBOR
STONEBROOK COTTAGE
THE CABIN
THE CARRIAGE HOUSE

Stand-Alone Novels

THE WATERFALL
ON FIRE
KISS THE MOON
TEMPTING FATE
CUT AND RUN
BETRAYALS
CLAIM THE CROWN

Look for Carla Neggers' next novel
in the Sharpe & Donovan series

KEEPER'S REACH

available soon from MIRA Books

CARLA
NEGGERS

HARBOR
ISLAND

MIRA®

MIRA®

ISBN-13: 978-0-7783-1779-1

Harbor Island
Copyright © 2014 by Carla Neggers

Rock Point
Copyright © 2013 by Carla Neggers

For questions and comments about the quality of this book, please contact us at CustomerService@Harlequin.com.

www.MIRABooks.com

Printed in U.S.A.

To Uncle John and Aunt Martha

HARBOR ISLAND

One

Boston, Massachusetts

As she wound down her run on the Boston waterfront, Emma Sharpe could feel the effects of jet lag in every stride. Three days home from Dublin, she was still partly on Irish time and had awakened early on the cool November Saturday. She'd strapped her snub-nosed .38 onto her hip, slipped into her worn-out running shoes and was off. With less than a half mile left in her five-mile route, she was confident she hadn't been followed. Not that as an art-crimes specialist she was an expert at spotting a tail, but she *was* an FBI agent and knew the basics.

Matt Yankowski, the special agent in charge of the small Boston-based unit Emma had joined in March, hadn't minced words when he'd addressed his agents yesterday on a video conference call. "This Sharpe thief knows who we are. He knows where we work. It's also possible he knows where we live. If he doesn't, he could be trying to find out. Be extra vigilant." Yank had looked straight at Emma. "Especially you, Emma."

Yes. Especially her.

This Sharpe thief.

Well, it was true. She was, after all, the granddaughter of Wendell Sharpe, the octogenarian private art detective who had been on the trail of this particular serial art thief for a decade. Her brother, Lucas, now at the helm of Sharpe Fine Art Recovery, was also deeply involved in the stepped-up search for their thief, a clever, brazen individual—probably a man—who had managed to elude capture since his first heist in a small village on the south Irish coast.

Emma slowed her pace and turned onto the wharf where she had a small, ground-level apartment in a three-story brick building that had once been a produce warehouse. Her front windows looked out on a marina that shared the wharf. A nice view, but people passing by to get to their boats would often stop outside her windows for a chat, a cigarette, a phone call. Although she'd grown up on the water in southern Maine, she hadn't expected her Boston apartment to be such a fishbowl when she'd snapped it up in March, weeks before the boating season.

Had the thief peeked in her windows one day?

She ducked into her apartment, expecting to find Colin still in bed or on the sofa drinking coffee. Special Agent Colin Donovan. A deep-cover agent, another Mainer and her fiancé as of four days ago. He'd proposed to her in a Dublin pub. "Emma Sharpe, I'm madly in love with you, and I want to be with you forever."

She smiled at the memory as she checked the cozy living area, bedroom and bathroom. Colin wasn't anywhere in the 300-square-foot apartment they now more or less shared. Then she found the note he'd scrawled on the back of an envelope and left on the counter next to the coffee press in the galley kitchen. "Back soon."

Not a man to waste words.

He'd filled the kettle and scooped coffee into the press,

and he'd taken her favorite Maine wild-blueberry jam out of the refrigerator.

Still smiling, Emma headed for the shower. She was wide awake after her run, early even by her standards. After three weeks in Ireland, she and Colin had thoroughly adapted to the five-hour time difference. Their stay started with a blissful couple of weeks in an isolated cottage, getting to know each other better. Then they got caught up in the disappearance and murder of an American diver and dolphin-and-whale enthusiast named Lindsey Hargreaves. Now, back home in Boston, Emma was reacquainting herself with Eastern Standard Time.

Making love with Colin last night had helped keep her from falling asleep at eight o'clock—one in the morning in Ireland. He seemed impervious to jet lag. His undercover work with its constant dangers and frequent time-zone changes no doubt had helped, but Emma also suspected he was just like that.

Colin would know if someone tried to follow him. No question.

She pulled on a bathrobe and headed back to the kitchen. She made coffee and toast and took them to her inexpensive downsize couch, which was pushed up against an exposed-brick wall and perpendicular to the windows overlooking the marina. She collected up a stack of photographs she and Colin had pulled out last night, including one of herself as a novice at twenty-one. Colin had put it under the light and commented on her short hair and "sensible" shoes. She wore her hair longer now, and although she would never be one for four-inch heels, her shoes and boots were more fashionable than the ones she'd worn at the convent.

Colin had peered closer at the photo. "Ah, but look at that cute smile and the spark in your green eyes." He'd grinned at her. "Sister Brigid was just waiting for a rugged lobsterman to wander into her convent."

Emma had gone by the name Brigid during her short time as a novice with the Sisters of the Joyful Heart, a small order on a quiet peninsula not far from her hometown on the southern Maine coast. In September, a longtime member of the convent and Emma's former mentor, an expert in art conservation, was murdered. Yank had dispatched Colin to keep an eye on her. He'd tried to pass himself off as a lobsterman—he'd been one before joining the Maine marine patrol and then the FBI—but Emma had quickly realized what he was up to.

"I bet you were wearing red lace undies," he'd said as he'd set the photo back on the table.

Emma had felt herself flush. "I don't wear red undies now."

He'd given her one of his sexy, blue-eyed winks. "Wait until Valentine's Day."

They'd abandoned the photos and had ended up in bed, making love until she'd finally collapsed in his arms. He was dark-haired, broad-shouldered and scarred, a man who relied on his natural instincts and experience to size up a situation instantly. He didn't ruminate, and he wasn't one to sit at a desk for more than twenty minutes at a time. She was more analytical, more likely to see all the ins and outs and possibilities—and she was a ruminator.

As different as they were, Emma thought, she and Colin also had similarities. The FBI, their Maine upbringings, their strong families, their love of Ireland. Their whirlwind romance wasn't *all* an "opposites attract" phenomenon, a case of forbidden love that had come on fast and hard. They hadn't told anyone yet of their engagement. On Monday night in Dublin, Colin had presented her with a beautiful diamond ring, handmade by a jeweler on the southwest Irish coast. She'd reluctantly slipped the ring off her finger when they'd arrived at Boston's Logan Airport from Dublin late Tuesday.

Emma was so lost in thought, she jumped when her cell phone vibrated on the table. She scooped it up, expecting to see Colin's name on the screen. Instead, it was a number she didn't recognize. A wrong number? She clicked to answer, but before she could say anything, a woman spoke. "Is this Emma Sharpe? Agent Sharpe with the FBI?"

"Yes, it is. Who are you?"

"What? Oh. My name's Rachel Bristol. I need to talk to you. It's important."

"All right. Please go ahead."

"Not on the phone. In person. Meet me on Bristol Island. It's in Boston Harbor. There's a bridge. You don't have to take a boat."

"Ms. Bristol, what's this about?"

"It's about your art thief. Bristol Island, Agent Sharpe. Be at the white cottage in thirty minutes or less. There's a trail by the marina." She paused. "Come alone. Please. I will talk only to you."

Rachel Bristol—or whoever she was—disconnected.

Emma sprang to her feet. Thirty minutes didn't give her much time.

She ran to her bedroom and dressed in dark jeans, a dark blue sweater, a leather jacket and boots. She grabbed her credentials and strapped on her service pistol. She didn't leave a note for Colin. She would text him on the way.

Meeting confidential informants was a tricky business even with protocols, training and experience. But it didn't matter. Not this time.

Her thief.

Her problem.

Two

"Check the bathroom," Matt Yankowski said, making an obvious effort to hide his mix of urgency and irritation over the whereabouts of his wife, Lucy.

Colin Donovan frowned as he stood on the uneven wood floor in the sole bedroom of the senior FBI agent's hovel of an apartment near Boston's South Station. It was bigger than Emma's, but it had roaches and rusted appliances and a shower out of *Psycho*. He'd had a quick peek into the bathroom. He hadn't gone in and checked for signs of Lucy's presence. What was the point? If he'd been Lucy Yankowski, he'd have gone running from this place, too.

But this was Yank, technically Colin's boss and a man on his own in Ireland, worried about his wife and his marriage. Colin didn't want Yank to have to explain. Easier, smoother and more tactful just to check the damn bathroom.

Colin pushed the bathroom door open the rest of the way and stepped onto the cracked black-and-white hexagon tile, so old and worn that the black tiles by the shower stall were now gray. With his cell phone pressed to his ear, he glanced at the pedestal sink and the towel rack. "Yank, do you know your towel rack is on crooked?"

"Yeah, and I don't care. It does the job. See anything?"

"Guy stuff. Shaving brush, shaving soap, razor. Nothing remotely feminine."

"Check the shower. See if she left her shampoo in there."

"I guarantee you she didn't use the shower. She'd have gone to a hotel before she used your shower, Yank. Damn."

"Just check, will you?"

"That means I have to touch the shower curtain."

"It's clean. It's just stained. It came with the place. I didn't want to spring for a new one."

"You can get a new shower curtain for next to nothing."

Yank made no comment. Colin pulled open the curtain. He figured he could wash his hands when he was done. Yank was tidy and clean despite his rathole apartment, but the shower and shower curtain were disgusting. Only word for it.

"No shampoo at all in here," Colin said, stepping back from the shower. "Just a bar of orange soap."

"My coal-tar soap. I didn't bring it to Ireland with me."

"I could have gone my whole life without knowing you use coal-tar soap, Yank."

"Think I like having you search my place?"

Colin sighed and went back into the bedroom. "Lucy wasn't here, or if she was, she didn't stay long. Your bed's made. Your fridge is empty. Your bathroom and kitchen sinks are clean. The roaches—"

"I don't need to hear about the roaches," Yank said. "I've been living there almost a year. I know all about the damn roaches. I got a cheap place and rent month-to-month because I thought Lucy would move with me. We would sell our house in northern Virginia and buy a place in Boston. Made sense to rough it a little."

He'd roughed it more than a little, but Colin let it go. He returned to the kitchen. A roach was parading across the floor. Where there was one cockroach, there were a hundred cockroaches. Often like that in their line of work, too. But Yank didn't need to hear that right now.

"Where do you think she is?" Colin asked.

"Off stewing."

"Where?"

"Paris. Prague. Tahiti. How the hell do I know? I'm just her husband."

Colin could hear the strain in Yank's voice. He was in his early forties, a classic, square-jawed, buttoned-down FBI agent with hardly ever a wrinkle in his suit. He and Colin had met four years ago when Colin had volunteered for his first undercover mission. Matt Yankowski, a legendary field agent, had been his contact agent through two years of grueling, dangerous, isolating work. Then the director of the FBI had called in Colin for another mission—one even more grueling, dangerous and isolating. It had ended in October with the arrest of the last of a network of ruthless illegal arms traffickers. They'd almost killed his family. A friend. *Emma*.

"When was the last time you were in contact with Lucy?" Colin asked.

"Sunday. Before I left for Ireland. It wasn't a good conversation. Leave it at that. I called her on Thursday and left her a message. She didn't call back. I texted and emailed her yesterday and again this morning. Zip."

"Did you tell her you were going to Ireland?"

"No, I did not." Yank grunted, as if he was already regretting having called Colin. "All right, thanks for taking a look. I just wanted to be sure she wasn't in Boston passed out in my apartment."

"What about passed out at home in Virginia?"

"Not your problem."

"Yank, I don't have to tell you that you need her back in touch soon. With all that's going on, we can't have your wife AWOL."

"That's right, Donovan. You don't have to tell me."

"Yank…" Colin hesitated a half beat. "Have you talked to the director lately?"

"Yeah. He says he's retiring." Yank sounded relieved at the change in subject. "He's moving to Mount Desert Island to be a grandfather and write his memoirs. That's why you two bonded, you know. He loves Maine."

"Maybe he and I could do puffin tours together."

"I could see that, but I don't know who'd scare tourists more, you or him. I've heard some rumors about his replacement. All the names give me hives, but it'll be what it'll be. Hey, you wouldn't want to spray for roaches before you leave my place, would you? There's a can of Raid under the sink."

A can of Raid and a million roaches. Colin debated, then said, "I'll spray for roaches if you stop at the Celtic Whiskey Shop on Dawson Street in Dublin before you leave and pick me up a good bottle of Irish whiskey."

"Done."

"Let me know when Lucy is back in touch."

Colin disconnected. He sprayed for roaches—and sprayed actual roaches—and then got the hell out of Yank's walk-up as fast as he could. The only reason the place didn't have rats was because it was on the third floor. Needless to say, there was no security in the building. There was barely a front door.

Colin welcomed the bright, cool November air. He had woken up to Yank's email asking him to check his apartment for Lucy and telling him where to find a spare key in his office a few blocks from Emma's place. She'd already left on her run. Bemused by Yank's request, Colin had walked over to the highly secure, unassuming waterfront building that housed HIT, short for "high impact target" and the name Yank had chosen for his handpicked team. Yank had shoehorned Colin into HIT in October. Colin had packed his bags for Ireland a few weeks later to decompress. He'd expected to hike the Irish hills and drink Irish whiskey and Guinness alone, but Emma had joined him in his little cottage in the Kerry hills. She hadn't waited for an invitation, but that was Emma Sharpe. His ex-nun, art historian, art conservationist, art-crimes expert—the love of his life—was the bravest woman he knew. Which had its downside, since she'd do anything regardless of the risk.

He saw he had a text message from her.

Meeting CI on Bristol Island. Back soon. Had a good run.

A confidential informant? Emma? Bristol Island? Where the hell was Bristol Island? Colin texted back.

Are you alone?

He buttoned his coat and continued toward the HIT offices and her apartment, looking up Bristol Island on his phone. It was one of more than thirty Boston Harbor islands, unusual in that it was privately owned and not part of the Boston Harbor National Recreational Area. He waited but Emma didn't respond to his text. He didn't want to call her in the middle of a delicate meeting. As with Lucy Yankowski, Emma's silence didn't necessarily mean anything.

It didn't necessarily not mean anything, either.

Three

Emma picked her way across the cold, hard sand beach at the far end of Bristol Island, which was connected to a mainland peninsula by a short, private bridge. It barely qualified as an island. She'd parked at a marina—the upscale Bristol Island Marina, quiet on a Saturday morning in late November—and found the trail her caller had mentioned. She'd followed it through a tangle of mostly stunted, mostly bare-branched trees and brush, a few rust-colored leaves hanging from the occasional gray branch. The trail ended at a crescent-shaped beach dotted with a half-dozen run-down cottages that looked as if they were one good nor'easter from being swept into the harbor.

The only white cottage was the second one, tucked between a gray-shingled cottage that had all but collapsed into the sand and a tiny brown cottage, the only one with its windows boarded up. Water, sand, trees and brush had encroached on what yards the cottages had once had. They looked to be about a hundred years old, probably a former summer colony of families who had once enjoyed sea breezes and clam-digs on this refuge in the shadows of the city.

Emma didn't see any footprints in the mix of sand and sea grass between her and the white cottage. Her caller could have come by a different route, perhaps an offshoot of the trail she had taken. It was low tide. A few scrappy-looking seagulls were investigating the offerings in the lapping waves. The biggest of the lot flew onto a rickety pier and watched her as if it knew something she didn't.

She was aware of the city just across the water, but it seemed as if it should be farther away. In early July, she had taken the inter-island shuttle and explored a few of the islands in the outer harbor. She'd enjoyed a solo picnic with a panoramic view of the Boston skyline. She'd been glad to be back in New England and a member of Matt Yankowski's team, and she'd just played a vital role in the arrest of Viktor Bulgov, Colin's notorious arms trafficker and a Picasso enthusiast. She hadn't known Colin then. She'd only surmised that a deep-cover agent had been tracking Bulgov, gathering evidence on him and his network and their illegal activities.

She stepped over broken beer bottles next to a fire circle piled with charred logs and came to the white cottage, its sagging porch no more than six inches off the sand. Its front door was ajar, but sand that had blown onto the worn floorboards of the porch appeared to be undisturbed.

"Rachel Bristol? It's Emma Sharpe."

A seagull cried behind her, and a breeze stirred in the snarl of bare brush between the white cottage and the ones on either side of it. As she stepped onto the porch, she noticed a red smear and splatters, wet, oozing into the peeling gray paint and cracks of the floorboards to the left of the front door.

Blood.

And pale, slender fingers—a woman's hand, limp and unmoving, on the edge of the porch.

Emma pulled back her jacket and placed a hand on the butt of her nine-millimeter. As she drew her weapon and moved to her left, she saw a woman sprawled on her back in the grass and sand next to the cottage, her left hand flopped onto the porch floor.

Emma responded instantly, leaping off the side of the porch, squatting next to the woman. There was more blood. A lot of it, seeping into the sand, soaking the woman's sweater. Emma checked for a pulse but already knew there was nothing anyone could do. The woman was dead.

Rachel Bristol? Or someone else? Someone her caller had wanted Emma to find?

The dead woman had short, spiked, white-blond hair and wore black toothpick jeans, an unzipped black wool jacket and a light blue sweater, the chest area now red with blood. Her black flats and thin black socks were muddy, unsuited to the conditions on the island.

Emma took a closer look at the wound.

Not a knife wound. Not a wound from an unfortunate fall onto a sharp object. It was, without a doubt, a gunshot wound.

Emma quickly stepped behind a clump of scrawny gray birches, but an active shooter who wanted to target her could have done so by now. She dug out her cell phone and dialed 911, identifying herself as an FBI agent. She related the situation as succinctly as possible. The dispatcher offered to stay on the line with her. She declined.

She disconnected and called Colin. "The woman who wanted to meet me. She's dead, Colin."

"Where are you?"

"I told you. Bristol Island." But she realized what he

meant. "I took cover. I'm safe. I've never seen this woman before. I'm sure I'd remember. If it's the same woman who called me, her name is Rachel Bristol. At least that's what she said her name was."

"We'll figure that out later. You're alone out there. No one else is in danger. Right now, your only job is to stay safe. That's it, Emma. Nothing else."

That would be the case for anyone in her situation. She knew that. "I'm in a good spot."

"I'm on my way," Colin said. "I'll stay on the phone with you until the police get there."

She heard the gulls, their cries sharper, louder, as if they sensed the tragedy that had unfolded up by the white cottage. She leaned forward, without exposing herself as a target, and peered down at the dead woman, seeing now that her right arm was flopped at her side with the palm up.

Emma edged a bit closer, noticing something in the woman's palm.

A small, black stone, polished smooth.

There was some kind of etching that she couldn't make out—but she didn't need to. The stone would be inscribed with a simple Celtic cross and a sketch of Saint Declan, an early medieval Irish saint.

The cross was the signature of an international art thief who had first surfaced ten years ago in the tiny village of Declan's Cross on the south Irish coast.

Her thief, as Yank had put it.

Eight times over the past decade, the thief had laid claim to a recent art heist by sending a small cross-inscribed stone to Wendell Sharpe, Emma's grandfather. Then last week, that pattern changed. Out of the blue— unrelated to any recent art theft—she and her grandfather had both received cross-inscribed stones in Ireland.

So had her brother in Maine, and Matt Yankowski, her boss, in Boston.

"Emma?"

The sound of Colin's deep, intense voice brought her out of her thoughts. "I'm here."

"You're sitting tight, right?"

She heard the urgency in his voice—the fear for her safety—and tried to reassure him. "I am." She ducked back within the branches of the birches. "I'm the patient one, remember?"

By the time the Boston homicide detectives finished up with Emma, the rest of the HIT team had gathered at their waterfront offices. She and Colin were in her car, on their way. He'd taken a cab to Bristol Island and flashed his credentials at the police officers securing the scene, and that was that. No one had stopped him. When he and Emma walked back to the marina, he'd had her toss him her keys. She hadn't argued. She ached from tension, jet lag, her run—from the searing reality that she had come upon a woman who had just been shot to death.

"You didn't charm the detectives," Colin said when they were almost to HIT's building. "I thought you might."

"I'm not in a charming mood."

"As in a mood to charm or a mood that charms?"

"Both. Either."

"I never charm anyone."

He'd conducted more than a few death investigations during his three years with the Maine marine patrol. She didn't have that experience. Didn't want it. But she knew what to do in an active shooter situation, and she'd done it.

"You're right, though," she said. "The detectives aren't happy with me."

"Can't blame them. A woman shot as she's about to meet an FBI agent about an international art thief they didn't know about. An FBI agent with a unit based in their city they didn't know about."

Emma sank into the passenger seat of her small car. "I told them HIT is discreet, not secret. I was being honest, but they took it wrong—said I was being cheeky."

Colin glanced over at her. "Did they really say *cheeky?*"

"Maybe they just rolled their eyes."

The police had cordoned off the small island while they searched for evidence, but there were no additional victims and no signs yet of the shooter, who could have exited the scene by boat, on foot or by car, truck, van or—as one of the detectives had put it—stork. Emma had nothing concrete to offer beyond a description of the call and her reasons for going to the island. She had stuck to the broad brushstrokes of her history with the thief. Details could wait for more information on the dead woman.

She glanced out the passenger window at the harbor, eerily still under the clear sky. "We don't know if the dead woman is Rachel Bristol or if either one—the dead woman or Rachel Bristol—is the one who called me."

"Odds are, Emma."

She nodded, turning back to him. "Yes. Odds are."

"She had a stone cross on her exactly like the crosses your thief has sent to your grandfather after every theft for the past ten years. Add in the crosses sent to you, Lucas and Yank last week, and I don't blame the Boston homicide detectives for being pissed that we didn't bring them up to speed on this thief. I told them to calm down but they have a point."

"None of the thefts occurred in Boston," Emma said. "We can't get tunnel vision. That won't help."

"We also have to look at the evidence right in front of us."

She took a quick breath as she pictured the woman's face. Her dead eyes. The stone cross in her palm. "I've heard of suicidal people manipulating someone to find their body, but that's not what happened here. This wasn't a suicide. I didn't see a weapon, and the police haven't found one, at least not yet."

"She wasn't shot by aliens, either."

Emma ignored his muttered comment. "The police said the area is sometimes used for illicit target practice. I suppose this could have been an accidental shooting. I didn't hear gunfire. Planes were landing and taking off at Logan but I didn't notice any close overhead. I was focused on the island and what I was doing, though, not on the sky."

The police were in the process of interviewing everyone at the marina. People at a busy harbor marina presumably were accustomed to frequent comings and goings. Even at a quiet time of year, they wouldn't necessarily pay attention to someone wandering off onto an island trail. As far as Emma knew, no one had paid attention to her when she'd arrived.

Colin slowed, downshifting as they came to their building. "Emma, did you tell the police everything?"

"What do you mean by *everything?*" His eyes held her for a fraction of a second, but it was enough. "Colin, are you mad at me?"

She saw him tighten his grip on the wheel. "We can talk later."

She sat up straight. "You *are* mad."

"It's your nature to hold back, Emma. You don't want to do that now, with this killer at large."

"I'm not holding back. I'm doing my job."

"If I'd been with you when this woman called, would you have told me?"

"I did tell you. I texted you."

"That was one hell of a cryptic message you sent," he said.

"You don't think I should have gone out there alone."

"To a deserted island to meet a stranger who called you about a thief who could be escalating to violence? Damn right I don't think you should have gone out there alone."

Emma didn't answer immediately. She appreciated his intensity and his honesty, if not his conclusion. But he thought she kept secrets. He thought she had layers that he would never be able to peel back to her core. Love and sex were one thing. Knowing her was another. She got that and attributed it to their different natures—his hot to her cool—and not to anything fundamentally wrong with their relationship, or with her.

Finally, she said, "I made a judgment call."

"So you did."

"What about you? The note you left on the kitchen counter wasn't exactly packed with details. You went off on your own." She gave him a cool look. "You weren't at Starbucks, were you?"

"I didn't find a dead body."

Not one to back down, her Colin. "I was careful. I was aware of my surroundings. If the shooter had wanted me dead—"

"Then you'd be dead right now, and I'd be explaining to the homicide detectives that I didn't know what the hell you were up to out on that island."

"I wouldn't have thought twice if it'd been you going to meet a CI."

"For good reason."

"Because you have field experience that I don't. Okay. Fair enough. That doesn't mean I didn't know what I was doing."

Colin sighed through clenched teeth. "I'm not saying you didn't know what you were doing. I'm saying you shouldn't have gone alone." He turned onto the gated entrance at their building. "And if you want to see mad, wait until you talk to Yank."

"Does he know?"

"Not unless someone else told him."

"I thought you might have called him while I was with the detectives," Emma said with a grimace.

"Ha. Not a chance, sweetheart." He glanced at her, his eyes that deep, sexy blue that made her spine tingle. They were uncompromising now, certain and if not annoyed, at least frustrated. Then, without warning, he reached across the small car and touched her cheek with one curved finger. "I'm glad you're safe."

"It was good to hear your voice when I was out there hiding behind a tree. Are you going to tell me where you took off to while I was on my run?"

"It involved cockroaches."

"The six-legged kind or the two-legged kind?"

"Six."

Emma shuddered. "Gross."

Colin winked at her, any hint of irritation gone. "There's something we have in common. We both hate cockroaches."

Four

~~~⌒⊙⊙⊙⌒~~~

Sam Padgett had organized the conference room and gathered the team at the big table. He'd joined HIT in August—late compared to the other members. He was one of the hard-asses, struggling to understand the role of art and art crimes in their mission. Emma knew little about him. Mid-thirties. Single. Native Texan. Extensive field experience in Texas and the southwest. Ultrafit with short-cropped medium brown hair, brown eyes and what he knew—clearly—was a sexy smile. He liked to gripe about Boston's high cost of living, and he got along well with Colin, also new to HIT, also a hard-ass.

Padgett had put on a trim, dark suit with a tie before coming into the office unexpectedly on a Saturday. He'd placed the stone cross that Matt Yankowski had received a week ago on the table. He'd also set up a monitor in the middle of the table for Yank to talk to them from Ireland. Specifically, from Dublin. Even more specifically, from Wendell Sharpe's Dublin apartment. Emma recognized the unlit fireplace in her grandfather's living room. She said nothing, preferring to let Yank explain his whereabouts if he so chose.

He didn't so choose. He led off the meeting with a nod

to his gathered team, agents with expertise in everything from hostage rescue to finance, cybersecurity, forensics and art crimes. Officially on duty, he wore a charcoal-colored suit, but his gray-streaked hair looked as if he'd been trying to tear it out, without success. That was unusual for Matt Yankowski, a senior agent with supreme emotional control.

"I just got off the phone with an irate lieutenant in BPD homicide," Yank said. "He thinks I should have invited him to coffee and explained what we were up to when I decided to set up this unit in his city. Probably would have wanted me to bring my crystal ball, too."

No one said anything. Colin stayed on his feet, leaning against the door as if he didn't consider himself a true member of HIT. Everyone else was at the conference table. Only a few were missing. Emma sat on the chair Padgett had directed her to, one that gave Yank a good view of her. She'd taken a few deep breaths, centering herself, wishing color back into her cheeks.

"The lieutenant brought me up to speed," Yank continued. "The victim is positively identified as Rachel Bristol, forty, of Brentwood, California. Beverly Hills, basically. She was an independent movie producer, divorced eighteen months ago from Travis Bristol, fifty-three, also a producer. Travis has an apartment in Hollywood and a house here in Boston. Beacon Hill. His daughter, Maisie, thirty, is one of the hottest producers in Hollywood. The three of them planned to meet for a catered brunch at the Bristol Island Marina. The Bristols own the island. There's talk—according to the lieutenant—of expanding the marina and developing the outer part of the island where Rachel was killed. The cottages are owned by individual families but most of them are condemned. The Bristols own the land they're built on. They've bought out a few of the families, but basically the cottages are rotting while the Bristols figure out what to do with the island. Meaning Maisie. She's the one with the money and the vision."

"Was that what brunch was about?" Padgett asked. "The future of the island?"

"The detectives hadn't gotten that far when I talked to the lieutenant," Yank said. "It looks as if Rachel got out there early and called Emma to come meet her. BPD doesn't have any information on where Rachel got the cross or if it has anything to do with why she was shot. It obviously has something to do with why she called Emma. I told the lieutenant to expect us to work this thing. We agreed to keep each other informed."

Yank's gray eyes settled on Emma. She cleared her throat, knowing she was expected to say something. "Did the police recover Rachel's phone?" she asked.

Yank nodded. "It was in wet sand not far from her body. She probably dropped it when she was shot. It's in bad shape. They'll see what they can get off it. Someone else could have used it, but there are no other footprints near the body besides yours and hers." His gaze bored into her. "How did this woman get your number, Emma?"

Colin and the BPD detectives had asked her the same question. She gave Yank the same answer. "I don't know. It was one of the things I planned to ask her. I don't hand out my number to everyone, but it's not top secret."

"Who all has it besides us?" Padgett asked.

Emma knew it was a loaded question but answered, anyway. "My family. A few friends."

Yank hadn't shifted his gaze away from her. "Declan's Cross has been in the news recently with the murder of Lindsey Hargreaves."

It had been almost two weeks since Lindsey had been

found dead on cliffs near the village of Declan's Cross. Emma leaned forward, trying to relax the tensed muscles in her lower back and legs. "A few of the news accounts mentioned Declan's Cross is the site of a celebrated unsolved theft of three landscape paintings—two of them by Jack Butler Yeats, arguably Ireland's greatest painter."

"And a fifteenth-century Celtic cross like the one found on Rachel Bristol this morning," Padgett added in a combative tone.

"Somewhat like it," Emma said, matter-of-fact. She didn't want Padgett to succeed in getting under her skin. "The stolen cross is a rare silver wall cross inscribed with Celtic knots and spirals and the figure of Saint Declan, one of the Irish saints who helped Christianize Ireland in the fifth century. Some scholars believe he could even predate Saint Patrick."

Padgett stretched out his long legs. "How do we know it's Declan on the cross and not some other Irish saint?"

Emma reined in any irritation with Padgett. He was testing her, she decided. Letting her know that he was going to ask any and every question he had if he thought it would help get to the bottom of what had happened on Bristol Island that morning. "We know it's Saint Declan because the figure is holding a small bell," she said. "Tradition holds that the bell was given to Declan by God and led him across the Celtic Sea to Ardmore, on the south coast of Ireland, where he established a monastery."

"I didn't find any photographs of the stolen cross in the files," Padgett said.

"We don't have one, only a detailed description by its owner, who died five years ago, and copies made by his niece, Aoife O'Byrne, an artist."

Emma was aware of Yank eyeing her from Dublin,

and Colin from his position by the door. No one else in the room spoke.

Finally, Padgett scratched the side of his mouth. "Got it," he said.

"It's a lot to remember." Emma kept any sarcasm out of her voice. "The third painting stolen that night is the work of an unknown artist, an oil landscape that depicts a scene in Declan's Cross—three nineteenth-century Celtic Revival crosses on a hill next to the ruin of a church dedicated to Saint Declan. The largest of the crosses is a copy of the stolen wall cross."

"No picture of the unsigned painting, either," Padgett said. "We only have photographs of the two Yeats paintings. Jack Butler Yeats was related to William Butler Yeats?"

"His younger brother."

"Good to know."

Emma heard a slight edge of sarcasm and even belligerence creep into her colleague's tone. Sam Padgett hadn't signed on to HIT to chase art thieves. She doubted he'd ever read William Butler Yeats and was certain he'd never heard of Jack Butler Yeats until the stone cross had shown up for Yank. It was a much smaller, modified version of the wall cross, minus the knots and spirals and inscribed onto a polished stone rather than carved out of silver.

Yank settled back in his chair next to Wendell Sharpe's fireplace. "It's not common knowledge that the thief who hit Declan's Cross ten years ago has been active since then, striking in eight cities around the world, or that he's the nemesis of a renowned octogenarian art detective. Maybe our murdered Hollywood producer figured it out."

"And wanted to make a movie?" Emma asked.

"It's possible. Did she sound scared on the phone?"

Emma shook her head. "Breathless. Excited. Definitely not scared."

"Okay. Keep me informed. Watch your backs." Yank shifted his gaze from her to take in his entire team. "I want this Sharpe thief."

Emma stayed behind in the conference room as the rest of the team filed out once the monitor went blank and Yank left them. Colin ducked out, saying nothing. He didn't have his own desk yet. He would go down to her office or park himself at one of the cluster of desks in the open workroom. Yank had designed the space so that his agents could work quietly, alone, behind closed doors or in small or big groups.

"Yank was at your grandfather's place in Dublin, wasn't he?"

The question came from Sam Padgett. He hadn't gone anywhere. Emma nodded. "I recognized the fireplace. How did you know?"

"I recognized the fireplace, too. It's pictured on the Sharpe Fine Art Recovery website. I did my homework." He walked over to the large casement window that looked out on to the harbor. The sky had turned overcast. "I should have taken a picture of the sun while it was out."

"Making a joke, Sam?"

"Nope. Serious. Might not see the sun again until April."

"Winter days can be bright and sunny in Boston. Those are often the frigid-cold days, too."

"Something to look forward to. I like you, Emma. You're smart, and you're good at what you do, but it bothers me that you didn't tell us you'd been a nun."

Not what she'd expected, given the circumstances. "Yank knew." She kept her tone even, without any defensiveness. "It wasn't a secret. It's just not something I talk about that often. Do I know everything about your past?"

Padgett turned from the window. He seemed almost to smile. "I wasn't a monk for three years in my early twenties, that's for damn sure."

"What were you?" Emma asked him.

The almost-smile broadened into a genuine one. "Trouble." He returned to the table and pointed at the small stone cross. "Where did Rachel Bristol get her cross?"

"I don't know."

"Could it be one of the ones this thief sent to your grandfather?"

"Possibly. I haven't talked to him yet. I don't know if any are missing."

"He didn't turn them over to law enforcement?"

"No."

"Interesting guy, your granddad. Has he told us all he knows about this thief?"

"I can't say for sure," Emma said, noticing beach sand on her boots. Her stomach lurched, but she tried not to show any emotion or discomfort as she continued. "It's been ten years. There's a lot of information. Blind alleys he's gone down, people he's talked to and leads he's followed that haven't worked out. He doesn't write everything down. It's hard to know what he's forgotten, what he's deliberately left out that he thinks doesn't matter."

Padgett grimaced. "An honest answer, I guess. Have you told us all you know?"

"Yes."

He pulled out a chair and sat down, nodded again to the stone. "What's the significance of the bell? Besides it leading Declan to Ireland. Does it have any special powers?"

"Declan and his followers were at sea, returning to Ireland, when they realized they had left the bell behind on their stop in Wales. They prayed for its return, and it appeared on a large boulder that they followed to Ardmore."

"Right."

Emma ignored Padgett's skeptical tone. "The bell is gone now, but a boulder on the harbor beach is said to be the one that carried the bell to Ireland."

"More than fifteen hundred years ago."

"It's called Saint Declan's Stone. On Declan's feast day in July, the faithful crawl under it with the hope it will bring them good health, or restore them to good health. Saint Declan was a healer credited with many miracles."

Padgett ran one finger over the small cross-inscribed stone in the center of the table. "Think our thief is hoping for a miracle?"

"It's one theory. We have very little to go on, unfortunately. Even the artwork he's stolen over the past ten years doesn't tell us much. We can speculate but not much more than that."

"Well, our long-departed Irish saint and his little bell must have meaning for our thief or he wouldn't copy them onto a rock every damn time he makes off with a work of art."

"I'm glad you said *our* thief."

Sam's dark eyes hardened. "Yeah. I don't like that he sent Yank this cross. I don't like that he could have followed any one of us here. He's out there taunting us. And if he—or she—killed that woman this morning, then we've got a violent perpetrator on our hands. This scumbag's in Boston, Emma. Mark my words."

"He could be in Maine by now."

"Heron's Cove?" Padgett got to his feet. "Home of the Sharpes. I haven't been up there yet. I hear it's pretty."

"It is. Not that pretty matters to a rugged guy like you."

"Making a joke, Emma?"

She managed a smile. "Nope. Serious."

He gave a short laugh and again looked out the windows toward the harbor. "Did the shooter know you were on the way this morning? Who would have discovered Rachel Bristol's body if you hadn't?"

"Her ex-husband or stepdaughter, I imagine."

"The cops said that Travis and Maisie didn't know Rachel had gone onto the island. She didn't have her own car in Boston. She had to have hired a car, taken a cab or the subway or walked." Padgett shifted back to Emma. "Was Rachel Bristol killed to keep her from talking to you? That's the question of the hour, isn't it, Emma?"

"Right behind who shot her."

He shrugged. "That's a given. You okay? I've been in the situation you were in this morning a few times."

"I'm okay, Sam. Thanks for asking."

"Once the adrenaline wears off, you think—hell, I could have been shot dead myself out there." He grinned as he started toward the door. "But I'm not an ex-nun." He paused in the doorway and looked back at her. "Were you thinking as a federal agent this morning, or a Sharpe?"

"I'm a federal agent at all times."

"I know that. Do you? Deep down? Or does part of you think you still work for your family?"

He left without waiting for the answer. Emma knew the entire team would be sifting through her files on the Declan's Cross thief. Her grandfather hadn't investigated that first theft in the small Irish village until six months later, after two Dutch landscapes were stolen from a small museum in Amsterdam. He received the first of the crosses, along with a museum brochure, and recognized the image of Saint Declan and his bell. That and subsequent crosses not only allowed the thief to take credit for his heists but also to keep Wendell Sharpe on the case—and to taunt one of the world's great art detectives.

Her cell phone vibrated in her jacket pocket. She fished it out and answered without looking at the screen. "Emma Sharpe."

"Emma…Agent Sharpe…it's Aoife O'Byrne."

Emma sat on the edge of the conference table. She hadn't expected the Irish accent and cool voice of the Dublin artist, the younger niece of John O'Byrne, the man who had owned the artwork stolen ten years ago from his home in tiny Declan's Cross. "What can I do for you, Aoife?"

"I need to see you. I'm in Boston," she added quickly. "I'm staying at the Taj Hotel. Can you meet me here? Now? It's important."

Emma eased to her feet. "I'll be right there. Are you in your room?"

"I am, yes."

"Wait there. I'll come to you."

Emma got Aoife's room number and disconnected, aware of Colin watching her from the doorway.

"Are you going to tell me who that was?" he asked.

"Aoife O'Byrne."

"The Irish artist who threw you out of her studio in Dublin a few days ago?"

"She didn't throw me out. She almost threw me out. She threw Granddad out. Well, she slammed the door in his face. But that was ten years ago." Emma pushed a hand through her hair. "She's in Boston."

"Boston," Colin repeated. "Old Wendell told me she's one of the most beautiful women he's ever met."

"She is very attractive," Emma said.

"Good." Colin handed her a sandwich in a small plastic bag. "I stole it out of the fridge in the break room. I think it's Padgett's. He won't miss it. He probably has a stash of MREs in his desk. You need to eat something."

"You and Sam Padgett are going to give Yank a headache, aren't you?"

"Lots of headaches, I imagine," Colin said lightly.

The sandwich looked good. She noted crisp-looking oak-leaf lettuce poking out of the edges of the soft marble rye. She didn't care whether it was ham, cheese, roast beef or some weird concoction Sam had come up with. She was suddenly starving.

Colin grinned at her. "You eat. I'll drive."

Five

Colin followed Emma through a revolving glass door into the Taj, located in an iconic 1927 building on Arlington and Newbury Street in Boston's Back Bay. "Mike and I slipped in here when we were in town for a Red Sox game," he said as he and Emma entered a gleaming elevator in the lobby. "He was thirteen. I was eleven. It was the Ritz-Carlton then. Doorman made us in two seconds flat."

"Did your parents know what you were up to?"

"They still don't. They were doing a swan boat ride with Kevin and Andy. We said we'd stay in the Public Garden." He stood back as Emma hit the button for Aoife's floor. "Mike gets bored easily."

She smiled. "And you don't," she said, openly skeptical. "Did the Red Sox win?"

"You bet. Against the Yankees, too. Ever attend a Red Sox game, Emma?"

"Not yet, no."

"But you've done high tea here, haven't you?"

The elevator rose smoothly up into the five-star hotel. She leveled her green eyes on him. They were the best green eyes. "I have," she said.

"Alone? With your family? With the good sisters?"

"With my family. My Sharpe grandmother was still alive. We all came down for a December weekend in Boston. Granddad, Gran, Lucas, my folks and me. We went to the *Nutcracker* and the Museum of Fine Arts and did high tea. I was nine. Gran bought me a maroon-colored coat with a matching dress with white lace." Emma smiled again, some color returning to her face. "It's a special memory."

Colin could picture the Sharpes trooping into the elegant hotel. From what he'd seen of them so far, they were the sort of people who were comfortable anywhere—high tea, a gallery opening, an Irish pub or a struggling Maine fishing village. Emma's great-grandparents had moved from their native Ireland to Boston when Wendell, their only son, was two. They'd ended up in the pretty village of Heron's Cove in southern Maine, where Wendell had launched Sharpe Fine Art Recovery from his front room sixty years ago. Fifteen years ago, a widower, he'd moved to Ireland and opened an office in Dublin, although he insisted Maine was still home.

Emma could take over the Dublin office now that her grandfather was semiretired, Colin thought, but here she was, an FBI agent who had just come upon a shooting death.

Then again, Rachel Bristol could have called Emma that morning because she was a Sharpe, not because she was an FBI agent.

The elevator eased to a stop, and the doors opened. Emma led the way down the carpeted hall. Halfway down on the left, a slender woman with long, almost-black hair stood in the open doorway to one of the rooms. She was addressing a man—shaved head, denim jacket, cargo pants, late thirties—in the hall. "I don't understand," she said. "Who are you? What do you want with me?"

"Rachel is dead." The man's voice was raised and intense, but he wasn't shouting. "That's what I'm telling you."

The woman seemed to have trouble digesting his words. "Rachel Bristol? She's dead? But how can that be? What happened? You must tell me."

Colin heard the woman's accent now. Irish. Without a doubt.

Aoife O'Byrne. Pronounced *Ee-fa*.

He'd met her older sister, Kitty, almost two weeks ago, when he and Emma had ventured to Declan's Cross and ended up in the middle of a murder investigation. Kitty was attractive, but Aoife was drop-dead gorgeous—in her mid-thirties, with shiny black hair that hung to her waist, porcelain skin, vivid blue eyes and angular features. Wendell Sharpe hadn't been exaggerating when he'd said she was one of the most beautiful women he'd ever met.

"Rachel was shot this morning." The man with the shaved head lowered his voice. "That's the word, anyway. I wasn't given an official report."

"*Shot?* But I— We—" Aoife broke off, then took in two quick, audible breaths. She placed a hand on the doorjamb as if to steady herself. "I don't know who you are or what you want with me, but you need to leave now, before I call hotel security."

The man didn't budge. "Rachel came to see you here last night. Why? What did you two talk about? I'm not leaving until I get some answers." He gave a quick glance at Emma and Colin, then turned back to Aoife. "Believe me, the police are going to want answers, too."

Colin stepped past Emma and reached the man a half step ahead of her. "Easy, my friend. What's your name?"

The man cast him a cold look. "None of your damn business."

"Think not." Colin produced his credentials from inside his jacket. "I'm Special Agent Colin Donovan, and this is Special Agent Emma Sharpe. FBI."

"FBI? No kidding." He put up both palms, as if he knew to keep his hands where the two law enforcement officers could see them. "Name's Palladino. Danny Palladino. I don't have a beef with the FBI. I'm private security. The Bristols are a client."

"Are you carrying?" Colin asked.

Palladino nodded. "Right hip. Glock. It's legal. I'm out of Las Vegas. I got into town last night. I went to Bristol Island for a Bristol family meeting and it was crawling with cops. What's the FBI doing here? You guys don't investigate local homicides."

"I called Emma—Agent Sharpe," Aoife said, her voice less combative.

"Wait." Palladino pointed at Aoife, then Emma. "You two know each other?"

"We met in Ireland because of Agent Sharpe's work in art crime," Aoife said without elaboration. "When I called her just now, I didn't know…" She took in a deep breath. "I didn't know about Rachel. She was a friend of yours, Mr. Palladino? I'm so sorry."

"She wasn't a friend," Palladino said. "Why did you—"

Colin held up a hand, cutting him off. "One thing at a time." He turned to Aoife. "Okay if we talk in your room?"

"Yes, of course." She pushed open the door behind her and motioned into the room. "Please, come in."

It was a one-bedroom suite, complete with a fireplace and view of the Boston Public Garden, spectacular even in November. Palladino went in first, then Emma and Aoife. Colin stayed by the door. He would let Emma handle the situation and jump in if needed. Right now, Palladino looked more shocked, confused and frustrated than menacing.

Aoife walked over to the fire. Although she was dressed warmly in a black sweater, leggings and socks, she was shivering, hugging herself tightly as if she was cold. She wore no jewelry or makeup. A pair of black ankle boots was cast off on the rug in front of the couch. If she'd been out of the hotel that morning, she'd had enough time to warm up. There was no sign in her pale skin of rosy cheeks from the November cold.

Palladino walked over to the windows and looked out at the Public Garden. "I still can't figure out why a well-known Irish painter would call two FBI agents—or even one FBI agent."

Emma ignored him and sat on a chair across from Aoife. "When did you arrive in Boston?" she asked the artist quietly.

Aoife tucked her feet under her. "Yesterday afternoon. I flew in from Dublin."

"You must be jet-lagged," Emma said. "I'm still waking up at the crack of dawn, and I've been home for several days."

"I was very tired last night. I managed to sleep until six this morning. Not too bad."

Palladino nodded to several small sheets of plain paper spaced out on a small, elegant desk. "What are these?"

"Random sketches," Aoife said. "I did them this morning when I realized I wouldn't be going back to sleep. They're Celtic crosses."

"So I see," Palladino said. "Any particular reason?"

"Many particular reasons."

Her cool, prickly response didn't seem to affect Palladino. "Have you left your room today, Miss O'Byrne?" he asked.

She shook her head. "I haven't gone out of here since last night. I had breakfast in."

Emma sat forward in her chair. "I overheard you tell Mr. Palladino that Rachel Bristol was here last night."

"That's right," Aoife said. "She met me here around eight o'clock. I ordered wine and cheese, and we chatted for perhaps a half hour. Here—by the fire. She'd just arrived from Los Angeles and had dropped off her things at her ex-husband's house and walked over. We were both tired from our trips and agreed to meet again today. She said she would phone me this morning and we could set up a time."

"Travis Bristol," Palladino interjected, glancing at Emma. "That's the ex-husband."

"Is he the Bristol who hired you?" Emma asked him.

"No. Ann Bristol, Travis Bristol's first wife. She lives in Las Vegas. I'm here to check on Maisie, their daughter—not for any particular reason, except that Maisie is rich, naive and stubborn." Palladino lifted one of the sketches as if he wasn't paying close attention to the conversation. "Maisie got in from L.A. late yesterday, too."

"I don't know her," Aoife said. "Rachel came here on her own last night."

Colin leaned against the door, shifting his gaze from Palladino to Emma. She seemed more centered than when he'd found her on Bristol Island, pacing, cold, tight with contained anger and the shock of having found a woman dead.

"Aoife," Emma said, "why are you in Boston?"

She hesitated. "Rachel phoned me at my studio in Dublin a few days ago. She wanted to talk to me about a film project she was working on, and I agreed to let her interview me. I've been wanting to come to Boston. This was an excuse. I booked my flight, and now here I am."

Palladino frowned. "What project?"

"She said she was working on an independent movie inspired by the theft of artwork from my uncle's house ten years ago. The stolen art has never been recovered, and the identity of the thief remains unknown. Rachel made the distinction between *inspired by* and *based on*. I'm not sure what she meant."

"I don't know anything about this," Palladino said.

"Rachel was going to get into more detail when we saw each other today, but now…" Aoife gulped in air, sliding her feet out from under her and letting them drop to the carpeted floor as she addressed Emma. "Was she murdered? Her death wasn't an accident, was it?"

"That's not for me to say." Emma rose, no sign of stiffness. "The investigating detectives are going to want to talk to both you and Mr. Palladino."

"I understand," Aoife said, subdued. "Thank you for coming under such terrible circumstances. I didn't know about Rachel's death when I called you. Emma…" The artist glanced at Palladino, then shifted back to Emma. "Might we have a private word?"

"Of course."

Palladino frowned, but Colin nodded to him. "Let's go, Danny. We'll wait downstairs for the detectives. They're going to want to talk to you, too."

"I think I should stay and hear what Miss O'Byrne has to say."

"You can think what you want, but you're not staying. Come on. I'll let you push the buttons in the elevator. I thought that was the best thing when I was a kid."

Palladino glowered. "An FBI agent who thinks he's funny. Just what I need."

But he walked past Aoife and Emma. He had one of the cross sketches in his hand and started to tuck it into his jacket. Colin snatched it from him and set it on a small table. Palladino shrugged and went out into the hall without a word.

Colin glanced at Emma. He didn't like leaving her alone. He wanted to tell her that he had his phone, but she knew that—knew that she could call if she needed to. Reminding her might not undermine her in any real way, but it would sure as hell annoy her.

He went into the hall and walked down to the elevators with Palladino.

"I'm from Las Vegas," Palladino said. "We have lots of elevators. You go ahead and push the button, Agent Donovan. Give that inner seven-year-old of yours a thrill."

Colin grinned at him. "Will do."

When they reached the hotel lobby, Palladino looked less cocky and argumentative—more as if he'd just realized someone had beamed him to another galaxy without his permission. "I want to finish up here and catch the next flight back to Las Vegas."

Colin shook his head. "That probably won't be tonight."

"Not unless we catch this killer."

"We?"

"Figure of speech."

"Right."

"You said you and Rachel weren't friends. How well did you know her?"

Palladino shrugged. "Not well. I've only been working for the Bristols a year. Rachel and Travis were divorced by then."

"You're a bodyguard?"

"I provide personal security. Whatever it takes to keep a client safe. Sometimes that means being a bodyguard, or contracting one. Depends on the client and the situation."

"When you say 'the Bristols—'"

"I mean Ann Bristol. She's my client."

"She sent you here to check on her daughter?"

"It's part of the package," Palladino said vaguely.

"Does the daughter know? Maisie?"

"She knows I'm in town."

His answers left a lot of room for interpretation. Colin didn't push him. "Come on," he said. "I'll buy you a cup of coffee."

They went into the Taj restaurant and were seated at a table overlooking busy, upscale Newbury Street. Colin called the lead detective on the shooting. Not a happy man. He asked Colin twice to spell Aoife and mispronounced it both times. Hadn't appreciated Colin correcting him. He instructed Colin to wait with Palladino at the Taj and to tell Emma and Aoife to wait, too. Back in his state marine patrol days, Colin had dealt with his share of federal agents. He didn't blame the detective for his attitude.

He ordered coffee. Palladino ordered iced tea and grinned across the table. "I'm not violating an FBI order by not having coffee, am I?" He didn't wait for an answer as he glanced out the window at Newbury Street. "Day's turned gray. If I lived out here, I'd have to go on Saint John's Wort or some kind of happy pills this time of year."

"It's still hot in Las Vegas?"

"Cooling down. Ninety degrees when I left yesterday. Ninety doesn't feel as hot there as it would here. It's a desert. Dry air. I could feel the humidity today out on that island. Smelled like dead fish. I hate the ocean."

"Do you like lobster?"

"I've never had it."

"It's good. One of my brothers is a lobsterman."

"Ah. I don't eat much shellfish, but I bet I'd love lobster. If it's good enough for a G-man's brother to haul out of the ocean, it's got to be good, right? Where do you catch lobster around here?"

"The ocean."

"Yeah. I know that. Funny."

"We're from Maine," Colin said. "My brother Andy just got back from Ireland. He spent some time in a little village on the south coast. Declan's Cross. Ever hear of it?"

Palladino shook his head. "I've never been to Ireland. I don't know how Rachel got interested in Aoife O'Byrne, if that's what you're getting at." His iced tea arrived. He gulped a third of it before he continued. "Rachel's death doesn't have anything to do with your brother, does it?"

"There was a murder in Declan's Cross last week. Andy's girlfriend was there. It was in the papers."

"I don't read Irish papers."

"It was in the papers here, too. The victim was an American diver, Lindsey Hargreaves. Her killer is dead."

"Case solved then," Palladino said.

Colin ignored him. "The uncle Aoife mentioned whose house was burglarized ten years ago is in Declan's Cross. Several valuable works of Irish art were stolen. Aoife's sister, Kitty, converted the house into a boutique hotel after their uncle's death a few years ago."

Palladino yawned. "Okay. One of those small-world

things. Or not?" Palladino watched in silence as their waiter delivered Colin's coffee in a silver pot. When the waiter withdrew, Palladino leaned over the table, speaking in a conspiratorial whisper. "You think Rachel saw news reports of the murder and this unsolved theft and that's how she got interested in Aoife and this movie idea of hers?"

"I'm just asking questions." Colin drank some of his coffee. It was ultrastrong. Perfect. He kept his gaze on the man across the table. "This is all news to you?"

"Totally." Palladino sat back. "No wonder you and Agent Sharpe have your knickers in a twist. What I know about art, Irish or otherwise, could keep us talking for thirty seconds. Emma Sharpe—did she investigate this Declan's Cross theft? She seems young to have been a fed ten years ago."

"Her grandfather investigated. Wendell Sharpe."

"Don't know him. Obviously, I came out here not knowing a whole hell of a lot about what's going on. Could this have been a random shooting—some yahoo target practicing who pops Rachel by mistake? Where was she hit?" He waved a hand. "Never mind. I know you won't tell me. Did Rachel call Agent Sharpe? Is that what happened?"

"The detectives can fill you in as they see fit," Colin said, drinking more of his coffee.

"Yeah, yeah. I know the drill." Palladino grinned, clearly not a man easily intimidated. "Don't get excited. I'm not an ex-cop. I'm ex-military. Navy. I was on fast-attack submarines for twelve years. See why I hate the ocean? The only thing worse than being on the ocean is being under it. I grew up in Las Vegas, and I signed up for the navy. Go figure." He polished off the last of his iced tea. "You and Agent Emma?"

"We're both with the FBI. It stands for the Federal Bureau of Investigation."

"That's not what I meant."

Colin knew it wasn't. "What about you? How did you start working for Ann Bristol?"

"She's a client. I don't work for her. I'm an independent operator. She called my office one bright, hot, sunny Las Vegas day. A mutual friend had referred her to me. Nothing out of the ordinary. She was worried about her daughter more than about herself. I've done work for high-profile people. I know what I'm doing."

"The daughter—Maisie—is okay with her mother sticking her nose in her business?"

"I didn't say that."

"Are you married, Mr. Palladino?"

"Nope. Never. I might get a dog, preferably one who likes the desert." He glanced out the tall windows at the street. "I rented a room near Mass. General Hospital. I can walk from here. Can I wait there for the detectives?"

Colin shook his head. "I'll order you more iced tea."

"Won't the detectives be pissed that you and Sharpe are talking to Aoife O'Byrne and me first?"

"We did them a favor."

"Bet they won't see it that way."

Danny Palladino was right. The homicide detectives didn't appreciate that two FBI agents had talked to him and Aoife O'Byrne before they could. Not a surprise, Colin thought as he followed Emma out of the Taj onto Newbury Street. The detectives also hadn't appreciated his point that without said two FBI agents—particularly Emma—they wouldn't have found out about Danny and Aoife as soon as they did.

Emma had been more diplomatic.

She buttoned up her jacket as two women in high-heeled boots breezed past them. "I've never been much of a shopper, but I could go for a Burberry coat."

"Our friends in the BPD would love for us to go shopping." Colin resisted the temptation to put his arm around her. They were in public, working. "I'll start saving now and buy you a Burberry coat on our fifth anniversary."

She grinned at him. "I'm going to hold you to that, Agent Donovan."

He could see the strain in her eyes. "The police aren't going to like what Aoife has to tell them, are they?"

Emma started walking up Newbury. "Aoife is in Boston as much to see me as Rachel Bristol. A stone cross arrived at her studio in Dublin on Thursday—by mail, just like the ones Granddad, Lucas, Yank and I received late last week."

"That's a couple days after you stopped to see her at her studio on Monday," Colin said.

"It's impossible to know if my visit and the cross are connected. I was careful when I went to see her. I don't think I was followed."

"The thief could have been watching her."

Emma nodded. "She's done similar crosses herself, designs inspired by the one stolen from her uncle's house."

Colin slowed his pace. "Emma, where is the cross Aoife received?"

"She debated calling the police in Dublin, and even my grandfather, but she had Rachel's invitation to come to Boston and decided it would be more efficient—her exact word—to bring the cross to me herself." Emma pulled her hands out of her pockets. "Aoife had the cross out on the desk in her suite last night when Rachel stopped by. When she went to look for it this morning, it was gone. She says she searched every inch of her suite."

"That's why she called you when she did."

Emma nodded. They approached the intersection at Arlington Street. The wind picked up, blowing a few stray, brown fallen leaves on the sidewalk. Colin pictured Emma on windswept Bristol Island, alone with a dead woman with a cross in her hand identical to the ones a serial art thief had been sending to Wendell Sharpe for ten years.

"You're not having a great day, Agent Sharpe," he said.

She almost smiled. "You could say that. Rachel must have helped herself to Aoife's cross last night and then called me this morning. Aoife has my number. She says she had it out on her desk last night, too. Rachel could have jotted it down or memorized it when she swiped the cross."

"Did whoever shot her know she had the cross and didn't care?" Colin stopped on the wide sidewalk. "Or know but didn't have time to grab it without shooting you, too?" He gritted his teeth, not liking any of the possibilities. "Why did Rachel steal this cross? Only a handful of people know it's the signature of a serial art thief. She wasn't one of them."

"Neither is Aoife. She knows only that it is similar to her uncle's stolen cross."

"Could Rachel have thought it was Aoife's work?"

"Maybe, but I don't think so."

They walked to a light and crossed Arlington to the Public Garden. Colin wasn't one for a lot of pondering and analyzing, but he also wasn't one for jumping to conclusions ahead of the facts. Rachel's killer needed to be identified and apprehended. The role of the Declan's Cross thief—if any—in her death needed to be sorted out. The lines were blurred between the jobs of the Boston Police Department, the FBI and the Sharpes.

Not *that* blurred, Colin thought.

The BPD had the lead in the homicide investigation. The FBI had the lead in the investigation into the thief. They would coordinate their efforts as appropriate.

The Sharpes of Sharpe Fine Art Recovery were private citizens.

More fallen leaves blew alongside the Public Garden's Victorian black-iron fence.

"Rachel stole the cross and called you," Colin said. "Why?"

"My guess? She believed she knew who sent it."

"Our thief."

"That's right," Emma said quietly. "Our thief."

Six

Dublin, Ireland

Matt Yankowski parked in front of what he hoped was Aoife O'Byrne's building on the Liffey River in Dublin. Somehow, he'd managed to navigate Dublin's maze of streets without veering into the wrong lane or the wrong direction down a one-way street. It was a bleak November evening, early by Irish standards. He turned off the engine and wipers, wondering if he should have stayed at Wendell Sharpe's place and left Aoife O'Byrne to the Irish police. *An Garda Síochána.* Guardians of the Peace. The garda, or gardai—or just the guards.

A popular Irish artist in the middle of a homicide investigation in Boston.

The gardai wouldn't like it.

Hell, he didn't like it, either.

He got out of his little rental car and buttoned his overcoat against the cold mist. So far, the only positive of his day was that his red Micra hadn't fallen to pieces on the drive from the southwest Irish coast to Dublin that morning. In fact, it was growing on him. It did a decent job handling any size Irish road—including roads he didn't consider roads—and, given its size, made his occasional lapse about driving on the left slightly less terrifying.

Since arriving in Ireland earlier in the week, he'd imagined exploring back roads with Lucy, no agenda, no idea where they would have their next meal or spend the night. It'd been a long time since they'd left room for that kind of spontaneity in their lives.

"A long time," he said under his breath.

After Colin's report earlier that day, Yank had called Lucy's sister, who lived in Georgetown. The two sisters had gone to Paris together in October. Yank had suspected Sherry had been stoking Lucy's fears and resentments about moving to Boston, but she'd been pleasant on the phone. "I don't need to check your house for Lucy, Matt. She's gone to Boston. She wanted to surprise you. I take it you're not there?"

"I'm in Ireland."

Sherry had sighed. "Did you tell her you were going to Ireland?"

"That's why I've been trying to reach her. I didn't expect to stay this long."

"And you wonder—" Sherry had broken off. "Never mind."

"She's in a snit, you think?"

"Wouldn't you be?"

He'd disconnected without answering. He'd tried Lucy's cell phone again and left another voice mail. *"It's me, Luce. At least let me know you're okay. Call, text, send a carrier pigeon. Whatever works for you."*

That had been four hours ago.

Still no response.

She was carrying her snit too far. He wouldn't give her much longer before he sounded the alarm. It wasn't easy to be objective, but if one of his agents came to him with the same story, he wouldn't care if the wife was sticking it to the husband for being a jerk. He would want to find her.

A man approached him on the sidewalk. Wavy black hair, blue eyes, a mix of Colin Farrell and Liam Neeson about him. He had to be Sean Murphy, a garda detective with a family farm in tiny Declan's Cross. He'd been in the thick of the events there last week, and he'd agreed to meet Yank at Aoife O'Byrne's studio.

"Matt Yankowski," Yank said. "Thanks for coming, Detective."

The two men shook hands. "I'm sorry about this woman's death in Boston," Murphy said. "It's good to hear Emma wasn't hurt. How is she?"

"Annoying the Boston police. That's not hard to do right now. I've already had a chat with an irate lieutenant in homicide."

"Ah, yes. So have I. The lieutenant was reluctant to share information but delighted to have me talk. I suppose I'd have done the same in his position." Murphy nodded toward the unprepossessing stone building behind them. "Shall we?"

It was an informal meeting—a senior garda detective and a senior FBI agent having a look at the art studio and apartment of a prominent Irish painter, sculptor and jeweler who had found herself in the middle of a Boston homicide investigation. Yank hadn't met Aoife O'Byrne, but Sean Murphy knew her from her and her sister's visits to their uncle's country house in Declan's Cross. According to Emma and Colin, though, it was Aoife's sister, Kitty, who'd caught the Irishman's eye as a teenager. The two had had something of a star-crossed relationship ever since. Kitty had gone on to marry another man, but they divorced and she eventually moved to Declan's Cross to transform her uncle's house into a thriving boutique hotel. Sean had devoted himself to his career, rising up through the garda ranks. Then early this past summer, he'd landed at his family farm in Declan's Cross for a long recuperation from injuries he'd sustained in an ambush. Kitty was there with her teenage son and her newly opened hotel.

"I gather you're back on the job?" Yank asked.

The garda detective shrugged. "It was time. Declan's Cross isn't that far from Dublin, and it isn't going anywhere." He winked at Yank. "Neither is Kitty O'Byrne."

A way of saying this time he and Kitty would make things work.

Hope for Lucy and me, too, maybe, Yank thought irritably as he followed Murphy into the building. There was no doorman or security guard. "I know Ireland has a low crime rate," Yank said, "but Dublin is still a big city, and Aoife is well-known."

"She doesn't like to change her ways based on her fame."

"Might come a time when she doesn't have a choice."

Murphy glanced back. "That time might already have come. I have a key," he added. "Kitty gave me one before I left Declan's Cross."

They went up wide stairs to the second floor. No one else seemed to be around late on a dreary Saturday. Murphy explained that the building had a half-dozen studios owned or rented by artists. Each studio included an efficiency apartment—kitchen facilities, bathroom, place to sleep—but only Aoife actually lived in hers.

Her cop almost-brother-in-law clearly didn't approve. "Aoife's doing well financially," he said as they came to the top of the stairs. "She can afford to live anywhere she likes. She doesn't have to live in her studio. She says the other artists in the building come and go at all hours, but you see what it's like now. Quiet as a church. I don't like her being here on her own."

"Does she appreciate your concern?"

"Not a bit. She tells me I know nothing of the art world. It's true. I remember her as a girl tinkering with paints and brushes, hammers and chisels—she was always working on something. Kitty's visual but not in the same way. You'll see her talents when you come to Declan's Cross one day." Murphy gave a small, unreadable smile. "I'll buy you a drink at her hotel."

"Did Aoife tell you she'd received the cross that's now missing from her hotel room and presumably is the one in Rachel Bristol's hand in Boston this morning?"

The Irishman's mood palpably darkened. "No."

"Wendell Sharpe says she didn't tell him, either," Yank said, feeling a draft in the dimly lit hall. "What about her sister?"

"Aoife told Kitty she was going to Boston but didn't mention the cross."

"What did she give Kitty as her reasons for going?"

"Impulse," Murphy said, as if that made sense where Aoife O'Byrne was concerned.

Yank said nothing. Sean Murphy had to be worried and annoyed at the situation in which Aoife had found herself—put herself—but he obviously wasn't letting his emotions affect his actions and concentration. He looked like any other senior detective on the job as he approached a door at the front of the building. Yank could appreciate the difficulties when the professional and the personal collided in their line of work.

Murphy got out a set of keys, then went still. He held up a hand, and Yank came to a halt behind him. He saw immediately what had caught the Irishman's attention.

The heavy door to Aoife's studio was shut now, but had clearly been pried open, the brass lock popped, with gouges and scratches on the door itself.

Murphy looked back at Yank. "Stay close. I don't need a dead FBI agent on my hands."

They entered a large room with high ceilings, exposed brick and stark, white-painted walls. Industrial-style windows were splattered with rain, reflecting the city lights and casting eerie shadows. A scarred-wood worktable occupied the center of the room. Utilitarian wood-and-metal bookcases that lined the interior wall had been cleared of their contents and one section upended, as if whoever had tossed the place had reacted in frustration.

Murphy dipped into an adjoining room—presumably the living quarters—and came back out again, nodding to Yank. "Clear."

While the Irishman switched on lights, Yank walked over to the bookcases. Most of the contents appeared to be art supplies and photographic equipment. A few books and sketchpads. As he leaned forward, he saw a hand extending from under the upended bookcase and its spilled contents. At first he thought it might be a work of art. Some sculpture.

It wasn't. It was a woman's hand.

"Murphy."

The Irish detective stood next to him and cursed under his breath. They moved in unison, dropping down to the bookcase and the woman pinned under its heavy metal-and-wood frame.

Yank saw dark hair. Fabric—dark red fleece. A jacket.

Murphy checked the exposed hand for a pulse. "She's alive," he said.

He and Yank lifted the heavy bookcase off the woman and shoved it aside. It had landed on top of her, trapping her but not crushing her. Murphy knelt next to her upper body, checking her breathing. Yank pulled sketchpads, a camera case and a tripod off her. He couldn't see her face, but she was a small woman, dressed in jeans, walking shoes, the fleece jacket. She must have come in from the street. Had she surprised whoever had broken into the place? Or was this their perpetrator?

Murphy moved back slightly, exposing her other hand.

Yank's gaze fixed on the simple gold wedding band.

He touched the Irishman's shoulder. "Murphy. Move back a bit. I need to see her face."

The detective gave him a sharp look. "Do you recognize her?"

Yank stared down at the pixie haircut and pixie face. The smooth, milky skin of her throat and her small body as she lay on her side, crumpled into a fetal position. His throat tightened. He couldn't speak.

"Agent Yankowski," Murphy said, cutting through Yank's shock. "Who is this woman?"

Lucy.

Yank sank onto his knees next to her. "She's my wife."

Seven

❧

"I played dead," Lucy said, trembling under the blanket a paramedic had given her. Yank had placed the blanket around her shoulders himself. She was sitting on the floor, leaning back against the exposed brick wall of Aoife O'Byrne's studio. She licked her chapped lips. "I heard you and Detective Garda Murphy come in, but I didn't know who you were."

Yank knew he had to contain his emotions, but it was damn hard. Lucy. His wife. In Dublin, trapped under a bookcase for at least thirty hours. Likely left for dead. She'd managed to protect her head and vital organs when the bookcase had come down on top of her, and she'd had access to her water bottle, although it had been nearly empty when she was attacked. She was bruised, but she had no broken bones, lacerations or other internal injuries. And she was shaken. More shaken than she would want to admit. She'd martialed her limited water supply and was mildly dehydrated, but she'd been lucky. They both knew it.

The gardai were doing their work. Sean Murphy was definitely the guy in charge. The living quarters had been tossed, too. Murphy had been firm but not a jackass when he'd reminded Yank this was now a criminal investigation. Yank knew he had no choice and had to stand back and let Irish law enforcement do their jobs. He had no authority in Ireland.

"What are you doing here, Lucy?" he asked finally, sitting next to her on the wood floor.

She attempted a weak smile. "I wanted to surprise you."

"Consider me surprised."

"Because you found me in Dublin or under a bookcase?"

"Take your pick."

Her dark eyes leveled on him. The same dark eyes he'd fallen in love with at twenty-three at the University of Virginia. He'd been getting his master's in criminal justice. She'd been a senior majoring in psychology. Ten years they'd been married, and yet some days—like today—he wasn't sure he would ever know her.

"I'm sorry, Matt," she whispered.

"Did you break in here and pull the bookcase on top of yourself?"

"No, of course not."

"Then nothing to be sorry about."

"Cut-to-the-chase Matt Yankowski. There's a reason you're in law enforcement." She sighed, again licking her chapped lips. He noticed a small cut at the corner of her mouth, probably from dehydration and biting down as the hours had dragged on. She eased a hand out from under her blanket and placed it on his thigh. "I'm sorry I didn't tell you I was coming to Dublin."

"Water over the dam."

She gave a tight shake of her head. "We have too much *water over the dam* and not enough real talking. Real listening. I flew to Boston on Thursday morning and went to your apartment, and you weren't there. I saw a printout of your flight information. I had my passport with me. I booked a flight on Aer Lingus for that night, then turned around and went straight back to the airport."

"Did you have any idea where I was?"

"Ireland," she said, and this time her smile revealed more of the ultraconfident Lucy Yankowski he knew so well.

"Were you mad?" Yank asked.

"Incensed."

A Lucy word. He covered her hand with his. Hers was cool, and he could feel its slight tremble. "I'm glad you're okay. There was a moment…" He breathed. "Lucy. Damn."

"It's been a long two days." She glanced at the studio, as if seeing the mess for the first time. "Does whatever happened here have anything to do with why you're in Ireland?"

"Probably."

"Aoife O'Byrne is a well-known artist. Where is she? I thought she'd come back. Then I realized it was the weekend, and maybe she was away."

"She's in Boston," Yank said.

"Boston? Why—"

"We'll get to that. Why did you come here?"

"I was curious. I arrived in Dublin at the crack of dawn. You know those overnight flights. I'd booked a room while I was at the airport in Boston, but it wasn't ready. I dropped off my bags, took myself to breakfast and read about the murder in Declan's Cross early last week. That's what brought you to Ireland, isn't it?"

"Sort of."

"Aoife O'Byrne was mentioned in the article. I checked out her website. It lists her address. I decided to kill time by coming by to have a look. I guess I expected a public gallery. I didn't think too much about it. It was a spur-of-the-moment thing."

"You've told all this to the Irish police?"

She nodded. "I figured you would want to know, too."

"I do, Lucy. I want to know everything. When you're ready. You've come through a hell of an ordeal. Aoife flew to Boston yesterday. Someone could have wanted to take advantage of her absence and see what was in here."

"An ordinary burglar, you mean. Then I walk in and startle them." She swallowed, sinking back against the wall. "I don't know why I walked in. I didn't see that the door had been jimmied. I can't explain. My mind didn't grasp it. Lack of sleep, being in a foreign country, irritation with you. I just don't know."

"It's okay. You don't need to make sense of it."

"Maybe not yet, anyway. I remember being in here, wondering where Aoife was. I heard someone in the other room. I called Aoife—except I mangled the pronunciation of her name. Sean Murphy's already set me straight. Anyway, next thing I was falling, things were crashing around me, and I was trapped under a bookcase. I thought I could push it off me, but I couldn't. It's heavy, and I was afraid I'd dislodge something and do real damage to myself."

"Did you yell for help?"

"Some. Once I was certain whoever had pushed the bookcase on top of me wouldn't hear me. I wanted to preserve my energy—I didn't want to waste it screaming if no one was around to hear me—but I also didn't want…" She broke off with a small shake of her head. "Never mind. You know what I'm saying."

He did. His wife—trapped, scared and in pain—hadn't wanted whoever had broken into Aoife's studio to come back and kill her. He wanted to scoop her up and carry her to his little car and disappear into the Irish hills with her. Protect her, keep her safe. A little late, he thought bitterly as he saw the bruise on her forearm where she'd fended off a falling object from the bookcase.

"I thought you were in a snit and that's why you didn't call me back."

"I was in a snit," she said. "I wanted to strangle you when I realized you'd gone to Ireland without telling me. Then I thought…I'd surprise you. I'd get you off to a cute Irish hotel and we'd talk, finally. And if you couldn't come—if your work wouldn't allow it—then I'd see the sights on my own. It wasn't a well-thought-out plan, but it was a plan."

"It would have been fun to see Dublin with you, Lucy," Yank said softly.

"I have my list of sights I want to see. The Book of Kells, the Long Room, Temple Bar, Grafton Street, Saint Stephen's Green, Georgian Dublin." Lucy sank her head against his shoulder. "Then I wanted to find a cozy Irish cottage and get you to take a few days off."

"I know just the one," Yank said. "I stayed there this week. It's in the Kerry hills. It's owned by an Irish priest, one of Emma and Colin's friends. I'm here because of work, but it's not the only reason. I needed some time on my own."

"To think about us," she said.

He put his arm around her. "Every time I saw rainbows and sheep, I thought of how much you love them."

"You never see rainbows."

"I did this past week. Gorgeous rainbows. They made me wish you were with me. I saw one this morning when I left the cottage…" He heard his voice crack. "And you were here, trapped…"

He glanced around the room. Sean Murphy was in close conversation with two other gardai. Yank knew he had to update his team back in Boston. Someone needed to talk to Aoife O'Byrne, keep an eye on her. Could she have faked the break-in for reasons of her own? Could someone have broken in looking for the stone cross that had ended up in Rachel Bristol's hand on Bristol Island?

If Rachel stole the cross from Aoife last night, why call an FBI agent? Had she figured she had information so important that Emma would overlook the theft?

What if Rachel *hadn't* stolen the cross? What if that was a story Aoife O'Byrne had made up?

Those were the first questions off the top of his head. Sean Murphy would have the same questions, as well as ones of his own. Despite their personal connections to the events of the day, Yank knew he and Murphy would do their jobs. They wouldn't go off half-cocked. They wouldn't leap to conclusions based on emotion or urgency.

Lucy's trembling eased. She seemed ready to fall asleep. "Do your thing, Matt. I'm fine."

"Are you hungry?"

She stirred, smiling suddenly. "Starving." Her eyes sparked with mischief. This was the Lucy he'd known and loved for so long, and had seen too little of the past year. "And my first Guinness on Irish soil sounds damn good about now."

Eight

Boston, Massachusetts

Maisie Bristol sank onto a frayed leather sofa in the front room of the classic nineteenth-century bow-front house her family owned on a tree-lined section of West Cedar Street on Beacon Hill. To maintain eye contact with her, Emma sat across from her on an equally frayed wing-back chair. Colin stayed on his feet by the foyer door. As they'd arrived on West Cedar, Yank had called them about the attack on his wife at Aoife O'Byrne's studio in Dublin. It wasn't something they planned to bring up with the Bristols, at least not right now.

Danny Palladino had led them inside, explaining the place was getting a much-needed face-lift. Maisie, he'd said, was more Southern California than Beacon Hill and didn't want the house to feel like a museum. He'd seemed out of place, not sure what he should do with himself, but finally settled on standing behind the sofa where Maisie was sitting. Travis Bristol, Maisie's father and Rachel's ex-husband, was pacing in front of the windows overlooking the tree-lined street. He and Maisie were both clearly struggling to come to terms with the news of Rachel's death.

"I saw Rachel just this morning," Maisie said, half to herself. "She was looking forward to our brunch at the marina. She was excited, she said."

Maisie grabbed a set of rolled-up architect's drawings on the coffee table and stood them on the floor. She looked younger than thirty, with her unkempt reddish-blond hair and spray of freckles across her nose and upper cheeks. She wore an unassuming outfit of a green-plaid flannel shirt untucked over boyfriend jeans and dark orange suede ankle boots.

"Rachel didn't do anything if she wasn't excited about it," Travis said, taking a seat next to Maisie on the sofa. His eyes were the same shade of pale blue as hers, but his hair was gray and he had no freckles. He wore a navy sweater that had to be too warm for the room and wide-wale corduroys a tone lighter than the sofa's cognac leather. Hours after his ex-wife's death, he still looked gut-punched, ashen and in shock. "The Rachel I knew could fire up a room with her excitement and passion for whatever she was doing."

"That was Rachel," Maisie echoed with a small smile. "Pushy, intense, generous, formidable, especially when she was convinced she was right."

Travis nodded sadly. "She had clarity of vision but she was also tenacious."

"She could be exhausting, though. She'd wear you out to get her way. There wasn't one thing wishy-washy about her." Maisie leaned her head against her father's shoulder. "We're going to miss her."

"You didn't go to the marina together?" Emma asked.

Maisie sat up straight, shaking her head. "We all had things to do later and went on our own. Rachel left early and said she would meet us there. I didn't think twice about it." She raised her chin at Emma. "I told the detectives all of this."

"Rachel loved the island and this place," Travis said. "I invited her to stay here whenever she was in town. Last week was her first time back since we split. I put her in a guest room upstairs. I've been back and forth between here and L.A. more often than usual because of the renovations. I used to tease Rachel that she married me because I came with an island and a Beacon Hill house."

Maisie nodded to the blueprints. "She wanted to know about the work we're doing. She'd had her own ideas about renovations when she and Dad were together."

Travis glared up at Danny Palladino. "How could you have let this happen?"

"I didn't let anything happen," Danny said, his voice even. "Rachel wasn't my responsibility. Neither are you. Technically, neither is Maisie. I'm not here in a protective capacity."

Maisie sprang to her feet, her freckles standing out against her pale skin. "You're here snooping on me. You never liked Rachel."

"I barely knew her," Danny said, matter-of-fact.

Travis slumped back against the couch. "Are you sure you didn't kill her yourself, Danny?"

Maisie spun around at him. *"Dad!"*

Danny didn't seem surprised at Travis's outburst, but the older man winced and immediately waved a hand in apology. "I'm sorry. That was uncalled for. I didn't mean it. Truly. It was raw emotion. Nothing more. Danny, please. Have a seat. Rachel's death is a shock for all of us."

Danny shrugged but made no move to sit. "Let's just hope the cops find her killer soon. Even if it was an accident, someone is responsible for her death." He settled his steady gaze on Emma. "That's not why you and Agent Donovan are here, though, is it, Agent Sharpe?"

Emma didn't answer, instead keeping her focus on Maisie. "What do you know about Rachel's relationship with Aoife O'Byrne?"

Maisie frowned. "Why don't you ask Aoife? Why ask me?"

Despite her unpretentious appearance, Maisie Bristol was clearly used to being in charge. Her father leaned forward, fingering one of the decorating magazines on the table. "We'll be happy to answer any questions you have, Agent Sharpe. I've never met Miss O'Byrne. I only learned of her last night when Rachel told us she had invited her to Boston, and she had just arrived. I understand that she's a remarkable artist."

Emma glanced at Colin, his expression unreadable, then shifted back to the Bristols. "Rachel told Aoife she was working on an independent film inspired by an Irish art theft. Were you involved, Maisie?"

"It's complicated," she said, her voice almost inaudible.

"It's Maisie's project," Travis said. "Rachel knew that. I'm sure she'd say the same thing if she were with us right now."

Maisie seemed hardly to hear him. "Rachel had her ideas about the direction we should take. We were going to talk about everything this morning at the marina. I have so many ideas. It's easy for me to get ahead of myself. I wanted to get more details on what Rachel had in mind and get Dad's take. We were also going to talk about plans for the island." She blinked back tears. "It was supposed to be a good get-together. Fun. Stimulating."

"We all love the island," her father said. "Rachel as well as Maisie and me."

Maisie nodded. "Mom, too. Some of my fondest memories are of the three of us digging clams on the beach. She'd like us to let the island become part of the national park system along with most of the other islands. That's an option, but I've been exploring the idea of launching a film school and production company on the island. It would be nonprofit. Who knows, maybe it could be part of the Boston Harbor Island Recreational Area, too." She waved a hand. "None of that matters right now."

"What time did you arrive on the island?" Colin asked from the foyer door.

Maisie looked startled, as if she'd forgotten he was there, but recovered quickly. "Just before the police did. I knew something terrible had happened. I threw up."

"I arrived a few minutes later," Travis said.

"It's been a long day. I know you understand." Maisie pointed vaguely toward the back of the house. "Why don't I show you my workroom? It's just downstairs. I don't like sharing the details of a project too soon, but…" She tried to smile. "But you're the FBI, and you want to know. And I have nothing to hide."

"I'll go with you," Danny said.

Maisie bristled visibly. "You don't have to stay, Danny. You can go anytime. Dad and I will be fine."

He shifted his impassive gaze to Emma. "Maisie is independent. That's cool, but it doesn't occur to her that someone might not wish her well."

"That's not what today is about, Danny," she interjected, clearly annoyed with him. "I'm not the one who was in danger, obviously, and we don't know that Rachel's death has anything to do with me. In fact, I can't imagine how it could."

"Rachel had her own life apart from Maisie and me," Travis said.

Maisie nodded. "She could have had her own enemies, too. More likely, what happened this morning was just a stupid accident. With the cottages falling into disrepair, vagrants and people out for a good time have been using that side of the island. Developing it would end all that. But we don't know what happened today, except that Rachel is gone."

Travis eased in next to his daughter. "Danny, you're welcome to move in here. If we'd known you were coming, we'd have had a room ready for you."

"I'm good with my rental," Danny said. "No rats or roaches."

Maisie gave him a cool look before turning to Emma. "Shall we go downstairs?"

Danny made a move to join them, but Colin shook his head. "You sit tight, Danny. We'll be back."

"Feds," he said, good-naturedly. "Love you guys. Go do your thing."

Maisie Bristol's workroom was down a half flight of stairs at street or "garden" level. French doors opened onto a brick courtyard with a stone fountain, statues and pots now mostly empty with the cooler weather. In the fading afternoon light, Emma noticed chips and cracks in the fountain. Moss and crabgrass covered patches of the brick. A six-foot stepladder leaned up against the back wall, reminding her that the Bristols were having work done on the place.

Maisie grabbed a book off a worktable pushed up against multipaned windows. "I'm sorry, I don't have many chairs in here, and the few I have are stacked with books. I've been collecting them like a madwoman. I don't know when I'll get to read even half of them."

"We don't mind standing," Emma said.

Colin walked over to the window. He'd said little since arriving at the Bristols' house, but she had no doubt he was paying close attention. That she'd found a dead woman and Yank had found his wife trapped in Aoife O'Byrne's Dublin studio hadn't sat well with him—as an FBI agent or as Emma's fiancé and Yank's friend.

Maisie set her book back on the table. Emma saw it was on Jack B. Yeats. "I wasn't familiar with his work until recently," Maisie said, brushing her fingertips across the cover, one of his western Irish landscapes. "Rachel told me about him, as a matter of fact. I didn't realize at first that her interest in Yeats cuts to our different approaches to the film we were working on together. She wanted flash and dazzle. I want…" Her eyes shone with fresh tears. "Well, I don't know what I want."

"When did Rachel introduce you to Yeats's work?" Emma asked.

"About a week ago. She'd done some research and thought she'd found the perfect hook for our movie."

"And you weren't sure?"

"I wasn't, no. I'm interested in the intersection of pagan Celtic Ireland and Christianity and the integration of those two worlds. I've been gobbling up everything I can." Maisie gave a broad gesture to more books stacked on the worktable. "It's fascinating."

Maisie—or someone—had turned the end wall into a collage of color printouts of photographs of Irish Celtic scenes. Emma recognized ogham stones, Celtic crosses, beehive huts and church ruins, pages from the Book of Kells.

"I wasn't upset by Rachel's ideas," Maisie added

quickly. "Differences are to be expected in a creative endeavor. I like to throw everything out onto the table—without self-censorship—and see what develops. Let things simmer and percolate until what's meant to be emerges. It's not always a neat and tidy process, but it works, at least for me."

"You've had a great deal of success," Emma said.

"I support good people and get out of their way and let them do their work."

"That takes a certain vision, doesn't it?"

Maisie smiled, brushing at her tears with the heel of one hand. "And luck."

"Did Rachel—"

"All my successes were flukes according to Rachel. She said it was a positive viewpoint. If they were flukes, I wouldn't expect to duplicate them in the future. I wouldn't be disappointed."

"She was lowering your expectations?"

"Helping me to a soft landing," Maisie said. "She and my dad started seeing each other when I was fifteen. I was even more awkward than the average awkward fifteen-year-old. Living in Las Vegas with my erratic but loving mother. Traveling back and forth to Los Angeles and Boston to see my father. It's not like not knowing where your next meal is coming from or going to bed hungry, but I coped by watching movies, talking movies, eating and sleeping movies. Rachel was very kind to me in her own way, and she taught me a lot."

"But part of her still thought of you as that awkward fifteen-year-old," Emma said.

"She admitted as much."

Colin turned from the window. "Was she hijacking your movie, Maisie?"

"She knew I wouldn't let that happen. She told me last

night that she realized I wasn't the insecure girl breathless for whatever words of wisdom she had for me—that
just because I'm open to ideas doesn't mean I don't have
ideas of my own, or a strong vision of my own. That
I…I…" Maisie gulped in air, her face crumpling as she
sobbed, tears streaming down her pale cheeks. "I can't
believe she's gone. I can't believe someone killed her."

Emma pulled out the one chair that was pushed under
the table and lifted a stack of books from the seat. Colin
eased Maisie onto the chair. "Try not to hyperventilate,"
he said. "It won't help."

She nodded, still gulping in air. "I know. I'm sorry.
I've been in such a state of shock that I've hardly cried
at all. I don't know what all Rachel was up to—I think
she was trying to manipulate me or bully me into doing
the movie her way. I'm sure that's why she invited Aoife
O'Byrne here. How awful it must be for her to arrive in
Boston and not twenty-four hours later, the woman who
got her here is shot to death in cold blood. I can't believe—" She clutched her shirt at her solar plexus. "I'm
going to be sick."

Colin placed a hand on her shoulder. "Easy, Maisie.
Just breathe normally."

She squeezed her eyes shut, tears leaking out of the
corners. Her nose was running. She sniffled, letting go of
her shirt and wiping her nose on the sleeve. She opened
her eyes and sniffled again. "Sorry. I never seem to have
a tissue. I'll change in a few minutes. God, what an awful
day." She raised her gaze to Emma. "I know you're the
one who found Rachel this morning. The police asked
us—Dad and me—if we knew that she'd called you.
We didn't. We've no idea what she wanted. Did she tell
you? When Rachel called—" Maisie stopped abruptly

and shook her head. "Never mind. I know you can't tell me things."

"How long had you and Rachel been working on the movie?" Emma asked.

"Since October. In the last week or so I could see it was turning into two different movies. Hers and mine. Rachel wanted to take my interest and knowledge of the Irish Celtic pagan and Irish Celtic Christian worlds and use them as the backdrop for a movie about an art thief and the private art detective chasing him."

Emma kept her expression neutral. "What prompted Rachel to go in that direction?"

"She read a news story about the murder of an American in a little Irish village. Declan's Cross. It mentioned an unsolved art theft of two Jack B. Yeats paintings, and she was off and running. Obsessed. She looked into this art detective and Aoife O'Byrne. The art detective is in his eighties now. She said ours would have to be younger."

"Did she give you his name?" Colin asked.

Maisie shrugged her slender shoulders. "I don't know. Maybe. I wouldn't remember. I'm terrible with names."

Emma narrowed her gaze on her. "Wendell Sharpe," she said.

"Yeah, that's it." Maisie straightened, gaping at Emma. "Wait. Sharpe? You two are related?"

"He's my grandfather."

"Oh. *Oh.* No wonder Rachel called you this morning, then. Now it makes perfect sense."

Emma picked up the book on Yeats. "How so?"

"You're an FBI agent and the granddaughter of a renowned art detective. Rachel could have been shifting and thinking of making you the art detective in her version of our movie. Maybe doing a composite of you and your grandfather. It'd all be fiction, of course—as Rachel said, inspired by but not based on real events. Anyway, with Aoife O'Byrne arriving yesterday, I can see that Rachel would want to talk to you. Pick your brain. With my scheduling a meeting at the marina this morning, it makes sense she asked to meet you on the island. Pure convenience."

"Did she tell anyone she was going out there?" Emma asked.

"She didn't tell me. She died before she could go into much detail about what she'd learned so far about the thief and her art detective—your grandfather—but I know she was excited. I was resistant to letting her take over this project, but I was willing to hear her out with as open a mind as I could."

Colin walked over to a closed door. "What's in here?"

"A guest studio apartment. It has its own entrance onto West Cedar. A friend of mine is staying there."

He cocked a brow at her. "What friend?"

Color rose in Maisie's tear-stained cheeks. "His name's Oliver Fairbairn. He's a mythologist. He worked as a consultant on one of my films. We got to talking on the set one day—he inspired my interest in Celtic Ireland."

"He's Irish?"

"English, actually. His expertise isn't restricted to Ireland or even to Celtic myths and legends. They're what I latched on to."

"Where is he now?" Emma asked.

"He went out for a walk. He doesn't live here—he stays here when he's in town. Most of the time that's when I'm in town, too. I'm mobile, but I've been in Boston a lot this fall, mostly to pull together plans for the island. Oliver's latest movie-consulting job ended in October, and he took the opportunity to do some research in Boston. He comes and goes. As Dad mentioned, he's been back and forth a lot, too. He lives in Malibu. He grew up here, though."

"Got it," Colin said. "Have the police talked to Mr. Fairbairn?"

"I don't know. Not that I know of."

"Was he at your brunch at the marina this morning?"

"He was invited," Maisie said. "Of course, there was no brunch. We were about to get started when the police descended and we found out about Rachel."

She looked out the window at the courtyard. Darkness was descending fast now. She seemed more tired and preoccupied now than in shock and disbelief.

Emma moved from the table and stood next to her. "Have you settled anything for your movie—time period, location, theme, characters?"

"I was still casting a wide net when Rachel told me about Declan's Cross. I did some cursory research. I could see why the theft caught her interest, but I was captivated by Saint Declan. I'd love to visit Ardmore, where he established his monastery." Maisie smiled sadly, her energy clearly fading. "The photos I've seen on the internet are intriguing. Is it as beautiful as it seems?"

"As far as I'm concerned, it is," Emma said.

"It seems like such a leap to get from a theft in a small Irish village ten years ago to Rachel's death this morning. It must be hard to take things step by step in a criminal investigation and not get ahead of yourself." Maisie's eyes narrowed, her gaze again turning cool. "Does your grandfather's involvement complicate your role, Agent Sharpe?"

Emma had no intention of answering the question. Maisie Bristol might look as if she cut her own hair and had just flunked high school algebra, but Emma could see her tackling Hollywood and coming out on top.

She drew a business card from her jacket and placed it on the table. "Call me if you think of anything else, or if you want to talk more."

Maisie had gone pale again. She didn't pick up the card. She bit down on her lower lip as she touched the black lettering. "The FBI. My God." She seemed to force herself to breathe. "I get sick to my stomach and maybe a little bitchy—maybe a lot bitchy—when I think that something I did could have led to Rachel's death. Rachel said the murder in Declan's Cross last week has been solved and the killer is dead. That investigation is all wrapped up, isn't it?"

"Yes, it is."

"You say that with such certainty."

"Call anytime, Maisie," Emma said. "Day or night."

Her shoulders slumped but she gave a small nod. "Thank you."

Nine

After they left the Bristol house, Colin walked with Emma back to the Taj Hotel. They needed to talk with Aoife O'Byrne now that Lucy Yankowski had been found in Aoife's Dublin studio. At least, Emma needed to talk to the Irish artist. Colin decided he could wait when he glanced in the bar off the Taj lobby and spotted Finian Bracken at a small table by the fire.

Of all people, Colin thought.

Finian was from the southwest Irish coast but lately resided in Maine as the parish priest in Colin's hometown of Rock Point. He was also good friends with Sean Murphy, the Irish detective who had walked into Aoife's studio earlier with Matt Yankowski.

Had Murphy called Finian to look in on Aoife?

Or had Aoife called him?

A man Colin didn't recognize was sitting across the table from Finian. Emma hit the up button for the elevator. Colin nodded to the bar. "I'll go talk whiskey with Fin and find out who his new friend is."

Emma nodded. "I'll meet you back here after I talk with Aoife. She's expecting me."

The elevator doors opened, and Colin waited as Emma

disappeared inside. Then he stepped into the quiet, dimly lit bar.

"Please," Finian said, motioning to a cushioned chair, "join us."

That was the plan, but Colin kept his remark to himself as he pulled out the chair and sat down. Although Finian was in his priest duds, he still managed to remind Colin of Bono. "Hello, Fin. Who's your friend here?"

Finian, a whiskey expert as well as a priest, formerly an executive at Bracken Distillers, had only a glass of water with a slice of lemon in front of him. "Actually, I didn't get his name."

"Oliver Fairbairn," the man said in a distinct English accent, raising his glass and swirling its amber contents. "A Scotch-drinking mythologist. And you are?"

Finian supplied the answer. "This is my friend Colin Donovan, Oliver."

The Brit leaned forward and spoke in a conspiratorial whisper. "You're an FBI agent." He sat back immediately. "I wish I could say I had a nose for American federal agents, but I don't. Maisie just texted me. She said you and another agent—Emma Sharpe—asked about me. That was Agent Sharpe who came in with you? I gather she doesn't want to join us."

Oliver Fairbairn either wasn't on his first Scotch or was pretending not to be. He had unruly dark blond hair and blue-green eyes and wore a rumpled shirt under a wool vest, with gray wool trousers and a trench coat on the back of his chair. He looked to be in his late thirties even if he was dressed as if he'd stepped out of the pages of a Sherlock Holmes novel.

He sipped his drink. "Scotch or a tall Irish, Agent Donovan?"

"I'm good, thanks."

"I prefer Scotch to Irish whiskey, but our good Father here tells me the peated Bracken 15 year old stands up to the best single-malt Scotch. A rare thing, a peated Irish whiskey."

"The Bracken stands up as far as I'm concerned," Colin said. "Not that my palate is particularly sophisticated."

"I'll have to try Bracken 15 one day, then," Fairbairn said. "Right now, I'm quite content with my Glenfiddich 18 year old. Glenfiddich is Scottish Gaelic. It means *valley of the deer*. Doesn't that conjure up beautiful images?"

"It certainly does," Finian said with an awkward glance at Colin.

Colin didn't soften his look. His Irish friend had no business being here, and he obviously knew it. He could have at least alerted Colin that he was on the way. Finian Bracken, however, would have his own reasons for his choices. He was in his late thirties, a late-vocation priest ordained only a year ago. They'd become friends since Finian's arrival in Rock Point in June to fill in for Saint Patrick's regular priest, who was on a yearlong sabbatical in Ireland.

Seven years ago—long before Colin knew him—Finian had been the happily married father of two young daughters and cofounder with his twin brother, Declan, of a successful Irish distillery. Then, on a summer day he could never get back, a freak sailing accident had taken his wife and daughters from him. Finian had been on his way to meet them for a family holiday.

Garda Sean Murphy had investigated the drowning deaths of Sally Bracken and little Mary and Kathleen Bracken. He hadn't been a detective with a special unit then. The two Irishmen had become friends. Colin had been aware that Finian had visited Declan's Cross, where Sean had a family farm, and knew Kitty, Aoife's sister. He hadn't thought about Dublin-based Aoife.

Oliver Fairbairn savored his Scotch, cupping his glass in both hands. "I hope your visit with my good friend Maisie went well, despite the circumstances. Isn't she brilliant? The perfect, mighty blend of intelligence, talent and humility. She couldn't have accomplished what she has if she'd been just another narcissistic Hollywood blowhard." He grinned, a thick lock of hair falling on his forehead. "I can say that out here. I'd never say it on the West Coast. I'd never work on another movie."

"You like your movie work, do you?" Colin asked.

"Sure. Why not? It pays well, and I don't care if directors mangle the legends and myths they hire me to teach them about. That's what legends and myths are for, isn't it? Mangling. Or *telling anew* as one director put it." The Brit grimaced. "Rachel Bristol got a kick out of that one when I told her. A bloody awful day, isn't it?"

Colin said nothing. He noticed Finian lift his water glass and take a sip but kept his attention on Maisie Bristol's mythologist. "Did you just happen into the bar here and strike up a conversation with Father Bracken?"

"As a matter of fact, that's exactly what I did," Fairbairn said. "I wanted to give Maisie and her father time to themselves and walked over here, somehow thinking it would be a good idea to pay my respects or whatever to Aoife O'Byrne. Fortunately, I changed my mind and decided on Scotch, instead, and met Father Bracken. How do you two know each other?"

"We're friends," Colin said without elaboration.

The Brit set his glass down. "A good day to have a priest for a friend."

"Aoife called me," Finian said, addressing Colin. "Kitty called, too. And Sean."

Colin hadn't planned on asking for an explanation in front of Oliver Fairbairn. "Makes sense," he said.

Finian leveled his midnight-blue eyes on Colin. "Aoife has checked out of the hotel. She's driving back to Maine with me. She's on her way down with her things."

Fairbairn's eyebrows shot up. "Aoife O'Byrne is going back to Maine with you? A beautiful woman, a famous Irish artist? Good heavens, man, won't your parishioners have fits if you sneak her into the rectory?"

Colin pretty much had the same question.

Finian looked unruffled. "I've booked a room for her at a local inn," he said.

"Well, then. That solves it." Fairbairn sat back and picked up his glass. "How on earth did you end up in Maine? A long story, I gather?"

"Are there any short Irish stories?" Finian asked with a shrug.

Fairbairn seemed to know Finian had said all he planned to about his relationship with Aoife O'Byrne. "Good point." He downed more of his Scotch, not savoring it this time. "I'm afraid the shock of Rachel's death has led me to drink too fast. If I make an ass of myself, will you please excuse me? Or am I too late, and I should put that in past tense and beg your forgiveness?"

Finian cracked the smallest of smiles, the first break in his obvious tension since Colin had arrived. "You're doing fine, my friend. Glenfiddich 18 is a beautiful Scotch. At least you didn't ruin it with ice."

"I like how you think, Father Bracken. What about you, Agent Donovan? You won't join me for a dram?"

"Not tonight, thanks," Colin said.

"I suppose what happened today didn't faze you.

Nerves of steel and all that. I've only known Maisie a couple of months and hardly knew Rachel, and I'm flattened."

Colin thought of the moment he'd realized Emma was on Bristol Island alone, with a woman dead at her feet and a shooter on the run—or getting ready to fire again. He noticed Finian's scrutiny, but his priest friend made no comment.

Oblivious, Oliver Fairbairn polished off the last of his Scotch. "I suppose you're wondering what I do. As I told the detectives, I'm a useless academic who doesn't have a normal job. It's true."

"You're an independent scholar," Finian said.

"A nicer way to put it. I'm not affiliated with any particular institution. I was fortunate to find work as a Hollywood consultant. If you want to know about the real Thor, I can tell you. Of course, there is no *real* Thor, is there?"

Colin sat back, feeling the heat from the fire. "I just know he's the one with the hammer. You've been working with Maisie on understanding Irish Celtic myths and legends."

"She's an eager student. A sponge. She wants to know everything. It's refreshing. Exhilarating, really, as you can imagine, for someone like me to have this wildly hot Hollywood producer interested in everything I can tell her about ogham stones and holy wells."

"And Saint Declan," Colin added.

Fairbairn's face fell. He looked as if he wanted to crawl into his Scotch glass. He picked up his water glass, instead. "Saint Declan is a recent interest for Maisie, because of Rachel. Which, of course, you already know, Agent Donovan. The interaction of pagan Celtic culture and the early Irish Christian saints—like Declan—shows a dynamic relationship. Pagan culture didn't wither away and Christianity didn't smother it. It's not that black and white. It's the stuff of great movies, I've no doubt. I'm eager to see what Maisie does with her knowledge and interest." He turned to Finian. "I'm sure you know more about Saint Declan than I do, Father Bracken."

"Have you ever been to Ardmore or Declan's Cross?" Finian asked.

"I was in Ardmore a few years ago. Maybe it's been longer now—six years? I travel so much. It's hard to keep track. I suppose I could have wandered through Declan's Cross when I was in the area. I don't recall. There's a fabulous hotel in Ardmore. It's built into the cliffs above the village."

"I know it well," Finian said. "It has an excellent Scotch selection."

Fairbairn nodded. "I blew the budget and booked two nights. I crawled through Saint Declan's monastic ruins, walked on the beach and enjoyed a good dinner and a good Scotch. Then I went back to London."

"Were you a Hollywood consultant then?" Colin asked.

"Just a hopeful academic."

Colin kept his focus on the Brit. "Is consulting your main source of income?"

"Oh, you feds will ask anything, won't you?" Fairbairn seemed more caught up in the drama of the moment than offended. "For the past eighteen months, yes, it's been my main source of income. I don't know about the future."

"Do you teach?"

"Not any longer. In the past I taught a university course here and there."

"When did you arrive in Boston?"

"This trip? Yesterday. I flew in from London. Maisie had asked me to be back today if at all possible."

"When?" Colin asked.

"A few days ago. Wednesday, maybe?" Fairbairn waved a hand. "I'm still jet-lagged. I don't have a good sense of the days. Maisie told me she and Rachel weren't seeing eye to eye on Maisie's film project. She thought I might be able to help. I didn't get the impression that their differences were anything they wouldn't be able to work out. Maisie's the one with the checkbook, after all. Rachel was nothing if not about making things happen, and if it had to be Maisie's way for the movie to get made—then so be it. Rachel was certain in her convictions, but she was also pragmatic. That's my take, anyway, for what it's worth."

"And Maisie?" Colin asked. "Is she as certain in her convictions?"

"In a different way. Maisie picks which ships to launch and launches them, so to speak. She doesn't get involved with details. This project was to have been a bit different. She didn't want just to launch the ship. She wanted her fingerprints on everything. Rachel worked in the engine room—it's what suited her—but she wanted to move up, launch a few ships of her own."

Finian lifted his water glass. "What about her ex-husband?"

"Travis does his own thing. He's well respected in Hollywood from what little I know. Rachel was one of those ex-spouses who doesn't go away. Keeps a relationship with the family. I don't know whether that's good or bad. She and Travis didn't have any kids together, not even a shared dog." Fairbairn breathed out and let his shoulders sag, as if he'd suddenly lost all his energy. "I should get back there and let you two chat. Please give my best to Aoife, won't you, Father? We've never met, but I happened into a gallery in London that had several of her paintings on display. Irish sunrises and sunsets, and one cheeky-looking porpoise. If I'd had the money, I'd have bought that porpoise."

"I don't know if that painting has ever sold," Finian said.

"Then maybe there's yet hope." Fairbairn's voice cracked, as if the emotions of the day had finally caught up with him. "It's been a pleasure, despite the circumstances. If I can be of any assistance, Agent Donovan, please don't hesitate to get in touch with me. Father, I hope the tongues don't wag too much when you bring Aoife O'Byrne to town."

He started to pay for his drink, but Finian refused to let him. Fairbairn mumbled his thanks, and shuffled out of the bar.

Finian smiled at Colin. "You look as if you're thinking up an excuse to arrest me."

"Don't tempt me. Why didn't you let me know you were coming down here?"

"I didn't want to bother you."

"Bother me? When you know a woman in the middle of a homicide investigation?"

Finian looked longingly at Fairbairn's empty Scotch glass as the waiter took it away. "Aoife has nothing to do with Rachel Bristol's death," he said.

"Let's switch, Fin. You take my FBI credentials and I take your clerical collar."

"Glenfiddich would go down nicely after today, wouldn't it, my friend?"

Colin sighed. "Do you know about the break-in at Aoife's studio?"

"Sean told me. He'd already phoned Aoife. She's horrified by what's happened, but we didn't have a chance to talk much about it. I imagine we will on the drive to Rock Point."

"Fin…"

He held up a hand. "No worries, Colin. I'm a grown man. I'll be fine."

"The inn you mentioned to Fairbairn—my folks' place?"

"Yes." Finian smiled feebly. "Your brother Mike is there."

"No worries, then," Colin said with a grudging smile. Mike was ex-army, a Maine wilderness guide and outfitter and tough as nails. Tougher. Their father was a retired Rock Point police officer. "We have no reason to think Aoife's a target, but whoever shot Rachel Bristol is still out there, Fin. Watch yourself."

"The detectives know how to reach her if they have further questions."

"How long does she plan to stay in Maine?"

"I don't think she's thought that far ahead. She just wants to get out of here."

"Fight-or-flight mode."

The priest's expression softened. "No doubt."

Emma entered the bar with Aoife, who wore a sleek black trench coat cinched at her waist and looked as if she couldn't get out of there fast enough. She barely glanced at Colin as she and Emma walked over to the table. "I'm ready, Fin," Aoife said. "We can go."

Finian was already on his feet. He took Emma's hand and kissed her on the cheek. "How are you, Emma? I'm sorry about this morning. Is there anything I can do?"

"I'm doing fine, thanks," she said quietly.

He nodded to Colin and left with Aoife. Emma, still in her leather jacket, sat at the table. "I see the Taj isn't making anything off you and Finian. Who was Finian's friend?"

"Oliver Fairbairn."

"Our mythologist movie consultant," Emma said. "I see."

"He didn't have much to say. He had a pricy Scotch. How's Aoife?"

"Shaken. She says she doesn't know anything about the break-in at her studio. All was quiet when she left early yesterday morning. She hired a car to take her to the airport."

"One of the perks of success," Colin said.

"She didn't notice anyone hanging around the building then or in the past few days. She's positive the cross came by mail and wasn't hand-delivered. She says it's the first and only time she's heard from the thief in the past ten years. I debated telling her we believe the same person is responsible for other thefts in different cities but decided not to, at least not yet."

"Do you believe her?"

"I have no reason not to. I don't see why she would have faked the break-in and left Lucy Yankowski under a bookcase. Poor Lucy. Talk about being in the wrong place at the wrong time."

"Like you this morning," Colin said.

Emma ignored him. "I would love to sit here by the fire with you, but I've been summoned to BPD headquarters. Our friendly homicide detectives have talked to Yank about what happened in Dublin. Now they want to talk to me."

"They're going to grill you about you and your family's contact with Aoife and pry as much out of you as they can about this thief." Colin shrugged. "I would."

"No doubt. If they have evidence this morning was

an unrelated accidental shooting, I'm not going to share all my files with them. I wouldn't, anyway. I'll tell them what they need to know."

"Used to bug the hell out of me when feds told me that." Colin thought Emma attempted to smile, but she looked troubled, preoccupied. He leaned forward. "What else is going on, Emma?"

"Lucas called on my way up to Aoife's room." Emma raised her gaze to Colin, her eyes deepening to emerald in the cozy light. "Rachel Bristol was in Heron's Cove on Monday."

"Lucas spoke to her?"

She nodded. "I need to go up there, Colin."

"We can leave after you finish with the detectives."

She looked at the fire, and now her eyes reflected the orange flames. "What if Rachel figured out Declan's Cross was the first of multiple heists by our thief?"

"That's not public knowledge."

"It's not *common* knowledge. A determined researcher digging through press reports on unsolved art thefts could figure it out, or at least make an educated guess."

"All right," Colin said. "Let's say Rachel connected the dots. Let's say she loves the idea of a serial art thief one of the world's best art detectives hasn't been able to catch. She dives in and starts stirring up trouble. She visits your brother in Heron's Cove, she calls your grandfather, she calls Aoife. Let's assume the thief is already on edge because of Lindsey Hargreaves' murder in Declan's Cross."

"And now, here's this Hollywood-type messing around in his world," Emma said. "He breaks his pattern and sends the crosses to Granddad and me, Lucas, Yank and then Aoife. But why? If he was worried Rachel was getting close to identifying him—or actually had identified him—why draw attention to himself? Then again, that's always been the issue with him. He draws attention to himself. It's like his thefts are a game for him." She broke off, clearly frustrated. "I'm speculating."

"The crosses are a form of manipulation."

"Maybe so, but as far as we know, never to commit murder."

Colin noticed a middle-aged couple enter the bar. It was filling up. "Do you want me to go with you to BPD headquarters?"

Emma shook her head, springing to her feet. "I should get over there before they send a squad car for me. I'll meet you back at the apartment." She buttoned her jacket. "You don't have to go to Maine, Colin. I can go on my own."

"Not a chance." That didn't mean he didn't wish he and Emma could drink whiskey by the fire and talk about anything but thieves, murder and Celtic crosses. "I'll gas up my truck."

Colin stopped back at the HIT offices and found Sam Padgett alone in the conference room with his Texas boots up on the table. It was dark, and Padgett wasn't a happy man. He'd taken printouts of art believed to have been stolen by the Declan's Cross thief and lined them up on the table as if they were cards in a game of concentration. "I'm desperate," he said, half-serious. "I thought looking at them one by one and in different combinations might help. Emma looks at them like an art historian. I look at them like a guy who doesn't know anything about art, which, for all we know, our thief could be."

"Come up with anything?"

Padgett glowered. "No. What the hell, maybe our guy has some deep-seated bullshit neurosis that's driving him to steal certain types of art. Maybe he grabs pieces that all have green in them because green reminds him of his dead mother's eyes."

Colin dropped onto a chair. "That wouldn't get us far."

"I know. I planned to go for a bike ride out to Concord today. I should have." The Texan heaved a sigh. "You ever think this thief's playing us for fools?"

"Yep."

"He's been winning for ten years. Is he smart or lucky?"

"Probably both."

Padgett sat up straight, lowering his feet to the floor. "It was a close one for Lucy Yankowski. If Yank and that Irish cop hadn't come along, she'd have been in serious trouble. You like to think someone would have noticed something, heard her yelling—but people in that neighborhood obviously aren't going to be thinking a woman's trapped under a bookcase in a famous artist's studio."

It was a fair point. Colin updated Sam on Emma's visit with the BPD.

"She could be a while," Sam said. "Maisie Bristol has produced five movies for the big screen and made a ton of money. She's on fire out in Hollywood. I downloaded all five. Want to take a look?"

"Sure, Sam. I'll see if I can find some popcorn in the kitchen."

Colin wasn't positive, but he thought Sam Padgett might have smiled.

Ten

Dublin, Ireland

Wendell Sharpe wouldn't hear of the Yankowskis checking into a hotel. He insisted Yank and Lucy stay in the guest room at his apartment in the heart of Georgian Dublin with its stately squares and plain-front buildings with their brightly colored doors. Sean Murphy had arranged to have Lucy's luggage brought over from her hotel, and that was that. It was done.

Now Lucy was in flannel pajamas, snuggled next to Yank on the couch in Wendell's small living room. She didn't look as haunted and said she wasn't quite ready to give up and go to bed, but she had to be exhausted. Yank ached every time he looked at her and saw the bruises on her arms, the right side of her jaw. And every time, he thought…*I did this to her.*

It wasn't rational but it wasn't altogether irrational, either.

Wendell Sharpe sat quietly by the fire. Sean Murphy sat across from Yank—an improvement over the Irishman's pacing. Between the questions put to her by Murphy and his garda colleagues and the conversation among the three men for the past forty-five minutes, Lucy would have a fair idea of what all was going on. Even things Yank would prefer she not know. A serial art thief, Celtic crosses, a dead woman in Boston. A damn mess.

Gardai were canvassing Aoife's building and neighborhood for witnesses—anyone who had been there around the time Lucy had arrived and in the hours after she'd been attacked. So far, they hadn't produced a single person who'd seen or heard anyone or anything suspicious, and no one had come forward.

"We'll keep at it," Sean said, "but it looks as if whoever broke into Aoife's studio did so without drawing the attention of anyone in the area."

"One of her friends, maybe?" Yank asked. "Sees her leave with her suitcase and takes advantage. Lucy shows up. Bang. Panic, pull a bookcase down on top of her and run."

The Irishman shrugged. "It's possible."

"Could Aoife have trashed her own place? Made it look as if someone had broken in?"

"Why would she do that?" Sean asked, cool.

"Maybe she wanted to divert, misdirect and confuse authorities."

"Again—why?"

"Something to hide. Maybe something to do with our art thief." Yank reached for a basket of crackers on the coffee table. Wendell had put them out with a selection of Irish cheeses, grapes, apples and a bit of raw honey— along with two bottles of wine. "What about men? Does Aoife have any old boyfriends kicking around who might want to search her studio?"

"Aoife's very private."

"Does that mean you don't know about men in her life?"

"It's late. See to your wife, Agent Yankowski." The garda detective got to his feet. He looked down at Lucy, who'd nibbled on the crackers and fruit but hadn't touched any of the wine. "Mrs. Yankowski, if there's anything you need—anything at all—call me, okay? Anytime."

"Thank you, Sean."

"Have a good night."

Although he might have spent the past five months recuperating and tending sheep in Declan's Cross, the Irishman hadn't lost his edge as a law enforcement officer. He would know that no matter how annoying Yank was or how out of line he got, it was his investigation, too, even if he had no authority in Ireland. Sean Murphy needed to stay abreast of what was going on in Boston and therefore needed Yank's cooperation.

He turned to Wendell. "I'll be in touch."

The old man held up a hand. "Hold on. There's something I need to tell you two."

Sean's blue eyes narrowed. "Should I sit down?"

"This woman killed in Boston called me last week. I didn't think much of it at the time. She said she wanted to interview me for a film. I could choose where and when—but soon. I didn't ask any questions. I just said no. I've received numerous requests for interviews over the years. I always say no. Lucas might handle things differently, but that's my approach."

"You're certain it was Rachel Bristol?" Sean asked.

"Yes. I wrote down her name in case she called again. I dug out the note, and there it was. Rachel Bristol. She said she was from California. Of course, I don't know if it actually was her on the phone—it could have been another woman pretending to be Rachel Bristol."

"Do you have the date and time of the call?"

Wendell nodded. He was lanky, blue-eyed and if a bit

stooped these days, as alert as ever. He handed the Irish-man a business card. "Tuesday afternoon, shortly after two o'clock. I wrote the info on the back." He looked over at Yank. "I wrote it down for you, too. Card's in the kitchen."

Sean tucked the card into his jacket. "Did Rachel argue with you after you told her no?"

"Like mad. I told her that if anyone is going to tell my story, it will be me. She didn't give up. She said she didn't want to tell my story. She had her own stories. She didn't use charm—she wasn't trying to butter me up or anything. She assumed I would be flattered that my life's work would inspire a film. She was convinced it would be a blockbuster and asked me to keep our conversation to myself." The old man settled back into his chair, the cushions long-conformed to his bony frame. "I hung up and forgot all about her until just a little while ago."

Sean seemed marginally satisfied with Wendell's re-port. "Did she mention Declan's Cross or the thief? Celtic crosses? Jack Yeats? Anything specific at all?"

"No, nothing. I didn't give her the chance."

"All right, then. Thank you. I'll be in touch if I have further questions."

With a final good-night, Sean saw himself out the front door.

Yank felt Lucy stir next to him, but she said nothing. He sensed that any mention of the events in Boston that morning disturbed her, as if somehow she was partially responsible for what had happened. If she'd been able to squeeze out from under the bookcase and notify the police, maybe Rachel Bristol would still be alive. It was a leap, but Yank understood. He'd been thinking if he hadn't met Emma Sharpe four years ago—if he hadn't encouraged her to join the FBI—then Lucy wouldn't have spent thirty hours trapped in an Irish studio. It was the kind of thinking that got him nowhere, but it sickened him to think about his wife lying there, alone, cold, hungry, afraid to move.

Wendell refilled Yank's wineglass and then his own. They'd met three and a half years ago, at the Dublin offices of Sharpe Fine Art Recovery on some cobblestone street. Emma had been fresh out of the convent then, working for her grandfather while she decided whether to join the FBI. Yank had come to Ireland to press his point of view that she should head to Quantico. He'd been certain she would make a fine agent, given her expertise, her Sharpe contacts and her unusual and incisive way of looking at things, shaped by her background as a Sharpe and her years as a religious sister. He'd already been toying with the idea of HIT. When it came to fruition, Emma had been top of his list of agents he'd wanted on his fledgling team.

He wasn't one to second-guess himself, but if Emma Sharpe had stayed with her family's art recovery business, he'd have had fewer headaches than in the past few months. At the same time, she'd proven herself to be the asset he'd expected she would be. Having her on his team was just more complicated—more hazardous to his own career, even—than he'd anticipated.

He didn't know how a new director would take to Emma, especially if that new director was Mina Van Buren. She was at the top of the list of names Yank had heard bandied about for acting director. Good old Mina. She was ambitious, competent and by-the-book, a prosecutor to her bones and not one to suffer fools gladly.

And Yank didn't trust her.

She'd left him a voice mail after he'd found Lucy. "I just want to know how your wife is."

He hadn't called her back yet. Probably should.

"Hell of a day," Wendell said, sipping his wine.

Yank grunted. "That sums it up."

Lucy sat up, wincing, giving a groan. "I'm stiff. I guess that's to be expected. I'll leave you two to your wine. Wendell, I can't thank you enough for letting us stay here."

Yank stood to help her to her feet, but she got up on her own and mumbled that she'd see herself to the guest room. He sat back down, watching her as she shuffled into the hall off the living room. She wouldn't have to do stairs to get to the guest room, and he'd hear her if she called for help. But she wouldn't. She'd hated being as vulnerable as she had been the past two days—he could see that in the hours since he and Sean Murphy had found her. Yank wasn't surprised. He knew his wife well.

"She's tough," Wendell said.

"Yep."

"I don't mean tough because she doesn't want a hand but tough because she got through this thing. We all need a hand once in a while. Doesn't mean you're not independent. Means you're human." The old man made a face. "I've had too damn much wine. I'd have lasted two minutes under that bookcase. I get claustrophobic when I get tangled up in my bedsheets."

"Damn, Wendell, now I'm picturing you in your shorts."

He grinned. "Most of the time I sleep in the buff."

"Now there's a picture I don't want in my head."

"You ain't kidding, pal."

Yank suspected that Wendell had meant to lighten the mood in the room. "You never wanted Emma to join the FBI," Yank said, sitting back with his wine.

"Why would I? She's good. She and Lucas would have

made a great team. Of course, I didn't want her to become a nun, either." The old art detective stared into his wine a moment before he continued. "That she's a Sharpe isn't a liability in any way for me. It is for you, though, isn't it?"

"Moot point. Did you think this Declan's Cross thief would come back to haunt her? Is there anything else about this thief in the Sharpe Fine Art Recovery files I need to know? Anything else in the Wendell Sharpe mental file? Now's the time to tell me."

"Before Emma did her first push-up at the FBI Academy would have been the time," Wendell said. "Maybe it would have kept her in Dublin with me. But it's too late now, and I can't say that there is anything else—in the actual files or my mental files."

Yank pointed his wineglass at him. "That's a slippery answer, Wendell."

The old man shrugged his thin shoulders. "Want a tall Irish before you hit the sack?"

"Two glasses of wine is enough alcohol for me, but I did have a look at your whiskey cabinet. Finian Bracken would be proud." Yank downed the last of his wine and stood, feeling the long drive across Ireland that morning, the tension of finding Lucy—of hearing from Emma and Colin back in Boston. And Padgett. That guy was relentless, but it was one reason Yank had selected him for HIT. He focused on Wendell, the firelight adding color to his lined face. "Father Bracken met Aoife O'Byrne in Boston and drove her up to Rock Point."

"Did he now? Well, they're both Irish, and they're both friends with Sean Murphy. Makes sense, I suppose."

"Anything between them?"

"Between Murphy and Aoife?"

Yank sighed. Wendell Sharpe was being deliberately dense. "Between Father Bracken and Aoife."

"How would I know?"

"Because you know things, Wendell. Because Aoife is the niece of the first victim of this thief. Because she's refused to talk to you about what happened that night in Declan's Cross for the past ten years. Because, my friend, you're not that different from me, and I'd know."

"Seven years ago, Finian Bracken was a man in terrible pain. That's what I know. It's what everyone in Ireland knows."

"And Aoife O'Byrne is a beautiful woman."

"That she is." Wendell put his feet up on the coffee table. "I think I'll have that tall Irish. See you in the morning, Agent Yankowski."

Yank didn't pursue the subject. He was a guest in Wendell Sharpe's home, and he had his answer, anyway. If no one could confirm it, people—or at least an octogenarian art detective—suspected there was something, or had been something, between Aoife and the Irish priest.

He helped himself to another chunk of cheese. Wendell explained that it was Cashel blue cheese, then described the other cheeses on the tray. Yank grabbed a slice of apple. "Getting into Irish cheese now that you're retired?"

The old man gave him a steely-eyed stare. "Semiretired."

"Emma says you're going home to Maine for Thanksgiving."

"That's the plan. Where will you be for Thanksgiving?"

"I haven't thought about it." Yank glanced at the hall where Lucy had disappeared, then turned back to Wendell. "Maybe I should."

"Our work can be hard on relationships."

"You and your wife—"

"A different time. We worked things out as best we

could. We made compromises." He stared at the fire but Yank had a feeling the older man was seeing his lost wife. "She never wanted to live in Ireland."

And so he'd stayed in Maine and hadn't opened the Dublin office until after his wife was gone. Yank got it. If Wendell had died first, he'd have died in Heron's Cove.

"I love Ireland," Wendell said. "I've enjoyed living and working here these past fifteen years. It's been good for the business, but I'd give up Ireland in a heartbeat to have my green-eyed girl back with me." He rose stiffly and winked at Yank. "I think I'll have that tall Irish now."

Yank got to his feet. "A long day."

"Yes. I'm glad your wife is recovering from her ordeal. This thief's been a thorn in my side for a decade, Agent Yankowski. The crosses have been a thumb in my eye. Now they're a thumb in your eye."

"I'm going to find this bastard."

Wendell opened a glass-front cabinet. "It seems he's already found you."

"Did he kill that woman this morning, Wendell?"

The old man pulled a bottle of Bushmills 16 from the cabinet. "I don't know," he said quietly. "I wish I did."

Yank said good-night and headed down the hall to his wife, leaving Wendell Sharpe to his tall Irish.

Lucy wasn't asleep when Yank slipped into the guest room. "I can sleep on the couch," he said.

"No—no, Matt." She patted the space next to her. "I want you here next to me."

He went into the bathroom and washed up. He didn't like his reflection in the mirror. He looked tense, uncertain, pissed off. An unpleasant mix of emotions. He saw fresh lines in his face. He'd passed forty. There'd be more lines down the road. He'd noticed a few at the corners of Lucy's eyes that morning. She'd turn forty next year. They'd talked about having kids early on in their marriage, but it hadn't happened, and they hadn't pursued it—done the tests, adopted. She had her work as a clinical psychologist. He had the FBI. He'd always seen them retiring together, reading books in the shade, going to nice restaurants, traveling. Never—not once—had he considered that she might not come to Boston with him.

He returned to the guest room and got under the covers with her.

"Did you and Wendell have a good chat?" she asked.

"He told me he sleeps in the buff."

"On these cold, damp Irish nights?" She smiled sleepily. "He's a brave man."

"I could do it if I had a cute woman with a pixie haircut in bed with me."

Lucy placed a warm palm on his shoulder. "I wasn't mad at you. When I was trapped. When I realized that someone had broken into the studio and deliberately pulled that bookcase down on top of me, I knew it had to involve one of your cases, and I knew that meant you'd find me."

"I thought you'd gone off to Paris again, or maybe Prague."

"Did I tell you I bought an Hermès scarf when I was in Paris?"

"Yeah, Lucy, you did. And a Chanel jacket. They cost more than my first car."

"Your first car was one pothole from the junkyard."

He saw that she'd shut her eyes and knew she was drifting. "We'll figure things out, Lucy. I promise."

"I know we will. I can't keep my eyes open but I don't want to go to sleep. What happens tomorrow?"

"Whatever you want to happen."

"You need to see Declan's Cross, don't you?"

"It can keep."

"I looked it up on the map. It's an easy drive from Dublin." She opened her eyes, then shut them again, barely awake. "I know I don't have all the details—or even half the details—but I want to see where this thief of yours struck. I want to ride with you into the Irish countryside…"

She didn't finish, and he saw that she was asleep. He kissed her on the forehead. "We can talk in the morning," he whispered, nowhere near ready to sleep himself.

He lay on his back, his throat tight. It was still relatively early on the East Coast. Colin had texted him that he and Emma were off to Maine. Finian Bracken and Aoife O'Byrne would already be there by now. Even if he was in Boston, Yank knew there wasn't much he could do. Right now, he was where he needed to be.

Eleven

Rock Point, Maine

Finian Bracken eased his BMW into the November darkness of Rock Point, the southern Maine fishing village that had been his home since June. Aoife sat in silence next to him, as she had for most of the ninety-minute trip north from Boston. Seeing her—hearing her voice, the lilt of her accent—had brought Ireland close to him again, and the past, reminding him of what he'd left behind and the man he'd once been.

"I shouldn't have come to Boston," Aoife said, her near-black hair gleaming in the glow of a passing streetlight, one of the few in the small village.

"Why did you come, then, Aoife?"

She turned to him before answering. "You know why, Finian."

He slowed the car but made no response.

She put her hand on his arm. "Can I at least see your church?"

"It's late. You must be tired. It's the middle of the night in Ireland."

"I'm exhausted but I know I won't be able to sleep for

a while, if at all. Tea and a chat with a friend would mean a lot to me right now." She lowered her hand. "Just that, Fin. Tea and a chat. No pressure. No memories."

His BMW—his one indulgence—hugged the curve of the harbor with its bobbing fishing boats. As Aoife's slender hand fell away, his priestly garb suddenly felt foreign, as if someone had poured him into it while he'd been napping. He'd never experienced such a feeling since becoming a priest. Then again, he hadn't seen Aoife O'Byrne since he'd entered the seminary. In all his visits to Declan's Cross since then, he'd never run into her there. He didn't know whether it was a coincidence or she had deliberately avoided him.

Instead of continuing to the Donovans' inn farther out on the harbor, Finian turned onto the knot of residential streets above the village center. Aoife wouldn't know he was making a detour. She'd never been to Rock Point. She trusted him to know his way around and get her to the inn.

He parked in front of Saint Patrick's of Rock Point, a small, white-sided building that had started its life as an American Baptist church. Next to it was the rectory, a late-Victorian house in need of a bit of sprucing up.

Aoife gave a small shudder. "Oh, my. It's not terribly charming, is it?" She turned to him with a smile. "I had visions of a Jane Austen parish, I suppose."

He couldn't help but laugh. *Jane Austen.* Maybe in Heron's Cove, Emma Sharpe's hometown just down the coast. Not in Rock Point.

"I'll give you the quick tour, and we'll have tea."

"And a chat?"

"I'm here to listen to whatever you want to say, Aoife."

"But not to talk yourself," she said coolly, if also with

a quick smile. "A priest's duty, I suppose, to listen without talking—or is it because it's me?"

He didn't answer. She didn't seem to expect he would.
They got out of the car, a hard wind gusting off the Atlantic. Aoife crossed her arms on her chest and followed
him to the rectory. He'd left a light on at the back door
but took her in through the front, switching on lights and
leading her down the hall to the kitchen. The church-
provided furnishings were worn but serviceable. With
her artistic eye, Aoife would notice everything.

He filled the electric kettle—one of his few purchases
since moving into the rectory—and plugged it in and
switched it on to boil. "We can have tea in the dining
room if you'd like," he said, lifting a teapot off an open
shelf.

"Here's fine." Aoife pulled off her coat and sat at the
kitchen table. She fingered a manila file folder he'd left
there. "Parishioner secrets?"

"The menu for the annual Saint Patrick's bean-hole
supper."

"Good heavens, what's that?"

"It involves baking beans in holes dug in the yard.
There's roast pork, coleslaw, homemade applesauce and
pies—the menu hasn't changed in decades. Bean-hole
suppers are a popular fund-raiser with churches and other
nonprofit institutions in the area."

Aoife sat back, smiling at him. "No wonder Kitty worries about you."

He laughed. "How is Kitty?"

"Much better with Sean Murphy back in her life.
Those two. Such drama over the years. I think it will
work this time. They're ready for each other now, even
with him going back to work in Dublin. The hotel is
doing well. Kitty can afford to hire someone to take over

some of her day-to-day duties. I'd love to have her back in Dublin more often, assuming I stay there myself. How are your sisters, Fin? Any of them married? And your brother and his family?"

"They're all doing great. Two sisters are married. One thrives on being very hard to catch."

"I met Declan, you know. It's been several years. He was in Declan's Cross on distillery business. I thought it was you and you'd quit seminary and gone back to Bracken Distillers, but then I remembered you have a twin." Aoife's vivid, intense blue eyes leveled on him from her seat at the simple oak table. "A hell of a shock, let me tell you."

The kettle dinged, and Finian set to making tea, an orange-spice without caffeine that he expected Aoife would like. He was aware of her watching him. He told himself it was good that he'd brought her here. Let her see him as he was now.

Let him remind himself of what he was now.

Aoife rose, as if she was too restless to stay still. "Does Declan resent that you abandoned him at the distillery?" She gasped and held up a hand. "Don't answer. It was a rude, unthinking question. I'm sorry."

"No offense taken, Aoife."

"Do you have help here?" she asked him quickly.

"With cleaning, and there's a part-time secretary at the church."

She mumbled something and headed down the hall. Finian didn't know what she was up to but set the teapot and cups on the table and rummaged in the cupboard for a package of digestives. He put out a few on a plate. He and Aoife would have tea, and he'd take her to the inn and let her get settled for the evening. The Donovans would know what to say to her.

She returned with a bottle of Bracken 15 year old and sat at the table across from him. "I grabbed the unpeated expression. I'm not fond of peated whiskey. That was just for a bit of fun, wasn't it? It's won awards, though, I understand. *Rare and dear*, yes?"

Finian nodded, watching her uncork the bottle with its distinctive black-and-gold label. "You're going to put Bracken 15 into your tea?"

"Don't look so horrified. It's just a splash." She poured a small amount into her cup, then grinned at him. "Worse than adding ice?"

"You could have used a cheaper whiskey."

"Not tonight. Tonight," she said, lifting her teacup, "I want Bracken 15, triple-distilled, as fresh and gorgeous as an Irish spring morning. Did you know it would be this good when you saw it into the casks?"

"I wanted it to be," he said.

She touched the beautiful label. "Fifteen years ago I was living in Ardmore, deep into my work. Life's changed so much since then, hasn't it?"

"Aoife…"

"I should have called Sean Murphy when I got that cross. There was no note, but I knew it was from the thief. But I didn't, and now this woman is dead."

Two seconds after Aoife had snapped on her seat belt—before Finian had wound his way back to the interstate highway—she had told him about receiving the small stone cross, a modified version of the cross stolen from her uncle ten years ago.

"If not Sean, then I should have told Wendell Sharpe," Aoife said, swallowing some of her tea-and-whiskey concoction. She made a face. "Each is better by itself, I think. Orange-spice tea. Bracken 15. Not in combination." She slumped into her chair. "Sean's furious with me. He didn't say so when he phoned me about the break-in at my studio, but I can tell. He referred to himself as Detective Garda Murphy. That's ominous, isn't it?"

"It's what he is."

"I suppose. I like to think of him as a sheep farmer. If I'd stayed in Dublin, do you think my studio would have been broken into?"

Finian shook his head. "I don't know, Aoife. We can't change the past, even the recent past. What's done is done."

"Lucy Yankowski wasn't killed. That's something, at least."

"Yes, it is."

"I allowed Rachel Bristol to manipulate me because I wanted to see your life here in America. I didn't leave out the cross for her to steal, but I should have known she would be interested in it. I didn't know this FBI agent's wife was trapped in my studio."

"You couldn't have known that," Finian said.

"I didn't need to know it." She set her teacup onto its saucer. "I should have called Sean when I received the cross."

"You're hard on yourself."

"A woman is dead, Finian." She narrowed her eyes on him. "Or shall I call you Father now?"

He heard the note of sarcasm in her voice but didn't let it get to him. "Finian works," he said.

"As far as I could tell when I spoke with Sean, nothing was stolen in the break-in. Why attack that poor woman? Why risk it? Why not just run?" Aoife shuddered and drank more of her whiskey-laced tea. "Do you miss Ireland?"

"Every day, but I know I'm where I need to be."

"I haven't been to Declan's Cross in far too long. I'm desperate to see Kitty, and my nephew."

"Philip. He's a good lad."

She smiled. "He's been giving Kitty fits, but he should be at his age—within reason. He's determined to be a garda diver. Sean has a couple of friends who are guiding him. Do you remember the first time you saw Declan's Cross, Finian? Did it take your breath away?"

"It did," Finian said. "It's a beautiful place."

"Of course, you're from Kerry, and there's no prettier place on this earth than the southwest Irish coast." She breathed in deeply, shutting her eyes. "Oh, Finian. I can see Kenmare Bay glistening in an orange sunset, and the MacGillicuddy's Reeks on a perfect summer dawn."

"You painted them both."

She opened her eyes and grabbed a digestive. "Yes, and I will again when the time is right. I love sunrises and sunsets. I might rent a cottage down the Iveragh Peninsula and walk and paint for an entire summer."

"It's a grand place to walk," Finian said quietly.

Her cheeks flamed red, and she put the digestive back on its plate. Tears sprang to her eyes, shining in the dim kitchen light. "I forgot that you and Sally…" Aoife clutched her chest. "I'm so sorry."

"I still have the cottage. I haven't stayed there in a long time myself, but I loan it to friends."

"Emma and Colin. Kitty told me they stayed there."

"Agent Yankowski did, too, this past week. He only went to Dublin this morning."

"You've met him?"

"I have, indeed. He and Sean will get on. You got a taste of Sean in full-blown senior garda detective mode."

Aoife grunted. "I like Sean better when he's cleaning the barn and tending sheep. It must have been a shock when he and Agent Yankowski arrived at my studio today. They'd never admit it, but you know…" She gulped in a breath, tears spilling down her cheeks. "How will I ever go back there, Finian?"

"No one died, and you'll have answers soon. You're strong, Aoife. You'll get through this." Finian knew it was true and yet felt his stomach twist with tension, with fear for this beautiful woman. She looked so damnably alone. But wasn't that what she'd always wanted? A life on her own, as an artist unencumbered by a husband, children. She'd never wanted so much as a dog or a cat depending upon her. He resisted an urge to take her hand and instead got to his feet, his tea untouched. "We should go."

"You're happy as a priest, Finian?"

"I was called to this life. For me, happiness lies in embracing that call."

She flipped her hair back. "You know I don't believe any of that, don't you?" She sniffled, rising, taking her coat from the back of her chair. "It doesn't matter. I'm glad you have a good life here. I'm also glad it's only a year. Bean-hole suppers. Fishermen."

"Beautiful sunrises," he said with a small wink.

"Oh. Now there's a temptation. I could rent a cottage here and paint Maine sunrises. You know I worry about being an insufferable snob, don't you? Getting away from Dublin and the social whirl of being a so-called famous artist would do me good. I cringe at thinking I'll become pretentious and isolated, afraid to take creative risks because I might upset some gallery owner or critic or perfect fool." She made a face. "I think I might have added too much whiskey to my tea."

Finian unplugged the kettle and set the cups and saucers in the sink. "You've always been outspoken, haven't you?"

"To a bloody fault." She snatched up the Bracken 15. "I'll return this to your cabinet. Do the church ladies mind that you were a whiskey man at one time?"

"I still am, you know. In any case, most of my parishioners don't know, and those that do don't seem to mind."

"So long as you dig holes for their baked beans."

She spun off down the hall. Finian grabbed his keys and followed her. She plopped the whiskey onto the dining room table, covered in an Irish lace cloth a parishioner had thought he would like.

Aoife stared out the dining room window into the Maine darkness. "You refuse to remember, don't you, Finian?" She placed a hand on the back of a chair. "I know you won't answer. It's all right. I remember."

Finian felt a draft and realized he'd left the front door cracked.

Aoife pulled the tie on her coat tight and walked past him into the hall. She paused at the door, her hand on the knob as she cast him a look that was a mix of pain, pride, vulnerability and anger. *No small measure of anger*, he thought. "I remember everything about that weekend," she said. "Every minute. Every touch. Every kiss."

"Aoife."

She ignored him. "I remember the rain lashing the old windows of my uncle's house. I remember the wind rattling through the halls. I remember how you kept me warm."

He stepped past her and pulled open the door. The sharp, cold air seemed to take her by surprise. He hated to upset her further but knew letting her linger here, in the parish rectory that was now his home, wouldn't help her.

"It's been almost seven years," she whispered. "Why can't I let you go?"

He tucked a strand of her hair behind her ear. "Because it suits you not to."

She glared at him. "Well, isn't that a hell of a thing to say."

"You're a strong, lovely woman who wants what she wants."

"And you're the forbidden fruit?"

"I'm just a man, Aoife. Then and now." He kissed her cheek. "I fell in love with you that weekend, and I have no regrets, except for the pain I've caused you."

"Have I caused you any pain, Finian?"

He skimmed the back of his hand along her cool cheek. "Anything we think we might have been together is a mirage. You know that, don't you?"

"You're saying I'd have strangled you inside a year."

"Inside a week."

"Oh, no. You'd have kept me from having a single coherent thought for at least a week. If I'd known your god was going to steal you away from me—" She broke off, seizing his hand, kissing his fingertips. She quickly released him and smiled, fighting back more tears. "I'd have gone with you to Killarney and designed whiskey labels for Bracken Distillers and painted sunrises for your office, and I'd have been happy."

"I was drinking a lot in those days—"

"Not that weekend in Declan's Cross."

"No, Aoife," he said. "Not that weekend in Declan's Cross."

Aoife didn't speak again until they arrived at the inn, an old sea captain's house on Rock Point harbor. She looked out at the stars sparkling on the dark water. "I called Emma Sharpe as soon as I realized the cross was missing. I'd intended to call her about it, anyway. By then, though, Rachel was already dead." She shifted to Finian, her eyes luminous and beautiful even in the harsh light of his car's interior. "I haven't prayed in a very long time. Shall I pray tonight, Father Bracken?"

He didn't know what to say to her. He never had. "I will pray," he said finally.

"Thank you," she mumbled, and jumped out of the car. "Don't get out. I'll find my way inside and introduce myself. Go back to your rectory."

She shut the door hard. He got out, anyway, and carried her suitcase onto the front porch overlooking the water. The house was lit up, and the Donovans—Frank and Rosemary—were expecting Aoife. They invited Finian to come in for a few minutes. He shook his head. "Call me if you need me for anything," he said, then left before he could start second-guessing himself.

He drove back to the rectory but didn't stop. Instead, he returned to the village. He pulled into Hurley's, a rustic bar and restaurant on the harbor. It was quiet on a Saturday evening in November. There were three trucks in the parking lot, two of them owned by Donovans. Finian parked and got out. He wasn't ready to be alone yet.

He went inside and crossed the dining room with its worn wood floor and round tables covered in blue-and-white-checked cloths. An older couple who lived within walking distance occupied a candlelit table as they nursed glasses of wine and the remains of a fish dinner.

Finian joined Mike and Kevin Donovan—the eldest and the youngest of the four brothers—at a table by the back windows overlooking the harbor. They each had a pint of Guinness. Finian motioned to the bartender that he would have one, too. No whiskey tonight. At least not at Hurley's. Maybe later at the rectory, although he seldom drank alone. He had, often, in the first terrible months after the deaths of his family. And he'd drunk too much, whether or not he was alone.

It was during that period that he'd spent a weekend in Declan's Cross with Aoife O'Byrne. Beautiful, artistic, talented, independent and irresistible Aoife. He remembered their time together. Every second of it. Her laughter, her cries of passion, her touch. The feel of her warm, smooth skin. The sight of her sliding into bed with him.

He'd convinced himself that with Sally and the girls gone, there was no one left he could hurt.

He'd been wrong. So incredibly, unbearably wrong.

He hadn't come to his senses for a long time after that weekend with Aoife—and he hadn't come to senses on his own. It'd taken Sean Murphy dragging him out of the Kerry cottage that he and Sally had bought and fixed up together, carting him down to the beach and leaving him there.

"Live or don't live," Sean had said. It was up to him now.

When Finian had sobered up—more or less—he'd hit the trails of the Iveragh Peninsula and walked and walked and walked. Alone, for weeks. It was in the hills of the southwest Irish coast that he loved so much that he'd experienced the call by God to a religious life.

This life, he told himself as he realized that the two Donovan brothers were frowning at him as if he'd gone mad. His Guinness arrived. He picked it up and smiled at the two men. *"Sláinte."*

Kevin said *"Sláinte"* in return, but Mike said nothing. Both had the Donovan rugged good looks, but Kevin, a Maine marine patrol officer, was considered the "nice" Donovan. Mike was not. He fastened his dark blue eyes on Finian. "This Irish woman you dropped off at the inn is a friend of yours?"

"We're acquainted," Finian said.

"Attractive."

Mike was a man of few words. Finian nodded. "She is."

"Attached?"

Finian raised his pint to his lips. "To her work," he said, then drank.

"She's an artist," Kevin said, his tone such that Finian suspected he knew something of the events in Boston and Aoife's role. It wasn't unreasonable, given that he was a law enforcement officer and Emma—his brother Colin's love interest—had found Rachel Bristol's body.

"I planned to head back to the Bold Coast tomorrow," Mike said. "Should I stick around?"

"Not on my account," Finian said.

Mike wasn't giving up. "Is this Aoife in trouble—or is she trouble?"

"She's tired after a very long and troubling day."

"Probably good you set her up at the inn instead of the rectory."

Finian met Mike's gaze. "She'll be comfortable there."

Kevin pushed his glass aside. "She knew the woman who was shot in Boston this morning. Did you, Fin?"

"I did not, no. Aoife only met Rachel Bristol last night."

"But she's in Boston because of her, right?" Kevin asked.

"More or less," Finian said.

Mike's eyebrows went up, but if Kevin read anything into Finian's comment, he didn't show it. Both men were intense, serious. Finian sat back with his pint. He hadn't expected an inquisition, but he supposed he should have. He'd brought a woman who was involved—however tangentially—with a homicide in Boston to their town, to their parents' inn. He hadn't considered that might pose a problem.

"The Boston police and FBI are all over this thing," Kevin said. "It's nice and quiet in Rock Point this time of year. I hope Aoife enjoys her stay."

Finian thanked him as he and Mike got to their feet. They weren't yet across the dining room when Colin arrived. Finian drank more of his pint as he watched the three brothers interact. Andy, the third-born Donovan brother, was in Cork with Julianne Maroney, a marine-biology graduate student who worked at Hurley's. Julianne had found the woman murdered in Declan's Cross almost two weeks ago. She'd gone to Ireland in part to get over Andy, who'd ended their brief relationship in September. Now they were back together again.

Colin joined Finian at his table. The waiter had removed his brothers' pint glasses. He indicated he was sticking to iced tea. No alcohol for him tonight.

Finian picked up his own glass. "Definitely in FBI vein, aren't you, my friend?"

"Always, Fin. Always."

A reminder, perhaps, or even a warning. "I was just thinking about Julianne and Andy. They've left Declan's Cross and are in Cork, aren't they?"

Colin nodded. "They'll be back in time for Thanksgiving. I called Andy and told him to stick to helping Julianne get sorted out for her marine-biology internship there in January."

"They should stay away from my friends," Finian added.

"None of this is your fault, Fin. Wendell Sharpe investigated the Declan's Cross theft ten years ago. You were a whiskey man then. You didn't know the O'Byrnes or Sean Murphy." Colin's iced tea arrived, and he took a drink, then eyed Finian over the rim of the thick glass. "Or did you?"

"I didn't, no."

"Declan's Cross?"

"I'd heard of it. Sally and I visited Ardmore a few times. *Ahrd Mohr* in Irish, which translates as *great hill.* They say Saint Declan gave Ardmore its name when he established his monastery there."

"Wouldn't you like to go back in time and find out what's true and what's legend from that era?"

"Truth and legend aren't necessarily two different things."

"Historical facts, then."

"Do you think we always find truth in historical facts?"

Colin held up a hand. "All right, all right. We'll delve into a philosophical discussion when we're drinking Bracken 15 or another good Irish whiskey. To go back to your original question, Andy and Julianne are as safe in Cork as they would be in Rock Point and possibly safer."

"Especially now that I've brought Aoife here," Finian said.

"Beating yourself up tonight, Fin?"

He shrugged. "Questioning my judgment."

"Hard to think straight around Aoife O'Byrne?"

"I'm not accustomed to friends being mixed up in murder investigations."

"Right now, Rachel Bristol's death is a homicide investigation. That means police don't think it was suicide, but it doesn't mean murder charges—or any charges—will be filed. An accident can be a homicide."

"This wasn't an accident," Finian said. "Where's Emma?"

"She's at my house. We haven't been up here since we

got back from Ireland." Colin pushed back his chair and stretched out his legs. He looked preoccupied more than tired. "I told Emma to take a hot bath and never mind what might be growing in the refrigerator."

Finian studied his friend a moment. "Was she in danger this morning, Colin?"

"It's an active investigation, Fin. I can't get into details."

His eyes, however, conveyed his answer—if only because he wanted them to. Colin Donovan was as complex a man as Finian had ever known. On the one hand, a man who relied on his instincts and quick reactions. On the other hand, a man who knew how to conceal his thoughts and his emotions and to reveal them only on his own terms. It wasn't a skill he always employed, but he was now; of that, Finian had no doubt.

"I understand," he said.

"Just because you're a priest doesn't mean I can tell you everything." Colin reached for his glass. "Have you told me everything you know about why Aoife O'Byrne is here?"

"In Rock Point or in the U.S.?"

"Both."

"You'll have to ask Aoife."

"Because you don't know or because you're being discreet?"

"Perhaps we're again talking about truth versus fact."

Colin sighed and sat up straight. "I asked Emma to marry me."

Finian wasn't altogether surprised. "And she said yes?"

"Yes, she did. We were in a Dublin pub on a gloomy November night. I got down on one knee and everything. It was damn romantic, I have to say."

"Congratulations. I'm happy for you both."

Colin set his glass back on the table. "I think the idea of getting married is stirring up some of her nun stuff."

"Her *nun stuff,* Colin?"

"The path not taken." He settled his gaze on Finian across the table. "Is Aoife O'Byrne stirring up some of your guy stuff, Fin?"

"Are you asking me as an FBI agent or as a friend?"

"I'm always an FBI agent. It doesn't mean I'm not always a friend, too."

Finian wished now that he'd gone back to the rectory and straight on to bed. If he couldn't sleep, he could have cleaned up the tea dishes. He hadn't had to drink alone. He could have not drunk at all. A pint with three Donovan brothers on the heels of that morning's tragedy was proving to be a strain.

"There's a history between you and Aoife, isn't there?" Colin asked.

Finian pushed aside his pint. He hadn't quite finished, but that was fine with him. He rose, steady on his feet despite the long drive to and from Boston and being near Aoife again, for the first time in nearly seven years. He addressed Colin calmly, as if he hadn't heard his friend's question. "I was able to rearrange my schedule today in order to meet Aoife in Boston, but I have Mass in the morning. Give my best to Emma. If she'd like to talk about her experience in Boston this morning, she can call or stop by anytime. I'd be glad to talk to her—as a priest, and as a friend."

"No on-and-off switch with you, either?"

"That's right," Finian said, then left Colin to his iced tea. On his way out, he discovered that Mike Donovan had paid for his pint. These men were friends, he knew. That didn't change the fact that it had been a long and difficult day.

When he arrived back at the rectory, he saw he had a voice mail from Kitty. "Sean is coming to Declan's Cross tomorrow. Oh, Fin. Promise me you'll see Aoife safely home. Promise me."

It was very late now in Ireland. He texted Kitty instead of ringing her. "I promise."

He left the tea dishes for morning and bypassed the whiskey cabinet in the dining room as he headed upstairs for a bath, prayer and likely a sleepless night.

Twelve

Colin's refrigerator didn't contain enough fresh foods to have anything go bad after his weeks away in Ireland and Boston. Emma wasn't as satisfied as she supposed she should have been. Finding leftovers furry with mold on a shelf or in a drawer would have given her something to do besides pace in the Craftsman-style house while Colin was checking things out at his parents' inn—and likely at Hurley's, too. She'd kicked off her boots and pulled off her leather jacket, although the house was downright cold. She didn't care. Her mind was racing. She needed to slow it down and sort one by one all the events, facts, images and snippets of conversation that spun through her head.

Ten years of events, facts, images and snippets.

She was conflating everything she knew about the De-clan's Cross thief and her family's involvement and her in-volvement—as a Sharpe and then as an FBI agent—with everything she knew about the Bristols, the O'Byrnes, Sean Murphy and Finian Bracken.

For good measure, she threw in everything she knew about Saint Declan, too.

"And Jack B. Yeats," she added with a groan. "Don't forget him."

She'd spoken to her grandfather in Dublin, and to Yank, briefly. Rachel Bristol hadn't wasted any time once Declan's Cross had surfaced in the news with Lindsey Hargreaves' murder. Rachel had contacted Aoife O'Byrne and Emma's grandfather in Dublin, her brother in Heron's Cove and finally Emma in Boston that morning.

Emma slowed her pacing but didn't stop. The works of Jack Butler Yeats had skyrocketed in value since his death in 1957. John O'Byrne had bought his two Yeats paintings a half century ago. They would be worth far more now, but whether the thief had sold them, given them away or destroyed them—or still had them—Emma couldn't say, and neither could her grandfather. Had Rachel hoped to get her hands on them? Had she figured out Declan's Cross wasn't the thief's only heist?

Colin came into the kitchen through the back door. "I thought I'd find you in the tub," he said.

Emma smiled, and finally stopped pacing. "That could be arranged."

"But right now you're pacing?" He moved closer to her. "That's not an Emma Sharpe thing to do."

"If you'd had apples or a can of pumpkin, I'd have baked a pie."

"Pie-baking as a form of meditation."

"I was thinking about lighting a fire in your fireplace, but it's getting late. I didn't want to waste the wood. It's chilly in here, though. I didn't turn up the furnace."

"Waste-not, want-not Emma." He slid his arms around her middle. "Pacing keeps you warm."

"How's Aoife?"

"I didn't see her. She'd gone up to her room. The folks

have her on the second floor in what my mother calls the lilac room. It has its own bathroom and fireplace."

"And lilac wallpaper?"

"Lilac something, I imagine. I haven't been up there since they redecorated."

He'd had only brief trips home to Rock Point during his months deep undercover to penetrate Viktor Bulgov's illegal arms network. "I assume your parents know what happened in Boston today."

Colin nodded. "Mike's staying at the inn tonight. Kevin's keeping an eye out, too."

"I assume Mike isn't staying in something like the lilac room."

"He's in an unrenovated room."

Emma slipped her arms around Colin's waist. "And Father Bracken? Did you see him?"

"Briefly at Hurley's. He didn't have much to say."

"Wise not to have Aoife stay with him at the rectory, whatever their relationship," Emma said. "I think it's safe to assume he's part of why she came to Boston. Unless she hasn't told us everything about the cross she received and her contact with Rachel Bristol, I'm not sure they were enough by themselves to get her onto a plane."

"Add a priest who looks like Bono and has only been a priest for a short time, and we now have an internationally acclaimed Irish artist in the lilac room at the Rock Point Harbor Inn." Colin tightened his hold on Emma. "If Rachel stumbled on the thief's identity or was getting close and he found out and killed her, it means he was in Boston this morning."

"And in Dublin yesterday morning breaking into Aoife's studio and pulling a bookcase onto Lucy Yankowski? I suppose it's possible." Emma reined in an urge to spin out of Colin's arms and start pacing again.

"It's also possible our thief has an ally, but I don't believe that's the case."

"A solo operator."

Emma nodded. "That's been our assessment from the start."

She felt Colin open his palms on the small of her back, but she saw that his eyes were narrowed and knew he was focused on Rachel Bristol and why she'd called that morning, why she'd lured an FBI agent out to Bristol Island—and who else knew. "Aoife says she was alone in Dublin the night the thief broke into her uncle's house in Declan's Cross," he said. "She's never produced a witness or other corroboration. She was frosty with your grandfather ten years ago, and she was frosty with you last week. Have you and your grandfather ever considered she could be your thief?"

"I did, although not seriously," Emma said. "I don't know about Granddad. We have so few real leads it's tempting to consider everyone, including the trash man."

Colin smiled. "I vote for the trash man as your thief."

She settled back into his arms, letting him take her weight as she met his gaze. "Are you still annoyed with me for going off to Bristol Island this morning?"

"Steamed. I think you should help calm me down."

"Whiskey with Finian Bracken didn't do the trick?"

"I only had iced tea."

"Ah. You walked in here with an end game in mind." She leaned deeper against his arms. "You always do, don't you, Agent Donovan?"

"You're on to me," he said, drawing her to him.

Before she could say anything else, he had her swept off her feet and was through the dining room and living room and up the stairs. It was a little tradition they'd started their first night together in his house above Rock

Point harbor, but she was always amazed that he could carry her upstairs without breaking his stride or even getting winded. It wasn't just that he was fit. It was also—as he'd told her more than once—that he was incredibly motivated.

He pulled back the covers on his bed and laid her on the cool sheets. He gave an exaggerated shiver. "Why didn't you turn up the heat?"

"I figured you tough Rock Point guys like it cold."

He sat on the edge of the bed and touched the back of his hand to her cheek. "A hell of a day, Emma."

"I was never in any danger—"

'You don't know that."

She hooked her hand into his. "You're right. I don't know that."

"But you did great today. You're a damn fine agent, and I'm not saying that just because I want to tear off your clothes right now."

"It's not one of my best shirts. If buttons and such go flying, I won't be upset."

"Good to know." He leaned down and kissed her. "Except you're done in."

"I'm not…"

"Mmm. You can't keep your eyes open."

She couldn't, or just barely. "I'll rally."

"Not tonight," he said gently.

He pulled off her socks first, then her pants, shirt and underwear, then tucked the covers around her.

"Are you coming to bed?" she asked, failing at stifling a yawn.

"In a few minutes. I'll turn up the heat and pour some whiskey."

"Would you mind drinking it up here, next to me?"

He smiled. "That was the plan."

He kissed her on the forehead and was gone, turning out the lights on his way out of the room. She heard his footsteps in the hall. He was solid, reliable, tough-minded and absolutely the sexiest man she'd ever known or imagined knowing. During her days with the sisters, working in the garden, meditating, thinking about what her life might be like if she left the convent, she would look out onto the choppy waters of the Atlantic and see lobster boats and marine patrol boats. Not once had she envisioned she would fall for a man like Colin Donovan, or that such a man would fall for her.

She heard the heat come on, and she thought she heard the tinkle of a whiskey glass. She sank deep into his bed, warmer now, tired, determined not to dream about Rachel Bristol and her spiky blond hair and blood-soaked sweater, and the small stone cross in her palm.

They awoke early and made love in the presunrise light, with no need for tearing off clothes since that job was already done. Emma wanted to stay with Colin under the warm covers and then rake leaves or sit by the fire and read books, but instead she took a long, hot shower, contemplating the changes in her life in the past few months—never mind in the ten years since an elusive, provocative thief had slipped into a rambling old house on the south Irish coast.

Colin met her downstairs in the kitchen. He reached for their jackets on pegs by the door and tossed hers to her. "I'm reading your mind," he said. "You want to go down to my folks' inn to see Aoife O'Byrne."

"There's no rush."

He shook his head. "Mike texted me. She's checking out. Fin's taking her back to Boston this morning after he's done up at the church. Mike said Pop's got apple streusel muffins in the oven."

Emma smiled. "Apple streusel muffins alone would lure me to the inn."

"It's a nice morning for a walk, but we don't want to miss Aoife or muffins. We can take my truck. You can drive if you'd like. Second gear is balky, but you get used to it."

"You drive. I'll tackle your truck another day."

When they arrived at the inn, Mike was pulling the muffins out of the oven. He had on jeans and what had to be the rattiest gray sweatshirt in existence, and wool socks, no shoes. He'd made clear he viewed Emma's relationship with his second-youngest brother with extreme skepticism. A Sharpe, an ex-nun, another FBI agent. In Mike's view, she was trouble for Colin—for an FBI agent who did the dangerous work he did. He'd seemed to be warming up to her when she'd followed Colin to Ireland a few weeks ago, but the past twenty-four hours couldn't have helped.

"Welcome back," Mike said, placing the muffin tray on a cooling rack on the butcher-block counter. "I hear Ireland was a mixed bag. See any rainbows?"

Colin walked over to the counter. "Lots of rainbows." He tapped a muffin with one finger. "Apples cooked?"

Mike shrugged. "I don't know. I'm not that great with muffins." He watched Emma as she unbuttoned her jacket by the back door. "Except for that murder in Declan's Cross, how'd you like being back in Ireland?"

A loaded question, as he'd no doubt intended. "The first two weeks were great." She sat at the large table, decorated with candles and a pottery pitcher of yellow mums that had to be Rosemary Donovan's touch. "I think you'd like hiking the Irish hills, Mike."

"You're never too far from a pub," Colin added.

Mike grabbed a potholder with a rooster on it and dumped the muffins onto the cooling rack. "Sounds better than a lot of places I've been. Damn, these muffins smell good, don't they?"

He clearly didn't want to talk about muffins, but Aoife had just entered the kitchen, expensive tote bag in hand, her black hair slightly damp, gleaming from her shower. She smiled, looking awkward, a little pale, as if she hadn't slept well. "They do smell grand. What a treat to have a homemade muffin. I never do at home. Half the time I'll make tea and forget to eat anything at all."

"Tea's already made," Mike said, lifting a pot from the counter. "Earl Grey, as requested. The folks will be back any minute. They're at church."

"Saint Patrick's?"

"Since they were born."

"Do the church members like Finian, do you think?" Aoife asked, sitting across from Emma at the table.

Mike shrugged. "Beats me."

"He must be different from what they're used to."

"A good-looking Irish priest who drives a BMW? Yeah. Different."

Aoife flushed and seemed relieved when Mike placed the teapot and a mug in front of her. Colin put the hot muffins on a plate and set them in the middle of the table. She didn't seem at all hungry but took one of the muffins, breaking it open on a small plate. "It's a charming inn. Lovely. My sister would appreciate it, too. I spoke to Sean Murphy a little while ago. I was awake, and it's five hours ahead in Ireland. He's in Declan's Cross. He said Mrs. Yankowski is doing well."

"Good to hear," Colin said as he helped himself to a muffin.

"She and her husband are driving to Declan's Cross this afternoon. He's your boss, Sean said. I think I knew that but in all the emotions of yesterday, it didn't sink in. Do you know Lucy Yankowski?"

Colin leaned against the counter. "I've met her a few times."

"What is she like?"

"She's a psychologist. She's kind of a pain in the ass, but you can't help but like her, anyway."

Aoife's eyes sparkled with unexpected humor. "I have a feeling that's not an out-of-the-ordinary experience in your world, Agent Donovan."

Mike grinned at her. "Implying we're a bunch of likable pains in the ass, Aoife—I say that right?"

"You did, and I'm not implying anything."

He didn't look convinced. "What's Aoife mean?"

"Joyful, radiant. Nothing I feel at the moment, I can tell you."

"Aoife also means beautiful," Emma said.

Aoife shrugged. "As they say, beauty is in the eye of the beholder." Her expression turned serious again. "I'm glad Lucy Yankowski is doing well. Thank God she didn't die or wasn't seriously injured."

"She shouldn't have sneaked off to Ireland without telling her husband," Mike said. When Colin looked surprised, Mike added, matter-of-factly, "I got it out of Kevin last night. It's not like it's classified information." He turned to Aoife. "Matt Yankowski's been up here a few times. Straight arrow. Intense. I don't know what all he does for the FBI, but it couldn't have been good when he found his wife trapped under a bookcase in your studio."

Colin winced. "Mike…"

He looked at his younger brother, obviously mystified. "What?"

Emma smiled at Aoife across the table. "The Donovans are known for not mincing words."

"I can appreciate that," she said.

Mike pointed at her as he gave Colin a victorious look. "See?"

Colin rolled his eyes, but Frank and Rosemary Donovan entered the kitchen through the back door, followed by Finian Bracken. Emma noted Aoife's reaction to Finian's presence—a deepening of her flush, a lowering of her eyes to her muffin. The confidence and briskness Emma had encountered when she visited Aoife in Dublin less than a week ago were gone. She seemed awkward and uncertain, as if she'd awakened wishing she'd done anything last night except drive to Rock Point, Maine, with Finian Bracken. He was dressed in dark khakis and a dark wool sweater. Emma had no doubt that Aoife noticed he wasn't in his priest's attire.

Rosemary asked whether Aoife wanted anything else after all—she'd already turned down a full breakfast. She assured them the muffin was plenty. "I'll finish it in the car," she said, rising. "Finian, are you sure you don't mind driving me back to Boston?"

"Not at all," he said.

Mike pointed at the plate of muffins. "Want one, Father?"

Finian shook his head. "No, thank you." Aoife reached for her tote bag, but he grabbed it. "Anything else?"

"That's it." She smiled at her hosts. "Thank you so much for everything. Are you sure you won't let me pay you—"

"Positive," Rosemary said. "We hope you'll come back at a happier time."

Aoife thanked her again and left with Finian, who all but ignored Emma and Colin and didn't say a word to Mike.

Once the door shut behind the Irish pair, Mike raised his eyebrows. "What's up with Fin and this painter? If a woman I knew had just been murdered, I'd want to hang out with two FBI agents, not an Irish priest. No offense to our good Father Bracken."

Frank Donovan frowned. He was sturdily built, blue-eyed and square-jawed, his once-dark hair iron-gray now. "Did I miss something?"

His wife sniffed and breezed between Mike and Colin to the sink. She, too, was blue-eyed and sturdily built, her short curls dyed a soft, golden blond. "Anything between Aoife and Father Bracken is in the past. He's a priest now."

"Emma used to be a nun," Mike said. "Look at her now."

His mother scowled at him. "Mike."

He grinned at her. "Just saying. Come on. Where did your mind go when you saw Aoife and Fin together just now?"

"She is a beautiful woman," Frank said.

"Not every man thinks with his—" Rosemary stopped herself and looked at Emma. "Never mind them. How are you this morning, Emma? I know you're an FBI agent, but yesterday had to be difficult. Can I get you anything?"

Emma shook her head, getting to her feet. "Colin and I need to get back to Boston. We're stopping in Heron's Cove on the way. The muffins are great. Thanks."

"Take some with you," Rosemary said. "Frank and I can't eat them."

Her husband gaped at her in obviously feigned dismay. "We can't?"

"We've had our quota of simple carbs for the week."

"Come on, Pop," Mike said. "You can help me clear out the junk around the furnace so I can see if I can figure out why it's not working right. It'll take your mind off carb control."

"Think I'll get points for exertion and be allowed another muffin?" he asked, following his eldest son to the cellar door.

"It doesn't work like that," Rosemary said.

Mike looked past them at Emma. "You can get out now, you know. Tell Colin you've come to your senses before it's too late and you're in for the long haul with the Donovans."

"Mike," his father said, "Colin does go armed. As a matter of fact, so does Emma."

Rosemary sighed. "Those two. It's always worse when Frank and Mike are together, but they're just trying to lighten the mood after yesterday."

"Peas in a pod," Colin said. "Taking a few muffins with us sounds good."

Mike kept his gaze on Emma. "I hear your grandfather's coming to Maine for Thanksgiving."

"That's the plan," she said.

"Think he's ready to move back to Heron's Cove?"

"I don't know. Maybe at this point Dublin is home for him. I don't want him to come back here and start fading. He's such a force of nature." Emma waved a hand. "It'll be fine, whatever he decides to do."

"You bet," Mike said, and disappeared into the cellar with his father.

Colin put a couple of muffins into a plastic bag. Emma thanked Rosemary and followed him out the back door. The morning sun sparkled on the harbor, but the air was brisk and cold, more like early winter than late autumn.

She smelled a hint of burning wood. Fireplaces and woodstoves would be working hard until spring.

Colin tossed her his keys. "You drive. Tackling second gear will keep you from ruminating."

She squinted at him against the bright sunlight. "And if it doesn't?"

"You'll stall or run off the road."

"I learned how to be fully present when I was with the sisters, you know."

"But you never drove my truck when you were with the sisters."

She had not. And she quickly discovered it was an experience not to be missed. She took the coast road south. "You weren't joking about second gear," she said halfway to Heron's Cove.

Colin grinned at her. "I never joke about my truck."

Thirteen

Heron's Cove, Maine

Some days Emma second-guessed her decision not to stay with Sharpe Fine Art Recovery after she'd left the Sisters of the Joyful Heart. They were rare—more so while at the academy and her first year as an agent—but as Colin's truck rattled to a stop in front of the small Victorian house where her grandfather had gotten his start as an art detective sixty years ago, she felt the pull of that different path.

She shook off the thought. It was intrusive, unhelpful—a distraction she didn't need right now. She glanced sideways at Colin. "I feel like I've been in a wrestling match with your truck."

"It has a mind of its own."

The gray-shingled Sharpe house was situated between a marina and an inn at the mouth of the tidal Heron River, a short walk from the village of Heron's Cove with its upscale shops and restaurants. The house was undergoing a down-to-the-studs renovation, but no workers were there midday on a Sunday. Emma expected to have to use her key on the front door, but it was unlocked. Except for a small apartment on the first floor in the back, her brother was converting the entire house—including the attic—into office space. He'd never expected to run Sharpe Fine Art Recovery on his own, but he'd taken to the job with an eagerness and thoroughness that boded well for the company's future. Whether he was happy was another question, one he and Emma rarely discussed.

She and Colin headed down the hall to the kitchen, still largely untouched, and out to the back porch, where Lucas was eating a doughnut and drinking water. He was still sweating from his daily run. He actually relished running. One of the differences, Emma thought, between herself and her older brother. He was lanky and tawny-haired like their grandfather, but he had their mother's eyes and more fiery temperament. Lucas could be analytical, but he would err on the side of getting things done.

"I'll check out the renovations," Colin said. "Give you two a chance to catch up."

He went back inside. Most of the workers on the house were from Rock Point. Emma sat on the railing, the river at her back. The tide was up, the breeze off the water penetrating her leather jacket. Lucas had on wind pants and a fleece over his running clothes.

"Sorry to interrupt your day off," Emma said.

"No problem. Finian Bracken and Aoife O'Byrne just left. They were only here for a few minutes. I guess she wanted to see the place." He drank more of his water. "Granddad didn't exaggerate about her being attractive."

"Does he ever exaggerate?"

"Only about his undiminished driving skills."

Emma smiled. Lucas had objected to their grandfather driving across Ireland in October to hike the southwest Irish hills on his own, for however long it suited him. That he'd made it back to Dublin without incident was little consolation to his only grandson. The one-bedroom apartment included in the Heron's Cove renovations was intended for Wendell Sharpe, whenever and if ever he wanted it.

"Anyway," Lucas continued, "I gather Father Bracken is taking Aoife back to Boston. I didn't mention Rachel Bristol, and they didn't, either. I talked to Granddad before I left on my run. The Yankowskis are on the way to Declan's Cross. Sean Murphy's there already. Granddad plans to take the opportunity to go by Aoife's studio and check it out for himself without the FBI and garda looking over his shoulder."

"I hope he's careful," Emma said.

"I told him as much. He reminded me that not once in all his years working in fine-art recovery has he ever come upon a dead body—not even of someone who'd died of natural causes at a ripe old age. Then he hung up. He's not mad. He's preoccupied." Lucas finished his glazed doughnut. "Granddad worries about you, Emma. I do, too."

She stood up from the rail. "I'm doing my job."

"I guess I always pictured you as an analyst who was never in any real danger, never mind the whole gun and Quantico thing. I figured one day you'd take your experience with the FBI back here and rejoin the family biz." His incisive gaze settled on her. "You won't be with the FBI forever."

"I won't be with the FBI next week if Yank gets back and fires me."

"Being a Sharpe complicates his life more than he anticipated," her brother said.

"Lucas, do you think Granddad's told you—us—everything he knows about the Declan's Cross thief?"

Lucas dusted sugar off his hands. "I don't know. When

I was in Dublin in October, he said he wanted to tell me things that aren't in the files now that he's retired—or semiretired, as he insists on putting it. He told me a lot, but his idea of *everything* and mine aren't necessarily the same."

"You wanted to know his assessments—his suspicions, his instincts—about open investigations, and he wouldn't always tell you."

"Exactly."

"That's what he's been like since our Declan's Cross thief has resurfaced." Emma paused, walking over to an art easel. When she was in Heron's Cove, she liked to paint, although she wasn't particularly good at it. She turned back to her brother. "What about you, Lucas? Have you told me all you know about this thief?"

"I have. And you, Emma? Do Granddad and I have everything the FBI has on this thief?"

"I wish I could say no. I wish we were on the verge of catching this guy."

Lucas nodded. "Understood."

Colin joined them from the kitchen. Emma noted how at ease he looked. She'd never met a man so tough to intimidate, so comfortable in his own skin—not that anything about Lucas Sharpe, Sharpe Fine Art Recovery or Heron's Cove should have intimidated Colin or made him feel awkward. She wanted to tell Lucas about their engagement, but first they had to tell her parents.

Well, first she and Colin had to decide when they would tell *anyone*.

She stood next to him and glanced down at the river. Working boats and pleasure boats were still moored at the marina, but fewer now than in the warm-weather months. She knew that Colin sometimes felt the pull of his old life on the water, before the FBI. The might-have-been of lobstering with Andy, or starting up a tour-boat business with Mike. Right now, though, he was pure FBI, focused, unrelenting.

Emma turned back to her brother. "Tell us about Rachel Bristol's visit."

"It was short and uneventful or I'd have mentioned it sooner. Whenever we're in the news, we get a spike in interest in us and what we do. I filed Rachel Bristol under that heading. So did Granddad when she contacted him." Lucas sat on the porch rail, the breeze running through his longish hair. He didn't look cold despite the sweat from his run drying on his skin. "She stopped by on Monday about midday. She walked in as if she owned the place. I happened to be here. She introduced herself and gave me her card."

Colin handed Lucas his phone with a photo of Rachel. "This her?"

"Yes. No question." He handed the phone back. "She said she was working on a movie about art theft and asked me if I'd be willing to talk to her about Declan's Cross."

"Because of news reports about the murder of Lindsey Hargreaves?" Emma asked.

"Rachel didn't get into that much detail. I didn't give her a chance, to be honest. I gave her more time to talk than Granddad did when she called him, but not much more. She said she didn't intend to do a documentary but instead a big commercial movie—she was still fine-tuning the concept. She asked me if the Declan's Cross thief had struck again since then or only that one time. I told her I had an appointment and hurried her along her way."

Colin touched a bit of dried paint—cerulean-blue—on Emma's easel. "Did she go quietly?"

"Yeah," Lucas said. "I got the distinct impression that seeing this place and meeting me were about half of what she wanted to accomplish. The rest—whatever she was trying to get out of me—would take more time or another approach. She struck me as someone used to figuring out how to get her way."

"Determined?" Emma asked. "Committed to this movie idea?"

"Yes on both accounts. She didn't mention anything that wasn't public knowledge. She asked about the items stolen in Declan's Cross and whether I'd met John O'Byrne or either of his nieces. I didn't say much. She packed in a lot of questions and comments in a short visit."

"Watching you for your reaction?" Colin asked.

"Thinking back on it, yes. I can't say I paid any attention at the time. She wasn't rude or offensive so much as sure of herself and excited about this movie idea." Lucas grimaced as he stood, zipping up his fleece. "It sure as hell never occurred to me she'd be killed in a few days."

"We don't know for sure her interest in Declan's Cross had anything to do with her death." Emma paused, noticing a man and a woman down on the docks, clearly arguing. The woman gave the man a shove. He didn't budge. Emma thought she recognized them. "Colin, is that Maisie Bristol and Danny Palladino?"

"Looks like it to me," he said, already moving. "I'll find out what's going on."

He trotted down the steps to the small backyard. In seconds he was at the retaining wall, jumping down to the docks. Lucas frowned at Emma. "That's Maisie Bristol? I looked her up on the internet after Rachel's death. I knew she was young but she looks fourteen. Who's the guy with her?"

"Her sometimes bodyguard, Danny Palladino."

Lucas squinted at the pair on the docks. "She sure

has a hell of an eye for a good movie. She looks pissed right now, though."

"Let's go and see what she and Palladino have to say."

"Colin won't mind?" Lucas seemed to realize what he'd just said and held up a hand. "Sorry, Emma. I know he doesn't tell you what to do."

"And vice versa."

"No doubt," her brother said with a grin. "I guess I sometimes still think of you as my kid sister."

Emma smiled. "Just so long as it doesn't rub off on Colin, we're good."

Maisie Bristol and Danny Palladino looked defiant but also somewhat uncomfortable when Colin brought them onto the backyard above the docks, intercepting Emma and Lucas. "They decided to go on a Sunday drive," he said, his tone neutral.

"What's this all about?" Emma asked.

"Curiosity, grief, restlessness," Maisie said. "Nothing sinister."

The wind was picking up. Lucas nodded to the back door. "Let's talk inside."

He took them onto the back porch and into the kitchen. The carpenters would be gutting it soon. Before leaving for Ireland, Emma had emptied the cabinets, with Colin's help. She'd seen the plans. The new kitchen and apartment would be great, but the place wouldn't be the same. But that was the point, and things changed. Still, as she leaned against the counter, she could almost see her grandmother showing her how to roll out piecrust.

Colin stood on the threshold of the hall into the front room. Lucas turned to Maisie, pointing at the kitchen table, stacked with carpenter tools, catalogs and notebooks. "You're welcome to have a seat," he said.

She shook her head. "No, thanks." She walked over to the sink and looked out the window at the water. She had on a cargo jacket, jeans and ankle boots, but she seemed cold. "Coming up here was my idea. Danny's just along for the ride. He insisted, in case I got into trouble—in case someone decided to shoot at me."

Danny stayed by the back door, ignoring her sarcasm. "Erring on the side of caution. I know this thief Rachel was interested in is sexy and all that, but ten to one some idiot using Bristol Island for target practice shot her by mistake." He shrugged. "I do realize I'm talking to two FBI agents."

Maisie bristled, turning abruptly from the sink and her view. "I find it hard to believe someone would accidentally shoot a woman in the chest a few minutes after she'd called an FBI agent to come meet her."

"Weird stuff happens all the time in real life," Danny said.

"I know this isn't a movie, Danny."

He leveled his steady gaze on her. "Okay."

Maisie muttered something unintelligible under her breath and shifted to Emma. "It's okay for us to be here. The Boston detectives know how to reach us. I wish I could help. I'd like to nail whoever killed Rachel myself."

"That's why we have cops," Danny said.

She kept her eyes on Emma. "After you left yesterday, I remembered Rachel told me she came up here earlier this past week. I was hoping seeing Heron's Cove might help me better understand what all she was up to. At the same time, I needed to get out of the house—away from my father. You can imagine the emotional state he's in. He once loved Rachel. They stayed friends after their divorce."

"What do you know about Rachel's trip up here?" Emma asked.

"Not a lot." Maisie fingered a carpenter's notebook on the counter. "Rachel was absolutely convinced that her basic concept for the movie was the right one."

Danny gave an exaggerated shiver. "It's almost as cold in here as it is outside. Don't you people believe in heat?"

"The house is being worked on," Lucas said.

"Yeah. So I see. That means no heat, I guess."

Maisie rolled her eyes. "Danny needs to go back to the desert. Rachel raved about Heron's Cove. She said she could see why the Sharpes didn't move their business to New York or Los Angeles. It truly is beautiful here."

"Did you know Rachel called my grandfather in Dublin?" Lucas asked.

"No, I didn't," Maisie said, less self-assured. "When was this?"

"Tuesday. She was here on Monday."

"I talked to her on Monday evening, then again on Friday after we'd all arrived back in Boston. She didn't mention having called your grandfather. She told me she wanted to go to Ireland. She asked if I'd ever been there. I haven't. I've been to lots of other places but never Ireland. She was so enthusiastic. I can't believe she's dead, that she…" Maisie waved a hand. "I'm sorry. Rachel and I had our ups and downs—I won't pretend we didn't— but I never expected she'd be shot to death."

Emma found a clean glass and filled it with water from the tap and handed it to her. "I'm sorry for your loss."

"Thank you."

"Rachel was on your nerves, though," Danny interjected. "She was elbowing her way into your project, trying to take control and turn it into something you didn't want. She was sneaking around—"

"I know that, Danny." Maisie drank some of the water and set the glass on the table next to an overstuffed notebook. "I don't need you to tell me."

Danny remained calm. "I just don't want our two FBI friends here to be misled."

Her cheeks flushed red but she turned to Emma. "I hope you know I'm not misleading you. I'm telling you what I know. Danny's right. This project—my idea of it—has me in its grip. I wanted to rein in Rachel before she got too caught up in her own vision. I wanted to hear her ideas, but I wasn't interested in having her take over, despite her experience and passion for her own ideas."

"That doesn't mean Maisie hired someone to kill her," Danny said.

She spun around at him. "I'll drive myself back to Boston. You can find your own way back."

He didn't flinch at her steely, combative look. "We'll go back to Boston together."

"Bastard." Shoving her hands in her jacket pockets, she turned to Lucas. "Sorry for the intrusion."

"Not a problem," Lucas said.

"Danny doesn't think of me as a powerful movie producer." She smiled, making clear she was joking. "I don't think of myself that way, either."

Colin stood straight. "Did Rachel mention Agent Sharpe to you?"

Maisie shook her head. "Not that I recall. She mentioned Wendell Sharpe, Sharpe Fine Art Recovery, Heron's Cove, Dublin. I think I'd remember if she'd told me one of the Sharpes was an FBI agent, but I can't say for sure. As I mentioned yesterday, I'm not good with that sort of thing."

Lucas pushed out his chair at the table. He looked relaxed, but Emma could see he was trying to figure out if there was more to Rachel Bristol's agenda than her idea for a movie. He was thorough if not patient when it came to wading into details and possibilities. "Did Rachel have any theories about the Declan's Cross thief?" he asked. "Who it might be, reasons for choosing the particular items stolen that night—"

"Not that she shared with me," Maisie said irritably. "Why?"

Emma could sense Maisie's mounting frustration at being out of control and in the dark—neither of which she was used to—but Lucas didn't ruffle easily. "I imagine you've been asked a lot of questions in the past twenty-four hours," he said, his own tone mild, understanding. "I know it can be hard. I've been there. I've learned it's best just to answer questions without reading anything into them."

"But there's more going on here than I've been told, isn't there?"

Danny grunted. "No kidding, Maisie."

She glared at him. "Stop patronizing me."

He winked at her. "Just keeping you alert and engaged."

"Did Rachel tell anyone else about her interest in the Declan's Cross theft and my grandfather?" Lucas asked.

"I have no idea," Maisie said. "I never asked."

Lucas got to his feet. "Did *you* tell anyone?"

"No. Rachel was so excited. I was tired when I got in on Friday, and she was banging on about including Aoife in her version of the movie. She was interested in how the theft ten years ago, when Aoife was just starting out, influenced her art and her rise as a star. A beautiful, internationally acclaimed Irish artist, an art detective, an art thief, a gorgeous location. It's sexy. I don't deny it."

Danny turned to Lucas. "The art that was stolen—it's worth a lot?"

"The Yeats paintings in particular are," Lucas said. "Was Rachel aware of that?"

"Yes, of course," Maisie said. "I am, too."

And, her tone suggested, it was irrelevant since she didn't need the money.

Lucas took her water glass to the sink. "Are you going to move forward with the movie?"

"Despite Rachel's death? I don't know yet. I'm as fascinated by early Celtic Ireland as ever, and I know she would want me to, regardless of our creative issues. We were going to iron them out, coordinate our efforts and settle on an approach." Maisie faltered, then cleared her throat and squared her shoulders. "We didn't get that chance. She didn't tell me she was going to call an FBI agent, or why, and now she's dead because of it. Even if it had nothing to do with who shot her, it was why she went out to the old cottages on the island."

"Maisie," Emma said, "if Rachel believed she knew the identity of the Declan's Cross thief, would she have told you?"

Maisie didn't hesitate. "Not until she could prove it, and not until she could spring it on me. She'd go for the drama." Maisie studied Emma a moment. "Is that why she called you, Agent Sharpe?"

Emma didn't respond. Danny Palladino took out a car key. "Okay, we're getting off into the land of speculation. Come on, Maisie. Let's head on back to Boston." He gave a broad gesture that took in Lucas, Colin and Emma. "You all know where to find us if you have any follow-up questions."

Maisie didn't protest when Danny took her by the arm

and led her out through the back door. Colin eased past Emma and followed them.

Once the back door shut, Lucas sighed heavily at the sink. "That was intense." He watched out the window for a few seconds, then turned to Emma. "Maisie and Danny? More there than a successful movie producer and her bodyguard?"

"I suspect so," Emma said. "Can you think of anything else Rachel said when she was up here last week?"

Lucas shook his head. "But if she was doing research on us, she could have read about Sister Joan's death in September and decided to pay the Sisters of the Joyful Heart a visit."

Emma buttoned her jacket. "I'll check in with them. Thanks, Lucas. If you think of anything else, call me. And be careful, okay?"

"Always."

Fourteen

Colin asked Danny Palladino about his relationship with Maisie Bristol while she buckled herself into the passenger seat of her Mercedes, parked in the lot next to the inn and the Sharpe house. "Unsettled," Danny said, leaving it at that as he got behind the wheel.

Maisie didn't so much as glance sideways at either of them. Colin figured he had his answer and let them go on their way without pushing for more details. He walked back up to the Sharpe house, squeezing through privacy shrubs onto the trim lawn, where Emma was standing, the sunlight shining on her hair.

He noted her troubled look. "I gather we're not going for a Sunday walk in Heron's Cove. What's up?"

"I just spoke to Mother Natalie. Rachel came by the convent on Monday, after she saw Lucas."

"Next stop is the good sisters, then."

"I can go on my own and pick you up back here."

"That would be out of your way. The convent's a nice place. Good views. While you talk to Mother Natalie, I can see if I can spot a whale out on the water. I'd meditate in one of the gardens, but they're only for the sisters."

Emma squinted at him. "Have you ever meditated?"

"On purpose?"

She sighed, shaking her head, but a spark of humor had returned to her eyes.

They got back in his truck, but he drove this time. She'd handled second gear just fine as far as he was concerned, but with Maisie Bristol, Danny Palladino, Lucas and now the Sisters of the Joyful Heart—Emma didn't need to fight his balky truck.

The convent was located on the outskirts of Heron's Cove, on a former late-nineteenth-century estate that the founder of the Sisters of the Joyful Heart, Mother Sarah Jane Linden, an artist and friend of Wendell Sharpe, had chosen herself, saving it from the wrecking ball. The original stone mansion was now the mother house, complete with leaded-glass windows, dormers, several porches and a spooky attic that Colin had personally visited, accompanied by Emma, formerly Sister Brigid.

He parked outside the front gate. Young Sister Cecilia, who'd arrived at the convent as a novice after Emma's departure, greeted them and escorted them along curving paths, past well-tended flower gardens going dormant for the season. Cecilia wore a modified gray habit and mud-encrusted, highly sensible shoes, and she and Emma talked about the challenges of watercolor painting. Sister Cecilia was giving Emma lessons. Emma loved to paint but maintained that she wasn't any good at it. Most of the time, Colin didn't know a good painting from a bad painting, but Matt Yankowski insisted he did and agreed with Emma that she was better suited to the FBI. Then again, when Yank had said that, he'd been determined to keep Emma in his unit and would have said anything.

When they arrived at the sitting room outside the mother superior's office, Sister Cecilia withdrew. Emma settled right in, obviously comfortable at the convent.

Colin wouldn't describe himself as comfortable.

Tall windows offered a view of yet another flower garden and, beyond it, the ocean glistening under the sun. That was where he was comfortable, he thought. On the water, in almost any weather.

In another moment, Natalie Aquinas Williams joined them from the adjoining office. She was in her early sixties, a Ph.D. in art history and a dedicated member of the Sisters of the Joyful Heart and its mission of art conservation, restoration and education. She also wore a modified habit, as well as a cross and ring that indicated she'd made her final vows—something Emma had stopped short of doing. Not in all his wildest dreams had Colin ever imagined he would fall for an ex-nun. Not a chance.

Emma greeted Mother Natalie with a kiss on each cheek and thanked her for seeing them. The older woman invited them to sit on a sofa in front of the fireplace, where a steady fire was burning, but Emma shook her head. "We're on our way back to Boston. We won't keep you."

Mother Natalie and Emma stood by the windows overlooking the garden as the older woman explained that Rachel Bristol had stopped at the convent early last week. Colin produced Rachel's photo, and Mother Natalie nodded, obviously pained. "That's the woman who was here on Monday. I'm sorry about her death. What a terrible tragedy."

"What can you tell us about her visit?" Emma asked.

"She didn't stay long. She was a dynamic personality, asking lots of questions, interested in everything. She told me that she came alone, drove herself up from Boston in a car she said she borrowed from her ex-husband there—she made a point of telling me because she wanted me to know she was from Southern California. She said,

'I'm all West Coast. I'm not East Coast.'" Mother Natalie smiled. "That was obviously important to her. We met here, but it was a beautiful day, and we ended up walking through the gardens. She asked about our work. She said she was exploring options for a movie inspired by Wendell Sharpe and one of his cases."

Colin watched a red squirrel scurry up a spruce tree. "What did she tell you about the movie?"

"Very little. To be honest, I didn't ask. She wanted to know about Wendell and Sharpe Fine Art Recovery. I made clear that I'm not a gossip and suggested she contact them directly. She said she'd already stopped in Heron's Cove and had spoken to Lucas." Mother Natalie shrugged, moving back from the window. "Nothing she said raised alarm bells for me. She didn't ask about you, Emma. I assumed she knew you'd been here for a time and were an FBI agent, but I didn't mention you. She was aware your grandfather had been friends with Mother Linden. She'd read that in accounts of Sister Joan's death and our discovery of the Rembrandt."

The murder of Sister Joan Fabriani in September and the subsequent discovery of an authentic Rembrandt etching on the grounds of the convent—literally in the attic—would have made for an eventful fall all by themselves, Colin thought. Now here Emma was again, dealing with another dead woman.

"The Rembrandt is no longer here, of course," Mother Natalie added. "I explained that to Miss Bristol. She didn't seem disappointed. I don't think it was of any particular interest to her. She then asked about Celtic art and whether I knew anything about Saint Declan."

"Did she say why?" Emma asked.

"Only that it had to do with her movie. I told her I don't know that much about Saint Declan or Celtic art—

which is true—and she thanked me and went on her way. I thought it was a leap to go from Rembrandt to a fifth-century Irish saint, but Sister Cecilia reminded me of the unsolved art theft in Declan's Cross, and then told me that you and Agent Donovan had just been involved in a murder investigation there." Mother Natalie touched Emma's arm. "It's a hard job you do. The FBI is lucky to have you."

"Thank you. Mother Natalie, did Rachel talk to anyone else here?"

"No. Just to me. She was confident, excited. If she'd seemed awkward or nervous—I'd have called you at once, Emma. It didn't occur to me she was in any kind of trouble."

"We don't know if she was in any trouble," Emma said. "Thank you for your time, Mother Natalie. The homicide detectives working the investigation into Rachel Bristol's death might want to talk to you."

"Of course. Anytime. And you're always welcome here, Emma." Mother Natalie turned to Colin, took his hand. "You, too, Agent Donovan."

"Colin," he said.

She smiled. "Colin it is." But her smile faded quickly. "I hope you find the answers to this woman's death, and I hope no one else is in danger."

Sister Cecilia reappeared and escorted them out of the sitting room, down the hall and onto the front porch. Emma assured her they would be fine getting back to the gate, but the young sister insisted on joining them. "I don't mind, and I need to tell you something." She rushed ahead of them down the porch steps, then onto the walk, finally slowing as they approached the convent gate. She paused, turning to Emma. "I overheard your conversation with Mother Natalie…. Some of it…" She blushed, glancing among the trees as if she thought someone might be eavesdropping on her. "Sorry. I'll tell Mother Natalie, of course, but when I heard her mention Saint Declan…" She broke off and waved a hand. "It's probably nothing, and I'm being silly."

"Just tell us what's on your mind, Sister," Emma said gently.

"Well—there was a man in town on Monday, the same day as Rachel Bristol. He stopped by our shop in the village. I was there. He asked some of the same things she did about your family. He also mentioned Declan's Cross." Sister Cecilia stepped closer to Emma, continuing in a near-whisper. "He was maybe five-eleven, lean, frumpy tweeds. He spoke with an accent. English, I think. He didn't tell me his name, and I didn't ask."

Oliver Fairbairn, Colin thought. Maisie Bristol's mythologist. Had to be.

Emma was clearly thinking the same thing but kept her focus on Sister Cecilia. "Did he tell you why he wanted to know—why he was asking you about my family and Declan's Cross?"

"He said, 'I understand that one of the Sharpes is an FBI agent and a former nun with your convent.' It's not a secret, and I assumed he'd read about you in the accounts of what happened in Declan's Cross." She took in a quick breath, her face draining of color. "Emma, should I have called you?"

"I wouldn't have known who he was, but in the future, if someone asks about me or anyone in my family, yes, Sister, please do call. It can't hurt. Did you see if this man was with anyone?"

Sister Cecilia shook her head. "I would have followed him, but I was teaching a pottery class and had six-year-olds arriving."

"You're spunky, Sister," Colin said, "but don't be following people, okay?"

She smiled, her cheeks still pink. "Spunky? I think I like that. But you're right, of course." She motioned toward the mother house. "I should go tell Mother Natalie I accidentally, slightly on purpose overheard you all talking."

Colin grinned at her. "She won't feed you to the sharks."

"Oh, no. Not this time of year. She can just fling me into the cold Atlantic and that would be enough to teach me a lesson." She looked amused. "I suppose you had nuns who smacked you with a ruler?"

"Not me. My brother Mike did, though. He says he had it coming."

"What did he do?"

"Something involving frogs is all I know."

She laughed, but the strain was clear. "Well, I hope he doesn't hold a grudge." Any hint of laughter disappeared as she started back down the walk. "I'd be happy to talk to the police, too, if need be, and we will pray for all those involved in this tragedy."

"Thank you, Sister," Colin said.

When they reached his truck, Colin again climbed in behind the wheel. He waited as Emma said goodbye to Sister Cecilia. Emma said she would love to resume painting lessons now that she was back in the U.S. The two women clearly had become friends over the past few months, ever since the young sister's own run-in with a killer.

Emma got into the passenger seat and smiled as she looked out at the convent grounds.

"Pretty spot," Colin said.

"Yes, it is. I could have spent my early twenties in a worse place."

"Missing the good sisters?"

"I don't miss my life here, and I don't regret not staying," she said without hesitation. "It was a path not taken. A bit like you and puffin tours."

"Puffin tours don't involve a vow of chastity."

She buckled her seat belt. "There's that."

"I can always do puffin tours. You can't be a nun again." He started the engine. "Do you ever wonder what would have happened if Yank hadn't stopped up here four years ago?"

"I wouldn't have made my final vows. I know that much."

"The FBI?"

"Yank planted that seed and nourished it after I left the convent and was working in Dublin with my grandfather. Heading to the academy was the right move for me." She stared out her window as he turned onto the convent access road, leaving the meandering paths and quiet gardens of the Sisters of the Joyful Heart behind them. "I had a good life with the sisters. I have no regrets about my time at the convent or about leaving."

"I still think Sister Brigid sensed one day she'd meet a rugged FBI agent out here on the rocks."

Emma grinned at him. "And deep down I knew I had to get out of the convent for that to happen?"

He downshifted to balky second gear as he slowed for a stop sign. "Were you afraid of men when you walked through the convent gates as a teenager?"

"No."

"Sex?"

"I wasn't afraid of anything. I was embracing what I believed was a genuine call to the life and work of the

Sisters of the Joyful Heart. Being a postulant and then a novice is part of the process of discerning the call and determining what's right for you. It's not about failure or success."

Colin turned onto the main road, heading south toward Boston. "Do you think our friend Finian Bracken ran to the priesthood after the deaths of his wife and daughters?"

"That's not for me to say. He would have gone through a rigorous process of discernment to understand his call and what his next steps might be."

"There's something between him and Aoife O'Byrne," Colin said. "Or there was, anyway. He drank hard after he lost his family. Maybe he did some womanizing, too."

"Or maybe there was just one woman," Emma said quietly. "I can see Aoife falling for Finian back then. He was wounded, angry, tortured, the co-owner of a whiskey distillery succeeding against the odds. Good-looking."

"I can see him falling for her, too. She's attractive, talented, independent."

"It was just over a year between the deaths of Finian's family and his going into seminary. I doubt he and Aoife had a real relationship. More likely it was a fling, one of those one-night stands that haunts you."

Maybe so, Colin thought. Maybe that explained the tension he'd sensed between the good Father and the beautiful Irish artist that morning. "Yank and Lucy are probably in Declan's Cross by now," he said. "Maybe he can get Kitty to tell him about Fin and Aoife."

"Assuming Kitty knows."

Emma had a point. Colin realized he had slowed to a near crawl. Cars were stacking up on his bumper. He hit the gas, speeding up, feeling his sudden tension. "Any chance Fin's our thief?"

"What? Where did that come from?"

"We only have his word for how he ended up in Rock Point, up the road from Sharpe Fine Art Recovery in Heron's Cove." Colin spoke matter-of-factly, not really believing anything he was saying. "What if Fin didn't just happen upon a Maine priest looking to do a sabbatical? What if he knew Father Callaghan was going to be in Declan's Cross and arranged to be there, too?"

"Father Callaghan picked Declan's Cross because he'd heard about the unsolved theft and was curious. That makes sense because he's the priest in Rock Point, which—as you noted—is just up the road from Heron's Cove." Emma paused, then shook her head. "No way is Finian our thief, Colin. He was in Declan's Cross because of his friendship with Sean Murphy. Finian and Sean stopped at the O'Byrne House Hotel for a drink because it had just opened, and because of Kitty's on-and-off relationship with Sean. Father Callaghan was staying at the hotel. He and Finian got to talking, and one thing led to another—and now Father Callaghan is on sabbatical in Ireland and Finian is serving Saint Patrick's in Rock Point."

"I guess that all makes perfect sense," Colin said.

Emma seemed hardly to hear him. "Ten years ago, Finian Bracken was a happily married man with two small daughters and a thriving whiskey business. How and why would he steal paintings from a house in Declan's Cross? Then go on to steal from cities all over the world? I don't need to check his alibis, Colin. There's just no reason—"

"I know, Emma. It's just damn weird how things work out sometimes."

She nodded. "You weren't serious, were you?"

"Not really," Colin said. "Lucas would make a good

thief, though. He reminds me of a fair-haired Pierce Brosnan."

"That doesn't make him a thief. Pierce Brosnan only played one."

"Good movie. We could watch it one night curled up on your little couch in your little apartment."

"*Our* little apartment."

"It will be, but right now it's your little apartment. It's got your touch."

"My touch being?"

"Irish lace pillowcases for starters."

She looked out the window again, and he could feel her drifting, ruminating. He reached over and touched her thigh. She turned to him, her green eyes warm with emotion as she spoke. "I was just thinking about Lucy Yankowski in Dublin. The attack on her at Aoife's studio. Colin, if I brought this on her, how can I possibly remain in HIT?"

"You're jumping too far ahead. We need to talk to Oliver Fairbairn, and we need to let Padgett know about Fairbairn's and Rachel's trips up here last week. He'll want to know. He's putting together a timeline."

"He's thorough. Never mind Yank. I've complicated Sam Padgett's life because I'm a Sharpe. And yours."

"Yank knew you were a Sharpe before he met you as Sister Brigid. Trust me, Padgett knew all about your family before he agreed to join HIT. I know his type. And I knew you were a Sharpe before I lusted after you. I didn't know you were an ex-nun, but I survived by thinking about you singing '*My Favorite Things*' to the Von Trapps."

"Colin."

He grinned at her. "What? Julie Andrews was kind of cute in *The Sound of Music.*"

"You know you have never once pictured me singing to the Von Trapps."

"This is true, but it perked you up. Let's keep things simple. Shall we stop for lobster rolls on our way back to Boston? We can get them to go. You like lobster rolls, don't you?"

She smiled. "Of course."

"Good. You realize I know all the best places to get lobster rolls between Quoddy Head and Provincetown, don't you?"

"That's a lot of lobster rolls."

He patted her thigh. "My point exactly."

Fifteen

Declan's Cross, Ireland

The tiny village of Declan's Cross occupied a scenic stretch of the south Irish coast east of Cork and west of Waterford. There were sea cliffs, a crescent-shaped sandy beach, brightly painted shops and houses, at least two good pubs and the boutique O'Byrne House Hotel, open just a year and already a favorite with Lucy Yankowski.

Instant love, Yank thought as he settled onto a cushioned stool at the hotel's bar.

He wasn't surprised. Lucy had always liked her creature comforts, and this place had them, while keeping an approachable, welcoming feel. Upscale without any airs. She was off for a swim in the spa pool. He'd been reluctant to leave her, but she'd insisted. "I need to do this," she'd told him. "I need to know I can be on my own."

A low, steady fire was burning in the marble fireplace behind him. The silver wall cross had been displayed on the mantel before it was stolen ten years ago, replaced now by a collection of colorful pottery vases. The half-dozen tables were unoccupied. Yank wouldn't have been surprised if he and Lucy were the only guests—a Sunday night in November wasn't the high tourist season—but another couple had wandered downstairs and out to a pub in the village. He and Lucy would eat in tonight. He expected the swim would do her good on every level, but he also expected that it would wipe her out for the rest of the evening.

Kitty O'Byrne Doyle set the glass of whiskey he'd ordered in front of him. He'd let her pick. She was black-haired, blue-eyed and direct to the point—but not past it—of briskness. "Yellow Spot," she said. "It's a good one."

"Finian Bracken would approve?"

"Enthusiastically."

Yank took a sip and savored the clear, smooth Irish whiskey. Once he swallowed, he waited, noting the long honey finish. He set his glass back down. "Definitely a good choice."

Kitty nodded with approval. "I wasn't much of a whiskey drinker until I got to know Finian. You've met him?"

"A couple times in Maine."

"Sometimes I shudder to think of him alone there, but he's made friends. He has his work, too. I look forward to the day he returns to Ireland."

"Do you think that will happen?" Yank asked.

"Without a doubt. His brother and sisters are here. It's home."

Home. Yank didn't think in those terms the way he once had. Almost twenty years with the FBI had done that to him, he supposed. He picked up his glass again, savored another sip of the Yellow Spot. He'd considered himself lucky—*them* lucky—that Lucy's job as a psychologist was mobile and she could pursue her career even if they had to move. They didn't have to stay in one place. When he'd gotten the green light for his new unit, he hadn't considered she might balk at moving to Boston. She'd formed ties in northern Virginia that he simply hadn't noticed. He'd gone to Boston, expecting her to put their house on the market and follow him. Nine months later, she was still in northern Virginia, and he was still in his rathole Boston rental.

Hiking the Irish hills and sitting by the fire on rainy Irish nights, alone in his traditional little cottage, he'd realized he hadn't done due diligence in consulting Lucy about Boston, and now he was paying the price.

She was, too.

And that was before she'd boarded a plane to Dublin and found her way to Aoife O'Byrne's studio.

Maybe Boston had been the final push she'd needed to acknowledge that she was unhappy with him, their marriage, the life they had. She was thirty-nine. He was forty-two. He supposed couples got restless about this time.

Except he wasn't restless. He was as in love with Lucy as he had been the day he'd married her.

Didn't mean it was a two-way street.

He could feel the wind off the Celtic Sea buffeting the hotel. He tried to imagine what it had been like when it had been a house. John O'Byrne had bought it more than fifty years ago, expecting to refurbish it with his wife. She'd died of cancer before the work was finished. He'd hung on to the place, keeping it much the same until his own death five years ago. Having no children of his own, he'd left the property to his two nieces.

All that was in Emma's files on the thief who'd slipped in here one November night ten years ago. Yank had familiarized himself with the details while he was in his Irish cottage—which was owned, ironically, by Finian Bracken.

Or perhaps not so ironically.

Yank watched as Kitty sliced a lemon on a cutting board next to a small stainless-steel sink. Why had the thief struck here first? Why then on to bigger cities— Amsterdam, Vienna, London, San Francisco?

It was still an open question whether the thief had known what he was after in the O'Byrne house or had simply been opportunistic, grabbing the two Yeats paintings, the unsigned landscape and the valuable wall cross because they'd seemed the most promising. The paintings had been in a reading room on the second floor, at the top of the main stairs. The thief had slipped in through the French doors in the back, in what was now the bar lounge.

Yank would bet the thief had known exactly what he—or she—was after.

"Quiet here," he said to Kitty, still carving up her lemon.

"We get busy again at Christmas."

"I like the quiet. It's a change from Boston. Ever been to Boston?"

"Not yet, no. I keep thinking one day I'll get there." She scooped up the pieces of lemon into her hands and dumped them into a small bowl. "Although with what's happened there since Aoife arrived, I don't know. Maybe I'll stay right here in Declan's Cross."

"You could do worse."

"I could, indeed. Would you like another whiskey?"

"Still nursing this one, thanks. Has Sean Murphy been in touch?"

"He's up at the farm," she said, brisk now.

"Did you think he'd quit the garda after his injury and stay on the family farm?"

She shrugged, grabbing a lime. "I didn't think anything one way or the other. It was for Sean to decide what

he wanted to do. He says Emma Sharpe and Colin Donovan work for you?"

"One way of putting it."

"Yes. I can see that, having met them." She smiled
unexpectedly, her blue eyes lighting up. "They're independent to a fault, aren't they? But I imagine you don't
want robots in your work—people who won't argue, chal-
lenge, probe, cause trouble when needed. I think of my
sister, and I'd want Emma and Colin looking after her."

"What about Finian Bracken?"

Kitty's porcelain cheeks flushed red. She stabbed her
lime in the center, then cut it neatly in half. "I've no doubt
Fin wants what's best for Aoife, too."

Yank picked up his glass. "Unusual for her to go off
to Boston on impulse like she did?"

"Not particularly. She doesn't like having her life all
neatly scheduled. She says having an appointment can
ruin her flow when she's deep into her work. She'd rather
be spontaneous. It's different from being impulsive, don't
you think?"

"Amounts to the same thing, jumping on a flight to
Boston at the last minute."

"Aoife can afford to book flights late," Kitty said air-
ily.

"Did Rachel Bristol contact you, Kitty?"

His question obviously caught her off guard. "No. She
did not." Kitty raised her gaze to Yank. "You've no authority in Ireland, you know."

He smiled and winked at her over the rim of his glass.
"I know."

She sighed, dumping the cut lime into the bowl with
the lemon. "You remind me of Sean in some ways. You
think you've seen it all, don't you?"

Yank was aware of Detective Garda Murphy behind

him, entering the bar through the French doors. He turned as the Irishman grinned at Kitty. "We have seen it all. Haven't we, Special Agent Yankowski?"

"I don't know much about Irish sheep," Yank said.

Kitty waved her paring knife. "Neither of you is funny. Not a bit."

Sean sat on Yank's left and helped himself to a glass and a splash of the Yellow Spot. "No news from Dublin. Whoever broke into Aoife's studio either didn't draw attention or wasn't seen. Our American friends—" Sean raised his glass at Yank "—are keeping us informed about the investigation in Boston."

And now Maine, Yank thought. He told Sean what he knew. "Rachel Bristol was in Heron's Cove last Monday. She visited Lucas Sharpe and Emma's former convent, the Sisters of the Joyful Heart."

"Emma Sharpe a former nun," Sean said, shaking his head. "Will wonders never cease."

"Oliver Fairbairn was also in Heron's Cove," Yank added.

That perked Sean's interest. "The British mythologist. What do we know about him?"

"Damn little." Sean drank more of his whiskey. "It's difficult to guess at this stage—from this far away— whether Rachel Bristol's and Oliver Fairbairn's trips to Heron's Cove should raise red flags for us."

Yank agreed. "The Bristols are a wealthy family with a lot going on. We don't want to get sidetracked with dead ends."

Lucy wandered into the room, her hair still damp from her swim and shower. Her cheeks were rosy, and her movements were smoother, more self-assured. Only her eyes and stiff smile suggested that she was recovering from a nasty ordeal. She nodded to Sean, then eased up onto the stool on Yank's other side and spoke to Kitty. "You have a lovely hotel," she said graciously. "What a pleasure it must be to come to work every day."

"It is," Kitty said, beaming. "I'm glad you like it. What can I get you?"

"Whatever Matt and Detective Murphy here are drinking."

"Irish whiskey."

Lucy smiled. "Perfect."

Sean studied her a moment, then eased off his stool. "I'll see you both tomorrow. Have a good night."

He left the same way he'd come in. Yank felt the cold draft and noticed Lucy shiver. She forced another smile. "It's a dark night."

Yank could feel her mood slipping. "What sounds good for dinner?" he asked her.

"I haven't eaten much today. Swimming helped my appetite." She raised her gaze to Kitty. "Do you think you could do fish and chips? When I was…stuck…" She took in a breath, then smiled and continued. "I dreamed about having Irish fish and chips when I got out."

Kitty returned her smile. "I think I'd have dreamed about whiskey and chocolate."

Lucy laughed, her tension visibly lifting. "That sounds good, too. You know, I'm not much of a whiskey drinker. Beer would go better with fish and chips, don't you think?"

"I do," Kitty said. "You can sit here in the lounge or go down to the dining room, or I'll send a tray up to your room—"

"I'd like to sit here by the fire," Lucy said, then turned to Yank. "Does that suit you?"

"It suits me fine." He stood, taking the remains of his whiskey and offering his wife his free arm. She hesitated, then took it, steady when she got off her bar stool but clearly exhausted. He glanced back at Kitty. "Thank you."

"I'll put more peat on the fire and get your dinner." She licked her lips and blinked rapidly, as if to ward off tears. "If only we'd caught that thief ten years ago—if only we'd stopped him…"

"He had nothing to do with Lindsey Hargreaves' murder," Yank said, guessing that was what was on Kitty's mind. "It's also possible he had nothing to do with Rachel Bristol's death."

"Why don't you call it a murder?"

"Because we don't know what happened out on that island."

The Irish woman nodded, then reached for a beer glass. "One step at a time. I know that from Sean." She sighed, putting the glass under a tap. "Smithwick's, Mrs. Yankowski?"

Lucy nodded, saying nothing as she sat at the table closest to the fire. She pushed up the sleeves of her sweater. The orange glow seemed to bring out the bruises on her forearm. Yank fought his reaction—the twist of his gut—and sat across from her, talking about peat fires, the smell of the sea, the purplish cast to the November Irish light. It was what Lucy seemed to need, and she picked up the threads of his attempt at small talk and focused on late autumn in Ireland. "Tell me about Finian Bracken's cottage. I want to hear about Irish rainbows and sheep." She covered his hand with her bruised one. "And I want to hear about you," she added softly. "You don't do well with too much thinking and too little action."

"Ever the psychologist," he said.

She squeezed his hand. "No, Matt. Ever your wife."

Sixteen

Boston, Massachusetts

Finian crossed busy Arlington Street to the quiet, meandering walks of the Boston Public Garden. He'd spent little time in Boston since his arrival in the U.S. in June. He wasn't one for cities, but Boston had its charms. He'd left Aoife to talk to the homicide detectives in her hotel suite. They'd given him a suspicious look, and she'd explained who he was—"A friend from Ireland," she'd said—and they'd seemed satisfied, at least for the moment.

The Public Garden's deciduous trees were mostly bare of their leaves, and the swan boats had shut down for the season. Finian stood on the small bridge that arched over the shallow man-made pond and called Sean Murphy in Ireland. At least he assumed his detective friend was still in Ireland and not on a flight to Boston.

"I just left Agent Yankowski and his wife at Kitty's hotel," Sean said. "Where are you, Fin?"

"Boston. With Aoife."

His friend groaned. "Fin."

"You sound as if you have a stomachache."

"I'm getting one. What's going on with you and Aoife?"

"Nothing. I'm a calm port in a storm. Nothing more."

"Now, maybe. What went on in the past—" Sean broke off. "Never mind. I don't need to know unless it can help us figure out what's going on now. Lucy Yankowski is recovering, but we're fortunate, Fin, that her husband and I didn't find her body."

"Thank God for that."

"What are your plans now?"

Finian looked down at a duck parading along the edge of the pond. "I will stay with Aoife until she returns to Dublin or the police find out who killed Rachel Bristol and why."

"Fin. Are you sure about this?"

"I booked a room adjacent to her suite."

He could hear the relief in Sean's sigh. "All right, but take care. This woman didn't shoot herself. Even if it was an accident, the shooter could panic and do more harm."

"It wasn't an accident, Sean."

His friend was silent a moment, then said, "No."

"A year ago, why didn't you quit the gardai and I quit the priesthood? We could have run your farm together. Your uncle Paddy would have liked that. The three of us lads, tending sheep. You could still have reunited with Kitty."

"I don't know that we were ever united enough to re-unite."

Finian smiled for the first time since he'd left Aoife with the two Boston detectives. "But you're united now, Sean. It's good?"

"It's damn good, Fin."

After Finian disconnected, he headed off the mini sus-pension bridge and made his way down a paved walk to the ducks. John O'Byrne had enjoyed having ducks at his house in Declan's Cross. He'd been devoted to the place. He'd been an eccentric, white-haired old man by the time Finian had met him almost seven years ago. Aoife had his love of art and Kitty his head for business—neither of them, happily, had his bushy eyebrows and beaked nose.

Finian felt his throat tighten as he turned up the walk, barely aware he was in the middle of a major American city. He saw only Aoife on the cliffs past the Murphy farm on the headland above the village of Declan's Cross. He was there again, on that unusually warm February afternoon. The wind was whipping her dark hair in her face and every which way, and she was trying to hold on to a sketchpad and pencils. A loose sheet of the heavy white paper had blown onto the lane. Finian picked it up, handed it to her and felt his knees buckle at his reaction to her. Her beauty, her energy, her impatience. She snatched the sheet, stuffed it into the pad and grumbled about the wind catching her by surprise.

"What are you sketching?" he asked her.

"Nothing, as it turns out. I'm just holding on to paper." She squinted at him with those incredible blue eyes. "I was absorbing the colors, the light. I've been up here a million times but it's always different. Who are you?"

"Finian Bracken."

"Ah. Sean's friend." No immediate reaction beyond that. "I'm Aoife, by the way—Aoife O'Byrne. My uncle has a house in the village. He's off to Portugal at the moment. I'm staying there with the ducks and the bats." She tucked her pad and pencils into a slouchy canvas bag. "Sean's not here, you know. He had to stay on in Dublin at the last minute on some garda matter."

"I'm sorry I missed him."

"Yes, well—would you like to walk back to the village

with me and have a pint or a glass of wine together? I've got myself so worked up and annoyed with the wind, I need to settle down."

He didn't consider resisting. He expected to stop at a pub, but she took him to her uncle's house and dug out wineglasses and a bottle of Cabernet Sauvignon from a dusty cupboard in the drawing room. She wrapped up in a throw, sat on the couch and watched him light a fire in the fireplace. He felt her artist's eyes boring into him, seeing into his soul—past the blinding pain of his recent loss of his wife and daughters, past his unkempt appearance, to the man inside, or at least the man he'd been. Sally and the girls felt near and distant at the same time.

He almost left, but Aoife took his hand and pulled him onto the couch next to her. "Stay, Finian. Please. It's about the time bats start swooping around in here."

"Have you seen one?"

She smiled. "Not in years."

She gave him a little of her blanket. They drank wine and listened to the crackle of the fire, smelled the burning peat and enjoyed its heat. She had canvases leaned up against the wall by the fireplace and explained she was into sunrises and sunsets these days, especially over the sea. She was unpretentious and dedicated to her work, and he found her mesmerizing and completely fascinating.

Taking her wine with her, she slid out from under her throw and stood. He noticed the shape of her hips, the length of her back and her legs, as she pulled back a canvas that was covering two additional canvases. "These are rough," she said. "I'll probably end up painting them over. I rarely work with models, but I saw these little girls on the beach and decided to see what I could do."

He went ice still, staring at the half-formed figures....

Two little girls running on the beach. It was as if they were his own daughters. He could hear their laughter and squeals of delight at the encroaching waves, their pleas to stay out longer.

"Finian?"

He rose stiffly, glaring at her. "Why did you do this to me?"

"Do what? I have no idea what you're talking about..." Aoife stopped, horror turning her ghostly pale. "Oh, dear God. Oh, Finian. I'm so sorry. My sketch reminds you of your daughters. I should never have shown it to you. I wasn't thinking. I was caught up in my own vision. It was selfish." Tears spilled down her white cheeks. "I can't imagine what you've gone through. Please forgive me."

"There's nothing to forgive," he said, his voice strangled.

"What can I do? Finian—please, what can I do to help?"

He shook his head, but he was unable to take his eyes off her sketch. He could picture her with pencils in hand, her brow furrowed in concentration as she tried to get onto paper the images that were in her head. Not of his daughters—he knew that, at least intellectually.

Finally, he turned to her again, and he touched a curved finger to her cheek, capturing the flow of tears. She grabbed his hand and kissed his fingertips, apologizing again. It was more than he could take. The tears, the touch of her soft lips, the memories. He felt the heat of the fire on his back, then all at once it seemed to go through him, to penetrate every cell in his body. He was burning. Aching.

He wanted oblivion, and he wanted this beautiful woman.

And she knew it.

"Finian," she whispered, moving closer to him, threading her fingers into his hair. He held her, lifting her off her feet, smelling the ocean salt on her hair, and when he kissed her, tasting it on her mouth, her tongue. She was all angles and softness, eager and tender and irresistible.

Alone in the drafty house, they'd made love by the fire, as the sunlight faded and the clouds and rain moved in from the west, and then night fell.

A weekend to remember, and he did remember, Finian thought as he returned himself to Boston, to a cold November afternoon. Aoife was a famous artist now. Wealthy, successful and as beautiful and alone as she had been that weekend in Declan's Cross.

"I'm a free spirit, Finian Bracken," she'd told him with a wry smile as she'd packed to return to Dublin. "You don't have to worry about me."

He couldn't say for certain what Sean and Kitty knew or suspected, but Aoife had assured him she'd kept her promise not to speak of their weekend to either her sister or their garda friend—and Finian had kept his promise to do the same. He wasn't protecting himself, and he wasn't embarrassed or ashamed of the love they'd shared that weekend. When he'd tried to make sense of his call to the priesthood—to understand what it meant for him—he'd been straightforward and honest about what had transpired between Aoife and him. He'd gone into the process of discernment honestly, as the man he was. No better, no worse.

When Finian returned to the hotel, he spotted Oliver Fairbairn in the bar, enjoying a pint, eating nuts and watching a hockey game on the television. He abandoned all three when he saw Finian and joined him in the lobby. "Aoife O'Byrne is on her way down," Fairbairn said.

Fairbairn frowned. "Rachel?"

"She's the only one I saw. The police won't say if she had it with her when she died or if they found it in her things."

"I haven't seen it," Fairbairn said. "I'm sure it isn't in Maisie's workroom—I doubt Rachel would have shown it to her if she'd stolen it from you."

"The police haven't mentioned it to you?" Finian asked.

Fairbairn shook his head. "Not at all, but not surprising given the situation."

"I did several versions of the cross myself early in my career," Aoife said. "It was fun, and I learned so much in the process."

The Englishman smiled. "It's very Irish, isn't it?"

She smiled back at him, relaxing visibly. "It is. Come see us in Declan's Cross one day. You'd love my sister's hotel."

"I'm sure I would."

Fairbairn said goodbye and headed across the small bridge, back toward Beacon Hill. Aoife watched him, then turned to Finian. "I probably shouldn't have done that. Even if Emma and Colin understand, they won't like it. On the other hand, there are a lot of things in my life I probably shouldn't have done. Talking to a mythologist is the least of them."

"Maybe so," Finian said, keeping his tone neutral.

"You disapprove. Well, so be it." She edged in close to him. "We could hold hands and walk in the garden. Pretend we're not mixed up in a murder investigation. You're not in your priest clothes. No one would care if they saw us."

"The clothes don't make the priest, Aoife."

She pushed ahead of him without a word. Finian let her keep her lead as they returned to the hotel.

She was breathing hard when she stopped at the elevator and banged the up button. "I know you won't leave me alone until you're certain any danger has passed." She gave him a cool smile. "My priestly bodyguard."

"Your friend."

"Yes. That, too." Her eyes shone with tears. "I'm glad you're here. I'm sorry I brought up the past. I know there was never an *us*. We had a weekend together at a terrible time in your life and a free-spirited time in mine."

"I'm not running from the past or the truth."

"If you'd given yourself time—another day, and then another…you'd have made a new life for yourself."

"Let's not talk about the past."

"Our weekend was the best of my life," she said bluntly, stepping into the elevator, banging another button.

Finian debated heading straight to the bar, but he got in with her. "It's easy to say that now," he said as the doors closed.

"Because you're a priest, and any relationship with you is hopeless."

"Because what we shared that weekend can never be repeated. You've known that for years." He could feel her arm brush against him. "Sometimes we cling to the idea that happiness lies in what we know we can't have."

"I don't cling to it. I revisit it now and again." But any humor evaporated quickly, and she stepped away from him, her hands shoved in her coat pockets. "You're the forbidden fruit, I suppose. I can see that, but I expected nothing in return from you. I still don't. My feelings for you were and are real. Tell me, Finian, do you regret the time we spent together? Do you wish you'd never met me?"

"My only regret is that you—"

"Can't let go?" She spun around at him, her eyes fierce with emotion. "There's never been another man in my life like you. That's a fact. If it makes you uncomfortable, so be it."

"I don't want you to use me as an excuse not to live your life to its fullest."

"I'm not." She sounded more defiant than convincing, but some of the ferocity went out of her as they came to her floor. She pulled her hands out of her pockets and tightened the tie on her coat. "I've been deeply absorbed in my work. I have often wondered if daydreaming about you has helped. What I do can be all-consuming, but I have friends. I have a full life."

"I'm glad of that," Finian said, following her out into the hall.

"Can you say the same, Finian?"

"I can, yes."

She snorted, skeptical. "Ha. So you say. Don't you miss real life?"

"Nothing could be more real than the life I'm living now."

She stuck the key card into her room door, then pushed the door and let him go in ahead of her. She pulled off her coat, draped it on the back of a chair and stood in the open doorway to the bedroom, as if she were hyperaware of the king-size bed visible just inside. "Was I real to you that weekend?"

"Of course you were." He stayed by the entrance. He had no intention of sitting for a chat. "You are now."

"I know you were drinking too much then, but not that weekend. Was I just another form of oblivion?"

"Aoife, you helped me to see that I had to go on—that I could go on—without Sally and the girls. My call to the priesthood isn't a reflection on you."

"I wish I'd phoned you after that weekend," she said quietly, sinking onto a sofa. "I wanted to. I kept thinking I would. But I didn't. I was busy getting ready for my first show in London. The weeks ticked by. Next thing I knew, you were off to the seminary, becoming a bloody priest."

He smiled. "I heard your London show was a grand success."

She flopped back against the soft cushion. "It was. You know, I can't believe I'm thinking about sleeping with you right now, after all that's happened."

"You've had a difficult few days."

"Mmm. Yes, I suppose I could use a few hours of oblivion myself right about now."

At least, Finian told himself, some of the high emotion had subsided, but he knew her wry tone and flirty gaze were a cover for the fatigue and loneliness she had to be feeling. "How did your interview with the detectives go?" he asked her.

"As well as can be expected, considering they have no idea what to make of me. For all they know, I could be the Sharpes' art thief. Is that something you've ever considered, Finian? That I could be the thief who broke into my uncle's house that night? I was twenty-five then. Full of myself, impulsive, reckless. I could have helped myself to a couple of Jack B. Yeats paintings."

"Did you?" he asked quietly.

Her look turned cool. "I'm not going to answer that. It doesn't deserve an answer." She got up and walked over to the windows. "Maybe I should spend a year in Boston painting. I wonder if I could do it. You've been here since June. What's it like?"

"I'm not in Boston."

"You're in run-down but charming Rock Point, Maine, with its lobstermen, FBI agents and innkeepers. Oh, Finian. My dear Father Bracken. Why aren't you home in Ireland making whiskey with your brother?"

"Because I'm here."

"Meant to be, is it?" She looked at him, her blue eyes vivid, filled with pain, resignation, confusion—a cauldron of emotions. She gave him the smallest of smiles. "Don't answer. You can explain, and I can listen and try to understand—and we'll still be right where we are right now, because I won't understand. Our weekend of mad sex in Declan's Cross I can understand. You were in a sorry state. In my own way, so was I, if on a different scale from you. We needed each other then."

He didn't argue with her, and he didn't try to explain. Anything he said would only sound like rationalizing, or would hurt her further. He walked over to the window and stood next to her.

"I want to visit the Bristols," she said abruptly. "I should pay my respects."

He nodded. "I'll go with you."

She raised her gaze to him, then took him by the wrist. "There's no replacing your wife and daughters. I'm not the believer that you are, but I believe they're with God, at peace."

"I do, too."

"Are you at peace, Finian?"

He knew he wouldn't answer, and she seemed to know, too. He gestured toward the door. "I'll settle into my room. I'll go with you to visit the Bristols whenever you're ready."

"You'll know what to say to the bereaved. As a priest, I mean."

There was an edge to her voice—a touch of bitterness, perhaps. "All we can do is our best," he said, then left her.

He breathed deeply when he reached the hall. The murders in Declan's Cross two weeks ago and now in Boston had stirred up the past for Aoife, the longing for what might have been. Maybe she'd told herself she wanted to see him because he was a friend who was now a priest serving a church far from home, but that wasn't the whole story. She'd also wanted to wound an ex-lover. A man who'd done her wrong, and in doing her wrong, had done himself wrong, too.

"No regrets," she'd told him as they'd parted that weekend so long ago. "No regrets, ever, Finian. I promise. Now promise me the same."

He'd believed their weekend had meant little to her. An interlude of laughter and sex and fun. He'd seen her as uninhibited, uninterested in entanglements, particularly one with a tortured man who'd lost his family.

Easier that way for him, wasn't it?

He settled into his room next to hers. As he splashed his face with cold water, he heard a door shut hard in her suite. Aoife wasn't a woman to hold back her emotions. He looked at his reflection, seeing lines forming at the corners of his eyes—he wasn't a young husband with two small daughters and hadn't been for more than seven years.

He saw weariness in his face, and regret and grief and loss, but also, he thought, hope and faith and love. He touched a finger to his reflection, his throat aching with emotion, and he saw the man he was, not the man he had been—or the man he might have been.

Another door shut hard in the adjacent room.

Had she honestly expected him to fall in bed with her?

Had she expected him to be tempted?

Maybe he had been, he thought, drying his face with a soft towel.

He returned to the bedroom, unpacked and put on his clerical suit. He felt at peace. On that weekend with Aoife O'Byrne, he had finally realized, if not yet accepted, that he was still alive. He had delayed joining Sally and the girls on their sailing holiday by a day and thus hadn't drowned with them, and there was nothing he could do to change that fact, whether he lived another hour, day or fifty years. He'd left Declan's Cross—and Aoife—and gone back to Kerry. He raged and drank and taxed his friendship with Sean Murphy to its limits, but however unknowingly, he had started on the road out of desolation. It was a road that had led him into the priesthood and on to Rock Point, Maine, and now here in Boston, full circle, back with beautiful Aoife O'Byrne.

Seventeen

"You just missed Aoife O'Byrne and her Irish priest friend," Danny Palladino said from the front steps of the Bristols' Beacon Hill house. "Father Bracken, right?"

"That's right," Colin said.

Emma paused next to him on the brick sidewalk. They'd walked to Beacon Hill from her waterfront apartment. It gave her time to think about what she'd learned in Heron's Cove, as well as from Matt Yankowski. Colin had said little.

"He's cool," Danny said, smoking a cigarette. "I like his sunglasses. He and Aoife only stayed a few minutes. They wanted to pay their respects. They walked from the Taj. I suggested they stop on Charles Street on their way back. It has good shops and restaurants, and our two Irish friends look like they could use a break."

"That's where they are now?" Emma asked.

"Yeah, I guess." He flicked ashes from his cigarette onto the sidewalk. "My first cigarette in five years. I'll toss the rest of the pack. Travis and Maisie won't let me smoke in the house. Place smells like turpentine from the workers, but a cigarette would do them in. Acceptable versus unacceptable toxins, I guess. How was your drive south from Maine?"

"Quick," Colin said. "It's the time of year."

Danny nodded thoughtfully. "Fewer tourists. My drive down was quiet. Maisie sulked most of they way. She likes Heron's Cove, though. She wants to go back for wild blueberry pancakes and a fried fish sandwich. Not at the same meal." He held up two thick fingers. "Two different meals."

"There are some great restaurants in Heron's Cove and the surrounding towns," Emma said. "When did you learn Rachel had been up there last week?"

He leaned back against the steps. The stone had to be cold, but he didn't seem to mind. "When Maisie told me this morning. She was in Los Angeles on Monday. Travis was here in Boston. Rachel stayed with him and then flew to Los Angeles on Tuesday and then back here again on Friday. I'd feel like a yo-yo but Rachel liked the action." Danny tossed his burning cigarette onto the sidewalk. "Now I can see why she wanted to know more about you Sharpes."

"And why would that be?" Emma asked mildly.

Danny stood up and crushed his cigarette under the toe of his Western-style boot. "You're an interesting lot, and you're obsessed with this Declan's Cross thief. Makes me think there's more at stake than a few missing Irish paintings. This guy's responsible for other heists, isn't he?" He tucked the remains of his pack of cigarettes into his jacket pocket. "I'll bet Rachel wondered the same thing. Think it got her killed, Special Agent Sharpe?"

Emma didn't respond. The black glossy front door opened, and Travis Bristol stood on the threshold. He looked slightly less pale than he had yesterday. He motioned toward the interior of the house. "Please, come in. I don't want to alarm the neighbors. I know you must think you look like three ordinary people having a pleasant conversation about Thanksgiving decorations, but trust me—you all look armed and dangerous."

Danny grinned at Emma. "Is that a first for you?" He held up a hand before she could answer. "Sorry. That was out of line."

She ignored him but thought she saw Colin smile. "Where's Maisie?" she asked Travis.

"In her workroom." He opened the door wider. "Please, come inside or leave." He stopped at the distinct sound of a scream—a woman's scream—behind him. "Did you hear that?"

"That's Maisie," Danny said, starting up the stairs.

Colin bolted past him. "I'll handle this."

Travis sank against the door as Colin charged into the house. "Maisie." Travis's voice was strangled. "What the hell…"

Emma mounted the stairs, but Danny shoved Travis aside and ran into the foyer. Travis followed him. "Hold on," she called to them. "Both of you."

They were already down the hall, past the living room and library. Emma raced after them and managed to get in front of them as they came to the stairs down to Maisie's garden-level workroom.

They heard no other screams.

Danny seemed to calm down as he glanced at Emma. "Maybe something startled her. We're all on edge."

Colin appeared at the bottom of the stairs. He didn't have his weapon drawn. "Clear," he said. "Maisie's safe. Oliver Fairbairn took a door to the face. You can come down."

Travis's relief was palpable as he headed past Emma down the stairs. Danny sank against the stair rail, exhaling slowly. "Damn," he breathed. "Coast is clear and now I want to puke. This is why it's better not to have a personal connection to a client.... Not that I do." He grimaced, clearly more upset by Maisie's scream than he wanted to let on. He waved a hand, rallying. "Never mind. Let's go."

Emma said nothing and followed him down to the workroom. Colin glanced at her. "I've called the detectives."

Oliver Fairbairn was standing by the worktable, touching a fingertip to the swollen, bloody right side of his mouth. "I don't know which I could use more right now—ice or Scotch." He winced. "Hurts."

Maisie was pacing with such intensity that the tail of her flannel shirt flapped behind her. She clutched the T-shirt underneath as if she thought it might help reduce her heart rate. She was swearing, more to herself than to anyone in particular. She stopped abruptly and pounded a fist onto her worktable. "I can't stand this. I can't. Not another damn minute."

Travis glared at Colin and Oliver. "What the hell just happened?"

"Oliver came in through the garden," Colin said. "When he started into his suite, someone smashed the door into his face. He went down. He's not sure if he blacked out or how long he was down—he was on his hands and knees when Maisie came downstairs and found him. She screamed. Here we are."

Danny peeked into the suite. "Someone was in here searching the place?"

"I'm sure I surprised one of the workers," Oliver said. "The only exit onto the street from this level is through the suite. You can't go through the garden."

Colin stepped past Danny into the suite and returned

almost immediately with an ice pack. He handed it to Oliver. "It'll help with the swelling."

Oliver put the ice to his lip. "I'd rather have the Scotch."

Maisie crossed her arms on her chest. "I came downstairs from the kitchen and saw Oliver and immediately thought he'd been shot. I hadn't heard gunfire but it's the first thing that went through my mind."

"Understandably," Danny said, standing close to her. "You okay?"

She scowled at him. "I'm not the one who had a door shut in my face."

He didn't seem surprised or perturbed by her snapping at him. "Did you see anyone else?"

Travis stood next to his daughter. "Dwight Wheeler was here earlier. He's one of the carpenters working on the renovations. He stopped by to see if they would be working tomorrow, given what's happened. I told him they could take the day off."

"I saw a carpenter earlier, when I went out for a walk," Oliver said. "I don't know his name. Didn't think a thing of it. He must have decided to take the opportunity to get some measurements or whatever while he was here, and I startled him. Poor chap probably realized what he'd done and ran. I heard the street door open and shut. I didn't black out, but I did see stars, I'm afraid."

"Dwight's family owned a cottage on the island," Maisie said. "That's one of the reasons we hired him."

"Did you talk to him when he was here?" Danny asked.

"No." She turned her back to him and touched a book on Ireland open on her worktable, running her fingertips across a photograph of a cluster of ruins on a hillside. "I wish I were there right now." She took a breath and looked at Emma. "I didn't realize it until after I saw you this morning in Heron's Cove, but Rachel enlisted Oliver to help her. She led him to believe it was what I wanted."

"But it wasn't?" Emma asked.

"I didn't know about it. I didn't have a chance to weigh in."

Danny muttered, "Typical Rachel," under his breath. Maisie clearly heard him but didn't so much as glance in his direction. She struck Emma as someone who expected people to respect her boundaries without necessarily defining them. The *they should know better* approach. It would be easy for a woman as apparently talented, opinionated and assertive as Rachel Bristol to overstep, either deliberately or unintentionally.

Oliver lowered himself gingerly onto a tall stool by the worktable. "My teeth are all intact, at least," he muttered.

"You were in Heron's Cove on Monday," Emma said. "Rachel was there, too. Want to tell us about that, Oliver?"

"It's not a secret," he said, matter-of-factly. "I was curious about Rachel and what her angle might be with regard to Maisie's film project."

"So you followed her?"

"No." He seemed mildly offended. "Rachel told me she was going up there. I decided to go, too, and left shortly after she did."

"But you didn't tell her," Emma said.

"I did not. I'd never been to Maine. I stopped at Sharpe Fine Art Recovery and a shop in the village run by the Sisters of the Joyful Heart. Then I had a late lunch at a charming restaurant and drove back here. Rachel had taken me into her confidence at least somewhat. She showed me news articles about the theft in Declan's Cross ten years ago and asked my opinion on the stolen cross.

She had a million questions. I didn't answer all of them by any means."

Maisie flipped to a bookmarked page and several photographs of stone beehive huts on the Dingle Peninsula. She turned again to Oliver Fairbairn. "Why didn't you tell me?"

"There hasn't been time. You were in Los Angeles. Rachel was on her way there. I flew to London that night. When we all got back to Boston… Well, you know what happened."

"Someone shot Rachel to death," Maisie blurted.

Oliver placed the ice pack on his swollen lip. He lifted his gaze to Emma. "Rachel mentioned the value of the stolen art but no theories about who the thief might be. She was gathering information, but she said she wasn't worried about historical details and such. She said what she didn't know she could make up, since the movie she had in mind wasn't a documentary."

Maisie crossed her arms, agitated, impatient. "Rachel had no right to involve you, Oliver. I'm sorry." She shut the book and turned to Emma. "Oliver isn't an expert in art and art crimes. He's a mythologist. Rachel knew that."

"I wasn't aware of any of this," Travis said, visibly shaken as he addressed Emma. "Her interference with Maisie's movie, Heron's Cove, this Irish art theft—it's all news to me now that she's dead."

Maisie took in a quick breath. "Dad, I'm sorry. I was going to get everything straightened out. I didn't want this project to be high-stress. I wanted to take my time, but you know how Rachel could be once she got the bit in her teeth—which she did this past week. I also have my ideas for Bristol Island as well as all my other projects. I'm afraid I piled too much on my plate, and I neglected to tell you what was going on."

"It's not your fault, Maisie," her father said. "Rachel could be a damn bully. That's the truth of it."

Danny went over to the garden doors. "Security here is lousy. You need a proper alarm system."

Maisie bristled. "That's none of your business."

"It is if I'm to protect you—"

"I'm not the one who needed your protection. Rachel was." Angry, trembling, Maisie brushed past him. "I'm going upstairs."

Travis followed her. Danny ignored them both and touched a latch on one of the French doors. "There's no sign of forced entry," he said. "I guess the police will want to talk to this carpenter, though."

Oliver removed the ice pack from his lip. "I can expect more scrutiny now, too, can't I, Agent Sharpe?"

She shrugged. "Does that bother you?"

He smiled a little. "Wouldn't it you? I thought I was getting involved with an exciting film project about Celtic Ireland. Instead, I'm involved in a murder investigation. It's disconcerting, to say the least."

"Ever fire a gun, Oliver?" Colin asked casually.

He didn't seem perturbed by the question. "With friends in England. Fox hunting. Bird hunting once or twice."

"Ever hit anything?"

"Targets. Nothing live. The hunts were more about camaraderie and scenery than anything else. I don't like blood." Oliver examined the ice pack. "I don't even like this bit of blood I'm leaving on the ice pack."

"Lip doesn't look too bad," Colin said. "You won't need stitches."

"Doctor Donovan." Oliver touched two fingertips to his swollen jaw. "I suppose you have experience with split lips given your work with the FBI."

"Given three brothers," Colin said with a grin.

"That would do it. An only child myself." The Brit pointed up at the ceiling. "All right if I go up for that Scotch?"

"No problem," Colin said.

He headed upstairs with Oliver. Emma noticed that Danny was deliberately lagging behind. "I'm the unwelcome guest," he whispered then slouched past her to the stairs. Emma followed him. When they reached the living room, Maisie was curled up on the sofa, hugging a pillow to her chest. Oliver Fairbairn was standing by the windows, his ice pack back on his cut lip.

Colin was in the foyer door. When the police arrived, he would be the first to greet them and fill them in on the situation.

Travis brought two glasses and a bottle of Talisker from the library. He set the glasses on a polished coffee table and uncorked the bottle. "One for me, one for our British guest, but there's plenty to go around if you all would like to help yourselves." He nodded out the window as he poured some of the Scotch into one of the glasses and handed it to Oliver Fairbairn. "I see our detective friends have arrived."

"A party," Danny said, plopping onto the couch.

Maisie looked as if she wanted to kick him. "Are you sure you weren't the one who smashed the door into Oliver?"

"Looks to me like the so-called *attack* on your mythologist friend was really just a panic attack by a carpenter."

She rolled her eyes. "That isn't remotely funny, Danny."

"Not meant to be. This carpenter got scared and panicked. That's it."

Emma noticed that the chemistry between Danny and

Maisie was even more obvious now than it had been that morning in Heron's Cove.

Travis poured the second glass of Scotch and handed it to his daughter. "You need this more than I do." His expression was hard to read as he turned to the security consultant. "Danny?"

"No, thanks. I've had my shot of nicotine. I'll stay away from the Scotch."

Travis remained on his feet next to Maisie. "I was thinking, Danny, that since you aren't a witness to what happened downstairs, you can go on your way. We don't need to keep you here. Am I right, Agent Sharpe?"

"The detectives are here," she said. "It's their call."

"An accidental door in the face isn't a cause for concern," Travis said, his tone mild, no hint of distress or criticism. "I'm surprised you bothered to call the detectives."

"I'll go meet them," Colin said.

Oliver set his ice pack aside as he sipped his Scotch, apparently oblivious to his swollen jaw and lip. "The tension's getting to everyone. We need answers, Agent Sharpe. We need to know what happened to Rachel and why."

Danny stretched out his thick legs in front of him. "I agree. We need to know if she was shot because of Maisie's film project and this unsolved Irish art theft or for some other reason—like being in the wrong place at the wrong time when some idiot was firing a gun."

Maisie took in an audible breath. "Danny. Just shut up, okay? Shut. Up."

"No problem, Maisie," he said evenly.

Oliver cupped his Scotch in his palm. "You don't think the police will suspect I shut the door in my own face, do you?"

Maisie smiled at him. "That would be a trick."

He angled a look at Emma. "Agent Sharpe?"

"Just answer their questions truthfully and completely," she said.

"I should have told you about Heron's Cove and Rachel sooner." A thick curl flopped onto Oliver's forehead. "My apologies, Agent Sharpe."

"Me, too," Maisie said. "Rachel's death was such a shock. It's not as if Oliver and I have any experience with that sort of thing. My father, either."

"Neither do I, really," Danny said, getting to his feet, his gaze on Emma. "My job is to prevent violence. Even if Rachel wasn't my responsibility, I'm sorry I didn't do that yesterday."

Emma said nothing, but his words obviously took Maisie by surprise. She buried her face into the throw pillow, crying. The three men—her father, Danny and Oliver—seemed to be at a loss, but they were spared when Colin returned with the two BPD lead detectives investigating Rachel Bristol's murder. The detectives, Emma knew, would have a lot of questions, more, perhaps than Travis, Maisie, Danny and Oliver were expecting or prepared to answer given their state of mind. The detectives would also want to talk to the carpenter, Dwight Wheeler, and find out whether he'd smashed a door into Oliver Fairbairn—and where he'd been yesterday morning when Rachel was shot near a condemned island cottage the Wheelers had once owned.

Colin stepped back into the foyer. Emma eased in with him, but she knew the detectives would want to talk to her again, too.

Eighteen

After interviewing everyone at the Bristol house, the detectives whisked Emma back to BPD headquarters with them. Colin didn't blame them. In their shoes, he'd have demanded access to her files—FBI and Sharpe—on her serial art thief. She'd have told him to go to hell. Not in as many words, maybe, but he'd have gotten the message. He expected the detectives were getting that message now.

She'd be right to hold firm, he thought. It was tempting to cast a wide net in a homicide investigation, but it wasted time and seldom yielded results.

He found Finian Bracken standing outside a boutique women's clothing shop on Charles Street, the main retail and restaurant street for upscale Beacon Hill. Through the shop window, Colin saw Aoife O'Byrne unfolding a cobalt-blue scarf. "Boston's colder than she expected?" he asked Finian.

"She didn't say. It's not any colder here today than in Dublin."

"Maybe it's just a pretty scarf, then." Colin thought the weather was fine, but he'd done a lot of walking that afternoon. Finian didn't look cold, either. "Did you see or hear anything unusual when you stopped by the Bristol house?"

"Visiting people in shock over a murdered loved one is unusual in my world," the Irishman said. "Thank God for that."

Colin explained about Oliver Fairbairn's door to the face. "Did you see anything, Fin?"

He shook his head. He wasn't wearing his sunglasses. It was late afternoon now, gloomier, rapidly getting dark. "Only Maisie Bristol, her father and the bodyguard—I forget his name."

"Danny Palladino. I think he and Maisie used to be an item. A lot of sparks between them."

"I noticed."

"I don't necessarily have an eye for that sort of thing, but sometimes it's obvious." Colin stood back as two men went past them with a big, skinny, expensive-looking dog. He couldn't think of the breed. He watched the trio a few seconds, then turned back to Finian. "It's like you and Aoife. I don't need a two-by-four over the head to get it that you two have some kind of history."

"It doesn't matter. I'm a priest now."

"Before you became a priest. After your wife died." Colin peeked into the shop window again. Aoife now had the blue scarf around her neck. "During that year of torment and alcohol, maybe a beautiful artist showed up in your life. Maybe you two shared something that you haven't yet put to rest."

"I wouldn't be a priest if I were in love, Colin. It's not how it works. It's not how I work."

"Did I say love? I said *shared something*. Want me to spell it out? Because I can. I'm an FBI agent. I can spell out awkward things without breaking a sweat."

Finian gave him a small smile. "That's a way of saying you can be a heartless bastard, isn't it?"

Colin grinned. "It is."

The Irishman sighed. "I should have known that wouldn't bother you."

"I know you're a priest now, but before that—you were just a guy, Fin. Then you took the worst blow a man can imagine. You got through it, but it had to be pure hell."

"That doesn't excuse me." He looked into the shop window, Aoife at the register with her scarf. "After all this time, she's still alone. She uses me as the reason she doesn't have a man in her life. She told me she always dreamed of having a big family in Declan's Cross, but here she is…." He didn't finish.

"It's not too late for her," Colin said. "Or for you."

Finian didn't look as shocked as he might have. In fact, he didn't look shocked at all. "I am an ordained priest, Colin. I received the sacrament of holy orders. I made promises of celibacy and obedience, and I have kept those promises."

Colin was unmoved. "You can change your mind, you know. Being a priest isn't a prison sentence."

"Or a hiding place," Finian said.

"You're a deep thinker, Fin. You can handle Aoife being in love with you."

"She isn't in love with me."

"She just thinks she is? Try that line out on her. You'll be like Oliver Fairbairn and get a door shut in your face. He has a hell of a fat lip."

Finian tried to smile. "I'd deserve a fat lip, I suppose. Were you the one who discovered Oliver after he'd been injured?"

"I got to run down the stairs and find him nursing his fat lip."

"The danger had passed?"

"If there ever was any real danger."

"And Emma?"

"Conferring with the police."

"Is that a problem, for you, Colin?"

"Not for me. Maybe I was crazy giving her that ring and asking her to marry me, putting that pressure on her now." The words were out before he could stop them. "Maybe all those Irish rainbows got to me."

Finian shook his head. "You know that's not true." He gave a mock shiver. "It's getting chilly. I hope Aoife decides on her purchase soon."

Even as he spoke, Aoife burst out of the shop, the blue scarf around her neck. She smiled. "It's so soft and warm. I couldn't resist. How are you, Agent Donovan?"

"Colin."

"Ah. Good. We're friends now."

He wouldn't go that far, but he didn't contradict her. She seemed to resist an urge to hook her arm into Finian's and instead eased between both him and Colin, putting an arm around each of them. "Let's walk back to the hotel. I'm desperate for a drink." She grinned at Finian. "I think I'd like an Irish coffee. What do you think about that, Father Bracken?"

He shuddered. She laughed, but Colin saw that her laughter didn't reach her eyes, as blue as her new scarf. She lowered her arms and talked about the shops and restaurants they passed, pointing out temptations in window displays.

"*Temptations* is a dangerous word when one is walking between a priest and an FBI agent, isn't it?" Her laugh sounded slightly brittle. "The beautiful objects in the shop windows. How's that? Better, I think. In another life, I'd put together window displays. I'd love to do Brown Thomas at Christmas. Can you imagine, Finian? Have you ever seen it at Christmas?"

He smiled. "I have. Little Mary loved Brown Thomas at Christmas. A born shopper, she was."

Aoife went pale, her step faltering. "Oh, dear God, I keep putting my foot in my mouth."

"No, you don't, Aoife. People often avoid anything that would remind me of Sally and the girls. I feel their awkwardness and then don't talk about them—"

"So you don't make *them* uncomfortable."

"I thank God every day for the years I had with my wife and daughters. It's good to be reminded of those years. What's not good," he added quietly, "is to live in them instead of in the present."

Colin had never heard his friend of five months be so open about such feelings.

Aoife blinked rapidly, but he didn't see tears in her eyes. "Living in might-have-been and should-have-been is to live in a morass of regret, longing and futility. It can be a hard lesson to learn." She tucked her arm into Finian's and leaned against him, then let go and smiled. "And here we are, an Irish priest, an Irish artist and an American FBI agent in Boston early on a chilly November evening. Our present. It's where we are even if we can think of a thousand places we'd rather be. I, for one, would rather be in front of a fire with my Irish coffee."

They crossed busy Beacon Street. Colin debated leaving Finian and Aoife going on to the HIT offices, but he continued with them through the Public Garden and back to the Taj. He asked if Aoife had seen anyone at the Bristol house. She said no, which he'd expected, but it felt good to focus on something concrete, instead of wondering about whatever had transpired between her and his Irish friend after the deaths of his family, before the priesthood—and what was between them now, however unspoken. It reminded him of an Irish mist. You could see it, taste it, feel it, but you could never grab hold of it.

Aoife invited him to join her and Finian for Irish coffee. Colin declined, politely, and went back out to Arlington Street. It was dark now, the city lit up around him. He found himself wanting to smell the ocean and have a drink with his brothers, but he set off back across the Public Garden, toward the waterfront and the HIT offices.

He dug out his cell phone. It was well before midnight in Ireland.

He dialed Yank.

"Donovan? What's up?"

"Maisie Bristol's mythologist took a door to the face, probably by a scared carpenter."

Yank was silent.

"What," Colin said, "that doesn't move your needle?"

"The mythologist—Oliver Fairbairn? The Brit?"

"Right. I took charge of the situation. I didn't let anyone touch the door, and I gave him ice for his fat lip."

"And you got me out of the tub for that?"

"Yank. Don't put that image in my head. Just don't. Tell me you're kidding, and you're at the bar drinking Bracken 15 with your wife and Kitty O'Byrne."

"I am. Sean Murphy's here, too."

"He'll want to know about the door incident."

"You know you're not an official member of my team, Donovan. I can disown you at any moment. But go ahead," Yank said. "I'll pour more whiskey. You talk."

Sam Padgett was as unimpressed with the attack on Oliver Fairbairn as Yank had been, but they all knew—professionally—that it had to be investigated in light of

Rachel Bristol's death and her interest in the Sharpes and the Declan's Cross art thief.

Padgett was in the conference room, still working. "It's hard to think of a British mythologist getting smashed in the face leading to anything that concerns us."

"I know," Colin said, warming up to the guy. "What do you have? Anything new?"

"A damn mess is what we have."

"One thing at a time. You can't eat a whole buffalo in one bite."

"You can't. I can."

"Trying to be funny again?"

"I thought that *was* funny." Padgett sat back on his chair at the head of the table. He had files and papers stacked, and a legal-size spreadsheet printout. "I've been following the money. My policy, and I'm good at it. Maisie is worth hundreds of millions. Maybe a billion. She started out with money as a Bristol and from her mother, but not that kind of money. You get close to a billion, that's a different league. She's young and busy, and she doesn't care—she's been amassing wealth and putting millions into her movies. I doubt she's ever had a real budget in her life."

"Who manages her money?"

"No one person or firm in particular, at least that I can find."

"Spender?"

"Just on the movies she produces. She lives simply— same apartment she's had for the past two years—but she bought out her father's stake in Bristol Island, which they inherited as co-owners from his grandfather, her great-grandfather, who died in his nineties three years ago. The house on West Cedar is in both Travis's and Maisie's names." Padgett shrugged. "These are the broad brush-strokes. Public record. We can go deep if we need to."

Wading into finances wasn't Colin's favorite thing to do. He relied on people like Padgett who loved digging into numbers. In Padgett's case, he also loved holding his own out in the field. A man of many talents, and he obviously knew it. Colin didn't have a problem with a little cockiness, especially if it was earned.

"What about Rachel Bristol?" he asked. "Anything there?"

"Nowhere in Maisie's league financially but doing okay from what I've been able to figure out. Rented an apartment in upscale Brentwood. Didn't own her own place. She had money from her divorce from Travis, and she was self-employed. She was always trying to put deals together and find money for her projects."

"The big deal always around the corner?"

Padgett nodded. "That's my take."

Colin finally sat at the table, his chair scratching on the floor. Most of the other agents had gone home. He had no idea when Emma would be back from BPD head-quarters.

"I took a swipe at Aoife O'Byrne's finances," Padgett said. "She's doing well for herself. Exponential growth in recent years. She owns her studio in Dublin, but I can't see that she owns any other property. I'd have to go deeper. Maybe she's got a villa in the south of France or something." He glanced at Colin. "She as pretty in real life as in her pictures?"

"Prettier."

"And she's hanging out with this Irish priest? That'll get tongues wagging in little ol' Rock Point. You want me to look into Father Bracken's finances?"

Colin shook his head. "No, but I'm not calling the shots."

"Yankowski just wants this fixed before he gets back here. You know what's going on with him?"

"He's in Ireland," Colin said, as if that explained everything.

"Meaning you know more than you're going to tell me. Fair enough. Want me to look into the Sharpes' finances?"

"Padgett."

"We already know Emma's FBI salary."

Colin looked at him. "Funny."

"There's the old man, Wendell, and the son, Timothy, Emma's father chronic pain due to his fall on the ice seven or eight years ago. He must have had some hefty medical bills. His wife, Faye, used to teach art, but she doesn't anymore. They're spending the year in London."

"It's a diversion that seems to help him manage his pain," Colin said.

"Got it. If I get shot and survive, I'm going to request the FBI send me to Fiji for a year." Padgett made a face. "Hell. Sorry. That was over-the-line humor. Can't be fun for the guy. Still, the Sharpes know people. What if they know a collector who buys stolen art? I don't see old Wendell breaking into houses and museums, but what if he aids and abets our thief?"

"And the crosses sent after every theft?"

"Designed to divert, delay and distract."

"That's a lot of effort. If it's Wendell, why not send himself something easy—like a movie stub from the city he's hit, or a photograph of the stolen art? You've seen the stone crosses. They're not dashed off."

"I admit I'm speculating," Padgett said, sarcastic. "I've never met Wendell Sharpe. I don't want him to be this thief, Donovan. That would crop-dust all of us with its stink. I could end up back in Houston sweeping out my uncle's rodeo."

"Your uncle doesn't have a rodeo, Padgett."

"He could." He leaned back in his chair. "I figure Emma went through a thorough background check when she was recruited. Right? She didn't tell us she'd been a nun, but Yankowski and the director knew, didn't they?"

"Bark up another tree."

"No problem." Padgett grinned as Emma appeared in the doorway. "Hey, Emma."

She was grim, obviously tired. "The police have a warrant for the arrest of Dwight Wheeler, the carpenter who was at the Bristol house today. The Wheelers owned their cottage on Bristol Island for fifty years. The Bristols— more accurately, Maisie—bought them out a year ago."

"Means our guy, Dwight, knows the island," Padgett said.

Emma nodded. "He's done some target shooting out there. Physical evidence links him to Rachel's death, but the detectives didn't get into details with me. They now doubt Rachel's interest in the Declan's Cross thief and my family has anything to do with why she was killed."

Padgett grunted. "What'd Dwight do, miss a tin can and hit her in the chest?"

"A window. There was no tin can at the scene."

"Ah."

Emma walked over to the conference-room windows. The harbor was still and quiet, reflecting the city lights now that it was nightfall. "The case against Dwight Wheeler is solid enough for an arrest. I suggest we go home, have a good dinner, get a good night's sleep and see what's what in the morning."

"We want to talk to Wheeler," Colin said.

Emma nodded. "Oh, yes. Yes, we do."

Padgett got to his feet. "This guy didn't send the crosses to you and your brother and grandfather or to Matt Yankowski, and he didn't pull a bookcase on top of Yank's wife in Dublin."

"Separate incidents, according to the detectives' current theory."

"Or the thief is out there, manipulating events—he could have manipulated this carpenter into shooting Rachel Bristol."

"We'll know more once Dwight Wheeler is in custody and we're able to talk to him."

Padgett reached for his suit jacket on the back of his chair. "I hate this case."

"Another attempt at humor?" Colin asked him.

"No, sir. Dead serious. I want to figure this thing out before someone else gets killed. It's the kind of case that wraps itself up with a pretty bow and gets you thinking it's a present when really it's a stick of dynamite up your ass." Padgett looked over at Emma. "Sorry about the language."

"I speak English just fine," she said with a quick smile.

Padgett said good-night and left, and Colin stood next to Emma at the window. "Do the cops know where Dwight Wheeler is?"

Emma shook her head. "They don't think he'll be hard to find. He lives in Dorchester. He knows Bristol Island. They must have the murder weapon." She exhaled, touching a finger to the cold glass of the window. "Wheeler could have banged the door in Oliver Fairbairn's face this afternoon, too."

"What do we know about him?"

"He's forty, divorced, father of two teenagers, prior arrests for drug possession and driving under the influence but no convictions and apparently clean in recent years. He told some of the other carpenters that Bristol Island was a safe place to do some shooting, especially this time of year. Invited them out there, never mind that the Bristols bought out his family and are paying to remove their cottage. The Wheelers never owned the land, only the cottage itself. He probably didn't expect to find anyone out there on a cold November morning."

"Then he probably didn't know about Maisie's meeting at the marina," Colin said.

"The marina is on the other side of the island. If Rachel had met me there, she'd be alive today—assuming Wheeler shot her by accident, and it wasn't an intentional murder."

"You'd think someone determined to kill her would have found another way."

Colin could see Emma's stubbornness as she turned to him. She'd held up under his and Padgett's scrutiny and had refused to let it get to her—to feel as if she'd done something wrong in going out to Bristol Island to meet Rachel. Maybe she was wavering now, but Colin didn't think so.

Finally, she spoke. "It's up to the detectives what to tell the Bristols and Aoife O'Byrne about Wheeler. Do you want to join Aoife and Finian for dinner?"

"I do not," Colin said without hesitating. "It was awkward enough waiting for her to buy a scarf and then walking back to their hotel with them. If Fin's got any sense, he left Aoife to hotel security and went home."

"Do you think that's what he did?"

"No."

They headed out together. With no one around, Colin draped an arm over Emma's shoulders. "If our thief isn't a murderer, that's a good thing."

"If he manipulates others to commit murder?"

"Not a good thing."

She smiled, leaning into him. "I like your clarity of thinking. Dinner in tonight?"

"Sure. I'll cook."

"That means—"

"I have pizza delivered. It can have anything on it but broccoli and especially pineapple. Pineapple on pizza is just wrong."

"Have you ever had pineapple on pizza?"

"Never."

"Then how do you know it's not good?"

"I didn't say it wasn't good. I said it was wrong. But I bet it's not good, either." He pulled her closer, kissed the top of her head. "Emma, you okay?"

"Dwight Wheeler isn't the killer."

"I love it when you go with your gut."

"What's your gut say?"

"Dwight Wheeler isn't the killer, and pineapple on pizza is a bad idea."

When they reached her apartment, Colin's cell phone buzzed, and he answered without looking at the screen. His brothers, his folks, Yank, the director and Emma, who was with him, were among the few people who had his number.

"Agent Donovan. Mina Van Buren. Are you alone?"

"No."

"We need to talk when you are, but there's no rush. I'll find you when the time is right. Be prepared and tell no one. Agent Yankowski, Agent Sharpe, your Irish priest friend. Understood? No one."

Colin tightened his grip on the phone. "Okay."

"Sorry to be cloak-and-dagger, but that's the way it has to be."

She clicked off. Colin kept any hint of a reaction to her call from showing in his face, then winked at Emma. "Anchovies?"

She hesitated. He could see the questions in her eyes, but she smiled and said, "I love anchovies."

"You would," he said with a grin, and dialed her favorite North End pizza place. The number was on a small bulletin board next to the refrigerator, along with pictures of her family and of sheep in a green Irish field.

Nineteen

~~~◦◦◦~~~

Declan's Cross, Ireland

Yank woke to an empty bed, or at least empty of Lucy. He sat up in the dark room and remembered he was in Declan's Cross, at the O'Byrne House Hotel—not at Wendell Sharpe's townhouse or Finian Bracken's tiny cottage, or back at his dumpy apartment in Boston. Definitely not at his home in northern Virginia. He could hear the wind buffeting the sturdy old building. There wasn't a clock in the room. Kitty had mentioned something about proper sleep hygiene. He'd have to grab his cell phone to figure out what time it was. One in the morning? Two?

"Lucy," he said. "You in here or did you go down to the reading room?"

Of course, if she'd gone down to the reading room, she wouldn't hear him. He threw back the covers and climbed out of the warm, cozy bed. Damn, it was chilly. In his cottage in the Kerry hills, he'd stoke up the stove for the night and sleep up in the loft, capitalizing on the fact that heat rises. He'd only been cold when the stove went out and he'd been too lazy to go down the ladder-like steps to fire it up, instead piling on the extra blankets in a small chest in the loft and waiting until daylight. He remembered wishing Lucy was with him on one particularly frosty morning.

He checked the bathroom. She wasn't there. He went back into the bedroom, figuring maybe she hadn't been able to sleep and had, in fact, gone down the hall to the reading room. But his eyes had adjusted to the dark, and he saw her silhouetted against the drapes in front of a window.

He stood next to her. "Can't sleep?"

"I had a nightmare. I couldn't breathe…" She stopped. "I don't want to think about it."

"I don't blame you. I hate those kind of nightmares."

"Have you ever had one?"

"Yeah. Not in a while. I had them after my first undercover mission."

"What did you do?"

He stood a little closer. Not too close, in case she was still spooked by her nightmare. "I woke you up."

"Sex as the antidote to a post-trauma nightmare."

"Worked."

She slipped her hand into his. "Did it really?" she asked softly.

"Lucy…"

She raised his hand and pressed it to her chest, above her breasts. She had on just her nightgown—no robe—and her skin was cool. She must have crawled out of their warm bed a good fifteen minutes or more before he'd awakened.

"I can feel your heart racing," he said.

"It's quieted down some." She pushed his hand lower, until he could feel the soft swell of her breast. "I didn't break any ribs. I'm a little bruised but not…not so that I would be uncomfortable if we…" He could hear her swallow, could almost make out the angles of her face. She eased his hand under her cottony nightgown, onto the bare skin of her breast. "Matt. I've missed you."

He felt himself respond. He had on boxers and a T-shirt. He'd be cold soon, too. How long since they'd made love? Weeks…months. They'd had grudge sex well before she'd gone off to Paris with her sister in October. When had that been? When he was in northern Virginia over Labor Day weekend? He'd initiated it. They'd gone to bed mad, and she'd slept on the very edge of the mattress, as far away as she could get from him without sleeping on the floor or in another room. He'd worked his way over to her and touched her hip, eased his fingers between her legs. She'd kept her back to him, pretending to be asleep or just giving him the cold shoulder. He'd felt her respond, reluctantly—grudgingly—at first, then less so.

Tonight was different. She eased closer to him, releasing his hand and slipping her arms around his middle. She lowered his shorts. He swore softly at how much he ached for her. And she knew it—he could sense just how well this woman he had loved for so long knew him.

She cast aside his shorts and grabbed his hips, then whispered, "I'm ready. So ready. Matt…"

He lifted her, hoisting up her nightgown, feeling how hot and wet she was as she lowered herself onto him. He hadn't taken her this way in years. He didn't want to hurt her, but she rocked and ground, eager for his deepest, hardest thrusts. He responded, not holding back, until his love for her and his driving need for her obliterated any sense of time or place. He lowered her to the floor, still inside her, still with her fingers buried deep into his hips. She writhed under him, taking what she wanted from him.

Oblivion, he thought. That was what she wanted. Needed.

Then she moved under him, into him, and he was lost…totally lost…and yet also where he was meant to be, with his wife, this woman he would grow old with and one day laugh with about the time they made love in the dark, on the floor of an Irish boutique hotel.

She managed not to cry out. He knew she wanted to. His Lucy could be quite the screamer. Spent, sweating now despite the cold air, he carried her to the bed. She was limp and loose and warm as he pulled the covers over her, then climbed in next to her. He still had no idea what the hell time it was. He didn't care. Things were under control in Boston, and he was here in Ireland, with Lucy.

"It feels great to walk," Lucy said, tucking her hands into her jacket pockets. "What a gorgeous day."

Yank noticed the wind blowing through her pixie-cut hair. It was a sunny, breezy morning with hardly a cloud in the sky. They'd indulged in a late breakfast at the hotel—a "full Irish" breakfast, complete with rashers, sausage, fried eggs, mushrooms, tomatoes and black and white pudding. Toast and scones on the side. Coffee, juice. Lucy's appetite was back in full force, but she'd suggested a walk. A long one, she'd said. They'd set off through the hotel garden and into the village and now were making their way up a narrowing lane onto Shepherd Head. Sea cliffs dropped to their left. Green pastures spread out to their right and up ahead of them. Even with the wind, Yank could hear sheep baaing.

Lucy smiled. "I love the views, but sheep, Matt?"

"You won't see lambs this time of year."

"Next trip."

They passed a simple farmhouse and a cluster of outbuildings off to their right. The Murphy farm, Yank knew from Emma and Colin. An old man was climbing onto an ancient tractor. Paddy Murphy, Sean's uncle. It was Yank's first trip to Declan's Cross, but he knew the names and places from the report on Lindsey Hargreaves' death here two weeks ago. An American diver with secrets, with dreams that she'd tried to fulfill in all the wrong ways.

"I wish you could enjoy the day without so much on your mind," Lucy said.

"Yeah. Me, too."

"It's not really a day off for you, is it?"

"Not today. Soon." He grinned at her. "I'm not wearing a coat and tie, though."

She returned his smile. "Did you get special dispensation from the director?"

"He's retiring. We're getting a new director."

Her smile faded, and she squinted up at him with knowing eyes. "What does that mean for you?"

He shrugged. "New thorns in my side."

"Matt…I asked because I want to know."

"I don't know what it means," he said. "The name floated as the acting director isn't making me turn cartwheels."

"Mina Van Buren," Lucy said without hesitation.

He gave a mock shudder. "Ruin the day, why don't you? That's like the good wizards not wanting to say Voldemort out loud. How'd you guess?"

"I live in northern Virginia, remember. I hear things, and Mina Van Buren is one of the few possibilities for acting director who could make you shake in your boots."

"I never shake in my boots."

"You don't like her."

"I don't trust her. I don't have to like her, but I do have to trust her."

"What about her don't you trust?"

"Her law enforcement instincts," he said without hesitation.

"For good reason?"

He glanced sideways at his insightful wife. "Yes. That doesn't mean I'm right about her. I hope I'm not." They came to a barbed-wire fence. Fat sheep ran toward them, bleating, butting each other. "Can you tell a boy sheep from a girl sheep?"

"I imagine we both could with a closer look. They're so cute, aren't they? I want to buy a mug with a silly sheep painted on it. It'll make me smile in the morning."

"We'll buy two mugs. I need to smile in the morning, too."

They continued farther out onto the headland, the lane turning to dirt as it curved away from the cliffs, fields on both sides now. Then it narrowed to a pitted, treacherous track that Yank wouldn't want to navigate even in his little Micra. The ocean was close again, and more cliffs. Then the lane descended slightly into a cluster of windstunted trees. The ruins of a church were just through the trees, above a low, very old stone wall.

"Holly trees," Lucy said, touching the waxy, evergreen leaves of one of several similar small trees growing along the stone wall. "They're supposed to bring good luck—bad luck if you cut one down." Her hand fell away. "I need to replenish my supply of good luck. I have a feeling I used up my good luck when I ventured to Aoife O'Byrne's studio."

"I can see how you would feel that way. It wasn't just luck that got you out of that situation, Lucy. It was your reactions, how you handled yourself."

"I couldn't even reach my cell phone, but it wouldn't have mattered. I used up the battery on my flight." She nodded up to a trio of Celtic crosses out past the church ruins, on a green hillside at the tip of the headland. "They're awe-inspiring, aren't they?"

"I guess."

"You're looking at them like an FBI agent. Because of the thief? Aoife O'Byrne?"

Something in Lucy's tone made him turn to her. "What's up, Lucy?"

"Aoife had a sketchbook of these crosses—this scene—on one of the shelves of her bookcase."

"She did copies of the crosses early in her career. Actually, copies of a fifteenth-century silver cross that was stolen from her uncle." He pointed up the hill. "The center cross is a larger version of that one."

"Amazing. Can we go up there?"

"Just have to mind the sheep—and sheep droppings."

She grinned, obviously game. This was the Lucy he knew and loved, he thought, watching her scramble over the stone wall onto a muddy trail. She'd always been eager, inquisitive, willing to try anything, provided it wasn't illegal, unhealthy or totally insane. The tightness and bitterness of the past year had disappeared.

At least for now, he thought, following her onto the trail.

The ground was soft and uneven, but Lucy had no trouble as she climbed up the hill to the biggest of the crosses. Yank stood in its shadow. They were back in the wind now, blowing at them from every angle and tasting of the sea. He couldn't tell if the tide was in or out, but the waves were white-crested as they surged against the rockbound coast.

"A hell of a sight," he said.

Lucy nodded, tracing a spiral on the cross with her fingertips. "I know very little about Celtic markings and symbols. Saint Declan was an interesting character, though, wasn't he? Imagine roaming this coast fifteen hundred years ago."

"We think the thief hid out here after breaking into the O'Byrne house."

"By choice?"

Yank started up the hill closer to her. His right foot sank into a muddy spot. "I don't know." He watched her move her palm over the worn gray stone. "The stolen landscape by the anonymous painter depicts this scene. Then the thief ends up here."

"Interesting."

She turned and looked out at the sea. Her jacket flapped in the steady wind but she didn't seem to notice. Yank glanced behind them and saw a fence that marked off the field and more sheep in the distance.

"I suspect your thief has a hole he can't fill no matter how many paintings he steals," Lucy said, continuing to stare out at the water. "The thefts give him temporary relief."

Yank rubbed the back of his neck. *Your thief.* He supposed it was now. "He likes the adrenaline rush?"

"No doubt that's part of it. Are the thefts brazen—as in he takes huge risks that could get him caught?"

"Kitty could have been in the house ten years ago. She wasn't. She was with Sean Murphy. Sean's uncle was looking after the place, but turns out he was sleeping off a pint too many. The other thefts were brazen but well planned. Our thief isn't impulsive."

"What's more important, the works he steals or the places he steals from?"

"I couldn't tell you," Yank said.

"Could Emma?"

"She could make an educated guess. Her grandfather, too, and probably her brother. I don't know about her parents."

Lucy pulled up her hood and turned again to the crosses. "I wonder if these first stolen works here in Declan's Cross presage the others somehow, not from an artistic standpoint, perhaps, but from an emotional one. What's this thief's inner world like? That's what I would want to know."

"Could he escalate to violence after ten years?"

"You're sure he hasn't committed acts of violence in ten years? What about before he started stealing art? What if he became a thief to make peace, at least in his own mind, with violent acts in his past?"

"That he committed?"

"Or were committed against him, perhaps." Lucy touched the simple figure of Saint Declan and his bell on the centerpiece of the elaborate cross. "Saint Declan was a healer."

"Backaches," Yank said. "I don't see our thief justifying a decade of stealing and taunting to get over a backache."

Lucy rolled her eyes. "It wasn't just backaches."

"Your nose is red. Let's get out of this wind."

She slipped her hand into his. "Tell me about the taunting. In confidence. Make me a professional consultant if you need to." She nodded down the hill. "We can have a look at the church ruin while we're here."

They took another route down to the church, pretty much a pile of ivy-covered rubble with the odd tree poking up out of it. On the way, Yank told Lucy about the crosses sent to Wendell Sharpe and then, after Lindsey

Hargreaves' murder, to Wendell, Emma, Lucas Sharpe and him.

Her dark eyes narrowed on him. "That's why you're here in Ireland?"

"It's one reason. I also had to make sure Colin Donovan was returning to the fold, and I needed some time."

"Because of me," she said quietly.

"Because of us."

She sank onto an intact wall made of stones now splotched with white lichen. Her hood was half on, half off. Her nose was even redder, but she wasn't shivering. "With this woman's murder two weeks ago, the thief could feel as if he set off a chain reaction that now, a decade later, has resulted in violence."

"He's losing control."

"The law of unintended consequences at work. He could be trying to regain control somehow by sending the crosses. Or warning you," she added. "Putting you on alert."

"You're here because of this damn thief."

She shook her head, getting to her feet. She winced, then rubbed the inside of her wrist. "I forgot it's bruised. Maybe that's a good sign. Anyway, do you know why I'm here? Why I wanted to surprise you? What triggered me? I'll tell you." She let go of her wrist and shoved her hands back into her jacket pockets. "Because of that absolute disgrace of an apartment of yours."

"What? It's fine. It's cheap, and it's close to the office."

"It's a dump. It has roaches."

"It's being renovated."

"Then the rent will triple and you'll move to another dump." Her tone was crisp and matter-of-fact at the same time. "When I walked in there, I knew you had put your life on hold. I knew you were waiting for me to make up my mind. I knew…" She glared at him as if he'd said something wrong when he hadn't said a damn word. "Matt, I knew I wanted to be with you. Whatever it takes."

"So you hopped a cab to Logan and boarded a flight to Dublin?"

"Exactly."

"Without telling me," he said.

She nodded. "Without telling you."

In the world of Lucy Yankowski, that made perfect sense. Yank pulled her hood back on top of her head. "You're a whirlwind, Lucy. Always have been."

"I've been playing head games with you. Seeing how you've been living made me realize how selfish and unthinking I've been. I put aside how selfish and unthinking you've been—or I think you've been. I considered the pressure you're under. The responsibilities you have. You deal with major criminals and agents with complicated lives. You don't do things easy, and you don't do easy things. You never have. It's one of your greatest strengths."

"But it can be hard to live with," he said.

"I've been telling myself that I was comfortable in our old life, and you were willing to throw that away without a proper discussion. Without truly taking me and what I wanted into consideration. Then this nasty freaking cockroach scampered across your kitchen floor, and I realized that I don't want a commuting marriage, and I don't want to leave you."

"Was it a big cockroach?"

"It was huge. As big as a tarantula."

"I know him. I named him Hugo."

She looked as if she wanted to laugh, but she didn't. "Matt. I just poured my heart out to you."

"Yeah, and I'm your knight in shining armor, and I have a cockroach to slay. I need intel."

"No, you don't. I dealt with Hugo myself. Then I booked my flight and headed to the airport."

"My intrepid Lucy. You've always said your career is portable, you know."

"Things change. I thought you'd noticed."

"I didn't notice until you stayed in Virginia. Then I noticed, but it was too late. You were pissed—"

"I was *upset*. I was figuring things out."

"Figuring things out means you take a long drive in the Blue Ridge Mountains. Pissed means you go to Paris with your sister and buy Chanel jackets and Hermès scarves."

"One jacket, one scarf. I also bought a purse, but I got a good deal."

"How good a deal?"

"Not so good that I didn't feel guilty about your roach-infested dive of an apartment, but good in Paris terms." She pulled a hand out of her pocket and reached up and placed a cool palm on his cheek. "When I was trapped under that bookcase, trying to stay coherent, I knew you would find me. I knew it in my heart and soul. I trust you more than I trust anyone on this earth."

"Lucy…"

"I don't want to be your damsel in distress, but you are my knight in shining armor." She sniffled, tucking her hand back into her pocket. "Nothing like a heavy bookcase falling on top of you to knock some sense into you."

"I'm sorry you had to go through that, especially since Hugo had already knocked some sense into you." But he gave up on the humor, the flippancy, and stood back, sinking into the Irish mud. He could hear birds above the wind. He didn't know birds. He didn't know vegetation or the different kinds of rocks out on their hillside, and he didn't know sheep. He knew his work, and he knew Lucy. He leaned toward her and kissed her on the forehead. "I love you, Lucy. Always and forever."

They climbed back over the stone wall to the lane. Lucy said nothing until halfway to the Murphy farmhouse. Then she looked up at him and made a face. "There's one more thing."

There was always one more thing. He'd been expecting something. "What?"

"I quit my job."

He almost tripped over a rut in the lane. "When?"

"Middle of September. I've been consulting but I don't go in every day. How do you think I've been able to flit off to Paris and Ireland?"

"I was going to offer to quit my job for you."

"And do what? Get underfoot? Grow vegetables?"

"Lots of things I could do in the D.C. area. I'm an experienced senior federal agent..." He stood straight, eyeing her. "You really quit your job?"

"I did." She paused and looked down the lane, toward the tip of the headland. "What if your thief finds solace in the crosses? What if he's not taunting Wendell Sharpe so much as inviting him to find solace, too, and now you and the rest of the Sharpes?"

"Your theory of the case?"

"I wouldn't go that far, but having been out to the crosses, these are questions that come to my mind."

"They're good questions, Luce."

Sean Murphy met them at the hotel. He had agreed to join Yank on a video conference call with Emma and Colin in Boston. Kitty had set them up in the reading room on the second floor. It had been a musty library ten years ago, the spot where her uncle had hung his treasured Jack B. Yeats paintings and the landscape by the unknown artist. Now it was bright and cheerful, with a mix of contemporary and traditional furnishings.

Lucy went over to a moody watercolor seascape done by Aoife O'Byrne. "Her studio is plain—no distractions—but her artwork is colorful, emotional. Incredible. It's real and not real at the same time." She turned to Sean. "Are Aoife and Kitty close?"

"Very close," he said.

"Nice. I have a sister. We like to spend money together." Lucy smiled. "I'll leave you two. I'll be downstairs having lunch. I intend to have a glass of wine, and dessert."

Sean watched her leave. Once she'd shut the door behind her, he spoke. "She seems to be recovering well. I saw you two walking out past the farm."

"Yeah. Nice spot. I can see why you were tempted to be a sheep farmer."

"I'll always be a sheep farmer," he said. "Right now, I'm also a detective."

"Not a bad way to think."

"It helps." The Irishman's expression darkened. "Tell me about Dwight Wheeler. What do you think, Agent Yankowski? Did he kill Rachel Bristol?"

Yank looked out the windows at the quiet garden and the churning sea, not a boat in sight. He wanted to be downstairs having wine and dessert with his wife, but he could picture Emma and Colin arriving at the HIT offices. It was lousy weather in Boston. He'd checked. Finally, he answered Sean Murphy. "A guy goes out one Saturday morning to do some target practice on an island within spitting distance of downtown Boston, just as a woman whose family he works for shows up to wait for an FBI agent to come meet her. He decides to shoot at the very same cottage where she happens to be standing, and he hits her in the chest and kills her."

"The worst shot of his life or the best."

Yank sighed. "Yeah. What are the odds it was either?" He turned on his laptop. "Let's get started."

Sean didn't look ready to get started.

"What's up, Detective?" Yank asked.

"Rachel Bristol was in Ireland last week. She arrived early Tuesday morning and left again on Friday, an afternoon flight. She stayed in Dublin all three nights." Sean paused, glancing up at the seascape by Aoife O'Byrne. "I showed a photograph of Rachel to Kitty just now, while you were on your walk with your wife. Rachel had lunch here at the hotel last Thursday. She rented a car for the day and drove down from Dublin herself."

"Alone?"

"As far as Kitty knows."

"So Rachel was here in Ireland, not in L.A. Why lie to her family?"

Sean shifted his gaze to Yank. "Perhaps because she surprised your wife at Aoife's studio—or she knew someone had—and didn't want to explain herself."

"She stole the cross from Aoife in Boston. She could have been looking for it at her studio." Yank sucked in a breath, pushing back an image of Lucy trapped in the Dublin studio. "All of that's speculation."

"That's right," Sean said, then nodded to the laptop. "Let's talk to Emma and Colin in Boston."

Twenty

Boston, Massachusetts

Emma wasn't prone to throwing, kicking, pounding or overeating when she was frustrated, but that didn't mean she never wanted to. An hour after the video conference with Yank and Sean Murphy ended, she looked longingly at the shelf of art books in her office and considered what it would be like to pitch them against the wall one by one.

Instead, she changed into running clothes and headed out into the cold November rain for a run on the waterfront. She went alone. She went armed.

A run wasn't the same as throwing things, but it helped.

When she returned to the HIT offices, Colin was stretched out on her office couch. "I'm on my lunch break," he said, making no move to sit up. "This is a cheap couch. Yank pick it out?"

"I don't know who picked it out. It was here when I arrived in March."

"Having seen Yank's apartment, I bet he picked it out."

Emma frowned as she sat on her desk chair and unlaced her running shoes. "When and why did you see Yank's apartment?"

"Saturday morning while you were on Bristol Island alone. He had me check to see if Lucy was there. She wasn't." Colin threw his feet onto the floor and sat up in one swift, utterly masculine motion. "It's a hole, in case you were wondering. Explains why he doesn't have us all over for cocktails."

"As if he would if he lived in a decent place. He was worried about Lucy?"

"She hadn't been answering his calls and texts. I'm smelling a reconciliation in Ireland. Maybe he'll be easier to live with, but I doubt it. He was a pain in my backside when he and Lucy were getting along."

"Because he was your contact agent and you don't like anyone looking over your shoulder. That seems to be Yank's lot in life. Attaching himself to highly independent people he then worries about."

"The worrying's a facade. Trust me. If the alligators had gotten me in October, Yank would have given me a nice sendoff and then found someone else." Colin leaned back against the couch. "He'd have done the same with you if you'd told him to go to hell and made your final vows. Or whatever it is Sister Brigid would have told him. Peace be with you?"

"You're cranky. Did I wake you from your nap?"

He grinned at her. "I was thinking."

"Ah. Let me call a meeting. Colin Donovan has been thinking." She grinned back at him. "Did you have lunch yet, or did you think through lunch?"

"I had a hot dog with Padgett. He wanted to follow you on your run. I assured him you were capable of defending yourself. He's not convinced. You two will have to go shooting one day. You could go out to Bristol Island. Shoot some tin cans."

The bantering mood in the room evaporated, and Colin got to his feet and seemed to look as longingly at her art books as Emma had. "The detectives didn't call you while you were on your run and tell you they'd brought in this carpenter they like for killing Rachel?"

"They did not. I'd have said something before I let you tell me about you and Padgett eating hot dogs together." But Emma felt her comment go flat, any attempt at humor now feeling off, out of place. She raked a hand through her hair. It was wet from the rain, all in tangles. She should have pulled it back and worn a hat. "Next year, let's go on a Mediterranean cruise in November."

"Sounds good. You don't know any Greek art thieves, do you?"

"I'd have to check my files."

"And your grandfather's files." Colin touched a fingertip to her nose. "Raindrops. It's nasty out there."

"If Rachel was in Dublin, why did she call my grandfather and Aoife instead of stopping in to see them? If she was right there—why the games?"

"Maybe she was shy or intimidated."

"*Nothing* we've learned about her suggests—"

"I was kidding, Emma."

"Of course. Sorry. But why invite Aoife to Boston when they could have had a pint together at a Dublin pub?"

"Cagey. Protective of her film idea. Onto the thief and nervous about turning herself into a target. Those are just off the top of my head. I can think of other reasons, but they're all a leap from where we are now."

Emma shoved her running shoes into her closet and grabbed her street clothes. "Do you think Rachel had figured out the Declan's Cross theft was only one of a number of thefts?"

Colin shrugged. "Who the hell knows? She could have assumed we're after a serial thief without doing any research, or she could have looked up unsolved thefts and connected the dots herself. The police have her computer, don't they?"

"Actually, no. Apparently, she didn't have one. Just her phone."

"Too important to have her own computer?"

Emma didn't answer, since there was no answer. Ever since the conference call from Declan's Cross that morning, she'd felt less and less confident about her understanding of Rachel Bristol. It was as if the pieces they had of Rachel's life didn't fit together. It wasn't just a matter of missing pieces.

Colin headed for the door. "I'll let you change. We don't want people thinking I've seen you in your Skivvies."

"Colin…"

"I know, Emma," he said, serious again. "We're missing something. We need to figure out what before it bites us in the ass or someone else gets hurt."

"I won't screw up life for you or anyone else on this team. I'll quit first."

"The police think Rachel was killed by mistake by a carpenter. She could have stumbled on our thief when he was already stirred up after Lindsey Hargreaves' murder. He breaks into Aoife's studio to find out what she might know and panics when Lucy shows up. It almost makes more sense that there's no connection between Rachel's death and her interest in the thief." Colin opened the door and looked back at Emma with a wink. "Defies logic, maybe, but makes sense."

"This is what you've been sorting through on my couch?"

He gave her a quick smile. "I'm always on the job."

"Yank would string us both up for wild speculation."

"We'd deserve it. Good thing he's chasing rainbows and Lucy in Ireland."

Colin left, shutting the door behind him. Emma quickly changed out of her running clothes, drying off and figuring she'd take a shower later back at her apartment. With the cold and the rain and her slow pace, she hadn't done much sweating. She combed out her hair and sat at her desk, debating what to do next. Finally, she called her brother in Heron's Cove. He didn't pick up, so she left a message. "Why would our thief be interested in Aoife O'Byrne?"

She disconnected and stared at her blank computer screen, visualizing Aoife's studio with its exposed brick and stark white walls and minimalist industrial furnishings. Her art was lush, but her workspace was the opposite. What if Rachel Bristol had decided Aoife was the thief? Could that have influenced her actions? Could it make them logical, sensible—fit together into a coherent whole that explained why she'd called an FBI agent on Saturday morning and her subsequent death?

A text message came in. She saw it was from Colin. The man was down the hall but he was texting her.

Bet old Wendell has told you everything he knows about this thief?

She sat back in her chair and typed her response.

Not a bet I'd take.

His answer was immediate.

Didn't think so.

Emma left it at that and decided to call her grand-father in Ireland. She barely took time to say hello and find out how he was, but he still managed to cut in before she could get to the point. "Rachel Bristol was in Dublin last week. Sean Murphy told me. As I told our detective garda, Rachel didn't take me out for a pint, and I forgot to tell you. I'm old but not senile. I didn't recognize her from her picture. If she spied on me, she did so without my knowledge."

"We tend not to think people are following us."

"We're not wired for paranoia. You sound tired, Emma."

"I'm preoccupied. Did Rachel give you any indication that she was after the thief herself? That she knew who it was or thought she knew? Think, Granddad. Maybe there's something—"

"She didn't say anything of the sort, but her tone of voice—high-pitched, excited, determined. She knew she was on to something big. I figured half of it was in her head. I regret that. I wish now I had taken her more se-riously. If she'd told me she was in Dublin, I might have invited her over for coffee. Easy to say after the fact, I suppose. At least I wasn't rude when I blew her off."

"Did she mention other names? Her ex-husband, Tra-vis. His daughter, Maisie. His daughter's bodyguard, Danny Palladino. This mythologist, Oliver Fairbairn. Anyone, Granddad?"

"None of them."

"What about a carpenter?"

Emma heard her grandfather's sigh. "A carpenter,

Emma? No. Go work on something else for a while. You're baked. It happens. You must have other cases."

A stack of them. She made herself smile into the phone. "Take care of yourself. I'll be in touch, and you call me if you think of anything else—I don't care how stupid or inconsequential it might sound to you. Call."

"Will do, Special Agent Sharpe."

After she disconnected, she went out into the hall and found Sam Padgett in his office with the door open. She rapped on the doorjamb. He didn't look up. "You smell like a wet squirrel, Emma."

"You're such a charmer, Sam."

He looked up at her and grinned. "A wet bunny rabbit? Would that suit you better?"

"'What can I do for you, Emma?' would suit me just fine. If Rachel lied about flying into Boston from Los Angeles, did anyone else lie? Oliver says he flew in from London, Maisie from Los Angeles, Danny from Las Vegas. Travis was already in Boston."

"You want flight confirmations," Padgett said.

"You sound as if I just said I want us to dig a hole to China. I'll find out what's up with the detectives first."

"I hope they have this carpenter in custody. I did some more digging on him. There's no way he's our serial art thief. It's not just that he's a die-hard Red Sox and Celtics fan with no hint of any interest in art. Ten years ago when your thief was breaking into a house on the south Irish coast, Dwight was on his honeymoon. They went to Disney World. He posted pictures on their anniversary. Him, the wife and Mickey." Padgett's chair creaked as he leaned back. "It's sad. I'm an FBI agent in a small, elite unit, and I just was looking at pictures of Mickey Mouse."

Emma couldn't resist a smile. "You hate me, don't you, Sam?"

"Like the plague," he said with a grin.

"Thanks for the information."

"Anytime." He was serious now. "We're going to figure this thing out, Emma. I know this woman's body was
still warm when you found her. I kid around, but I don't
ever lose sight of what we're doing here."

"I know, Sam. I've never doubted you."

He snapped up straight in his chair. "You will when
I tell you I had a tofu hot dog with your boyfriend. I'm
dating a vegan woman. Or is it a woman who is vegan?
Anyway, I figured I'd try a meatless hot dog on my own,
in case I needed to spit it out."

"Did you?"

"Nope. Only because I'm one tough son of a bitch."
He laughed at his own remark and waggled his finger at
her. "Shut the door as you leave, would you? I'm diving
deep into numbers. I need quiet."

Emma shut the door and found Colin alone in the
conference room. "You didn't tell me about the tofu hot
dog," she said.

"Padgett's tale to tell. These macho brilliant types
can be hard to figure. Fin called. He's still in Boston and
wants us to have dinner with him and Aoife. She plans
to fly back to Dublin tomorrow. Can't say I blame her."

"What are they up to now?"

"No idea. I didn't ask. I suggested if they get bored
they could walk the Freedom Trail. Fin had no idea what
I was talking about."

"I imagine Aoife would appreciate a little boredom
right now."

"Wait until Fin has to explain to the church ladies why
he disappeared for a couple of days."

"He has a right to his own life."

Emma left it at that. Her cell phone rang, and she saw

it was a text from the lead detective on the Rachel Bristol death investigation.

We have suspect in custody.

She showed it to Colin. He was already on his feet. "Grab your coat. I'll drive you over there."

She was already on her way back to her office. She noticed the rain had picked up and was lashing against the windows, the gray fog blanketing the harbor. If nothing else, at least she'd have a good excuse for smelling like a wet squirrel.

Four hours later, dinner with Finian Bracken and Aoife O'Byrne struck Emma as the perfect way to end the day. She showered at her apartment, changed into a long skirt, boots and a dressy leather jacket and suggested that she and Colin take a cab. He didn't argue. He'd joined her in interviewing Dwight Wheeler, but it had been a waste of time. Wheeler hadn't had much to say. He'd met Rachel Bristol a few times at her ex-husband's Beacon Hill house. He'd done some shooting at the cottages on Bristol Island from time to time but hadn't been out there on Saturday.

Emma was reluctant to believe he was responsible for shooting Rachel. Then a search of his truck produced damning evidence—spent shell casings, a magazine of a gun like the one used to kill Rachel and a whole lot of beach sand.

The BPD was in the process of conducting further searches. They assured Emma they were keeping an open mind, but they were clearly unmoved by Dwight Wheeler's protests of innocence and believed they had their guy. While provocative, Rachel's interest in a ten-year-old theft in Ireland and the cross found on her body didn't appear to be connected to her death.

The rain had stopped when Emma climbed into a cab next to Colin. She slid in close to him. He was warm, dressed in a sportcoat over a dark sweater and trousers. She smiled at him. "You could pass for a regular G-man."

He laughed. "That would make Yank happy."

"You're a very good-looking man, Colin Donovan."

"Well, thank you, Emma Sharpe. Your skirt's a little sexy for the Bureau, but I like it."

"My skirt is almost to my ankles."

"I'm not talking about your legs, as cute as they are."

She knew they were engaging in a diversion, taking a break from the intensity of the day with the arrest of Dwight Wheeler. It hadn't been a normal couple of weeks, even by her and Colin's hectic standards. Before that, they'd insulated themselves from the demands of their work—and families—with their stay in Finian Bracken's cottage above Kenmare Bay. She shut her eyes for a moment, recalling sitting with Colin by the fire with nothing more serious on their minds than turning the page in the books they were reading. Only on their last few days in the cottage had the unsolved theft in Declan's Cross come up, and then the disappearance of Lindsey Hargreaves and subsequent discovery of her body on the cliffs.

The cab dropped them off at the Arlington Street entrance to the Taj. They joined Aoife and Finian in the bar, at a table by the fire. Aoife wore a close-fitting deep red dress that set off her dark hair, pale skin and dazzling eyes. "Dinner with an Irish priest and two American FBI agents," she said with a smile. "How perfect."

Finian settled his gaze on Emma. "The Bristols will be here soon. They're joining us for a drink."

Emma nodded without comment. She had noticed the extra chairs at the table. She and Colin had postponed talking to Aoife and the Bristols about Rachel's trip to Dublin until after having a chance to speak with the BPD detectives and their carpenter suspect.

Travis and Maisie Bristol entered the bar. Danny Palladino followed them but sat at a high stool at the bar by himself while father and daughter sat at the table. "Oliver sends his regrets," Maisie said. "He's working. He says it helps steady his nerves."

"He's a funny guy," Travis said.

Maisie folded her hands on the table as if she didn't know what else to do with them. "The police stopped by and told us they've arrested Dwight Wheeler. That's upsetting, but I guess it's better that Rachel's death was a terrible accident than…well, premeditated murder."

Her father winced. "Maisie."

"Sorry. I don't know how else to say it. Maybe it's best I don't say anything." She unfolded her hands and let them drop awkwardly to her sides. "I'm always tripping over my words."

"But you're good at attracting money and success," Travis said, softening. "You're centered, Maisie. You know who you are at your core, and you have a great eye. Sometimes you see things other people miss—"

"I wish I'd seen that Dwight was a reckless idiot," she muttered. "I liked him. I wanted to do him a good turn. I knew he hated to lose the cottage, but it was inevitable and we paid a fair price."

Aoife touched Finian's shoulder. "Perhaps you could choose a whiskey for us?"

He ordered Jameson for the table, but Emma and Colin both stuck to iced tea, a reminder to everyone that this wasn't a social occasion for them. She noticed Danny had a beer. He glanced back at Maisie but she ignored him. Travis seemed oblivious to any tension between them.

"I understand you're an expert in whiskey, Father," Travis said. "You're one of the Brackens who founded Bracken Distillers. Miss the whiskey business?"

"Only the good parts," Finian said smoothly.

Maisie smiled. "Excellent answer. Every career has its bad parts. It's easy for people on the outside to think someone else's work is without any negatives." She held up her glass and swirled the caramel-colored contents. "I want to learn more about whiskey. How should I go about it?"

"Start drinking it and decide what you like."

"That simple, huh?"

"Nothing with Finian is ever that simple," Aoife said. "Is it, Agent Donovan? You two have become friends since Finian came to America."

"Whiskey's not simple," Colin said. "I used to think it was."

In the few months Emma had known Finian Bracken, he had seldom looked uncomfortable, but he did now. He held up his glass. *"Sláinte."*

Maisie and Travis joined in with their whiskey, Emma and Colin with their iced tea. Aoife remained quiet, her glass untouched. "I suppose you want to talk to us about what you've learned about Rachel's visit to Dublin last week," she said finally.

"The detectives told us," Travis said, his shoulders slumping. "I had no idea. I took her at her word she'd been in Los Angeles."

"Same here," Maisie said.

Aoife stared down at her glass. "I never saw her in Dublin. I'm not always that aware of my surroundings when I'm deep into a project, but she had a distinctive look—I'm certain I would have remembered her."

Travis nodded. "Memorable. Good or bad, you remembered Rachel once you met her." He looked at Emma across the table. Shadows from the dim light and flickering fire seemed to dance on his pale, grim face. "Isn't that right? You only saw her after she was dead, but—"

"Dad." Maisie's voice was low but intense. She grabbed his arm. "How much have you had to drink already? Maybe you should skip the Jameson."

"I'm quite all right, Maisie. Relax." He picked up his glass. "My apologies, Agent Sharpe. Do you think Rachel broke into Aoife's studio?"

"Did she give you any indication that she could have?" Emma asked.

Travis shook his head. "No, nor did she give any indication that she saw who did it or knew anything about it. But I only saw her for a few minutes Friday night and Saturday morning. She was on a plane from Dublin on Friday?"

"That's right," Colin said.

"The same day I flew," Aoife added. "I'm sure she wasn't on my flight."

"She wasn't," Emma said.

Aoife's expression turned cool. "Of course, you would know by now."

"I've been picking up bits and pieces of the history of your family and this unsolved art theft in Declan's Cross." Travis sipped his whiskey, his eyes on Aoife as he lowered his glass. "Have you offered a reward for the return of your uncle's stolen art?"

Aoife tossed her head back. "My uncle did immediately after the theft. Kitty and I added to it, but it's been several years. That can't be what this is about, can it?

Reward money?" She held up her hands, as if warding off an attack. "Of course not. It was my studio broken into. I couldn't possibly…" She seemed to stop breathing as she stared at Emma, then gulped in air. "Emma… Agent Sharpe…you can't possibly…" Breathing rapidly now, on the verge of hyperventilating, Aoife turned to Finian. "Finian, do they think *I'm* the thief? Do *you*?"

Emma felt Colin go still next to her. Travis and Maisie gaped at Aoife. Finian calmly said her name, and her breathing quieted, more under control as she bit back tears. Danny Palladino eased off his bar stool with his beer and walked over to the table. "Whoa, easy, everyone. Imagine the fuss if Maisie Bristol gets herself thrown out of the Boston Taj bar."

"Maisie hasn't said a word," Travis said, testy.

"Doesn't have to."

"Have a seat, Danny," Colin said. "No one's getting thrown out."

"I'm sorry," Aoife whispered.

Travis rose. "We should be going, anyway. Thank you for the whiskey, Father Bracken. Agent Sharpe, Agent Donovan—we'll be at home if you have any additional questions."

Maisie had taken off her shearling jacket and let it fall around her on her chair. She shrugged it back on, catching her hair. She didn't seem to notice. "I'm going out to the marina tomorrow. Oliver and Dad are going, too. We're having breakfast and then walking out onto the island. I have such a vision for what it can be. I don't want it to be a place of death anymore."

"We'll be scattering Rachel's ashes there when the time comes," Travis said. "She was so young—she never specified what she wanted done with her remains. Although we were divorced, she had me listed as next of kin or whatever it's called nowadays. She loved the island. I know she'd approve."

"Join us tomorrow," Maisie said. "All of you. You're all welcome. It's truly a beautiful place. Agent Sharpe, I know you're a federal agent and trained and all that, but I think it would be a healing experience for you to go out there."

"This is still an open investigation," Danny said.

Maisie didn't so much as glance at him as she buttoned her expensive jacket. "I'm aware of that."

She breezed out, her father right behind her. Danny didn't follow them. He made a face. "Artistic temperament or do I have cat hair on my jacket?" He pretended to check his shoulders for cat hair. "Some people would say she's strictly a businesswoman, but she's not. She makes her choices about projects based on her artistic eye."

"It's been a difficult few days for her," Aoife said.

"For all of us. Well. Kick-ass FBI agents and holy Irish priest excluded. You all don't have difficult days, do you?" He grinned. "Couldn't resist. See you all in the morning."

He left, catching up with the Bristols in the lobby.

"I'm not very hungry," Aoife said. "And my head's spinning, not entirely from the whiskey, either. Emma, Colin—do you believe this carpenter killed Rachel? What about the cross she stole from me? What about her trip to Dublin?"

Colin leaned over the table. "The best thing you can do, Aoife, is be sure you've told us and the detectives everything you know about Rachel's interest in you, your conversations with her, your calls, emails and texts. Everything."

"I have," she said without hesitation.

"Then leave the rest to us," Colin said.

She relaxed visibly. "Thank you. Yes, that's what I will do. Leave law enforcement matters to you." She smiled. "Sean Murphy would be pleased."

Finian raised his glass. "Sean's a good man and a great friend. Did you visit him when he was in bits after his encounter with those smugglers last June, Aoife? I can see him knee-deep in mud and sheep dung, pitchfork in hand."

"He loves those blasted sheep," she said, rallying.

Emma welcomed the change in subject and saw that Colin did, too. They ordered appetizers and another round of whiskey and iced tea, and if Aoife O'Byrne knew anything about Rachel Bristol's visit to Ireland the week before, she hid it well. What she didn't hide at all, Emma thought, was how much she was in love with Finian Bracken, the only priest in Rock Point, Maine. He was staying at the Taj again tonight and would, he said, until Aoife was safely on her way home.

Twenty-One

"I'm in an unpleasant mood," Aoife said, gathering pencils she'd left on the desk in her suite. She looked at them in disgust. "I tried sketching the view, just to keep my mind and hands occupied. It was a disaster, as you can see."

Finian looked at the half-finished sketch on the desk. He recognized the Public Garden and the gold-domed Massachusetts State House at the top of Boston Common—which he knew from his walk with Aoife earlier in the day.

"Your work is never a disaster, Aoife," he told her.

"Thank you for saying so, but you have no idea what you're talking about, do you?"

"I know what I like."

"And you like these scribbles?" She shoved the pencils into a bag open on the desk chair. "I feel like a five-year-old begging for positive reinforcement and attention. You know what you like. I know what's good. What's good of mine, I mean. I'm in an unpleasant mood, but I haven't become a snob. You know when you've delivered a good sermon, don't you?"

"Most times."

"Or should I make a whiskey comparison? There's artistry in producing whiskey."

"There is," he said. "Aoife, would you like me to order you some herbal tea to help you sleep? Chamomile—"

"I don't want tea." She snatched the sketch and crumpled it up with two hands. "Emma and Colin are perfectly lovely people, and I can see why they're your friends, but I felt a bit as if I was under a hot interrogation lamp. They can't think I'm the thief, can they? That I sent those crosses—sent one to myself?"

Finian was tempted to rescue the sketch from her but instead watched her shove it into the rubbish. He kept his tone mild, neutral. "I didn't notice anything different in their behavior. You're on edge, Aoife. It's understandable."

"Your bloody Jameson didn't help." She raked her long fingers through her hair. "I hope I don't vomit."

"I hope you don't, either."

She laughed a little. "You weren't a fish out of water tonight. You still know how to handle yourself at a dinner despite your priest's garb. Of course, why would I think otherwise?"

"You handled yourself well, too, Aoife."

"My uncle taught me how to behave, even when I didn't want to, although he was happiest alone in his rambling house. Well, happiest when my aunt was alive and with him there. They loved Declan's Cross. It was home for them more than Dublin ever was. For Kitty, too."

"Do you think about moving there?" Finian asked.

"Always." She cleared her throat, as if she needed to push back unwanted thoughts. "You're welcome to sleep on the couch in here. I promise I won't come out in a sexy nightgown. Save yourself the money and cancel your room."

"It's already paid for."

"In all these years, Finian, I never once thought this thief was watching me, following me. Now I do. I feel so unsettled." She folded her arms over her chest and paced in front of the windows. She paused long enough to kick off her shoes. "I'm trying to be practical, but the thought of going back to my studio…" She shuddered. "I don't know if I can do it, Finian."

"No one died there. It's your home."

"I've always thought of it as temporary. I assumed I would buy my own place in Dublin, or move to Declan's Cross." She paused, lowering her arms, calmer. "Oh, Fin—Father Bracken, my great friend. Thank you for being here." She smiled. "Aren't you glad I didn't throw a drink in anyone's face tonight, considering my mood?"

"Have you ever thrown a drink in someone's face?"

"I've been tempted a time or two. Who's to say I'm not tempted now? You've been at my side all day, Finian. Do you think that could be part of why I'm out of sorts?"

"I hope not," he said simply.

She flopped onto the couch and looked up at him, her dress bodice pulled lower, exposing more of the curve of her breasts. He wasn't sure if she was aware of how close she was to popping out of her dress, or if she would care if she did. "I wish I could go home satisfied that you've turned into a boring man of the cloth with whom I have nothing in common, but I can't."

"We have Ireland in common. That must seem like more than enough right now."

She stretched out her slim legs and placed her bare feet on the coffee table. "You're also not a judgmental, critical bastard of a man of the cloth."

He smiled. "That's good."

"Do your parishioners love you?"

"They love Father Callaghan."

"The priest you're replacing for a year. Will you go back to Ireland?"

"We'll see what happens. Right now, I'm serving St. Patrick's of Rock Point, Maine, to the very best of my ability."

"You know half the women in Ireland cried when you entered the seminary, and the other half cheered you on. You were our project."

"The tormented man," he said.

"We all wanted to save you." Aoife shrugged, crossing her ankles. "I'm not telling you anything you don't know." She threw her head against the back of the couch and blew out a breath at the ceiling. "Do you think the police really do have Rachel's killer?"

"They have a man in custody."

She sat up straight and steadied her gaze on Finian. "That's not the same thing, is it?"

Finian shook his head. "Rachel sounds as if she was reckless, out of control—"

"And excited," Aoife said. "She knew she was on to something, whether it was just clarity about her vision of what this movie she and Maisie were working on should be. I know what that's like, when you know you've got it. You can feel it in the pit of your stomach. I can look at a blank canvas, and that's all it is. A blank canvas. Then I'll look at it, and it's a seascape. I can see that my next brushstroke needs to go here, not there. If Rachel was experiencing that kind of artistic clarity and vision, I can understand why she'd dash off to Maine and then dash off to Ireland. It doesn't mean she had a plan."

"You wouldn't break into someone else's home and work studio and push a bookcase on top of an innocent woman."

"Or even a guilty one," Aoife interjected. "But we don't know that was Rachel."

"No, we don't," Finian said quietly.

She smiled unexpectedly. "I can see Sean frowning at us now at all our speculating, can't you?"

Finian laughed. "I can."

"I used to imagine us all in Declan's Cross together. Sean, you, Kitty and me. I could paint, Kitty could have her hotel, and you and Sean could talk about sheep and whiskey over a pint at the pub. It'd be a good life, wouldn't it?"

"We couldn't ask for more."

"But it's not what you are meant to do, is it?" She swept to her feet, a little unsteadily. She took his hand and kissed him on the cheek. "Good night, Father Bracken."

Finian went down to the bar and watched a few confusing minutes of an ice hockey game on the television while he debated whether to order tea, whiskey or go straight up to bed. There were no other customers at the bar, which he appreciated. Nonetheless, he went into the lobby when he decided to call Sean Murphy in Ireland.

"Fin? What's happened? Where are you?"

"I'm having whiskey at the bar in Aoife's five-star Boston hotel."

"She's with you?"

"In her suite."

"Give me a blasted heart attack, Fin. I was dead asleep."

"It's later than I thought. What time is it there?"

"I don't want to know. Two in the morning. No sign of dawn yet. I'm at the farm."

Finian didn't ask his friend if Kitty was with him. "Sean, do you think this carpenter killed Rachel Bristol?"

"It's not my place to say."

"But you have instincts."

"Instincts aren't the same as evidence. Just watch yourself, Fin. Kitty says Aoife flies home tomorrow. That's good. Thank you for looking after her. We'll take care of her here."

"Am I being dismissed, Sean?"

"Take Aoife to the airport and go back to your church in Maine. I mean it, Fin. It's my best advice, as your friend as well as a detective."

"Are you any closer to finding out who broke into Aoife's studio?"

Sean gave an exaggerated yawn. "Good night, Father Bracken."

Finian could tell he wasn't getting more out of his garda friend. He wished Sean a good night and disconnected as Maisie Bristol entered the hotel lobby. She'd changed into casual clothes. Her lank hair was tucked inside her coat, her hands in her pockets, her eyes wide and haunted as she looked up at him. "Can I buy you a drink, Father?" she asked.

He motioned toward the dark, quiet bar. "I'll buy you one."

Maisie went in ahead of him and climbed up onto a bar stool. He sat next to her. She promptly ordered a glass of champagne. He ordered Scotch and let the barman choose.

"Do you know much about champagne, Father?" Maisie asked, facing him.

"Not as much as I do about whiskey."

"*Uisce beatha.* The water of life in Irish. Did I mangle the pronunciation?"

"Not at all," he said, then pronounced the Irish for her.

She smiled. "I love your accent. Do people tell you that all the time?"

"Not all the time. Often." He noticed the hockey game had ended. He didn't know who'd won. In fact, he didn't know who'd played. "You don't have a Boston accent."

"I didn't grow up here. I grew up in Las Vegas."

"Which do you like better?"

She shrugged. "I don't think that way." Her champagne arrived, and she picked up the glass. "I like the bubbles. They symbolize hope and fun, don't you think?"

"And celebration," Finian said.

"I'm not in a celebrating mood, or a fun one, for that matter. I do have hope, though." She tasted her champagne. "Very nice. How's your Scotch?"

"Smoky."

"I don't like the smoky ones. I always feel as if I'm drinking out of an ashtray. Not very sophisticated of me, is it?"

"Your palate may change," he said.

She laughed, her eyes catching the light from the television. "A diplomatic answer. Of course, no one challenges me on my lack of sophistication anymore. If my movies had been flops, they would. Funny how life can turn out. Did you always know you were going to be a priest?"

He realized then she didn't know about his past. He shook his head. "Not until a few years ago."

"I'm not Catholic. I believe in God, I guess, but I don't think much about it." She fingered the condensation on the outside of her glass, as if she wanted to capture just one bubble and follow it. "Rachel and I weren't going to iron out our differences, Father. I told the police and the FBI agents we were, but it's not the truth. I was going to drop the hammer on her. Get her out of my film project and out of my life."

"I see."

She gave him a thin smile. "Not what you were expecting, I know." Her smile evaporated, and she swept up her glass again. "She was obnoxious, she was out of control and she was trying to drag me in a creative direction I didn't want to go. It got unbearable this past week or so. I'd had it."

"Did you tell anyone?"

"No. I'm like that. I hold things in until I feel the time is right. I figured I'd tell her at the marina. Not in front of Oliver and my father, of course—or Danny, once I realized he'd decided to elbow his way back into my life. But I knew I had to deal with Rachel before she ruined the movie or drove me out of my mind."

"And you didn't tell this to the authorities."

"I didn't lie, exactly. I talked myself into believing there was a glimmer of a chance that Rachel and I *would* work out our differences. It seemed wrong to malign her after her death." Maisie gulped her champagne. "I was so pissed at her. Then damned if someone doesn't shoot her."

Finian sipped his Glenlivet, a single malt Speyside Scotch that was one of his favorites. He had resisted suggesting the bar manager stock Bracken Distillers. He set his glass on the polished bar, realizing he wanted to talk about whiskey with the barman. Sean Murphy would have him escort Maisie to the nearest police officer. Colin would do the same. Emma, too, no doubt, although her role in the investigation into Rachel Bristol's death was more complicated—as a Sharpe, and as the FBI agent who'd found her.

This young woman, however, hadn't come to him because he was friends with two FBI agents and an Irish detective. She'd come to him because he was a priest.

"When I found out Rachel was dead," Maisie continued, looking away from him, "for a split second I was relieved. Isn't that awful? I was so tied up in knots about confronting her that for one little instant, I was glad I didn't have to. At first I didn't know she'd been shot. I thought she might have had a stroke or hit her head on a rock or something."

"Your emotions didn't kill her, Maisie," Finian said.

"I suppose you're right. Imagine all the people who'd be dropping dead in the streets if wishing them dead actually worked—not that I wished Rachel dead. I didn't. I just wanted her out of my life." She grimaced. "I'm not good at confrontation."

"Is that why Danny thought he should follow you to Boston?"

"Maybe." She sighed, then shook her head. "*No*. He followed me because he thinks my mother hired him to check on me. My parents worry about me." She drank more of her champagne and glanced up at the television and its post-game report. "They worry because of the money. I've made a ton of it. Before the money, trust me, they didn't worry about me."

"Did Rachel worry about you?"

"Rachel wanted to best me. She had more experience in filmmaking than I do, and she felt superior to me— that any success I've had is just a fluke."

"Envious?"

"Maybe. I don't think that was it, though, as much as plain old superiority. She was good, but she'd had some bad luck lately. I know that can happen. I'm not naive. You're only as good as your last project in this business." Maisie set down her glass and turned on her bar stool to face Finian directly. "It's different as a priest, I guess. You're not judged by the souls you can and can't save, are you?"

He had no intention of discussing his life as a priest with Maisie Bristol. "Have you thought about how you can go forward after these past few days in light of what's troubling you now?"

"Get toxic people out of my life sooner rather than later? Never mind. That was uncalled for. I know I need to learn how to do a better job setting boundaries and confronting people. Maybe if I had with Rachel, she'd be alive today."

Finian frowned. "How so?"

"She wouldn't have been sneaking around in Maine, flying off to Dublin—calling an FBI agent to come meet her on a lonely island." Maisie inhaled deeply, tears rising in her eyes. "Oh, hell. I thought I was all done crying. You know, Father, Rachel was demanding and confrontational a lot of the time, but I always knew where I stood with her."

"Even though she was, as you put it, sneaking around?"

Maisie waved a hand. "That had more to do with Rachel being Rachel. The drama, holding her cards close to her chest. I had no doubts about her opinion of me. She and my father were married when I was a teenager. Rachel tried to be a decent influence, but we were too close in age. We never could be friends, and I already have a mother. Still…it's hard. Her death. How it happened."

"I'm sorry for your loss, Maisie," Finian said quietly.

"Thank you, Father. Rachel was positive what she wanted to do with this movie was the right way to go. Normally, I'm one to listen and take in all ideas, but not this time. I can't explain. Something about early medieval Celtic Ireland and its pagan roots got to me."

"It touched your soul, perhaps."

"Yes." She smiled, relief washing over her face. "Yes, maybe that's it. I haven't even been to Ireland myself. I'm probably a little envious that Rachel had the guts to go there, and I didn't. She was difficult and yet inspiring at the same time."

"And now she's gone to God," Finian said.

"I hope she's with God. I really do."

He noticed Danny Palladino in the doorway. "Shall we invite your friend to join us?"

"No." Maisie groaned. "He's twitching. I can see it from here. I should go." She slid off her bar stool. "Thank you, Father. Will you and Aoife come to Bristol Island in the morning?"

"That's up to Aoife."

"It would be good to have you there."

She headed out, pushing past Danny to the lobby. He paused, rolled his eyes at Finian, then grinned and followed her.

A man in love, Finian thought as he returned to his Glenlivet. He didn't know whether Maisie shared Danny's feelings for her. She was in such turmoil right now it would be hard to trust such emotions.

A basketball game was on the television. It made even less sense to Finian than ice hockey, but he watched it, wondering if Aoife was asleep up in her suite, and if her older sister had been with Sean Murphy at the farm. He shut his eyes, imagining himself in the rolling green fields of his own family's farm in south Kerry, dreaming of where life would take him—where he would be in twenty or thirty years. He was thirty-nine now, and as a boy of fifteen, he'd never once pictured himself as a priest…or as a husband and father who'd lost his family.

"Another round, Father?" the barman asked.

Finian opened his eyes and shook his head. "I'm done for the night, thanks," he said.

He paid for his Scotch and Maisie's champagne, and when he arrived back in his room, there were no sounds from the suite next door. He put his hand on the wall, as if somehow it could comfort Aoife in her nightmares. If he'd taken up her offer to sleep on her couch, would he have stayed there?

Yes.

He had no doubts, but it was a potent mix, this murder investigation and this beautiful, frightened woman alone so far from home.

Unless Aoife *was* the thief, of course.

Finian gave an inward groan and prepared for bed and another long night alone at Aoife O'Byrne's five-star Boston hotel.

Twenty-Two

Colin watched Emma as she sat cross-legged on her living room floor with printouts of photos of Celtic Ireland laid out in front of her. They had already been through her personal files on Jack B. Yeats. As the night wore on, Colin could see that what they needed now wasn't more information but some distance. Burning the midnight oil wasn't always the best course when the pressure was on, but Emma had a great capacity for working a problem.

He sat next to her and stretched out his legs. "No wonder you have your master's in art history," he said. "You have an endless attention span for spreadsheets, dossiers, files and theorizing."

"I wouldn't say endless."

He grinned at her. "It feels endless."

She raised her head from a photo and smiled. "Are you saying you're bored?"

"Not bored." He picked up a photo of the twelfth-century round tower in Ardmore, not far from Declan's Cross. "This isn't boring. It's pretty incredible. Maybe we can do more sightseeing our next trip to Ireland. I was more interested in wild Ireland and Guinness this last trip." He put an arm over her shoulders. "And you."

"We had a good time at Finian's cottage."

She'd changed into flannel pajamas that Colin found oddly sexy. He could feel her fatigue. "We should call it a night, Emma."

She sank into him. "I'm starting to go in circles with this stuff. Part of me is wishing I'd specialized in something else when I joined the FBI and left art crime to my family."

Colin understood her mood, her doubts. "Yank recruited you because of your background. He likes to forget the advantages of your being a Sharpe when the disadvantages cause him headaches."

"A serial art thief wouldn't be on HIT's radar if not for my being a Sharpe. Yank would have never received that cross. He wouldn't have gone to Ireland."

"He wanted to make sure I wasn't going to quit and do puffin tours."

"He also wanted to see about the cross."

"Yank's a big boy. He can take care of himself. You're twisting yourself into knots." Colin hooked an arm around her waist and picked her up. "Time for bed."

It was about three steps into her cell of a bedroom. More dramatic to carry her to bed at home in Maine, but easier to here—and irresistible with the feel of her under the soft flannel. He flung her over his shoulder, sack-of-potatoes style. A few long strides, and he was next to her bed. It was a double. No room for anything bigger. He hadn't quite gotten over wondering if she'd tried recreating her novitiate room. He was confident she hadn't had lace pillows in her tiny, plain room at the Sisters of the Joyful Heart, and she sure as hell hadn't had him.

He laid her on the bed. She smiled up at him, draping her arms over his shoulders. "I could carry you like that, especially from the living room into here. I should give it a shot sometime. Surprise you."

"Only way you're getting away with that is if I'm unconscious, and this place is on fire."

She clasped her hands behind his neck. "You're not going to tell me about Mina Van Buren, are you?"

"Tell you what?"

"That she's in line as the new director and already has something up her sleeve for you." Emma drew him closer to her. Her eyes were deep green in the darkened room. "That you don't trust her, and neither does Yank."

"I do what I'm told to do."

"Oh, right. Compliant Colin Donovan." But her teasing didn't last. "What if she tells you we can't be together?"

He shook his head. "That's not going to happen."

"Would you lie to me about an undercover mission?"

"Emma…"

"I know you can't answer that. I've heard rumors about a history between Van Buren and Yank. Have you?"

"There are rumors about everyone."

"That's an artful answer."

"Artful. Good word. I'll remember that." He settled next to her on the cozy bed. "Mina Van Buren wouldn't be on the short list for acting director if she didn't know how to handle a viper pit and take care of herself. On my first undercover mission four years ago, she showed Yank just how capable she is on that score."

"Threw him into the viper pit?"

"That, Yank could take."

"You," Emma said quietly. "She threw you into the viper pit."

"She counted on Yank to get me out, which he did—with help from me, I might add."

"Then Mina Van Buren and Matt Yankowski do have

a history. I don't need to know the details. I know you won't tell me, anyway." Emma snuggled against him. "But you'll be careful, Colin?"

He lowered his mouth to hers. "I'm always careful."

"Don't be too careful right now." She kissed him back, flicking her tongue against his, smiling in the dark. "For my sake if not your own."

"Ha." He slipped his hands around her hips, lowering her flannel pajama bottoms. "Do you worry about being married to an undercover agent?"

"I don't worry about being married to you."

"What about getting cold feet at the altar? Does that worry you, Emma?"

She wiggled under him, even as his palms slid over the warm skin of her hips. "Because I decided not to make my final vows as Sister Brigid? No." Her hands drifted down his bare back, his skin, she knew, cool to the touch. When she got to his hips, she stopped, pressing her pelvis up to meet him. "I know now that you were always out there, ready to come into my life."

"What if I'd come into your life after you'd made your vows?"

"You're thinking of Aoife and Finian."

"Maybe. Leaving the sisters for the FBI wasn't like when I left the marine patrol for the FBI. Imagine if I hadn't. I might have met you when you were in your nun's tunic."

"Would you have lusted after me?"

"I'd have known pretty quick that you weren't going to stay a nun. I wonder what Mother Natalie would have done if she'd caught me sneaking into your room."

"I think of everyone at the convent, she was the first to sense I wasn't staying."

He'd managed to slip one hand between her legs, feeling her heat, her wetness. She gave a small moan, and

Colin kissed her again. She still had on her pajama bottoms. He had on his shorts. Then there was her shirt.

All that effort, he thought with a smile, deepening their kiss, easing his fingers inside her. She wasn't just wiggling under him now. She was pulsating, writhing with heat and desire. She shoved his shorts down over his hips. It would take only a few swift moves to dispense with them.

She breathed his name and arched under him.

She wasn't in a waiting mood—and he damn sure wasn't.

Her pajama bottoms were at her knees.

Close enough, he thought, thrusting into her. She cried out as if it was their first time. His heartbeat surged, and he raised his chest off her, looking down at her as she bit down on her lower lip. He thrust deep, hard, felt her dig her fingers into his hips. When she kicked off her pajama bottoms and wrapped her legs around him, he was lost, his blood pounding, a thousand sensations racing through him as he quickened the pace of their lovemaking. He knew she wouldn't last. He could feel her surrendering, letting go, quaking under him as he drove into her again and again, faster, until she threw her hands above her head and then cried out, this time with release. He could feel her going limp under him, but still he didn't stop, until finally he felt his own release, his own surrender.

Then they dispensed with their tangled bedclothes, and held each other naked in the dark. He might not be the man the sisters and the Sharpes had envisioned for her when she left the convent—the man she'd envisioned for herself—but it didn't matter, at least not right now.

Colin woke in the milky light of dawn to an empty bed. He heard Emma in the living room and realized she was on the phone with her grandfather, who was presumably still in Ireland, where it would be a decent hour. Colin had no idea if she'd called Wendell or he'd called her.

He threw off the covers, pulled on a pair of shorts and went into the living room. It was cool. Heat wasn't included in the rent, and Emma kept the thermostat down low. He did at his place, too. He didn't have a set of flannel PJs there, either. He had T-shirts in both places and wished he'd put one on.

Emma was pacing, barefoot, cell phone to her ear. "You do what's good for you, Granddad. There will be other Thanksgivings. I want Mom and Dad to meet Colin, but that will happen." She paused as she listened to her grandfather. Then she smiled at Colin. "Yes, Granddad. He's the one. Talk to you soon. I love you."

When she disconnected, she sat on the couch and stared down at the rug, saying nothing. Colin went over and sat next to her. "How's the old man?"

"He's in Declan's Cross. He just arrived. He drove down first thing this morning. He said he didn't want to pay Kitty's price for a room. Ever frugal, my granddad."

Colin could hear the fatigue in her voice. It wasn't just the early hour. She sounded distracted, preoccupied, as if only part of her was with him on the couch. "What's on your mind, Emma?"

"My father is struggling." She looked at the windows, their shades down and drapes pulled, but Colin knew that wasn't what she was seeing. "His doctor in London wants him to try a new approach to pain management. I don't have the details."

"It's been a rough road for him."

"Some days are better than others. This past week, there haven't been any good days. He tries to be optimistic. He's learned to meditate. He... Colin, I don't know how much more he can stand." Her voice cracked, and she cleared her throat. "Granddad wants to go to London to be with Dad instead of coming here for Thanksgiving."

Colin squeezed her hand. "That's understandable."

"I should have gone to London when we were in Ireland. I could have done a day trip, even, but I had it in my head that Mom and Dad would come to Heron's Cove for Thanksgiving. Somehow, they'd pull it off, and we'd all be together."

"It'll happen sooner rather than later. You'll make it happen."

She smiled at him. "Can-do Colin Donovan." She sniffled and sucked in a breath, held it for a few seconds, then let it out slowly before she continued. "We used to be together all the time in Heron's Cove. Then Grandma died, and Granddad moved to Dublin. My parents started traveling more and more after Dad's fall. They spend months at a time away—and now a whole year in London—but that doesn't mean we're not a close family."

Colin lifted her hand to his lips and kissed it. "It'll be okay, Emma."

"I want what's best for my parents, and I'll see Mom and Dad soon, one way or the other. I got my hopes up about Thanksgiving, and I shouldn't have. I know better. I know Dad has good days and bad days. We take them as they come."

"I'm sorry." He slung his arm over her shoulders and pulled her close to him. "This is a first, though. You're warmer than I am."

"No way. You're a tough guy from Maine. You never get cold." She snuggled close to him. "I love you, tough guy."

He kissed the top of her head and breathed in the smell of her hair. He would probably never fully understand the complexities of her life—of being a Sharpe—but he didn't need to, any more than she needed to understand everything about being from Rock Point and what having Mike, Andy and Kevin as brothers was like for him. "I'm always here for you, Emma. Anytime you want to talk, whatever you want to talk about."

"I know. I also know that one day you'll get another undercover mission, and when you can't be there for me—"

"Emma."

She got onto her knees on the couch and turned his shoulders so that he was facing her. "Colin, when you can't be there, I don't want you to worry about me. I don't want you to think about me except when it can help you. Promise me that, okay?"

He saw how serious she was. He touched the back of his hand to her cheek, felt her cool, soft skin. He thought of the long nights when he'd been in deep cover with scumbag arms traffickers. Dangerous, amoral sons of bitches. That was before Emma. Having her in his life would make undercover work both easier and harder, but there was no going back. She was wearing the ring he'd slipped on her finger a week ago in Dublin. Even if they hadn't told anyone yet, their engagement was for real.

"I promise," he said, "but if Mina Van Buren takes over the show, she could offer to help me pick out my boat for puffin tours."

"Yank wants to keep you. She won't get in his way."

"We'll see. Whatever happens, I won't let my work hurt you. I'll do something else." He smiled, wrapping his arms around her. "I'll sit behind a damn desk."

"Easy to say when the next undercover mission is theoretical. We know undercover work is dangerous, but on Saturday, I went out to a harbor island and arrived minutes after a woman was shot dead. Anything can happen anytime." She leaned into him. "We'll be okay, whether you're chasing arms traffickers or doing puffin tours with Mike."

"Mike. He'd throw rude tourists overboard."

"I've no doubt." She sat back on her heels. "I woke up thinking about Rachel Bristol. Seeing her. My heart was pounding. I got up and called Granddad. I didn't mean to wake you."

"Is Yank still in Declan's Cross?"

Emma nodded. "Granddad is meeting him. He says Lucy Yankowski is continuing to improve." She jumped off the couch and stood, obviously wide awake and restless. "He also says Yank and Sean Murphy are as skeptical about Dwight Wheeler as we are. Granddad is, too, but Rachel's killer isn't his focus. The thief is."

"Why did Wendell go to the trouble of driving to Declan's Cross this morning?"

"He and Lucas are trying to figure out what Rachel did while she was in Ireland. She was in Declan's Cross for at least a day. Granddad's hoping he can pick up a lead there."

"I bet Sean Murphy is keeping him on a short leash."

Emma switched on a light. "No one keeps Granddad on a short leash."

"Let's hope old Wendell and I never are at cross purposes," Colin said with a grin. He stood, giving an exaggerated shiver. "Are you up for the day or going back to bed?"

"Three o'clock and it'd be back to bed. Four o'clock, though—it could go either way. I'm still a bit on Irish time myself. What about you? Back to bed, or coffee with me?"

As if there was a choice. "Coffee with you. I'll make

it, but I need to get a shirt on first. I keep it cool at home but it's freezing in here."

"I can turn up the heat. I rather like the shirtless look."

"Only if you do likewise."

"Then we might as well go back to bed now."

He went over to her. "You have a practical streak I like," he said, and started unbuttoning her flannel top. She didn't stop him, and he got halfway done with the job before he gave up, scooped her into his arms and carried her back to bed.

Twenty-Three

Ardmore, Ireland

Yank had agreed to meet Wendell Sharpe in Ardmore. It was a warm morning, and he and Lucy had decided to have breakfast on the terrace at the O'Byrne House Hotel. Lucy had been enjoying her second scone when Kitty had come out and given him Wendell's message. He and Lucy had already packed up and checked out, assuming they would drive back to Dublin and make arrangements to fly home. Him to Boston, her to Washington. Whatever worked. Instead, they'd made the short drive from Declan's Cross to the pretty village nestled on Ardmore Bay.

The Micra was better with Lucy next to him. No question.

He parked on a narrow street in the center of the village. He didn't want to leave her. She wasn't ready to be on her own. *He* wasn't ready.

She touched his arm. "Go on, Matt. Do your thing. Some of these shops look intriguing."

"I'll stay within shouting distance."

"I have my cell phone. I can text you." She smiled.

"Maybe I'll find the perfect Irish wool sweater for you. Boston winters are cold."

"Lucy…"

"I'm not ready to go off on my own on city streets, but I can do this."

It was a perfect day, sunny and warm enough they didn't need to bundle up. Lucy crossed the street to a string of what looked like craft shops. Yank could go with her, and he'd probably enjoy himself despite his reluctance, but he'd never had much of an attention span for wandering through craft shops.

He headed up the street, which rose steeply out of the village. Wendell Sharpe was waiting at a concrete seawall above a rocky coastline that curved downhill to the village, eventually giving way to a sandy beach, quiet under a cloudless blue sky.

Wendell was in a charcoal-gray wool cap and a Barbour jacket that hadn't been new when Yank had been at the FBI academy twenty years ago. He stared across the seawall at the boulders and bay and said something in what Yank recognized as Irish. "It's an old saying," Wendell said. "It translates roughly as 'the left hand of Ultan against evil.' According to legend, Ultan warded off Nordic invaders by raising his left hand against them. Their ships sank, and Ardmore was saved from attack."

Yank stood next to Wendell at the wall. "Who's Ultan?"

"He was a follower of Saint Declan. He lived during the time of the Viking raids, hundreds of years after Declan walked this ground in the fifth century." Wendell sighed, his wool cap staying on his white hair despite the breeze off the water. "I wish I could ward off disaster by holding up my left hand."

"I wish you could, too, Wendell."

"Saint Declan has had a lasting influence on this area. It's known as the Deise. There's another Irish saying. 'Let Declan be the Patrick of the Deise, and let the Deise be with Declan until doom.'"

Yank was starting to regret not checking out the craft shops with Lucy. "Does any of this help us find your thief?"

Wendell pointed at a large, rounded boulder perched on smaller rocks on the beach. "Tradition tells us that's the same boulder that led Declan and his followers to Ardmore more than fifteen hundred years ago. They'd been praying after discovering they'd left behind a small bell—"

"I know all about the bell," Yank said. "A gift from God. Appeared on top of the boulder and led them here to Ardmore." He pointed at the boulder. "No bell now."

"It disappeared long ago."

"Mmm."

Wendell ignored him. "You can see that the stone in Saint Declan's boulder is a different kind than in the other rocks and boulders that form the coastline here."

"There was a pamphlet in our room at the O'Byrne House that says the boulder could have landed up here during the Ice Age."

"Brought down from nearby mountains," Wendell said. "Maybe so, but who's to say it didn't end up in the sea and appeared in time to lead Saint Declan to Ardmore?"

Yank was unimpressed. "It's a big damn rock, Wendell. It would have sunk."

"The ocean can be a fierce thing in a storm." The old man shrugged, standing straight. "Pilgrims still come here to wiggle under Saint Declan's Stone in hopes of healing."

"I'd be more likely to get a backache than cure one crawling under that thing."

Wendell sighed and pointed at him. "You, my friend, are a natural skeptic."

Yank grinned. "Pragmatist, but if someone is cured crawling under Saint Declan's Stone, that's great. Meanwhile, what's going on, Wendell? Why did you ask me to come out here?"

"I didn't want to talk in Declan's Cross."

"Avoiding Sean Murphy?"

"You're worse than a skeptic, Agent Yankowski. You're the type who always sees the dark side."

"Detective Garda Murphy is an Irish law enforcement officer. He can arrest you."

"Who said anything about getting arrested?" Wendell pointed up the sunlit street. "Let's walk. I don't waste beautiful weather in November in Ireland. Your wife is welcome to join us."

"She's looking for a sweater for me."

Yank texted Lucy and let her know what he and Wendell were up to. She texted him back immediately that she was fine. Yank didn't relax. He knew it would take time before he believed she was truly fine—maybe before she believed it, too.

He and Wendell walked uphill on a street that wound past houses built close together, many with spectacular views of the water, and the modern Cliff House Hotel, which hugged the steep, narrow strip of rocky coast on the bay. Wendell didn't seem to have any trouble handling the hill. When the street dead-ended, Yank figured they would turn back, but the old art detective led him through an open black-iron gate. They were on a dirt path high above the bay. This, Yank knew from his pamphlet, was a marked walk that would take them along sea cliffs, then back into the village, passing Saint Declan's grave and the ruins of his monastic settlement.

Yank balked. "I'm not doing a scenic walk with you, Wendell. If I'm doing a scenic walk, it's with my wife."

"Relax," Wendell said. "We can stop here."

They were at a grassy area just past the gate. Wendell settled onto a simple bench on the edge of the path, facing the sparkling bay. To the right was a wall of a church ruin, its dark stone splotched with white lichens. To the left was a holy well amid more stonework.

"Imagine Saint Declan here," Wendell said, staring out at the water. "Walking this same ground hundreds of years ago."

Yank stayed on his feet. They were on a headland above the village down to their left. He could see two kayakers riding waves onto the crescent beach. He didn't see any other walkers on the path but imagined it would be popular during the warm-weather months.

He'd done enough treks in the Irish countryside for now, though, and focused on Wendell Sharpe. "Talk, Wendell. I've got an active investigation on my hands."

The old man squinted at the blue-green bay. "Oliver Fairbairn came to see me in Dublin."

Yank tried not to look shocked, but Wendell's statement wasn't what he'd expected. Not even close. "Fairbairn? The mythologist? Maisie Bristol's research consultant?"

"That's right."

"When?"

"October."

"This October," Yank said, not making it a question.

"It was before that mess in Declan's Cross—before Emma and Colin arrived in Ireland. Fairbairn stopped by the office. He said he was researching early medieval

Irish Celtic crosses—he wasn't interested in nineteenth-century Celtic Revival crosses—and asked me if I had any special insights, any crosses that I could point him to that might not be among the usual suspects. That's the phrase he used. 'Usual suspects.'"

"Was his visit out of the ordinary for you?"

"It was unusual but not unheard of. I was busy with closing the Dublin office and getting Lucas up to speed on things that aren't in the official files."

Yank would love to know what all wasn't in the Sharpe files. Only Wendell Sharpe knew what he hadn't shared with his grandchildren—or law enforcement—about his decades as an art detective and remained locked up in his bony head.

A candidate for a Vulcan mind meld, Yank had often said.

"Why didn't you mention Fairbairn's visit sooner?" he asked.

"I didn't think of it until I talked with Emma this morning. Asking me about Celtic crosses isn't a crime."

"Wait. You talked with Emma this morning? When? It's five hours earlier there."

"She couldn't sleep."

Yank grimaced. No more details required. "Go on."

"I called Lucas after I hung up with Emma. Got him out of bed." Wendell didn't sound that repentant. "Oliver Fairbairn was working with Maisie Bristol when he came to see me. He's from London. It makes sense he would stop in Dublin for a little hands-on research into early medieval Ireland on behalf of a wealthy, successful movie producer. Makes less sense that he could choose me. One would think a mythologist would have access to real experts in the field, which I'm not."

"Fairbairn followed Rachel Bristol to Heron's Cove last week."

"That's what Lucas said." Wendell rose, brushing at a muddy spot on his trousers. "Well, you're the senior FBI agent, my friend. You will know whether this information is worth a further look."

Yank rubbed the back of his neck. "I'll get you a photo of Fairbairn," he told Wendell. "You can confirm—"

"Sean Murphy already did. I stopped by the Murphy farm before coming here. Fairbairn's tweedier in the photograph Sean showed me than the man I saw, but it's the same man."

"Emma, Lucas, Sean. What, Wendell, am I the last person you decided to talk to today?"

A glimmer of a smile. "Yes."

Yank looked at the old man and sighed. There was more. No question. "What else, Wendell?"

"Lucas did some digging. Oliver Fairbairn does his Hollywood consulting under the company name of Left Hand Enterprises."

"The left hand of Ultan," Yank said.

"It's not a coincidence." Wendell got to his feet, looking stiff now, preoccupied. "Oliver Fairbairn was interested in Saint Declan long before Maisie Bristol hired him."

Yank nodded, but he kept his gaze narrowed on the old art detective. "And?"

"And Oliver Fairbairn isn't his real name."

"What is?"

"I don't know."

"Hell, Wendell. Who is this guy?"

He didn't answer. They walked in silence back down the hill into the village and met Lucy in front of a restaurant. People were sitting at tables outside on a terrace, presumably likewise determined not to squander the perfect November day.

Lucy rhapsodized about an Irish wool sweater she'd bought at one of the shops she'd visited. "It's perfect for you, Matt. Don't worry, it looks rugged. Are you two done? Don't let me rush you." She gestured to the restaurant. "This place has the most fabulous-looking desserts on display. I took a peek inside. I can amuse myself for as long as necessary."

"Wendell and I are done," Yank said, hearing the heavy note in his voice.

Lucy tilted her head back at him. "What's going on, Matt?"

He knew what he had to do. He glanced at Wendell and saw that the old art detective knew it, too. Oliver Fairbairn and Left Hand Enterprises merited a closer look.

Yank turned back to his wife. "Change of plans, Luce. Are you up for a trip to London?"

She broke into an unexpected smile, her pixie face lighting up with what he thought was genuine pleasure. "London," she said. "It's been ages since I've been to London."

Twenty-Four

Bristol Island, Boston, Massachusetts

Emma turned up her jacket collar against the cold wind off Boston Harbor as a shivering Maisie Bristol greeted her in the Bristol Island Marina parking lot. It was nine o'clock in the morning, and Emma had already talked to her grandfather, her brother, Yank, her HIT colleagues and the BPD detectives investigating Rachel Bristol's death. Time to get everyone together, but Maisie was alone in the parking lot.

Alone, Emma thought, but less tight and preoccupied. Maisie smiled. She wore a hooded sweatshirt under a flannel shirt, on the light side for the conditions, but she didn't seem to mind the cold, despite her shivering. "Good morning, Agent Sharpe. I'm glad you and Agent Donovan could be here. Isn't it a glorious day? Chilly, but I love it. We don't get this sort of day in Los Angeles." She squinted against the bright sun. "It's good to be here after what's happened."

"Who else has arrived?" Emma asked.

"Dad's here. He and I drove out together. Aoife and Father Bracken were already here. I think they're walk-

ing out to the other side of the island to see where...
you know." Maisie's smile faltered. "Where Rachel was
killed. I'm sure it's a comfort for Aoife to have a priest
with her. Dad went to meet up with them."

"What about Danny?"

"He's here somewhere." Maisie rolled her eyes. "Of
course."

"He came on his own?"

Maisie nodded as Colin joined them. He didn't seem
to notice the wind. Maisie hunched her shoulders against
another cold gust. "Good morning, Agent Donovan. It's a
chilly one. We're only missing Oliver. He said he would
meet us here."

"Did you talk to him this morning?" Colin asked.

"I haven't seen him since last night. Why? What's
going on?" Maisie's teeth were chattering now. "Oliver's
eccentric. I'm not worried he's not here yet—I won't be
worried if he doesn't show up. It's not a big deal."

"Oliver Fairbairn isn't his real name," Emma said.
"Did you know that, Maisie?"

She gaped at Emma. "What? Really? No, I didn't
know. I had no idea. I don't pay him directly. I pay his
company. Well, my bookkeepers do. Left Hand Enterprises. Oliver says the name has mythological significance."

"Did he ever tell you what significance?"

"No. I never asked, either. It didn't seem important."
Wind blew hair in Maisie's face but she didn't seem to
notice. "You can't possibly think he has anything to do
with Rachel's death or your thief. He's just an eccentric
scholar. He doesn't even have a cell phone."

"We want to talk to him," Colin said. "One of our guys
is at your house now looking for him."

"Seriously?"

He nodded at her. "Seriously. Special Agent Sam Padgett."

When Emma had spoken to the BPD detectives, they'd confirmed that Oliver had identified himself only as Oliver Fairbairn. He hadn't mentioned it was an alias. By itself, it wasn't much—but coupled with Left Hand Enterprises, his trips to Dublin in October and Heron's Cove last week, it was enough to have a chat with him. Padgett had jumped at the chance to head over to Beacon Hill while Emma and Colin headed to Bristol Island.

Maisie crossed her arms on her chest, her freckles prominent against her pale skin. "Oliver had nothing to do with Dwight Wheeler. He's in custody. He shot Rachel. Isn't that the end of it?"

"We spoke to the detectives this morning, Maisie," Emma said. "They're not as confident Dwight is the shooter. He says he wasn't on the island on Saturday. He says he and his family accepted the cottages would never go back to being the oasis in the city that they'd been when he was a boy, but also that you paid more than a fair price to buy them out. They trust you to do right by the island for the future."

"Then he's not... If he didn't..." Maisie sucked in a breath. "Are you saying Rachel's death wasn't just a terrible accident?"

Colin eased in next to her. "Let's collect everyone and go from there."

"All right. I can read between the lines of your nonanswer." More subdued, Maisie pulled up the hood of her sweatshirt over her wind-tangled hair. "Danny's likely the closest." She pointed at the trail. "There's a rock outcropping not far from here with a fabulous view of the skyline. He went to have a look. I'm sure he can see us through the trees. He's probably bitching about the cold. I told him he can go back to Las Vegas anytime."

Colin looked at Emma. "I'll see if I can find him."

Maisie waved a hand. "I can go. You two are starting to freak me out. Talk about intense." She apologized immediately. "Sorry. That came out wrong. I know you have a job to do."

"Not a problem," Colin said.

"I'll go with you. I know every inch of this island." She wrinkled her face, self-conscious. "And I know Danny."

Emma saw Colin wasn't thrilled by the idea of having Maisie Bristol tagging along, but he gave in. "All right," he said, "let's go."

They headed up the same trail Emma had taken on Saturday morning, alert but not expecting to find Rachel Bristol dead. This morning was clearer, brighter, colder, feeling more like early winter than late fall. Maisie tucked her hands up into her sleeves. With her casual attire, disinterest in grooming and unassuming manner, it was easy to forget she was a successful—and powerful—Hollywood producer, but Emma had gotten glimpses of a young woman becoming accustomed to being in control.

Danny Palladino wasn't at the rock outcropping where Maisie had expected he would be. She threw up her hands. "The son of a bitch expects me to inform him of my whereabouts at all times, but he can disappear whenever it suits him. What if I got into trouble and was counting on him to jump out of the woods and come to my rescue?"

Colin dipped into the birches between the trail and the outcropping, fallen leaves cushioning his feet. Sunlight glistened on the quiet harbor. Waves rolled onto the sand and rocks.

Emma turned to Maisie. "Could Danny have gone

back to the marina? Could he have passed you in the parking lot without your noticing?"

Maisie shook her head. "Absolutely not. He'd have said something. Pinched my butt. Something."

"Maybe the cold got to him, and he went to find a spot to warm up."

"Nothing gets to Danny."

Prickly, Emma thought, but also conflicted—and worried. "If you don't want him here, why don't you ask him to go home?"

"Yeah, why don't I? Maybe because he's the most reliable and loyal man I've ever known. That doesn't mean we can be together. He didn't like Rachel. He doesn't like my father. He likes my mother okay, but it doesn't matter. I'm…" Maisie pushed windblown hair out of her face. "I'm Maisie Bristol, movie mogul. You know what I mean?"

"Your success gets in the way of your relationship with Danny?"

"His nosiness doesn't help. Plus he has a keen eye for dysfunction. Some people like to keep the blinders on. I would be one of them."

"You own the island," Emma said. "You bought out your father earlier this year."

"So? Now you sound like Danny. He keeps saying that Dad doesn't own so much as a grain of sand here and it's got to bother him that he doesn't have a say in what happens to it. But he *does* have a say. I'm not that person, Agent Sharpe. I would never shut him out. Danny doesn't get that."

"Did your father need money, Maisie?"

She gave Emma a cool look. "Everyone needs money."

It wasn't an answer, but Emma let it go for the moment. "Sometimes Danny doesn't see the nuances between people," Maisie said. "Dad and Rachel were divorced but here he is, ready to scatter her ashes on an island she loved. She was in a rough patch. He gave her a place to stay. He encouraged her work. Danny says there has to be more to it. He's always one to lift up the rocks and see what scurries out from underneath them." She drew herself up straight, looking out at the water. "It's difficult to be here. Harder than I imagined."

"It's so soon," Emma said.

"Too soon, maybe."

Colin emerged from the brush onto the trail in front of them. "No sign of anyone."

Maisie balled up her hands into tight fists. "Danny's probably at the cottages. I can't believe he went without me. I wanted us all to go together. Now everyone but me is there." She caught herself and smiled. "People have minds of their own, I guess. Nervy, huh?"

"We can head over there," Colin said.

"Thanks. I guess two FBI agents are a good substitute for… Never mind. I know I'm emotional right now."

"Do you come here often?" Emma asked her.

"More so in recent months, because I want to figure out plans. It's also a great place in warm weather. Well, it's a great place now, too, despite the cold. Everything is so crisp and clear and beautiful." Maisie pulled in her lower lip, then blew out a breath, clearly fighting tears. "Damn. I'm tempted to go home, but I'm not going to. If the rest of them can go out there, so can I."

They walked a few yards in silence, the trail barely wide enough for two people. Colin went ahead, and Emma stayed with Maisie. "Does your father come out here often?" Emma asked.

"Some. I don't know. We're not always in Boston at the same time."

"He's been spending more time in town. Is he working on a film project here?"

Maisie shook her head without comment.

"We've been doing some research, Maisie. Your father's in a rough patch, too. He's had a series of projects fall through."

"Nature of the beast, and he always has a lot of irons in the fire. It's natural for a few of them—even a lot of them—to fail. He throws a lot of darts and hits the occasional bull's-eye." Maisie's lips were starting to turn purple, but she wasn't shivering any longer and didn't appear to be in any real distress from the cold. "My approach is a bit different. I don't have as many darts, and so I aim each one carefully and don't throw it until I'm pretty sure I'm going to hit that bull's-eye."

"Have you and your father talked about his situation?"

"No, why would we? He's fine. He's excited about a project he's working on now, but he's not ready to talk about it. He has his work, and I have mine."

Maisie struck Emma as practical and unassuming, influenced, perhaps, by being in a business of sometimes startling ups and downs. At the same time, Emma sensed a certain defensiveness on Maisie's part when it came to her father.

Emma got a call and saw it was Sam Padgett. He barely waited for her to answer. "I'm at the Bristol house," he said. "The gardener let me in. I'm in the guest apartment. Oliver Fairbairn has flown the coop. All his belongings are gone, but there's a laptop on the dresser, left in plain sight."

"His laptop? Why would he leave it behind?"

"Rachel Bristol's laptop."

"Supposedly she didn't have a computer. Why do you think it's hers?"

"It says so. A computer printout is taped to the outside with her name and a list of a dozen unsolved art heists around the world. She's missing the London heist and has a few extras, but she was on to our serial art thief. There's no note saying 'To Emma Sharpe with love, Oliver,' but it's got to be his doing."

"We need to find Oliver, Sam."

"Yep. I'm walking through the rest of the house to see if he's playing Goldilocks and taking a nap in one of the upstairs rooms." He paused, then said, "I'm not liking this, Emma. You and Colin be safe out there."

He disconnected, and Emma looked at Maisie. "When were you in your workroom last, Maisie?"

"This morning but only for a minute."

"And you didn't see Oliver?"

"I told you no. His door was shut."

"Did Rachel have a laptop?"

Maisie frowned. "A laptop? What difference—"

"Just answer the question, Maisie," Emma said.

"All right, all right. Gad. You're scaring me. I have no idea if Rachel had a laptop. The police didn't find one in her things. No one touched anything of hers at the house before the police got there. We were all here at the marina, in shock. Why? Has a laptop shown up?"

"In your guest apartment where Oliver was staying. He's gone."

"Oh." Maisie grabbed her stomach with one hand. "It was taken before she was killed? Oliver took it? Why would he do that?" She gulped in air as if she was having trouble breathing. "Oliver didn't kill Rachel. It's impossible."

"We don't want to jump ahead too far," Emma said, then saw that Padgett had texted her. She glanced at her screen.

No Fairbairn. Called BPD. They released Wheeler. On their way to you.

She showed the text to Colin. He turned to Maisie. "We're going to hand you off to the marina security guard—"

"Wait. No way. What are you going to do?"

"We're going to collect everyone," he said. "The detectives are en route. We'll all meet back at the marina. You sit tight. Understood?"

Maisie was still arguing. "But I know the island. There's no reason to shut me out." Colin looked at her, and it was enough. She held up her phone. "I'll call the security guard and have him meet us. He's two seconds out."

Colin winked at her. "Good idea."

Twenty-Five

Finian stood in the sand and tall grass in front of the dilapidated white cottage where Emma was to have met Rachel Bristol and instead discovered her body. A sobering place to be, he thought. He didn't know enough details to pinpoint where Rachel had died. Not *in* the cottage, he was certain. In this spot? Where he was standing in the cold harbor wind?

He didn't think so. As if pulled by an invisible force, he looked to his left, to the overgrown area next to the cottage.

There.

That was where Rachel Bristol had been shot to death.

It wasn't just instinct on his part. It was also the scene itself. The subtle and not-so-subtle signs that the police and forensics personnel had been through there. It had a cleaned-up look that the rest of the area didn't. He noticed flattened grass, brushed footprints, bits of yellow crime-scene tape.

Aoife was on the porch. She'd been pale and withdrawn since they'd arrived at the marina and walked out to the cottages. She wore her travel clothes—black coat, black leggings and ankle boots—and her hair was pulled back. It was as if she was pretending she was already on her flight home to Dublin, but it wouldn't leave until early evening.

Finian suddenly longed for Ireland. He could see himself hiking with his brother as lads. Invincible they'd been, ambitious and filled with dreams. Most of Declan's dreams had come true. Finian's, too, he knew, at least for a time.

Aoife turned, the bright sun catching the highlights of her near-black hair. "This place must have been magical when these cottages were first built."

Finian stepped onto the low porch. She walked to the side edge and looked into the grass, brush and stunted trees where he believed Rachel had died.

"Do you think she knew she was in danger?" Aoife asked softly.

He knew what she meant. "If it was a bullet gone astray during target practice, then probably not."

"Do you believe that's what it was?"

He heard the skepticism in her tone but didn't pursue the subject. "It's a shame the cottages have to be torn down, but seeing them for myself—it's clear they can't be saved."

Aoife nodded. "I like Maisie Bristol's idea of launching a film-production facility here. It's a great location. It's close to the city, but also removed—and beautiful," she added, her voice choking. "If I ever come back to Boston, I want to visit some of the islands, especially in the outer harbor. During famine times, people fleeing Ireland were quarantined on one of the islands. I don't know which one. Imagine the disease and suffering on the ships that were taking their passengers away from more disease and suffering." She gave a small, tight laugh. "Thank God for air travel, right, Finian?"

He felt his throat tighten. "Aoife…"

She held up a hand. "I'm okay." But her eyes now glistened with tears. "You can still see faded stains on the floorboards where Rachel must have bled. She was probably standing where I'm standing right now when she was shot." Before Finian could respond, Aoife plunged on. "She stole the cross from me because she believed I was the thief. She wanted the big get. The big revelation. Irish artist launches her career by stealing from her uncle."

"Maybe Rachel was after the stolen art," Finian said.

"For a reward? To sell to a collector? I suppose it's possible, but I don't think so. She was obsessed with her idea for this movie she was doing with Maisie. Maisie has plenty of money. It wasn't an issue."

It would have been if Maisie had fired her from the project, Finian thought. He noticed there was no porch rail. Aoife stepped off the side into the mix of sand, grass and brush. The wind was dying down. He heard gulls… and something else. A movement in the trees and brush between the white cottage and the one next to it.

Aoife jerked up straight. "That wasn't a bird. Finian— someone is here."

"Get down." A man's voice, urgent, coming from within the brush and small, bare-limbed trees. "Both of you. *Down now.*"

Finian leaped for Aoife, enclosing her in his arms and taking her down into the sand and brush with him, shielding her as he heard a loud sound—a crack of gunfire.

Aoife shuddered with shock and fear. "Finian…what was that?"

He heard an unintelligible yell. "I'm hit." A moan. "Damn it…"

Danny Palladino crawled from the cover of the brush and trees. He collapsed onto his stomach and rolled onto the grass and sand close to where Finian held Aoife. The bodyguard was ashen, blood oozing onto his T-shirt from a wound in his left shoulder. He grabbed it, pressed his palm to the blood. Blood immediately seeped through his fingers.

Aoife gasped, clutching Finian. "He's hurt. We have to help him. Finian—"

"No," Danny said. "Stay down. I've been shot. Bastard's still here."

Finian tightened his hold on Aoife as she went still. She didn't make a sound.

"Danny," Finian said. "How bad, my friend?"

"I'm okay. Pissed off, Father. Really pissed off, but I'm pretty sure the bullet went in and out the other side." Despite his bravado, his voice was hoarse. "Shooter's behind the cottage next to us. Stay down. Don't make yourself a target."

"Do you know who it is?"

"Yep. Yep, I do. The son of a bitch. Call the FBI agents. They'll be at the marina by now. Let me talk to them."

Finian spotted a gun in the grass where Danny must have dropped it when he was shot. He started to crawl toward it, but Travis Bristol emerged through the brush and trees. He had a gun and pointed it at the wounded man. "Don't move, Danny."

"Bastard," Danny whispered. "You shot me."

"It was self-defense, and you know it."

"That's bullshit." Danny's color worsened, his pain evident as he struggled to talk. "I don't care. I'll do whatever you want. Just let Aoife and the Father go."

Finian kept Aoife shielded as best he could as he focused on Travis. "The FBI agents will be here soon. They'll have heard the gunfire. Let's wait for them."

"I'm fine waiting," Travis said, then he smirked. "Are

you, Danny? Do you want to tell Agent Sharpe what you've been up to? I'm not going to let you try to shoot me again."

Danny's eyes shut, and he seemed to sink deeper into the soft ground. "They'll be able to tell you shot me from a distance. They'll know the only reason I'm alive is because I ducked, and you missed my chest. Center mass. That's how you killed Rachel, isn't it?"

Travis didn't flinch. "You're done, Danny. You won't get away with this."

"Give it up, Travis. Think of Maisie—think of your daughter. The feds are going to see you with a gun on me, and they're going to shoot you." Danny bit down hard, clearly in agony, before he continued. "Do you really want Maisie to hear that shot? She'll have nightmares about it for the rest of her life. Give them a choice."

"The police are releasing Dwight Wheeler," Travis said as he held his gun steady. "They know you killed Rachel."

"Whatever. You and me, we can sort it out. Your attempt to frame the carpenter didn't work out. Now you're trying me. Okay. Fine. But Aoife, Father Bracken..." Danny licked his lips, his color worsening. He coughed, unable to go on.

"What do you want, Travis?" Finian asked quietly. "Tell me, and I will help you."

"This is all on Danny." Travis spoke through clenched teeth. "Whatever happens, it's all on him."

Finian prayed Emma and Colin in fact *were* on the way. He felt Aoife tense, but she maintained her composure. Danny's breathing was ragged, blood continuing to pour between his fingers. Finian believed him. Danny Palladino wasn't the killer. Travis Bristol hadn't shot him in self-defense. But Travis wasn't willing to give up on his plan. Finian could see it in him—the tunnel vision, the entitlement, the violence. No doubt he'd hoped to kill Danny before anyone else showed up.

"Your daughter is a joy," Finian said softly. "Maisie is a great name. I know you love her more than anything in this world."

The older man was past hearing. "I found Rachel's computer. She figured out that Aoife here is this thief the Sharpes and FBI have been hunting. She's hit at least a half-dozen places around the world, starting with her uncle's house in Declan's Cross."

Finian shook his head. "You're wrong, Travis. Aoife isn't the thief."

"I don't trust any of you. Danny figured out what Rachel knew and decided he wants to get the reward for the stolen paintings or maybe sell them himself. He killed Rachel, and he planned to blackmail Aoife."

"None of this is true," Aoife said, sounding weary more than combative.

Travis motioned at her and Finian with his weapon. "Did you and Father Bracken here work together? Ten years ago, he was a married man. Did you two have the hots for each other back then? It's convenient that his family died a few years later. Did he sabotage their boat, or did you do it together?"

Finian felt his entire body go still as he looked at this madman.

Danny stirred. "Let him talk," the bodyguard mumbled, semiconscious. "Keep him going…"

Spittle had formed on the corners of Travis's mouth. "Or did you kill the Brackens on your own, Aoife? Eliminate the competition so you could have Finian Bracken all to yourself?"

Aoife surged in Finian's arms but he tightened his

hold on her, kept her from leaping for Travis. The man would shoot her without a qualm. "Rachel got it wrong, my friend," Finian said. "Let's not compound her mistake with more mistakes."

"I have a right to defend myself," Travis said.

He pointed the gun at Danny Palladino. Danny opened his eyes and kicked out at Travis with both legs, catching him off guard, knocking him backward. Travis kept his grip on his gun. He raised it, but Colin was there, leaping from the brush, firing before Travis could.

Aoife screamed. Finian held her. Emma ran to them, her own weapon drawn, trained on Travis as Colin moved in and took Travis's gun, then checked him for additional weapons. But it was clear Travis Bristol was past hurting anyone else.

Colin glanced over at Danny. "That was a hell of a risk."

"Worked."

Danny shut his eyes. Aoife pushed away from Finian and knelt next to the wounded man, pressing the heel of her palm into his bloody shoulder.

Finian assisted her, aware of Emma's gaze on him and he looked up at her. "Aoife isn't your thief."

She nodded. "I know."

"Fairbairn?" It was Danny again. A relentless man. This time, he didn't open his eyes. "It's a fake name. He took off last night."

"Do you know his real name?" Emma asked.

Danny shook his head. "I know that Travis is deep in debt to the wrong people in Las Vegas." He shut his eyes again. "*Was*. Hell. Maisie…"

Finian could see that the bodyguard was stubborn, resilient and as deeply in love with Maisie Bristol as ever.

"She needs to remember the good times," Danny whispered. "That's what you do when your father turns into a monster."

Aoife smiled gently at him. "She will. She's strong, and so are you."

He tried to return her smile. "I want to go back to the desert."

"And I to Ireland," Aoife said with a pained look at Finian as Danny's blood seeped through her fingers.

Twenty-Six

~~~~~~~

Colin walked next to Finian on the hard, wet sand of Bristol Island beach. Aoife was a few steps behind them, obviously wanting to be alone but not too alone. It was low tide, but the wind had subsided to a slight, intermittent breeze. BPD marine patrol boats had come in close to the island.

Shaken, ashen, Maisie had wanted to ride in the ambulance with Danny, but the BPD detectives—and Emma—needed to keep them separated for questioning, at least for the moment.

Finian put on his sunglasses. "You and Emma aren't easy friends to have, Colin."

"Us? We just saved your ass, Fin."

"Thank you, but that I needed your help makes my point, doesn't it?"

"You're the one whose friend is the pretty Irish artist Rachel Bristol thought was a serial art thief."

"Aoife was to have been part of Rachel's big break. She didn't care about the stolen art. She wanted the drama and publicity to help convince Maisie to do the movie her way and revive her career. She couldn't see anything else."

Colin didn't disagree. "She and Travis were toxic together. Nothing was working out the way either of them wanted and hadn't been for a long time. Danny found out that Travis was in debt with the wrong people out in Las Vegas. He was hiding behind his ego, building a house of cards that was about to collapse on him. He couldn't face telling Maisie."

"Rachel found out and threatened him, didn't she?"

"Looks that way."

Aoife sped up and eased in between the two men. She hooked one arm into Finian's arm and the other into Colin's. "An FBI agent and a priest. A woman in danger couldn't ask for more." She leaned her head against Finian's upper arm. "I'm so sorry. I never should have called you when I arrived in Boston."

"I wouldn't have had it another way, Aoife."

"You protected me. You'd have let that man kill you before he could kill me. Then what would I have done?"

"You'd have gone on with your life.

"Try not to spool yourself up over what might have been," Colin said.

She leveled her vivid blue eyes on him. "Would you have shielded Emma?"

"Nah. She's got her own gun."

He saw a smile. A start of one, anyway. Aoife patted his hand and then slipped her arm out of his. "You and Emma are good together. It's nice to see after witnessing even a little of what Travis and Rachel Bristol did to each other. The games, the anger, the pride, the lives of entitlement and scarcity. I can't imagine. I don't want to imagine."

"Travis knew this frame of Dwight Wheeler wasn't holding up," Colin said. "He needed another fall guy, and not only did Danny fit the bill—he knew that Travis was in financial trouble and lying to Maisie."

"Poor Danny. Poor Maisie." Aoife shuddered. "They need each other right now. He's a man who doesn't want anything but the woman he loves. She's a woman who wants to do her work but her enormous success has changed everything. She needs someone solid in her life. Someone who understands her and her work."

Neither Finian or Colin responded as they came to the pier. Sam Padgett had arrived, and he and Emma were conferring with the BPD detectives. Colin figured Padgett had been in his element in the Bristol house. Action and answers had put him in a better mood, but so far, Rachel's laptop hadn't yielded any insights into Oliver Fairbairn and his real identity.

"I guessed that the thief who broke into my uncle's house hadn't stopped there," Aoife said. "I never mentioned my suspicions to you or your grandfather, or even to Sean Murphy and my sister—certainly not to Rachel. I assumed you knew more than I did, and I didn't want to come under scrutiny. I wanted to focus on my work. I didn't want my reputation to become entangled with that of an art thief." She turned to Finian. "I want to go home."

He slung an arm over her shoulders. "As soon as the police allow it, I will take you to the airport myself."

She smiled. "Thank you, Father Bracken."

He glanced at Colin and Emma. His eyes were hidden behind his dark glasses. "Will you be looking for Oliver Fairbairn?" he asked.

"Our mild-mannered mythologist," Emma said.

"He has a passport. He travels." Colin shrugged. "We'll find him."

Emma picked up a small stone and pitched it into the harbor. "It's off to London via Ireland, I think." She grinned at Colin, but the tension was in her eyes. It'd been a close call getting to Travis before he started shooting again. She took Colin's hand, squeezed it. "Best to tell Yank about our engagement in a foreign country, don't you agree?"

Finian didn't leave Aoife's side until they were at the airport and he had no choice but to buy a ticket to Dublin himself or go home to Maine. Colin wouldn't take a bet on what his friend would do. He and Emma were on the same flight as Aoife. She was even flying coach to be closer to them after her ordeal. They would see her into the care of Sean Murphy when they landed.

Unless Finian *did* buy a ticket to Dublin.

Aoife was holding back tears. "I love you, Finian. I always will."

Colin backed up as if someone had stomped on his big toe. Finian shook his head at him and kissed Aoife on the cheek. "Goodbye, Aoife. Give my love to Sean and Kitty."

"We'll see you soon." She smiled as she stood back. "Maybe one day the church will allow noncelibate priests."

Finian winked at her, and the twinkle in his midnight-blue eyes reminded Colin that his friend had had a sex life before the priesthood. It was a good guess it had included beautiful Aoife O'Byrne.

Aoife left him and didn't look back as she caught up with Emma and they went through security together.

Colin lagged behind with Finian. "Think she'd be happy as a priest's wife?"

"Who? Emma?"

"Ha, Fin."

"Emma will be happy as your wife, Colin. Your life together will be complicated and difficult at times, but it will work."

"It is working. It's great." Colin sighed. "It was a hell

of a moment, Fin. Seeing you and Aoife with this crazy son of a bitch."

"He would have killed us all. He was past reason." Finian looked out at the Boston skyline, as if somehow he'd forgotten where he was, then turned back to Colin. "Aoife will return to her life in Dublin, and I will see you and Emma back in Rock Point soon."

"You will. I've been away for weeks on end this fall. If you get bored, feel free to stop by my place and wash the windows. Window cleaner's under the kitchen sink."

Finian grinned at him. "I'm never bored in Rock Point."

Emma, Aoife, Colin and their half-full plane of passengers landed in Dublin early the next morning, at least on Irish time. It was still the middle of the night in Boston. Emma had stayed awake for most of the flight. Colin had known she would. She was deep into dots among more dots and trying to figure out which ones connected. She had the window seat next to him and spent most of the six-hour flight staring into the darkness. Never mind her grandfather's vault of a mind, Colin thought. Emma had her own.

Across the aisle, Aoife O'Byrne had slept little, but, he knew, for different reasons.

He hadn't slept because they hadn't slept.

Sean Murphy met them at their gate. He and Aoife embraced, the relief at her return to Irish soil palpable. He took her carry-on bag, and he escorted them through the terminal.

Colin checked his watch. Ninety minutes until the connecting flight to London. He appreciated being on his feet. He and Emma had jammed a few things into two small carry-on bags. They didn't plan to stay on this side of the Atlantic long. He would have offered to carry her bag, but she had it hooked tightly against her side, as if someone might steal it, but he knew that wasn't it. Her fatigue and tension had caught up with her. Ex-nun and trained FBI agent that she was, she wouldn't want to admit she was anything but cool, calm and collected. Colin had had his own brush with overload in October. Hence, two weeks in an Irish cottage.

"I'll see Aoife home, but I'm tempted to fly on to London with you," Sean said. "I would like to talk to Oliver Fairbairn myself. So far he is a dead end here in Ireland. To be expected since Fairbairn isn't his real name."

Emma slowed her pace in the seemingly endless corridor. "Fairbairn is a Scottish name. It means 'beautiful child.'"

"And you think his choice of alias has significance?" Sean asked her.

"Myths, legends, fairy tales and folklore are filled with stories of children and young people surviving against deprivation, loss and evil," she said, her bag still tight against her side. "Hansel and Gretel shoving the wicked witch into the oven. Snow White surviving biting a poisoned apple given to her by her wicked stepmother."

Colin tightened his hold on his own bag. "You think our mythologist survived a childhood trauma."

"It's possible," Emma said. "One name rose out of my files. Oliver York. He's a high-living English aristocrat. He bought one of Aoife's paintings a few years ago. Look him up, Sean. See if he was in Dublin in October when Oliver Fairbairn met my grandfather, or last week when Rachel Bristol was here."

"Does your grandfather know anything about this Oliver York?" Sean asked.

Emma's green-eyed gaze steadied on the Irishman.

"You'll have to ask him. I suggested we meet at the airport but he said he's busy."

"You sound dubious, Emma."

"I do, don't I?"

Sean Murphy looked as if he was debating whether he could arrest Emma for being a Sharpe. He turned to Colin. "The Sharpes make for fascinating company."

"No argument from me."

"You and Emma are still together after two weeks in Fin's little cottage and two weeks of chasing this Sharpe thief—not to mention two transatlantic flights in a week."

"Stronger than ever," Colin said, and he saw Emma's smile.

"Good for you." The senior Irish detective sighed. "We'll see if it's good for Special Agent Yankowski."

"He's meeting us in London," Emma said.

"Says he can't wait," Colin added with a straight face.

Sean grinned. "I'm sure he can't. Kitty was impressed with him and liked his wife. Next time you're in Ireland, come by the farm, and we'll get my bottle of Bracken 15 off the top shelf." He looked up the corridor at Aoife, who was leaning against a wall, obviously exhausted as she waited for them. "My thanks to you and Emma for what you did for Aoife and Finian yesterday on that island."

"You're welcome." Colin winked. "Wish you could have been there."

Sean's blue eyes sparked with amusement. "I'll bet you do."

They caught up with Aoife. "One more question for you, Aoife," Sean said, clearly solicitous of her. "A few years ago, a man named Oliver York bought one of your paintings. Do you remember—"

"My porpoises," she interjected. "I remember. I thought that painting would never sell, but he loved it."

"You met him, then?" Emma asked.

"Yes. He was at my first London show. Wait. He's Oliver Fairbairn? No way. They're *nothing* alike." She shook her head. "Well, I guess that would be the point of an alter ego, wouldn't it?" She didn't wait for an answer and spun around at her future brother-in-law. "I want you to tell me the truth, Sean Murphy. Did you ever once suspect I was this thief?"

He put an arm around her. "For a few minutes one winter about seven years ago," he said.

"I'll bet it was in February in Declan's Cross," she said tartly, then smiled at him. "It's good to be home."

Twenty-Seven

〜◦◦◦〜

London, England

Oliver York's elegant, spacious apartment overlooked beautiful St. James's Park in central London. Emma hadn't slept on the short flight to Heathrow, or on the train into the city. She knew Colin hadn't, either. They had, however, managed to change clothes and freshen up. Yank had met them at Claridge's, where he was staying with Lucy—her pick. They'd walked over to the gracious, ivy-covered mansion, now divided into three large apartments for its wealthy residents. Oliver was well-known in British high society, but he was also solitary and ultraprivate.

For good reason, Emma thought as a thin, gray-haired man led what he referred to as "the agents of the American Federal Bureau of Investigation" down a hall. He knew Oliver didn't have to let three FBI agents into his home and obviously didn't approve that he had.

"Are you the butler?" Colin asked him.

"My name is Martin Hambly, sir."

Martin took them through double doors into a library, where Oliver York stood in front of a tall window. "I've missed running in the park," Oliver said wistfully, turning to his guests. He'd exchanged his frumpy Oliver Fairbairn tweeds for well-fitting khakis and a mustard-yellow polo shirt. "November is a great time to be in London. Welcome."

Yank edged over to a wall of bookcases, a wooden ladder propped up against them for easy access to the higher shelves. He'd told Emma and Colin that he would let them take the lead. He was there to observe and as backup should Oliver York have a few more surprises up his sleeves. That he and Oliver Fairbairn were the same man was without question. Once they'd started pulling the right strings, his dual identities had unraveled fast.

"Thank you for agreeing to speak with us," Emma said diplomatically.

Oliver gave a slight bow. He'd slicked his dark blond hair back. "Of course."

Colin stayed with Martin by the door. "Nice place," Colin said.

"I grew up here. This room is more Oliver Fairbairn than me. All the musty books. He became the scholar I might have become if I wasn't…well, Oliver York. I'm not known for my academic inclinations."

"You're skilled in a variety of martial arts," Emma said. "Tae Kwon Do and Tai Chi in particular."

He didn't seem surprised or disturbed that she knew. "They train the mind as well as the body." He gave her a small, knowing smile. "Much easier and much more fun than becoming a monk or a nun."

"Sweatier," Emma said.

Oliver laughed. "Touché, Agent Sharpe." He turned to Yank. "Agent Yankowski, I trust you and your wife are enjoying Claridge's. I assume it was her idea for you to stay there. There are many good hotels in London, but Claridge's is my personal favorite. An iconic Art Deco hotel in the heart of Mayfair London. An excellent choice."

Yank gave him a dark look. "How do you know we're at Claridge's?"

"Why wouldn't I know? London is my home. I've lived here my entire life. I turn thirty-seven in February, but I assume you know that. I'm a Pisces. Intuition, illusion, dreams, secrets. We Pisces often feel misunderstood and burdened by our feelings."

He didn't give off the air of a man burdened by his feelings or anything else, but that, Emma knew, wasn't true. One of his Pisces illusions, maybe. Yank pulled a slender volume from a shelf. She didn't catch its title. He'd left Lucy at Claridge's reluctantly, and only after asking hotel security to keep a special eye on her.

Emma walked across the thick Persian carpet to the windows and looked down at the park, the oldest and arguably the loveliest of London's royal parks. It was early afternoon, gray with on-and-off drizzle, and yet Emma found herself longing to be walking through St. James's gardens.

She was aware that Oliver was watching her. She looked over at him. "Why didn't you tell us Oliver Fairbairn is an alias?"

His eyes widened, and he barked an incredulous laugh. "Are you serious, Agent Sharpe? An ultrahot Hollywood producer introduces me as Oliver Fairbairn to the FBI agents and Boston police detectives investigating a murder I know I didn't commit. I went with it. Trust me, you would have, too."

"Lying to federal agents—"

"I didn't lie." He waved a hand. "It doesn't matter now, regardless. I'm sorry about what happened in Boston. Travis was far more fragile than I realized and certainly far more violent. I didn't see him often. I had no idea he'd killed Rachel or was a danger to anyone else. The carpenter was in custody when I booked my flight back to London. I was free to leave."

"Your lip's looking good," Colin said. "Did Travis shut that door in your face?"

"I didn't see him but it must have been him, part of his frame of the carpenter. Dwight. Nice fellow. I'm glad he's been exonerated. Now, is there anything else? I'm leaving for the country as soon as I can. I want to work in the garden, walk the dogs and laugh in the pub with friends."

Yank held up another book. "I see you have a number of how-to books on drawing, painting and sculpting. Something you and Agent Sharpe have in common. She's been taking painting lessons."

"I'm not very good," Emma said. "What about you?"

"I have many books I haven't read and never will. I sometimes draw at my house in the Cotswolds but rarely here." He took in what Emma recognized as a calming breath. "Those are my mother's books."

Yank returned the book to its shelf. "We know she was killed in this room, Oliver. That's a tough one. Sorry it happened."

"So am I. It has nothing to do with why you're here."

"It has everything to do with why we're here," Emma said.

Oliver's expression became unreadable. "You have a theory," he said with an edge of sarcasm. He tilted his head back, his eyes hooded. "Tell me. Take me through it, Agent Sharpe. I'm listening."

It wasn't what Emma wanted to do, but she knew she had to. She wanted his reaction. She needed him to understand what they knew and the confidence they had in their conclusions. She stepped back from the windows. "You were eight years old when two burglars broke in here," she said. "Two men who had worked as groundskeepers for your family but quit a few months earlier. They thought the house was empty. You and your parents were supposed to be in the Cotswolds. The men were looking for cash and valuables—anything they could take with them and easily fence. They weren't having any luck. They were frustrated, angry, panicked. Your mother heard the commotion and grabbed you. But it was too late. The two intruders killed your parents and kidnapped you."

"Amazingly enough, Agent Sharpe, I know this story."

"I know you do, Oliver."

"It has nothing to do with Rachel Bristol's death in Boston."

"The men held you in an isolated church ruin in Scotland while they contacted your maternal grandparents with a ransom demand and waited for payment. You escaped and were walking, dehydrated, in shock, down a lane when an elderly Roman Catholic priest picked you up and brought you to the local police, who returned you to your grandparents. They became your guardians. They've since died. It's their house you now own near Stow-on-the-Wold."

Oliver walked over to the bookshelves and withdrew a guidebook on the English Cotswolds. "Have you ever been to the Cotswolds, Agent Sharpe? Its honey-stone villages, walking trails, tea shops and antiques shops— and farms, of course. We love our farms in England."

Emma expected he already knew the answer. "I visited a few years ago with my grandfather. We went to Stow-on-the-Wold for the day. We toured an old church."

"Saint Edward's. It's a Church of England parish. It's right in the village."

"I remember. By all accounts, Oliver, you'd been a happy little boy."

He gripped the guidebook in one hand. "Yes, I was."

"After your escape, you went to live with your grandparents."

"They were splendid people, Agent Sharpe. They thought I wouldn't want to come back here, but I did. We divided our time between here and the farm. I wouldn't let them touch anything."

Emma ran her fingertips over the back of a leather chair. No one had taken a seat since they'd entered the library, but there were plenty of options. Leather chairs, a reading lounge, two sofas, assorted desk chairs. "I can see you as a little boy, wandering through this place. Eventually you went to Oxford but dropped out after a year."

"Our frumpy, dear Oliver Fairbairn is self-educated as a mythologist. He wouldn't have it any other way."

"You became quite a wanderer, didn't you?"

"I love to travel, Agent Sharpe."

"Is Oliver Fairbairn your only alias?" Emma waited, but he didn't answer. "You can tell us, Oliver, or we can find out on our own."

"Oh, by all means, find out on your own. I wouldn't want to rob you of your fun." He set the book on a table, next to a brass lamp that looked like one Winston Churchill might have used during World War II. Oliver winked at Emma. "Imagine what skeletons and dastardly deeds you'll turn up investigating a lonely British mythologist. The reason I've never appeared on your FBI radar is because until this past week, I've never stumbled on to anything more serious than fellow wanderers with sprained ankles—oh, and a nasty bee sting. A college student. A pretty girl. The bugger stung her on her left ass cheek. Poor me had to swoop to her aid."

Martin Hambly smiled. Colin and Yank didn't. Emma didn't fall for Oliver's diversion. "Did you find comfort in the Celtic crosses at the church ruin, Oliver?"

"I found no comfort anywhere, Agent Sharpe."

"Creating Oliver Fairbairn helped you manage a terrible childhood trauma. We have no quarrel with that. But it's also a good cover for a career as an international art thief."

Oliver groaned. "And here we have it. I suppose you're still on your theory—speaking hypothetically?" He snorted. "Do you people realize you scare the daylights out of the rest of us when you speak hypothetically?"

"Enough with the drama, Oliver," Colin said.

"Easy for you to say," he muttered.

Emma walked over to a curio cabinet, its top shelf crowded with diminutive Celtic crosses. "These didn't come with the place, did they? They look handmade. Did you carve them yourself?"

"In fact, I did. It's a hobby I took up as a teen."

"Nice." She knew she'd made her point and stood back from the cabinet. "Did you just happen on to Declan's Cross ten years ago, or did you go there on purpose?"

"That's a 'when did you stop beating your wife?' question, Agent Sharpe," Oliver said mildly. "I suppose by now you know I stopped in Dublin on my way back to Boston from London last week. I went to see Aoife O'Byrne at her studio but she'd already left for the airport."

Emma let him change the subject. Even if he confessed to being in Declan's Cross ten years ago, there was little she could do about it. The Irish garda would take another look—they would without a confession—

but a decade later, it was unlikely they would find new evidence. "What did you see at Aoife's studio, Oliver?" she asked.

"A toolbox in the hall on the first floor. I recognized sculptor's tools."

"Being one yourself," Emma said.

"Strictly amateur."

"Why did you go there?"

"I knew Rachel was interested in her." He flopped onto a leather chair. "I thought I was mixed up in a creative squabble between two headstrong women—Rachel and Maisie—not in thieves and murder and who knows what all." He gave a long-suffering sigh. "Maisie's sweet, but you don't want to cross her. Rachel was a harridan but had a lot of good ideas."

Emma noticed Yank came close to smiling. Colin was still serious, eyes narrowed on Oliver. "Where did you get Rachel's laptop?" he asked.

Sam Padgett and the BPD detectives were all over the laptop back in Boston. Padgett had loved finding it even if Oliver Fairbairn, aka Oliver York, had deliberately left it out.

Oliver folded his hands on his flat abdomen. "What if I told you Rachel gave it to me for safekeeping?"

"Did she?" Emma asked.

He shook his head. "I saw Travis with it in the garden the day Rachel went up to Heron's Cove. I didn't know whose computer it was and made an effort to find out. People sometimes underestimate the technical savvy of a tweedy academic. Travis was one of them."

"He sneaked it from Rachel," Emma said. "Then you sneaked it from him."

"He returned it to Rachel. Then he took it again. I didn't find it until yesterday. I took a peek and decided to leave it for Maisie." Oliver glanced from Emma to Yank and Colin and then back to her. "You didn't think I left it out for you, did you?"

She gave him a cool look. "As you know, the laptop contains Rachel's journal. She describes her plans for her movie, her hopes, her dreams. She also describes her theory about a string of unsolved art thefts over the past ten years and includes links to news accounts about them."

"Was she right, Agent Sharpe? Or did she include a few that you don't believe your guy committed?"

"Two," Emma said. As he also well knew.

Oliver eased to his feet. His movements were sure and graceful, those of an expert practitioner of a martial art—and also of a very fit man capable of brazen art thefts. "Rachel confesses in her journal that she broke into Aoife's studio looking for the stolen paintings or any proof that Aoife was your thief. She helped herself to a crowbar from the sculptor's toolbox. She expresses surprise at how easy it was to jimmy the lock." He snapped his fingers. "*Just like in the movies,* she wrote."

Yank walked over to the windows. He stared down at the park without saying a word. He had to be thinking about his wife, but Emma kept her focus on Oliver. He was looking at Yank with compassion, whether real or faked, Emma wasn't sure. "Then your wife came along, Agent Yankowski," he said. "Rachel had no idea who she was. A woman in the building, household help—no idea. She panicked, pushed the bookcase on her and ran. She thought everything would be fine. Her victim would squeeze her way out to safety and call the police. By then, Rachel would be on her way back to Boston."

"Lucy was trapped for thirty hours," Yank said.

Oliver shuddered. "Horrible."

Yank turned to him. "You were worried Rachel was on to you, but she decided Aoife O'Byrne was the thief."

"People should leave sleuthing to law enforcement professionals, don't you think, Agent Yankowski? Although things have gone swimmingly once the FBI got involved, haven't they?"

Yank let his gibe go without comment.

"Rachel made some mistakes," Emma said. "Some big mistakes. Breaking into Aoife's studio, stealing the cross from Aoife. She wanted this movie to work, and she wanted to be the one to catch this thief. Travis had become a means to an end. Disposable. She stayed at his house and had access to his daughter. Other than that, she had no use for him, and he knew it."

Colin walked over to her, but his eyes were on Oliver. "Travis didn't kill Rachel because she called Agent Sharpe. He killed her because he'd lost control of her. He couldn't handle her contempt. He believed once everyone else knew the truth of his situation—his failures—he would be in for more of the same. He was in debt to the wrong people and thought the paintings were his way out of his problems, and he couldn't let Rachel ruin that chance. Of all people. He didn't know she would call Emma on Saturday. He knew that Rachel was a problem, and he would get her out to the cottages and kill her."

"An unhappy state of affairs," Oliver said.

Emma suspected he was ready to have Martin usher them out, but she continued. "The murder of Lindsey Hargreaves in Declan's Cross must have shaken you. Then Rachel got the bit in her teeth. You sensed things were veering out of control. I appreciate that you wanted to put us on the alert, Oliver, but you could have involved us directly instead of sending us those crosses."

He looked her in the eye without flinching. "What crosses, Agent Sharpe?"

"The ones you sent to my grandfather, my brother, Agent Yankowski, me and, finally, Aoife." Emma ached with fatigue but tried not to show it. "You named your company Left Hand Enterprises."

"Did I? A play on words. The right hand doesn't know what the left hand is doing. Oliver York doesn't know what Oliver Fairbairn is doing."

Emma shook her head. "Nice try but you told Maisie the name has mythological significance."

"What possible—"

"Lamh chle Ultain id aghaidh," she said. "It's Irish."

"The left hand of Ultan against evil and danger," Oliver said. "I know the saying, and I could have used Ultan when I was kidnapped. My parents could have used him. Oliver Fairbairn doesn't have the complications of being that little boy cowering in the ruins, grieving for his murdered parents and certain he will be next. Nothing more, and nothing less."

"I know the crosses are a comfort to you, Oliver," Emma said quietly.

"I hope they're a comfort to anyone who sees them. The Celtic crosses I saw as a boy saved my life. There is no doubt about that. Saint Declan was a healer who made a place for himself in Ardmore. Ultan warded off attackers. They're good stories. Stories have real power, don't they? Especially the ones we tell ourselves. The theft at John O'Byrne's house is a good story, too. The unsigned landscape stolen that night is an early Aoife O'Byrne work, don't you suspect? Her Yeats phase. A local scene of beautiful Celtic crosses."

"I've never seen it, and there are no pictures of it."

"I'm speculating," Oliver said with a thin smile.

Yank stood straight. "We're done here. We'll catch you next time, Mr. York. So, no next time."

Oliver ignored him. "My best wishes to your wife, Agent Yankowski. Enjoy your stay in London. Now, if you find yourselves in Stow-on-the-Wold, do come see me. I'll show you the farm."

Colin buttoned his jacket. "You and Martin here remind me of Batman. Rich guy traumatized as a boy. Loyal manservant. Secret missions."

"Batman is American," Oliver said, as if that explained everything.

"That means there's no Batmobile in the cellar?"

Oliver made no comment, but Emma thought she saw Martin Hambly smile as he escorted her, Yank and Colin back down the hall.

St. James's was a gorgeous park, even in gloomy November. Emma found herself wanting to spend the rest of the day exploring its gardens and meandering walks. Yank joined her and Colin. "Don't worry, I'm not staying. I won't ruin your walk in the park. Lucy just texted me. She's wrapped up her spa appointment and now she wants to see Buckingham Palace and experience a real London pub."

"You could ask Oliver York for a recommendation," Colin said.

"Not in the mood for humor, Donovan." Yank turned to Emma, his eyes narrowed on her. "Your grandfather told me the Ultan thing yesterday in Ardmore. He knows about York."

"You're not asking me my opinion, are you, Yank?"

"No. He knows."

Yank brightened when he spotted his wife entering the park from the street. She waved, smiling as she approached them. "I didn't make a single wrong turn or freak out at being on my own again. It feels great."

"I'll bet it does," Colin said, kissing her on the cheek. "You're looking good, Lucy."

"Thank you, Colin."

"I'm glad you're on the mend," Emma said.

"My bruises are healing, and so are my emotions, although they will take more time. The spa helped. And I made reservations for Matt and me to have high tea at Claridge's tomorrow." Her dark eyes gleamed with pleasure. "I *know* that will help."

Emma laughed. "A spa and high tea, Yank. I like how she thinks."

"You might keep that in mind, Colin," Yank said, then slipped an arm around his wife's waist. "We're off to Buckingham Palace."

A break if only for the moment, Emma thought, watching Yank and Lucy swing off into the park. He'd scheduled HIT video conference in ninety minutes. She and Colin would meet him at his hotel. She sighed. "I could curl up on a park bench for a quick nap."

"I bet Oliver would let you take a snooze on the library couch," Colin said with a grin.

"He probably would."

"Good job with him just now, Agent Sharpe." He slung an arm over her shoulders. "I love watching you work. You're smart, empathetic and kick-ass."

"So are you, you know."

"With the emphasis on kick-ass." He drew her close. "Are we spending the night in London or going straight to Dublin to hunt up your grandfather?"

"I'd take you to meet my parents but they're in Dublin. Lucas is flying in tonight. They don't always tell me everything anymore because I'm an FBI agent."

"Sharpe secrets. We'll go to Dublin tonight then." He kissed the top of her head. "Let's take a walk in the park, touch base with Yank and the crew in Boston and then scoot off to Dublin."

Emma smiled. "You don't want to just spring for a room at Claridge's?"

Colin laughed and gave a mock shudder. "Imagine if we ended up in the room next to Yank and Lucy."

"Oh. Yikes. No. It's on to Dublin tonight."

"In the meantime," Colin said, sliding his arm down to her waist, "let's take that walk in the park."

Twenty-Eight

London, England

"Long day," Lucy said, easing into the chair across from Yank in Claridge's bar. "I can see it in your eyes."

"I'm fine, Luce. No worries."

"Mmm."

He reached across the small table and touched a dark purple-and-yellow bruise on her wrist. "Rachel Bristol did this to you. She panicked. She thought you'd be okay."

"She was right. I am okay."

"Lucy…"

"Who knows, Matt. I might have stopped in to see Aoife O'Byrne's studio even if she wasn't a part of your FBI work. She's an incredible artist, and I've been spending money like crazy. I could have decided to buy one of her sunrises." Lucy smiled, her dark eyes soft in the candlelight. "I won't be able to resist if she decides to do an Irish rainbow."

"I'll remember that."

There was mischief in her smile now. "I want to go shopping at Harrods tomorrow. It's another of my fantasies. Then tea here at Claridge's."

"All our years together, Luce, and the things I still don't know about you."

"You'll be saying that when we're eighty."

"I hope so. We don't have to jam everything into one day, though. Since you quit your job, and I have unused vacation, why don't we stay in London through Thanksgiving?"

Her face lit up with pleasure. "That would be wonderful. Not at Claridge's the whole time. We'll go broke. I'll find us a wonderful little boutique hotel. We need to save for a decent place in Boston. I can tolerate your apartment until we find something. I've been thinking about options."

"Did you start thinking before or after you saw Buckingham Palace?"

"Ha-ha. I need to figure out what's next for me. I think it might involve yarn. Remember when I loved to knit?"

"I thought you still did."

"I do. I just haven't in a while."

She rubbed one of her bruises, a distance coming into her eyes. She smiled, but Yank could see the effort it took.

"Knitting could be therapeutic," she said quickly. "Maybe I can open a yarn shop and get into knitting as therapy."

"Whatever you decide, Lucy, I'm there for you."

"Right now, let's enjoy London." She looked around the elegant bar and grinned. "This is all irregular, though, isn't it?"

"As long as the new acting director doesn't get the bill. Which she won't."

"You're a good steward of the public's funds. You—" Lucy stopped abruptly. "*She,* Yank?"

"Yes."

"Mina Van Buren?"

Yank sighed. "It'll be announced any day."

"I hate that woman," Lucy said.

He looked at the woman across from him. His wife, his best friend, his greatest champion and the woman he would love forever. He smiled. "If things don't go well, I can always learn to knit."

Their waiter appeared with a bottle of expensive champagne. Yank started to tell him he had the wrong table, but he handed him a note. *Compliments of Oliver York.*

"Thanks," Yank said. "Two glasses."

Simpler, he thought, just to drink the damn stuff.

Twenty-Nine

Rock Point, Maine

When Finian returned to the rectory after a long walk along the harbor, he found Maisie Bristol waiting for him on the back steps. She was shivering in a sweatshirt that was too light for the cold weather, and she looked pale and frail. She stood as he started onto the steps. "I thought you might be a kitchen-door type. May I come in, Father?"

He brought her into the kitchen. He took off his coat and hung it on a hook, a routine that was becoming more familiar to him, as was everything about his life in Rock Point. He'd had his life laid out at twenty-two, and it had changed—abruptly, tragically and irrevocably. He knew that ambitious Maisie Bristol would have to confront the unexpected changes in her own life.

"Do you believe in the bad seed, Father?" She didn't give him a chance to answer. "I'm so afraid of what might be inside me. Because of my father."

"Because of what he did in his last days. He made his own decisions."

"My mother is shattered. She never saw it coming. She

says what she and my father had was real, but it wasn't forever. He always let pride and greed and lust get the better of him." Maisie lifted her troubled gaze to Finian. "Do you believe in true love, Father?"

He thought of Sally, laughing at some silly thing he'd said, cradling their babies, crying at the death of her grandmother—and loving him, sighing in his arms. And then of Aoife, intense, beautiful, giving.

"I believe in loving others," he said. "Maisie, lay Rachel and your father to rest and then do your own soul work. Wherever that takes you. Put your trust in that work."

"In God, you mean?"

He didn't answer.

"That's for me to figure out, is what you're saying," she said, drawing herself up straight. "I will figure it out, too. I will. Danny's getting released from the hospital today. He'll make a full recovery. He's going back to Las Vegas as soon as he can travel. I'll arrange for a private jet for him. Least I can do."

"I'm glad he's doing well."

"He says you shielded Aoife." Maisie studied him for a moment. "You're both brave men. And the FBI agents. Definitely want those two on your side."

Finian smiled, hoping to ease some of her tension. "No argument from me."

She flipped some of her tangled hair out from under her sweatshirt. "Who knows, maybe one day I'll knock on Danny's door in Las Vegas. When I'm not in so many pieces."

"Do you know what's next for you, Maisie?"

"Ireland," she said. "I'm not telling anyone. I'm going alone. I'll load up a backpack and do the waymark trail in Saint Declan country. Being solitary is a necessity for

Oliver. It's natural for Aoife and self-imposed for Danny. For me, it's a luxury. What about you, Father Bracken? Is the priesthood a kind of a self-imposed exile for you?"

"It's a calling," he said simply.

"I'm sorry. I've no right to ask such a question. I'm leaving for Ireland as soon as I get Danny back to Las Vegas." She smiled, looking less haunted. "I'll think of Ireland as my soul work."

After she left, Finian put on the kettle for tea. There was a knock at the back door. He thought it was Maisie returning to talk some more, but it was elderly Franny Maroney with a casserole, a pie and assurances that the church ladies would do anything for him.

She paused on her way out, her hand on the door as she looked back at him. "We would all understand if you left the priesthood, Father. You were once a married man. That Irish painter…" Franny smiled. "God would understand if you fell in love again, don't you think?"

"I'm not going anywhere," Finian said.

"Not yet, maybe."

He remembered Franny Maroney was planning her own first trip to Ireland. A lifeline. "Did you order your passport?" he asked her.

"I did, indeed. Scared the living daylights out of me."

"You'll love Ireland," he said.

"I know I will."

After she left, when it was quiet again, he finished making his tea.

Thirty

Dublin, Ireland

The Irish National Gallery of Art was located on a busy street between Merrion Square and St. Stephen's Green in central Dublin. Emma had wandered through its galleries many times but never with an internationally acclaimed artist like Aoife O'Byrne. Their visit coincided with one of the three separate weekly hours when *The Meeting on the Turret Stairs,* a stunning watercolor by Irish artist Frederic William Burton, was on view.

Aoife sighed next to Emma in the second-floor gallery. "The colors. The emotion." Her voice was at once strained and filled with warmth. "It's a gorgeous painting."

"It rips my heart out every time," Emma said.

Aoife looked at her in surprise. "I guess I didn't expect that from you."

Emma made no response and Aoife turned back to the painting, which depicted the last meeting between ill-fated medieval lovers Hellelil and Hildebrand—a Danish princess and her bodyguard. They exchange a final embrace on the stone steps of a tower, knowing he is about to die. Her father, believing him to be an unsuitable match for his daughter, has ordered his sons to kill the handsome knight.

Aoife peered at the painting as if seeing it for the first time. "Forbidden love," she whispered. "What a terrible price they pay for falling in love."

"What I see and feel most is their love for each other."

"Yes." Aoife straightened, smiled through her tears. "It transcends everything else, doesn't it? I suppose you've figured out that Finian and I…" She paused. "It was before he went off to seminary. Most days I think I'm over him, or I don't think about him at all. But when Rachel invited me to Boston, I could think of nothing else." She laughed. "Talk about forbidden love."

"Do you think Oliver York has a thing for you?" Emma asked.

"Not romantically. I don't believe so. I suspect he feels a bit guilty for stealing from my uncle and tying himself to me. It's disconcerting to realize he's been watching me all this time. The cross he sent last week—it was a warning?"

"He put us all on alert. With Declan's Cross in the news and Rachel's interest, he sensed something could explode, but he didn't know Travis would turn to violence any more than anyone else did."

"He feared for himself, too, no doubt. Discovery, if nothing else. But you don't have enough to arrest him?"

"There's what we know to be true, there's what we suspect to be true—"

"And there's what you can prove," Aoife said, finishing for Emma.

"Our thief does keep things interesting," Emma said.

"You don't think you've heard the last of him yet, do you?"

Emma didn't hesitate. "No, I don't."

Aoife turned back to the painting. "You and Colin Donovan—forbidden love, Emma?"

"Depends who you ask," she said with a smile.

At first Colin didn't recognize Mina Van Buren when she entered the Dublin pub where he'd proposed to Emma just over a week ago. He was enjoying a pint on his own, waiting for his fiancée—he loved that word.

Mina sat on the bench across from him in his booth. "Hello, Agent Donovan."

"Soon-to-be Acting Director Van Buren. Damn. For a second I thought you were Judy Dench."

"She's a lot older than I am."

"I meant in her younger years."

"I heard you were a mix of charm and killer instinct. It can be disconcerting, can't it?"

"I don't know. I don't think I've ever been disconcerted."

She didn't react. She was thickset with dyed blondish hair and glasses, and she was dressed like a tourist. "I'm glad you settled things in Boston. The thief?"

"You've read Agent Yankowski's report, haven't you? It's all there."

"I'm on my way to London to see Agent Yankowski. We have things to talk about."

"Disbanding his team?"

"No. Not if I have the final say." She clearly didn't plan to go further. "Emma Sharpe? She's with you, isn't she?"

"That's right. She is. Always."

Van Buren sighed. "I'm keeping HIT and keeping Yank in charge. No doubt he wishes it had been me under that bookcase last week, but it wasn't. I'm sorry it was Lucy. I'm sorry it was anyone. We need you, Donovan.

Now more than ever. You need latitude and independence, and you need us to trust you." She eyed him a moment. "I'll let you chew on that for a while and figure out what it all means. I want to meet Emma. It was fast, the two of you."

"What, you want to have dinner together, or just have her bake you a pie?"

"A pie would be good. Apple. I'll bring wine. Invite the priest. Father Bracken. I want to meet him, too. A quiet dinner. Just the four of us."

Colin had no idea if she was serious.

"It will get tough on you and Emma when there are things you can't tell her," Van Buren said. "Tough on you, too. We'll cross that bridge if and when we get to it. Emma is relatively high profile for an undercover agent's wife. If you had to make a choice—"

"I'd do puffin tours."

"With the wilderness-guide brother. Mike. You'd be miserable."

"I bet you've never been on a puffin tour."

"There's a lot you don't know about me, Donovan. I know you had a special relationship with the outgoing director. I'm good with that."

Colin knew she was stewing on a new mission but there was no point asking. "Do you have a security detail yet?"

"Sure. They think I'm at the spa."

"That woman thing can come in handy."

She cracked a smile. "I was joking. I've never been to a spa in my life. I had a massage once. I hated it. I kept thinking the masseuse would cut my throat." She got to her feet. "You don't have to fight me or hide from me, Agent Donovan. Neither does Agent Yankowski, or Agent Sharpe. I'm a fifty-eight-year-old grandmother who wants a safer world for her grandchildren, and I'm on your side."

When she left, Colin was tempted to see if she did have a detail or if she was on her own. But Mina Van Buren could take care of herself, and Emma had entered the pub.

Time to head to Declan's Cross and an Irish Thanksgiving with the Sharpes. He'd conspired with Lucas, his future brother-in-law, and set Kitty O'Byrne Doyle to the task. It should be good, he thought, although Kitty had said something about cooking a goose instead of turkey.

Thirty-One

∽⤙⤚∽

Declan's Cross, Ireland

"Quite a family I'm marrying into," Colin said as he and Emma entered the bar at the O'Byrne House Hotel.

She smiled. "It is, isn't it?"

Her grandfather, parents and brother were gathered at tables Kitty had pushed together and covered with white tablecloths for the occasion. She had created a centerpiece out of rust-colored candles and small pumpkins and had whole cranberry sauce, mashed potatoes, squash, green beans, roast goose—which drew a sigh from Colin—and American-style apple pie. A Thanksgiving feast that Emma quickly discovered had been arranged on the sly by her brother and her fiancé.

She didn't know if Colin had envisioned taking her father aside to formally ask for his daughter's hand in marriage, but she couldn't wait. "Everyone," she said, beaming, holding up her glass of champagne. "Colin's asked me to marry him, and I've said yes."

She held out her hand and showed off her ring.

"It's beautiful," her mother said.

Her father clapped a hand on Colin's shoulder. "Welcome to the family."

Lucas grinned. "Big surprise."

Across the table, her grandfather sighed. "Two FBI agents in the family. Just what I need."

Her parents stayed through pie and coffee. Her father's pain had flared up. Emma could see it in his eyes, the tightness at his mouth. Lucas eased to his feet. He would take them to Cork for the short flight back to London. He would go with them and see what else he could find out about Oliver York.

Colin was pouring the last of the champagne when Kitty emerged from the lobby with a small package. A glossy white box tied with a white cloth ribbon.

"It was on the front steps," Kitty said. "It's addressed to The Sharpes."

Emma opened it. Inside, tucked into white tissue paper, was a small lamb carved out of some kind of white stone. It had a little bell tied around its neck with a narrow white ribbon. She held it up for Colin and her grandfather to see. "White. A lamb. Symbols of hope and new life…"

"There's a note," Colin said, lifting a small card out of the box and handing it to her. "You do the honors."

The note was typed on what appeared to be an old manual typewriter. Emma read it aloud. *"In honor of the sheep who graze the grounds of Saint Declan on Shepherd Head. Imagine the Irish homecomings they have witnessed."*

Colin stood, already reaching for his jacket. "Let's go up there."

They decided to walk, including her grandfather. The late November afternoon had cast the hills in a purplish light. Waves washed onto the rocks of the sea cliffs. Emma held hands with Colin and watched woolly sheep prance in the fields of Murphy farm. There'd be lambs by Saint Patrick's Day.

When the lane came to an end at the church ruins, Emma could smell the mud and dampness along the ancient stone wall.

"Give me a minute," her grandfather said. "I'll meet you at the crosses." He pulled off his wool cap, then sank onto the low wall. "We don't need to add a fourth cross up there."

"I can wait with you," Emma said.

He shook his head. "No, go on."

Colin had already climbed over the stone wall. Emma joined him, and they made their way up the green hillside to the trio of crosses.

A carefully wrapped waterproof package sat under the tallest of the crosses—the one that was a copy of the elaborate silver wall cross stolen from the O'Byrne house a decade ago.

"It'll be the Yeats paintings and the cross," Emma said. "Oliver will have kept the unsigned landscape."

"It's Aoife's early work, isn't it?"

"I'm almost positive."

Colin nodded down the hill. "Here comes Granddad Sharpe. He doesn't look winded to me."

No, he didn't, Emma thought as she narrowed her gaze on her grandfather. He didn't look that surprised to see the package, either. "Well, Granddad," she said. "The only question I have now is this—how long have you suspected Oliver York was our thief?"

Her grandfather shrugged. "He was on my short-list after he bought the porpoise painting, but I couldn't place him in any of the cities at the time of the thefts. I didn't know for sure he was our guy until Oliver Fairbairn stopped to see me and then I found out about Left

Hand Enterprises. Maybe I didn't ask all the questions I could have. Maybe I couldn't. You can and have to." He met Emma's gaze. "It's one of the differences between us, FBI and private citizens."

"You let him taunt you," she said.

"I didn't let anything. I had a name and a history that provided a reason for interest in Celtic crosses, not a reason to steal—and no proof. Oliver isn't easy to track. He has resources, and he's smart. The FBI wouldn't have had enough evidence to nail him. Looking back from what we know now, it's easier to connect the dots."

"You had dots I didn't have." Emma knew she wouldn't get anywhere trying to convince him he should have confided in her. "Were you worried he would progress to violence?"

"If the thief had progressed to violence, then it wasn't Oliver York. It was someone else. Oliver isn't violent." He adjusted his wool cap atop his white hair. "He really is a cheeky bastard, though."

"We need to get Sean Murphy out here," Colin said.

Wendell pointed grimly down the hill. "He's already on his way. Kitty probably called him after that package turned up on her doorstep."

"Oliver needs to return all the stolen artwork," Emma said.

"He will when it suits him—which means when he knows he won't be caught. If you had enough evidence against him for the U.S. thefts, you'd arrest him, but you don't, and you never will." Wendell fingered the plastic on the package leaned up against the cross. "He's a talented fellow. He needs a new way to keep his demons at bay. I'd help him find something else to do with his energy if I were you."

Emma noticed Sean Murphy making his way up the hill.

"When do you two go home?" her grandfather asked.

"Tomorrow," Colin said.

"I'll see you before you leave." He winked at them. "Unless you sleep in."

"Granddad, we'll stay and walk you back to Kitty's—"

He shook his head. "After I talk my way out of Detective Garda Murphy arresting me, I'd like some time on my own." He looked at the trio of Celtic crosses, his expression turning serious. "Emma, Colin—Agent Sharpe, Agent Donovan—it was a good thing you two did, stopping Oliver. The lamb says it all. He's making a fresh start. He is cheeky, though." Then he kissed Emma on the cheek. "God willing, I'll be back in Heron's Cove for Christmas."

That evening, Colin ordered Bracken 15 and two glasses and had them delivered to their room at the O'Byrne House Hotel, overlooking the garden where, fifty years ago, John O'Byrne had found a fifteenth-century silver cross.

Emma sat on the floor in front of the fire. Colin joined her with the whiskey. "We have a full plate at work when we get back," he said, "but Thanksgiving in Rock Point is not to be missed. Wait until you try Mike's eggnog. He says the cheap whiskey makes it. He can't wait to get Fin's opinion."

"I'm invited?" Emma asked, smiling.

He kissed her on the cheek. "Pop says bring a pie."

"We can announce our engagement."

"My family isn't as easygoing as your family. They're going to want a wedding date."

"A wedding date," Emma said half to herself. "Colin…"

"I'm thinking spring. What about you, Emma?"

She could see it—the two of them surrounded by flowers and greenery, their families and friends, the ocean in the distance. "The gardens at the convent are incredible in June," she said.

"It's a great place for a wedding," he said.

She watched him sip his Bracken 15, noticed the small scar by his eye. "On paper we shouldn't be perfect for each other."

"We're not on paper." He set his whiskey on the floor next to him. "You know, there's a fireplace in our room."

"So I noticed. We're sitting in front of it."

He smiled. "Have you been envisioning us making love by the fire at our house in Rock Point? Because I have."

"Our house," she echoed. "I like the sound of that. I like it a lot. Any reason we shouldn't make love by an Irish fire?"

Emma could feel the heat of the fire as Colin took her in his arms. "No reason I can think of," he said, and his mouth found hers.

* * * * *

· Author's Note ·

Thank you for reading HARBOR ISLAND! I hope you enjoyed the story. It's the fourth in my Sharpe & Donovan series that launched with SAINT'S GATE, then HERON'S COVE and DECLAN'S CROSS. I've also written "Rock Point," a novella prequel about Finian Bracken's departure from Ireland for Colin's coastal Maine fishing village. It's available as an e-book and, for print lovers, as a "bonus" story in the hardcover print edition of HARBOR ISLAND and the paperback of DECLAN'S CROSS.

Boston is "my" city, and I loved creating Bristol Island, but the Boston Harbor Islands National Recreation Area is a real place, beautiful, rich with history and open to the public. I have more islands yet to explore! Likewise, tiny Declan's Cross is fictional, but Ardmore is real, one of my favorite stops in Ireland for its scenic beauty, ancient ruins and contemporary shops and restaurants. I've stood where Yank and Wendell stood and checked out Saint Declan's Stone. *A Walking Tour of Ardmore, Co. Waterford,* by Siobhan Lincoln was a big help in my understanding more about the history and lore of this lovely village.

The Meeting on the Turret Stairs is on display at the

National Gallery of Ireland just a few hours a week. I happened to catch one of the viewings as I was writing HARBOR ISLAND, and I highly recommend it to anyone visiting Dublin.

As always, many thanks to my friend John Moriarty, who graciously answered all my questions and allowed me to interrupt a truly wild Irish winter. I'm ever grateful to John Brennan for handing me an article several years ago about an Irish art theft…it got the wheels of my imagination turning! My husband, Joe, and I look forward to being back in Ireland, hiking the hills, tasting whiskey and enjoying the good company.

Special thanks to my editor, Nicole Brebner, my agent, Jodi Reamer, Tara Parsons, Margaret Marbury and everyone at Harlequin MIRA. We work hard and have fun!

My next Sharpe & Donovan novel is in the works… I'm excited!

To stay up-to-date with my books and goings-on—and for giveaways, recipes and photos of Ireland, Boston and Maine—please visit my website www.carlaneggers.com (you can sign up for my newsletter, too!) and join me on Facebook and Twitter.

Thank you, and happy reading!

Carla Neggers

Turn the page for bonus novella
ROCK POINT
available for the first time in print.

One

In all his travels, Finian Bracken had never been to America. London, Paris, Rome, Prague, Amsterdam, Vienna, Berlin, Budapest, even Moscow…but never New York City, San Francisco or Dallas. Certainly not Rock Point, Maine, where portly, thoughtful Father Joseph Callaghan served a struggling parish. Finian was a priest himself. His days of rushing from airport to airport, hotel to hotel, seemed distant, as if it had been a different man and not him at all. He didn't know if he'd ever leave Ireland again. He wasn't sure he wanted to.

He and his friend Sean Murphy, a preoccupied garda detective if ever there'd been one, had happened upon the American priest in the bar lounge of the lovely O'Byrne House Hotel in Declan's Cross, a tiny village on the south Irish coast.

Father Callaghan had explained he was winding down a month-long visit to Ireland and didn't want to go home. He said he was captivated by the land of his ancestors. *Father Joseph,* he called himself. Finian doubted he'd ever be a *Father Finian.* Even *Father Bracken* still sounded strange to him. He noticed his priestly black suit and collar were newer, crisper, than Father Callaghan's rumpled attire.

"Rock Point isn't one of those charming Maine villages you see in the tourist ads," the American priest said, halfway through his pint of Guinness, clearly not his first of the blustery March evening. "What do they call them in England? Chocolate-box villages? If you want that, you go to Heron's Cove a few miles away. Rock Point's a real fishing village."

"When do you return?" Finian asked.

"Monday." Father Callaghan counted on his stubby fingers. "Just three more days on the old sod."

Next to Finian, Sean took a big gulp of his Guinness and didn't say a word. Sean could be a conversationalist, but not so far tonight. Finian smiled at his fellow priest. "Is this your first trip to Ireland?"

"Yes, it is. I'd been wanting to go for ages. I buried a man last fall who for years said he wanted to see Ireland, but he never did. He died suddenly, still thinking he'd get here. He was seventy-six. I just turned sixty-two. Jack Maroney was his name, God rest his soul." Father Callaghan picked up his pint glass. "I booked my flight the day after his funeral."

"Good for you," Sean said, raising his pint. "To the old sod."

Finian, unsure if Sean was sincere or trying to be ironic, raised his whiskey glass. "To Ireland."

"To Ireland." Father Callaghan polished off the last of his Guinness. "I was feeling sorry for old Jack Maroney, and for myself, truth be told. Then I thought—do I want to die with no dreams left to pursue? Or do I want to die with a dream or two still in my pocket?"

Sean jumped in before Finian could come up with an

answer. "Depends on the dream. Some dreams you know are unattainable."

"I'm not talking about playing center for the Boston Celtics."

Sean pointed his glass at the priest. "Yes, you're right, Father Joseph, that's different. Romantic love. Now, there's an unattainable dream. For me, anyway. I'm not a priest." He winced and took a sharp breath as he looked at Finian. "Ah, blast it, Fin, I wasn't thinking. Forgive me."

"No worries," Finian said quietly, then turned again to Father Callaghan. "Will you come back to Ireland one day? Perhaps when it's warmer?"

"I'd love to spend a year here. Maybe take a sabbatical." The American priest sat up straight on his barstool as if to emphasize this idea wasn't a whim but something he was determined to do. "As soon as I can swing it, I'll be back, even if it's just for a couple weeks. I want to see more ruins and stone circles and such, and walk the ground of the Irish saints. I was in Ardmore today. We're in the heart of Saint Declan country."

Finian had visited Ardmore's monastic ruins and twelfth-century round tower, and also a particularly good hotel with an excellent whiskey selection. "Ardmore is quite beautiful."

"Sea cliffs, a sand beach, fascinating ruins. It's a wonderful place even if you don't give a fig about an early-medieval Irish saint."

"But you chose to stay here in Declan's Cross," Sean said.

"Another intriguing place." Father Callaghan glanced around the bar lounge, its half-dozen tables and upholstered chairs and sofas empty as yet on the quiet evening. "I wanted to indulge myself and spend a couple nights here. I'm in the smallest guest room, but the O'Byrne is still the most luxurious accommodation on my itinerary. It's been perfect. It only opened as a hotel last fall. It used to be a private home. Quite a history. I assume you know it?"

Sean buried his face in his Guinness, leaving Finian to answer. "We do, of course, sure. It was the country home of the current owner's uncle, John O'Byrne, who died a few years ago."

"A thief broke in here ten years ago, before it was a hotel, obviously, and made off with a fortune in art," Father Callaghan said. "The case has never been solved. A tiny, picturesque Irish village, a crumbling Irish mansion on the sea, an old widower with a taste for art—it'd make a great Hollywood movie."

He eyed Finian and Sean as if to see how they'd react. Sean set down his pint and made no comment. He was a strong, fit man, dark-haired and blue-eyed, dedicated to his work as a member of an elite detective unit in Dublin but still a child of Declan's Cross. Finian was more angular, his dark hair straighter, his eyes a darker blue, his roots in southwest Ireland—he wasn't as intimate with the details of the theft at the O'Byrne house as Sean would be.

With an almost imperceptible shrug, Father Callaghan continued. "The thief made off with three Irish landscape paintings and an old Celtic cross. Sneaked in through that door there." He pointed to French doors that led out to the terrace and gardens. "I gather it happened on one of your dark and stormy Irish nights."

Finian smiled, liking the American. Sean remained quiet, whether because he was from Declan's Cross or because he was a detective, Finian didn't know. He said, "November, in fact."

Finian's answer seemed to satisfy Father Callaghan.

The American priest's two nights at the O'Byrne House Hotel, he further explained, were an indulgence he'd saved for the end of his trip. The hotel had opened to rave reviews, its restaurant, spa, rooms, gardens and service all meeting the test of even the most exacting and discerning guests. Finian had to admit he still had an affinity for fine hotels. He couldn't call it a weakness when he thought about the many good people he knew who worked so hard and invested so much to provide their guests with a pleasant respite.

Kitty O'Byrne Doyle, John O'Byrne's niece and the proprietor of the O'Byrne House Hotel, had made herself scarce when Finian had arrived with Sean. No surprise there, although Finian had more suspicions than facts about the history between handsome Detective Garda and blue-eyed, black-haired, no-nonsense Kitty.

"How do you like being a priest so far?" Father Callaghan asked.

Finian welcomed the change in subject. "Is it something I'm to like or dislike?"

"Ah. You really are new. If you can remember this one thing in parish work, it'll save you a lot of trouble." The American eyed his empty glass on the polished wood bar. "Sometimes you're the first one to know something. Sometimes you're the last one to know. Sometimes you're the only one to know. Do your best to recognize which it is, and then forgive yourself when you get it wrong— because even if most times you get it right, there will be times when you will get it wrong."

It seemed like sound advice to Finian.

Kitty swept into the lounge and went behind the bar. She wore a simple black dress that made her look at once professional and elegant. She was always, Finian thought, lovely. She smiled at him and ignored Sean. "How are you, Fin? Will you be staying with us tonight?"

"I'm doing well, Kitty. It's good to see you. I'm staying up at the Murphy farm."

She still didn't look at Sean. "The spring lambs are starting to arrive, I'm sure."

"We lost one this morning," Sean said, casual. "A coyote got it. Bit its little head—"

Kitty stopped him midsentence with a stony glare, then turned back to Finian. "I love to see the lambs prancing in the fields in the spring." She looked at Father Callaghan. "Anything else I can get you, Father?"

"Not right now. I might have a look at your whiskey cabinet a little later."

"I recommend the Bracken 15 year old," Kitty said with a quick smile at Finian.

"Sean and I will be on our way," Finian said.

"All right, then. Good night, Fin. Sean." She spun into a small back room behind the bar.

Father Callaghan raised his eyebrows at Sean. "There's a story between you two, isn't there?"

"It'd take the full bottle of Bracken 15 to tell that tale," Sean said.

"I've no doubt." The older priest's eyes—a pale green—shifted to Finian. "Bracken 15? Father Bracken? A connection?"

"My brother and I started Bracken Distillers in our early twenties," Finian said.

Father Callaghan's surprise was obvious. "Then you decided to become a priest?"

Sean spared Finian from having to answer. "Another long story," he said, easing off his bar stool. "Good to meet you, Father Joseph. Enjoy your last few days in Ireland. I hope you get that sabbatical."

"Thanks. I enjoyed meeting you both, too. Finian, if you'd like to spend a year in southern Maine, maybe we can work something out with your bishop. You know where to find me."

Finian stood, smiling at the American. "Saint Patrick's Church in Rock Point, Maine."

"You're going to see about taking this parish in Maine?" Sean asked as he and Finian turned onto the quiet lane that wound onto Shepherd Head, the village lights twinkling beneath them in the darkness. It was a good walk—much of it uphill—to Murphy farm, but also a decent night for it, windy and chilly but dry.

Finian continued a few steps before he answered. "I'd be doing the old fellow a favor."

"And yourself."

"Maybe, maybe not. It would only be a year, while Joseph Callaghan got his fill of Guinness, Irish saints and Irish genealogy."

"You don't think he'll get his fill of Irish scenery?"

Finian could hear the Celtic Sea crashing onto the cliffs, and he could see stars and a half-moon in the sky above the black horizon. "One can never get one's fill of Irish scenery."

"You're only saying that because you're thinking about being away from it for a year."

"You're a cynical man, Sean Murphy."

"You know what ecclesiastic strings to pull to get this parish?"

"That's one way of putting it."

The village lights disappeared, and the hill became more steep, the cliffs closer—a sharp plummet across a narrow strip of grass and a low stone wall. Sean had grown up here on Shepherd Head. Finian had grown up on a farm in the Kerry hills, if not one as prosperous as the Murphy farm. He and his twin brother, Declan, were eldest of five. Declan was married with three small children. Two of their three younger sisters were married, also with small children.

Finian braked his thinking and returned himself to this moment, this quiet walk along the edge of sea cliffs. He could hear sheep now in the dark, distant fields. When he'd arrived late that afternoon, Sean and his uncle, who worked the farm, had just brought several vulnerable pregnant ewes down to the barn and an adjoining field.

"I suppose I should have been nicer to Kitty," Sean said.

"I wouldn't have mentioned the coyote killing the new-born lamb, I have to say."

"As if she's never heard of such a thing. She's been coming to Declan's Cross since she was a baby, and she's lived here for two years, fixing up that blasted house of hers."

"You wish it'd been torn down."

"Leveled," Sean concurred with a hand motion to go with the image.

Finian didn't know if his friend meant what he said. "Is that why you asked me here? You want to talk to me about Kitty—"

"Kitty? Why would I want to talk to you about her?"

"The art theft, then?" Finian asked.

"I didn't ask you here about Kitty O'Byrne or an old art theft."

Finian would have been surprised if he had. In their friendship of almost seven years, anytime Finian had brought them up, Sean had changed the subject. Sean came down to Declan's Cross as often as he could, given his demanding work in Dublin. He'd always wanted to be in the guards. *An Garda Síochána,* in Irish. The Guardians of the Peace. He'd never discussed with Finian the sacrifices his position required. He preferred, he'd said many times, to leave the job in Dublin when he was home in Declan's Cross.

Finian had sold his house in the southwest of Ireland years ago, but he still owned a traditional stone cottage in the Kerry hills. The home of his heart. His wife, Sally, had seen its possibilities, and they'd set to restoring it, doing much of the work themselves. He couldn't bring himself to stay there but loaned it to friends. He'd cleaned out all the personal items and put in a new bed, but it was still decorated with Sally's taste.

He hadn't slept there since the first anniversary of the tragedy that had taken her life, and the lives of their two small daughters. He'd been in and out of a drunken haze for months. Friends, family and even perfect strangers had tried to help, but he hadn't wanted help. He'd wanted oblivion.

He'd drunk bad whiskey that night. Why waste good whiskey on a man such as himself?

He'd been half asleep on the cottage floor when Sean Murphy had burst in, dragged his friend's drunken carcass to the bay and shoved him into the ice-cold water, swearing next time he'd let him drown.

Freezing, furious, Finian had crawled out of the cold water, staggered to his feet and taken a swing at Detective Garda. Sean easily could have sidestepped the blow but he took it square in the chest. Finian had been too weak—too pathetic—to hurt him.

He'd vomited on the pebbled beach until he collapsed onto his knees with dry heaves and then sprawled facedown on the hard, cold ground.

He'd wanted to die. For the past year, he'd wanted nothing else.

Sean had fetched a blanket and a bottle of water and set them next to Finian on the beach.

"Live or die, Fin. It's your choice."

Then he'd left.

Finian remembered mist, rain, wind, wails—a banshee, he'd thought at first, then realized it was himself. Keening, cursing, sobbing. He'd flung stones, clawed the cold, wet sand and attempted to dig his own grave with his hands, and he'd cried.

Dear God, he'd cried.

Sally, Kathleen, Mary.

My sweet girls.

Gone, gone, gone.

Sober, desperately sad, Finian had collapsed again, hoping to die in his sleep of hypothermia, or something— anything. Instead he'd awakened to sunlight streaming through high, thin clouds and the soothing sounds of the tide washing onto the pebbled beach.

He'd sat up and drunk Sean's water, and then he'd walked back up to the cottage.

He didn't stay. He'd loaded up a pack, emailed his brother not to worry and walked out of the cottage, past Sally's empty colorful flowerpots, hearing her laughter, and kept walking.

For days, he'd walked.

When his mind would wander off, he'd bring it back to where he was—he would notice the warmth of the sun, the crunch of stones, the cry of birds, the taste of cheese, apple and brown bread, the green of distant hills and the deep pink of foxgloves on old stone walls. He'd passed waterfalls and cliffs, cold lakes and misty bays, sheep wandering down grassy lanes, lively villages, lonely cottages and tourists *oohing* and *aahing* at the gorgeous Kerry scenery. He'd stopped in pretty places for a bite to eat, sitting in the sunlit grass, or on a hilltop, or amid wildflowers, taking in his surroundings.

When he heard the voice of God calling him to another life, he had no doubts. It wasn't the work of depression, grief, alcohol withdrawal, loneliness or insect bites. He couldn't explain and eventually realized he didn't have to. He just had to decide what to do.

It hadn't been an easy road. It still wasn't.

Finian slowed his pace as he and Sean came to the top of the hill. With the lights of the village no help to them now, Finian produced the key-size flashlight he had with him, a lesson learned from previous walks up to the Murphy farm with his friend. Sean would never have a flashlight. He didn't need one on this land.

"I have a favor to ask, Fin," Sean said, still clearly preoccupied.

"Of course."

"Don't be too quick. There's only so much I can tell you, even as a priest."

"It's about an investigation, then."

Sean gave a curt nod.

"I'll do anything I can," Finian said. "You know I will."

Sean walked a few steps ahead, then stopped, a dark silhouette against the shadows of the night as he turned to Finian. "This you won't want to do."

Finian heard a sheep close by, near a fence. "Let me be the one to decide. What do you need?"

"A name," Sean said. "I need a name."

Two

A ewe cried out in distress just before dawn. Finian went out to the barn with Sean and helped deliver a healthy lamb. With mother and baby safe and warm, Finian followed his friend back to the farmhouse, grinning as he hung his coat on a hook. "I hope I didn't misunderstand and this is the work God called me to do."

Sean laughed. "Farm work, Fin? Delivering lambs at dawn? I don't think so."

The kitchen was cool, a dampness in the air, but Sean got a turf fire going in the old fireplace and it was soon warm enough. Finian sat at the pine table. He'd jumped into jeans and a wool shirt. No clerical suit for working in the barn.

Sean put the kettle on to boil. "A full Irish breakfast this morning, Fin?"

"Perfect."

Sean set to work, and Finian's mind drifted, as it sometimes still did. He could see his fair-haired, beautiful wife, and he could hear her laughter when, years ago, facing the uncertainties of business, he'd wondered aloud if he should be a farmer.

"You a farmer? Oh, Fin. That's just so funny."

"We were farmers as boys. Declan and I."

"And now you're whiskey men."

He and Sally had been enjoying a pint and traditional Irish music at a Kenmare pub. She was such fun—and so smart. A young marketing consultant who'd just finished a project for Bracken Distillers.

He'd fallen for her on the spot and asked her to marry him three months later. They'd been hiking in Killarney National Park. She'd said yes without hesitation and burst into tears and laughter as she'd hugged him so hard they both fell to the ground.

He'd been twenty-four. She'd been twenty-three.

Kathleen had been born the next year. Mary three years later.

My sweet girls.

Finian returned himself to the present. He smelled the turf fire, and he noticed the chipped paint on the old-fashioned dresser, the plates lined up on its open shelves, the crooked lower doors worn with age and use. He watched Sean drop tea bags into a brown pot and then fill the pot with the hot water. His garda friend looked at ease, totally natural, in his torn flannel shirt and muddy work pants. Maybe at heart he was a farmer after all, meant for a life out here on Shepherd Head instead of the occasional few days off to help his uncle.

Sean Murphy had been a young, ambitious garda when he'd located Finian in his office at the old distillery he and Declan had returned to life, just outside Killarney. An important business matter had come up and Sally and the girls had started their sailing holiday without him. He would join them at their first stop that evening. He hadn't been enthusiastic about sailing, but Sally had thought it would be a grand adventure for them and the girls.

It was Garda Murphy who'd told Finian his wife and daughters were dead.

And who'd suspected him of having killed them.

It wasn't as full an Irish breakfast as Sean had promised because, it turned out, the tomatoes had spoiled. Finian didn't mind, but Sean shook his head and sighed. "I miss my grilled tomatoes."

He was only half joking. Finian poured more tea. "Next time."

"I think the rotten ones are from the last time I was down. Paddy doesn't stay up here as much. He's thinking about converting this place into a bed-and-breakfast or a holiday home. Can you imagine?"

"You could book it to people wanting an authentic Irish experience," Finian said with a smile.

Paddy Murphy, Sean's uncle, had been born in the simple farmhouse and had lived there until just a few months ago, when he'd moved into an apartment in the village. He was in his seventies, a longtime widower with no children. Sean's father was gone now, too. Sean wasn't a big talker, but Finian had pieced together the Murphy family story over a pint or a glass of whiskey. Finian's heavy-drinking days were in the past, and Sean had never been one for overimbibing. He was a driven man but one of great control.

Yet Finian could see that something was eating at his friend. It had to be this investigation. This favor. This name he wanted. He'd gone up to bed last night without telling Finian more. Finian had slept in a small bedroom off the kitchen, the barn just out back. Nonetheless, Sean had heard the distressed ewe first—a farmer's instincts or, more likely, an intercom system between the barn and his bedroom.

"You didn't invite me here to help with the sheep," Finian said finally.

"That would be the day, wouldn't it? You might have grown up on a farm, but that didn't make you a farmer."

"Nor did it make you one, Sean." Finian picked at the last of his grilled mushrooms. He'd had more of an appetite than he'd expected. Helping birth a lamb must have contributed. "You asked me here because of this name you want. Tell me more. If I can help, I will."

Sean settled back in his chair. "I'm looking for a man who's been in touch with you. Not as a priest. As a Bracken."

"I'm always a priest, Sean."

"I know that. I mean this man worked for Bracken Distillers."

"Ah. I see. He doesn't work for us any longer?"

"I don't think so. He contacted me a few days ago but wouldn't give me his name. He'd said he'd call again, but he didn't."

"Why don't you ask Declan about him?"

Sean scratched the side of his mouth. "It's not that simple." He leaned forward over the table. "This man called me because he knew you and I were friends. He sought you out because you're a Bracken and for no other reason. What did he tell you?"

"I haven't said I know the man you're talking about."

"But you do."

He did, indeed. Becan Kennedy was an itinerant carpenter who had done small jobs at the distillery over the winter and then moved on. Last week, Finian had stopped at the distillery, in his priest's garb. Becan had stopped by to do a few small touch-ups on a project he'd finished in February. He'd pulled him aside and asked to talk to him, in confidence.

They'd walked down to a field and old shed out behind the main distillery buildings. Becan had explained he was mixed up with "a bad lot" and deeply troubled by "some things" he knew. He didn't want to go to prison. He didn't want to anger his unsavory friends. He didn't want to get in deeper with them. Finian had encouraged him to get in touch with the proper authorities without delay.

Becan had said, *"I hear you know a detective in Dublin. Sean Murphy. Do you trust him?"*

"With my life, Becan. And so can you."

Finian hadn't seen Becan Kennedy since and didn't know where to find him—and he couldn't give Sean his name.

"You want to find this man," Finian said, "but you don't know who he is. Would it help if I encouraged him to contact you again?"

Sean got up from the table, shaking his head as if just realizing the implications of what his friend was saying. "No, Fin. Don't go to him yourself."

"If he comes to me?"

"Would he?"

Finian shrugged without answering. It was possible if not probable.

Sean rummaged on the dresser, produced an index card and a black marker and jotted down a string of numbers. He handed the card to Finian. "If he comes to you, give him this number. No one but me has it. Tell him to call me. Tell him nothing else."

"You know more than you're saying, aren't you?"

He pointed to the card. "*Only* if he comes to you, Fin. I mean it."

Finian looked out a window, across a sloping lawn and fields turning green to the sea. The sun was up now, burning off the morning mist. His throat tightened. He was certain of his call to the priesthood and the vows he had professed at his ordination. But Ireland…being a priest here…

He couldn't deny the truth. Everywhere were reminders of his loss. Of the man he'd been and was no more. Husband, lover, father, businessman.

"You'll be leaving Declan's Cross this morning?" Sean asked.

Finian nodded, turning from the window. "You?"

"Back to Dublin for me."

A dozen questions about why Sean Murphy was looking for Becan Kennedy rose up in Finian's mind, but he didn't ask even one of them as he saw his friend off to the barn and then headed out to his car.

Father Callaghan would still be at the O'Byrne House Hotel, enjoying his last days in Ireland. Given his melancholy mood, Finian wouldn't disturb the older priest, but he knew what he would do after he left Declan's Cross.

This tiny village, the O'Byrne House Hotel, Father Callaghan, Sean, the sheep….Becan Kennedy. All of it, somehow, was providential. Finian felt that truth deep inside him.

As soon as he could, he would get in touch with his bishop and talk to him about spending a year in Rock Point, Maine.

Three

Spring blossomed across Ireland, and it was done—Finian would leave in June to serve Saint Patrick's Church in Rock Point, Maine.

Joseph Callaghan would get his year in Ireland.

The next weeks flew by, and finally June was upon him. Finian spent his last few days in Ireland with his brother and his family at their home in the hills outside Killarney. He'd emailed Sean Murphy about Maine, receiving back only a terse "And you think Irish winters are bad."

Finian hadn't seen Sean since their visit in Declan's Cross in March, but he'd kept watch for stories on special criminal investigations. He hadn't noticed any that suggested Sean Murphy's or Becan Kennedy's involvement. Finian had been tempted to contact Becan, but he'd heeded Sean's advice—Garda advice—and focused instead on his preparations for his temporary move to Rock Point.

Until the morning before his departure to America when he received a cryptic text message that could only be from Becan Kennedy.

Becan wanted to meet.

* * *

Early the next morning, on his final day in Ireland before his year in Maine, Finian dragged Declan out to Old Kenmare Road, a trail that ran through mixed terrain between Torc Waterfall and the attractive market village of Kenmare. Declan's wife, Fidelma, and their children—two boys and a girl under the age of ten—dropped them off at the abandoned church near Ladies View, where Queen Victoria's ladies-in-waiting had admired the stunning views of the lakes of Killarney in 1861.

Finian paused and looked across the sunlit hills, tufts of white clouds floating high above Kenmare Bay in the distance. How could he last a year without seeing this place?

Yet he had to leave. Nothing was the same since the deaths of Sally and the girls, and yet everything was the same, but he knew that was only part of it. He was meant to be in Rock Point. He could feel that truth more than he could explain it.

"Ah, Fin, what a day," Declan said next to him. "We'll miss you, but you'll be back."

"I will."

His brother—so like him, so different from him—drank from his water bottle. Declan, too, looked out at the hills and the sweep of the barren hills and glens. "I don't feel abandoned," he said as he returned his water bottle to his pack. "You might be a priest now, but you've always been and always will be my brother."

"And you mine, Declan."

"No matter what madness we face in this life."

The bond between them had always been strong—as fraternal twins, as two brothers with three younger sisters, then as business partners.

Tilters at whiskey windmills, they'd called themselves in the early days.

They continued down the hill. The trail was narrower, rockier, even quieter. Finian felt the sun warm on the back of his neck. He'd dressed in hiking clothes. No need for the clerical suit out here. It told others who he was, but it didn't make the priest.

He imagined Sally's smile and amusement at the thought of him as a priest.

"Father Bracken... Oh, Fin, that's just delicious."

Seven years this summer since her death, and he thought of her and their daughters every day. How could he not?

Embracing grief, recovering from it, didn't mean forgetting.

Less and less did he let himself slide down into the dark hole of wishing the past could be different than it was. He had his regrets. They were a part of him now. If only he'd been with Sally and the girls that day. He didn't know enough about sailing to think he could have saved them, but at least he could have died with them.

At least they wouldn't have died without him.

A rogue wave it was, capsizing their small yacht.

Sean Murphy had explained several days after the tragedy. *"They went overboard, all three at once. They didn't stand a chance. They drowned, probably soon after. There were no other boats in the vicinity. The water was very cold. Hypothermia would have set in quickly even if they hadn't drowned."*

Drowned. Finian remembered trying to understand what that meant. He couldn't make sense of it. He'd been in his office at Bracken Distillers. He'd slept there, unable to go home. Divers had rescued the captain of the chartered yacht, but it was touch-and-go whether he would survive. Divers had also recovered the bodies of Finian's wife and daughters.

Gardai—led by Sean—were conducting a thorough investigation.

Sean knew he was under suspicion. Did he sabotage the small yacht? Hire someone who did?

"The captain is recovering from a head injury and hypothermia," Sean had continued. *"He regained consciousness and explained what happened. He tried to save your wife and daughters. They wore life vests, but they didn't help in this situation, at least not enough."*

"Then it was an accident? There's no question of anything else?"

Sean—Garda Murphy—had paused, leveled his gaze on Finian. *"We have no reason to suspect it was anything else."*

"Where are they now? Sally...Kathleen, Mary?"

"Their remains will be released to you. I'm very sorry for your loss, Mr. Bracken."

The investigation continued, and the sinking of the yacht was deemed an accident. A terrible, unforgiving accident that had resulted in three deaths. The captain left Ireland for Australia soon after, but he'd died of natural causes a year ago. He'd blamed himself for the tragedy, although no one else did. He and Finian had never met, never talked. After all, what was there to say?

Finian realized he had sped up his pace to a near-manic level. He stopped, letting his brother catch up with him. A soft breeze floated down from the hills, and Finian told himself he would remember its smell when he was in Maine. Remember its coolness on his face and its murmur among the rocks, fields, streams and knots of trees and shrubs.

"We've had our share of madness in our almost forty

years on this planet," Finian said, referring to Declan's earlier comment. He and his brother were like this— able to pick up conversations minutes, days, months after they'd started. "You've never said as much but you think it's madness that I'm a priest."

"Not madness, exactly." They walked a little ways, not another soul in sight, before Declan continued. "I worry you're running from your past."

"In becoming a priest or taking this church in Maine?"

"Both. I don't question that God called you to a different life. I question your interpretation of this call."

"I told Sean Murphy that maybe God meant for me to be a sheep farmer."

Declan managed a small smile. "That would be a sight. I see you in this Maine fishing village before I see you back on a farm. It never suited you."

"I helped Sean birth a lamb."

"Dear God."

They continued in comfortable silence. Declan, Finian knew, hadn't expected a response to his worries. He would speak his mind and let Finian decide what to do. It had always been that way between them. They'd worked side by side in the competitive world of international whiskey, brainstorming, arguing, laughing at setbacks and successes alike. They'd been tireless. Pragmatic when they had to be. Dreamers always.

Kenmare Bay was closer now, as blue as the sky.

"What a day, Declan," Finian said.

His brother smiled. "Yes. What a day."

Houses appeared on the lane, and soon Fidelma and the children greeted them in the village. The little ones hugged their father. They wanted ice cream.

"You'll join us, won't you, Fin?" pretty, red-haired Fidelma asked him.

"Of course."

They walked to a small ice-cream shop and bought cones made with local cream. Chocolate chip for Finian. They all headed down to Reenagross Park together, laughing, chatting, as if Finian weren't off to America tomorrow.

A hired car would meet him outside the park. He didn't want their goodbyes to be at the airport but here, in Kenmare, having ice cream together. "We'll come see you in Maine," Fidelma whispered, tears in her eyes, as she and Finian embraced. "Fin, my God… I've been thinking about Sally and the girls all day. I miss them so much. I always will." She stood back, tears streaming down her cheeks now. "I'm sorry. I shouldn't have said anything."

"It's all right, Fidelma. I miss them, too."

"It's part of the reason you're leaving us now, though, isn't it? You're not just escaping memories. You're escaping all of us, too. Our lives. Watching our three grow up while yours…"

"While Kathleen and Mary stay forever little girls," Finian said, finishing for her.

She went pale and whispered, "Pay no attention to me, Fin."

He hugged her close. "God be with you, Fidelma. I'm not escaping from my life here, and I'll come home. I promise."

Declan opened the door of the waiting car for his twin brother. *"Feck,"* he said, as only an Irishman could. "I hate goodbyes. We'll see you soon, Fin. Godspeed."

As he climbed into the car, Finian held back tears of his own. On their twenty-second birthday, he and Declan had taken a long hike in the Kerry hills and ended up deciding to go into the whiskey business. They'd built Bracken Distillers and made it a success against the odds—against the wise advice of most commonsense people they knew.

Now Finian had a different calling.

Declan would continue with the whiskey business they both loved, and Finian would spend the next year serving the people of little Rock Point, Maine.

Four

Finian had the car stop at Bracken Distillers, located in a restored seventeenth-century distillery just outside Killarney. He asked the driver to wait for him. Instead of going into the main building, Finian walked around to the back, then down a hill to a roofless stone shed he and Declan often talked about turning into a health club for employees. This was where, in March, Finian had walked with Becan Kennedy. Finian had assumed Becan, a carpenter who'd worked on many old buildings, had wanted to give his opinion on the shed's potential as a health club, but that notion had soon been dismissed.

Becan had requested Finian meet him in the same spot.

The partial walls and foundation of the old shed were covered in vines and moss, shaded by an oak tree. Becan eased out from behind the remains of the stone chimney. He was a thin, nervous man, no more than forty himself, in terrible shape despite his work as a carpenter. He had sagging, pallid skin and watery blue eyes that didn't connote midnight romances or quiet seas but, rather, a tormented soul. He wore nondescript jeans and a colorless T-shirt, and his trail shoes were crusty with dried mud. Finian hadn't changed back into his clerical suit—

he would in the morning, before his flight—but Becan recognized him from his work at the distillery, before Sean Murphy had invited Finian to Declan's Cross.

Without Becan Kennedy, Finian thought, he wouldn't have been at the O'Byrne House Hotel in March and met Father Callaghan, and he wouldn't be on his way to Maine.

"I was named for a saint," Becan said, tossing a cigarette into the mud.

Finian nodded. "So was I. There are a number of Irish saints named Finian, but the one I'm named for served here in the southwest. Do you know about Saint Becan?"

"He was a better man than I, no doubt."

"He founded a monastery in Kilbeggan."

Becan shifted from one foot to another; he was restless, distracted. "I only know Kilbeggan whiskey," he said with a snort.

"Saint Becan lived in the sixth century—at least a century after Saint Patrick." Finian kept his voice steady, hoping to ease the younger man's nervousness. "He was a religious hermit."

"Some days I'd like to be a hermit," Becan said. "Just skip the religious part."

"Why did you ask me here, Becan?"

He gave a crooked grin. "Not to discuss a lap pool in back of the health club. You know the guards are after me, don't you?"

The guards. Gardai. The Irish police. A certain detective Finian knew would want to be here now, and wouldn't be happy that his friend had come to meet Becan Kennedy alone.

Finian made no response. He felt his hike with his brother in the backs of his legs. He was in good shape but nonetheless hoped the exercise would help him sleep on the flight tomorrow.

"I talked to your detective friend in March," Becan said. "He tried to get you to give him my name, didn't he? But you didn't. You're a priest. You can't."

"What I'm wondering, Becan, is why *you* don't tell the guards who you are. They can help you."

Becan withdrew a pack of cigarettes from a back pocket. "You were decent to me." He tapped out a cigarette and pointed it at Finian. "You understand that men make mistakes."

"Spiritually or—"

"All kinds." He was nervous, fidgety, his eyes not meeting Finian's as he spoke. "I'm afraid, Father."

"Not of the guards," Finian said.

"Maybe. I don't know. I told your garda friend some things, about what I'm into. Then I got scared. I don't know what to do, Father. I don't trust anyone—except you."

"Did you come here alone?"

"Yeah, sure. Who'd come with me, you know? To see a priest?"

Finian had no answer for that question. "You didn't invite anyone else to join us?"

"God, no. Not the lot I'm with."

"And no one followed you?"

Becan stuck his cigarette on his lip and dug out a lighter. "No one followed me," he said under his breath, lighting his cigarette. "I didn't need that thought running in my head, you know, Father?"

"It was already there, though, wasn't it, Becan?"

He took a deep drag of his cigarette and blew the smoke off to the side, away from Finian. "I suppose you're right. I'm glad you're here, Father. Thanks for coming. I didn't want to involve you…" He waved his burning cigarette. "But here we are."

"What can I do for you, Becan?"

"I wish I'd stuck to carpentry work." He glanced at the

shed with an air of regret mixed with resignation. "But I didn't, did I? I got into things I wish I hadn't. I was almost hoping the guards followed you here."

"I understand," Finian said.

Becan threw down his partially smoked cigarette and ground it out with his heel. "You don't know we used this back field for one of our operations, do you?"

"What 'operation,' Becan?"

"Smuggling."

"Whiskey smuggling?"

"Whiskey, cigarettes, pills, counterfeit money. Not hard drugs or guns. Your brother doesn't know. No one here does. We didn't come onto distillery grounds, because of the security. We used the field." He nodded down past the shed to a quiet field outside of the grounds but owned by Bracken Distillers. "It's a good spot. You'd be surprised."

"I am surprised," Finian said.

"We distributed goods out across Ireland from here," Becan said. "I think the guards are on to us. I want out, Father. I want to tell the truth. That's all."

Finian reached into the pocket of his hiking pants and withdrew the card that Sean had given him in March. "It's Sean Murphy's number. He said to give it to you in case you contacted me. No one else has it. Only he will answer."

Becan seemed ready to bolt but snatched the card and tucked it into a pocket in his jeans. He sniffled. "The guards are watching us. We're watching them. It's a dangerous situation."

"You can make the call now, Becan. I'll wait."

"I need to think. I just don't know..." He shifted abruptly. "I have to go. You won't tell anyone about me. The guards. Anyone. Right, Father?"

"That's right. There's a time and place for each of us

to speak and for each of us to keep silent. You need to speak, my friend. Call the number I gave you."

Becan said nothing as he shuffled back to the old shed and disappeared.

Finian returned to his waiting car. He'd done what he could. His next stop was his hotel ahead of his flight out of Shannon Airport tomorrow.

He looked out the window as the refurbished distillery—his and Declan's dream come true—faded from sight. He remembered a warm June day like this one when Sally had greeted him at the gate after a walk out past the fields, sweaty, smiling as she'd leaned into him. *Let's go home early, Fin. I can't wait another minute to get your clothes off you.*

He could see her in the milky light of the endless June dusk as they'd made love.

He hadn't been a different man then. He'd been the same man he was now. To pretend otherwise—to try to make it not so—was to deny this life he'd been given, and the truth of who he was.

Suddenly he couldn't wait to be in Maine.

His hotel had dreadful food but a surprisingly decent selection of whiskey. No Bracken Distillers expressions, but Finian ordered an excellent Kilbeggan to take some of the edge off his soggy fish-and-chips. He'd ordered them before he remembered Rock Point was a fishing village and would presumably have restaurants that served proper fish-and-chips when the occasional urge struck.

He followed his bad fish-and-chips with a delicious bread-and-butter pudding. He doubted he'd eat much, if anything, on the plane tomorrow. He could excuse, or at least rationalize, the rich meal and hoped it would help him sleep tonight.

He was savoring the last bite of his pudding when Sean

Murphy slid into the booth across from him. Sean had a devil-may-care look about him at the same time as the air of a professional law enforcement officer—an uneasy combination that no doubt he used to great advantage.

Sean leaned back against the cushioned booth. "Your friend called."

"I have many friends, Sean," Finian said.

"Did you ask to meet him or did he ask to meet you?"

"Does it matter now?"

Sean's eyes narrowed. "Either way, Fin, you're playing with fire."

"I'm not playing with anything. I'm flying to Boston tomorrow." He abandoned his pudding and drank some of his whiskey. "Do you and your garda associates have Bracken Distillers under surveillance?"

"For what?"

"That implies you do, and there could be multiple reasons."

"It doesn't imply anything. Practically speaking, we'd have to have good reason to put anyone under surveillance. Do we, Fin? Do we have good reason to investigate Bracken Distillers?"

"You're a suspicious man, Detective Garda. You'd suspect your own sheep of wrongdoing if you discovered one of your fields was being used behind your back for untoward purposes."

Sean barely smiled. "No doubt I would. Blasted sheep."

Finian left it at that and sighed. "You're in danger, aren't you, Sean?"

"Comes with the territory." Sean's smile was genuine now. "Relax, Fin. Enjoy your flight tomorrow. Come back and see us soon, and stay in touch."

He didn't linger, and Finian sensed the seriousness behind his friend's easy manner.

"Be careful, Sean."

"No worries, my friend. No worries at all."

Finian had time for a breakfast that was worse than his fish-and-chips before he had to be at the airport. It wasn't really close enough to walk to the terminal, but he walked anyway. His luggage was no trouble at all. He'd always been a light packer, even before he'd become a priest.

"I have cousins in America, Fin. We should visit them one day."

"We will, Sally. We will."

"They're in New York and Savannah. They say Savannah is beautiful in early spring."

Finian shook off the image of his sweet wife lying in bed next to him on a warm summer night as they'd dreamed of their future together, whispering about trips to far-off places. She'd never worried when he traveled, and traveled often herself. They'd staggered their trips after the girls arrived, but had found themselves more and more reluctant to leave home, especially alone.

Finian entered the terminal. He wasn't a whiskey man now. He was a priest, on his way to serve a small parish in America. He looked up at the board to check the number of the appropriate Aer Lingus counter at which to drop off his luggage and collect his boarding pass.

Out of the corner of his eye, he noticed two men standing together in the wide, open doorway of a shop, next to a table piled with books.

Finian thought they were watching him but couldn't be sure.

He looked straight at them, but they turned away. Middle-aged, average size, dressed in casual clothes that wouldn't draw attention. No luggage. No air of urgency about catching a flight.

Gardai?

Becan Kennedy's cronies?

Finian ignored them and wheeled his luggage to the correct line. He was out of his mind, thinking they had anything to do with Sean's investigation—and if they did, they'd have to be crazy to try anything at a highly secure airport.

Was he half hoping they'd cause a commotion so he'd have an excuse not to board his flight?

After he checked his bag and got his boarding pass, he spotted the two men behind him on the escalator up to the gates. He pretended to check messages on his phone and snapped their photo as he stepped off the escalator.

In two seconds their image was off to Sean Murphy.

As Finian stepped into the security line, he noticed that the two men had disappeared. He'd missed them entirely and had no idea where they'd gone. He stepped into the duty-free shop and had a look at the whiskey offerings, including a nice display of moderately priced Bracken Distillers expressions.

He'd just paid for a bottle of water and was on his way into the lounge when Sean Murphy texted him, typically terse:

"If you see them again, notify security at once. Safe travels."

So the men weren't gardai, anyway.

Finian texted Sean an equally terse response, just as an announcement came over the loudspeaker that his flight to Boston would soon be boarding. His heart jumped as he realized he was officially on his way to America.

Five

Rock Point, Maine, was just as Father Callaghan had described. A bit run-down and struggling but located on a beautiful stretch of the northern New England coast. Finian had a car—not a parishioner or another priest—pick him up at the airport in Boston and then drop him off on the quiet street above the harbor where St. Patrick's Church and rectory stood side by side, sharing a lawn that was freshly cut but appeared to be mostly weeds. Father Callaghan had explained that the rectory was a Greek Revival house "due for a facelift," and the church was a granite-faced building that had originally been an American Baptist church.

Finian appreciated the mature shade trees as he carried his luggage to the back steps of the rectory. It was a warm, sunny afternoon, late in the day—even later if he considered that Ireland was five hours ahead. He'd slept little on his flight, but he'd be foolish to try to sleep now. Best to get on Maine time as soon as possible.

He left his luggage on the back steps and walked down to the village. He observed a bank, hair salon, pharmacy, liquor store, hardware store, insurance business—if not thriving, Rock Point was holding its own. He crossed the main street to a restaurant, Hurley's, a rough-wood building set on pilings and jutting out over the horseshoe-shaped harbor. High tide would reach under its floorboards. The harbor itself was crowded with working boats and a handful of pleasure boats, all bobbing in gentle waves.

Only when he walked past Hurley's down to the waterfront did Finian realize he'd been so caught up in taking in his new home he hadn't experienced his usual gut-twisting reaction at seeing sailboats.

It was a start, anyway, but as he walked out onto a pier, he felt the rush of excitement at arriving in Rock Point fade and melancholy creep in. He stood next to a stack of rectangular wire cages that smelled of dead things. It was low tide, which brought out more dead smells.

In his mind's eye, he could see the green of Ireland.

"They're lobster traps," a man at the end of the pier said, turning, giving Finian and his priest's garb a quick scan.

The American was solidly built, with dark hair, small scars on his eye and cheek and perhaps the most penetrating gray eyes Finian had ever seen. He wore a gray sweatshirt, jeans and trail shoes. A local man? Yes and no, perhaps.

"I'm not much of a fisherman," Finian said.

"Me, either, these days. You're the new priest at Saint Patrick's?"

"I am, yes. Finian Bracken."

"Colin Donovan. I'd heard we were getting an Irishman. My folks are members. I'm not much of a church-goer."

"Easter and Christmas?"

"Funerals and weddings. When I can. I'm not in town that often."

"But you live here?" Finian asked.

He shrugged. "I have a place a few blocks from the church, but I work in Washington."

"For the government?"

"I'm with the Federal Bureau of Investigation."

The FBI, then. The words seemed to come with difficulty, as if he wasn't used to identifying himself to strangers, at least not in his hometown. He was good-looking in a rugged way. Blunt. Physical. A man's man.

Finian wondered if Colin Donovan wasn't as removed from the church of his youth as he perhaps thought he was. But it didn't matter. Finian wasn't that kind of priest.

"Home for a few days, are you?" he asked the American.

"I am." Colin looked out at the water and bobbing boats. "It's good to get away from Washington for a few days."

Finian suspected the statement was true as far as it went and no further. "I haven't settled in yet. Where can I get a bite?"

"There." Colin nodded to the rustic restaurant on the water. "Hurley's. It's a local favorite. The clam chowder is good, but if you want anything fancier, you'll have to go into Heron's Cove."

"Hurley's sounds perfect. What should I call you?"

"Colin's fine, Father."

"Finian, or Fin, if you'd like."

Colin seemed to relax somewhat, but he struck Finian as raw, hyperaware of his surroundings, reminding him of Sean Murphy. Finian doubted the FBI agent was as convivial as Sean by nature—not that Sean had been particularly convivial last night at the hotel restaurant, or this morning in his texted reply, or, for that matter, in March during Finian's last visit to Declan's Cross.

Finian considered getting Colin's take on Becan Kennedy and the two men at Shannon airport, but it would serve no purpose. He was in a different country now. Sean's investigation in Ireland, whatever it was, whatever dangers he faced, wasn't for an Irish priest on a yearlong stay in a small town in southern Maine to sort out.

"Something on your mind, Father?" Colin asked him.

He pulled himself out of his wandering thoughts and smiled. "Whiskey."

For the first time, Colin offered a glimmer of a smile and warmth in return. "My kind of priest," he said.

"All things in moderation, even whiskey. Perhaps especially whiskey."

"Caution duly noted. Hurley's has a lousy selection, but maybe I'll see you there later."

With that, the FBI agent abruptly headed off the pier.

An interesting man, Finian thought, wondering if the good Father Callaghan had left any notes on the Donovans of Rock Point, Maine.

Finian arrived back at St. Patrick's to a welcome party in the recreation room. There was pie, coffee and well-wishes. In forty-five minutes everyone was gone, the place tidied and quiet. He wandered into the sanctuary. It had a foreign feel, despite all the requisite Roman Catholic accoutrements. The late-afternoon June sun streamed through a stained-glass window, adding a golden glow on the white walls, dark-wood pews and red carpet.

Father Callaghan had removed his personal items from the office, a small room off the side entrance. He'd left his books and files. A reader of Saint Augustine, the American was.

Finian locked the church behind him and walked over to the rectory. He carried his luggage into the worn kitchen and set it next to the table. Parishioners had left milk, bread, cheese, orange juice, a basket of fruit and a pie—wild blueberry, according to a handwritten note.

Ah, what would Sally think of him now?

He unzipped the outer compartment of his suitcase, an expensive black leather leftover from his days at Bracken Distillers. He withdrew a weathered case that contained a small antique hydrometer—a clever device that measured the alcohol content in spirits—and set it on the table next to the pie.

Then, with a whispered prayer, he withdrew two navy blue velvet pouches containing rosary beads a friend in Sneem had handmade for each of his daughters for their First Communion. He and Sally hadn't been particularly religious then, but they'd wanted to raise Kathleen and Mary in the church.

"Daddy, will you read me a story when we're on the boat?"

"I will, Kathleen."

Mary had piped up. *"Will you sing me a song?"*

He'd kept the rosary beads with him, but in seven years hadn't yet been able to take them from their velvet pouches.

Kathleen's were white glass, he remembered, and Mary's were pink glass.

He took the hydrometer and the pouches into the dining room and placed them in a glass-front cabinet.

The rectory was quiet, filled with late-day shadows and the faint odor of cleaning solution. It had obviously been scrubbed shortly before his arrival.

He bolted out of the dining room and left for Hurley's again. He walked, but he would have to see about a car. Father Callaghan had suggested leasing. Finian would look into it tomorrow. He was happy to have a restaurant within walking distance of the rectory—he wasn't a good cook and seldom drank alone anymore.

Hurley's was as simple and rustic inside as it was outside. He spotted Colin Donovan alone at a table in back, in front of windows overlooking the harbor, and told the waitress he was joining a friend. A stretch, perhaps, but he made his way past tables of locals and tourists—he'd spent enough time in Killarney to spot such a mix—dining on lobster, chowder, coleslaw, fried fish and pie. Rock Point seemed to be a place for pie.

Colin had no lobster, chowder, fish or pie in front of him. He held up his glass and named the American whiskey he was drinking. Finian gave an inward shudder but obviously not inward enough, because the FBI agent smiled and said, "It's rotgut, I know. You're welcome to join me."

Finian sat at the wobbly round table. The long June day was finally giving up its light, the harbor waters glasslike in the red-gold twilight. He examined a printed, plastic-coated menu that listed the establishment's limited whiskey offerings. He chose an acceptable whiskey from Tennessee.

Colin leaned back in his chair. "A whiskey connoisseur, are you, Fin?"

"My brother and I have a distillery in Ireland."

"Bracken Distillers," the FBI agent said, then tilted forward on his chair. "The church ladies didn't tell me. Father Joseph did. We'll have to work on John Hurley and get him to improve his whiskey selection while you're in town."

Finian's whiskey arrived, complete with ice and water he hadn't requested. The waitress must have read his expression because she blushed and said, "I just assumed. I'll bring you another—"

"No worries. In this case, water and ice are appreciated."

He thought he saw Colin Donovan smile.

Finian eyed the whiskey's medium caramel color, then took a tentative sip. It really was quite decent, a smooth, full-bodied, single-barrel sour mash Tennessee whiskey. He regretted leaving in the ice and water. He raised his glass to his new American friend. *"Sláinte."*

Colin smiled. *"Sláinte."*

In the morning, Finian again found himself at Hurley's. He had today to get himself settled before he started his duties at Saint Patrick's. He thought nine was a perfectly respectable hour for breakfast but soon learned it was late by Rock Point standards. The lobstermen had long been out. Hurley's apparently renowned cider doughnuts were depleted. As he sat at his table of last night, Finian swore he could smell chowder. It was early afternoon at home in Ireland, so he was hungry and ordered eggs, toast, ham and grilled tomatoes.

His waitress was a hazel-eyed young woman with a thick dark braid hanging down her back. She frowned at him. "I'll see if we can grill a tomato, Father, but if I get tossed out of the kitchen, you'll know that didn't go over too well. We do tomatoes in omelets, though. No problem with that. They're not grilled, though. Just cut up."

"Good to know."

"No black pudding or white pudding," she added, then smiled at him. "I can tell you're Irish. The accent. I'm of Irish descent. I'd love to go to Ireland someday. I'm thinking about doing an internship there. I'm a student—I pick up hours here when I'm in town." She took a breath. "Anyway, I'll see what I can do. White or wheat?"

"White or wheat what?"

"Toast."

Of course. Finian smiled. "Wheat."

He ordered coffee. He wasn't ready to chance Hurley's idea of tea. His waitress bustled off, and Finian looked out at the glistening harbor. The working boats were mostly out to sea. A small sailboat was moored off to his left.

Why couldn't Father Callaghan have been from Montana?

Finian tried his coffee when his waitress plunked it in front of him. It was perfect. He relaxed, and in another moment his phone vibrated on the table next to him. Declan calling to see how his first full day in America was going?

Ah, no.

He saw it was Detective Garda. "Sean," Finian said. "How are you?"

"Your friend and I arranged to meet, but he didn't show up. Do you know where he is, Fin?"

"I don't, no."

"If you did, would you tell me?"

"Depends how I knew, but it's not worth discussing since I don't know. Do you think something's happened to him?"

"If not yet, soon."

"The number I gave to him—I'm the only one who has it? That's how you know for sure it was me who gave it to him, isn't it?"

Finian could almost see Sean's smile. "You're catching on, Fin."

"I shouldn't try to sort out what's true and what's not true, should I?"

"Your friend is playing a dangerous game. Whatever he's told you, whatever I've told you, that much is true."

Becan Kennedy. The name was on Finian's lips, but

he didn't say it. "Have you talked to my brother?" he asked instead.

Sean was silent for two beats. Then he said, "No, I haven't."

"I think he's checking on a painting job at the distillery. We often need this or that done. Short jobs that we hire out. We've been thinking about converting an old shed that was part of the original distillery into a health club. Imagine that. A couple of poor Kerry sheep farmers planning saunas and treadmills."

"I'll go see Declan, then." Sean added, "I've always liked him."

"Does that mean he's not a suspect?"

"A suspect in what, Fin?"

"One never knows."

"It's good you're in this Rock Point. Watch your back nonetheless."

Finian started to say goodbye when he realized that Sean had already disconnected. He set his phone back on the table.

His breakfast arrived.

No grilled tomatoes.

Six

It took most of the day to find a proper car to lease and fill out the paperwork, but Finian finally had a black BMW in his possession. He hadn't taken a vow of poverty, but he wasn't one to flaunt his wealth. Nevertheless, he'd driven a BMW in Ireland and appreciated its familiarity. The traffic even in Maine was daunting. He'd had a taste of Boston traffic when he'd arrived yesterday. A BMW seemed less of an indulgence under the circumstances.

He took it for a drive around southern Maine, checking out places like Orchard Beach, Wells, Kennebunkport and York before parking in front of a marina in Heron's Cove, an attractive classic Maine village just down the coast from Rock Point. He got out, welcomed the cool breeze blowing off the water with the rising tide. There were more pleasure boats here. He remembered a time when he'd been fascinated by yachts.

No more.

He walked up a street lined with pretty shops and large residences, most with front porches that looked out on the Atlantic. He saw porch swings, hammocks, wicker chairs, most empty despite the perfect June afternoon. Heron's Cove reminded him of reruns of *Murder, She*

Wrote, but he supposed Jessica Fletcher's Cabot Cove was actually in California.

He sat on a bench on a narrow strip of grass between street and ocean, the tide crashing on rocks below him. Cormorants dove. Seagulls wheeled. Off in the distance, he heard the laughter of children.

He dug out his phone and called Declan. "I had a lobster roll for lunch and the sun is shining. How is Ireland?"

"Raining," Declan said.

Finian knew it wasn't true. He had a weather app with Killarney listed among his "favorites." He stretched out his legs, barely aware he was in a black suit while passersby were in shorts and T-shirts. "I miss Ireland. It's funny how life pieces itself together, isn't it? The threads all connecting as they should."

"Or not, as the case may be. Sean Murphy rang me."

"Ah."

"He asked if I could help him find a contract worker, probably a painter or a carpenter. I couldn't think of anyone off the top of my head. I'm checking the records, but it's a needle in a haystack. I don't even have a name for him."

"Maybe you're not the one who dealt with him."

"It's unlikely I would have. Sean is your friend. Do you know what's going on, Fin?"

"Just do as Sean says and not one thing more."

"Fin? Is this contract worker dangerous?"

"Sean Murphy's looking for him, isn't he?"

After he and Declan disconnected, Finian phoned Sean but his friend didn't pick up. Finian left a message for him to call as soon as he could.

Humidity had built up through the day, but Finian welcomed it as he took a scenic coastal road back to Rock Point. It was rougher than Heron's Cove. He parked in front of the rectory and got out into the shade of what he'd already learned was a sugar maple.

He tried to reach Sean once again but got his voice mail. He left a message. "I've missed something, Sean. Call me."

Finian was back at Hurley's that evening. Colin Donovan was at the back table with a bottle of Maker's Mark. "A fine Kentucky bourbon," Finian said. "It's not on the menu. You brought it?"

"Worked it out with Hurley's. I thought you might turn up tonight."

"Thank you," Finian said.

"We'll have to try Bracken 15 year old some time. We have a peated and a nonpeated version."

"You've been busy."

Colin winked. "Always like to know who I'm drinking with." He had a plastic pitcher of water—no ice—and two glasses. He poured a bit of the bourbon into each glass and then handed one to Finian. "Two of my brothers are joining us. Kevin and Andy. There's a fourth brother. Mike. He's farther up the coast."

"Four Donovans."

"That's right." He grinned. "You'll get used to us."

In a short while, Kevin and Andy Donovan joined them at their table. They wore jeans and T-shirts. Kevin, the youngest brother, was a Maine state marine patrol officer. Andy, the third-born Donovan, was a lobsterman who also restored boats. All three brothers were gray-eyed and strongly built.

Colin fetched two more glasses and poured bourbon for his brothers. After just a few minutes, Finian was convinced the younger Donovans didn't believe their FBI-agent brother worked at a desk in Washington, either.

Kevin and Andy left early, wishing Finian well. Andy apparently was quite the ladies' man.

Finian settled comfortably at the table and ordered a bowl of clam chowder. Colin said he wasn't hungry but didn't seem in a hurry to leave. "Is there a woman in your life?" Finian asked him.

"That would be complicated."

"Because of the nature of your work," Finian said. "You'll be leaving again soon?"

The FBI mask dropped in place. Colin ran a fingertip along the rim of his glass. "If anything happens to me, Fin, take care of my folks. My father's a retired town police officer. He'll understand. My mother won't."

"I will, of course, Colin."

He looked up then and grinned. "But nothing will happen. I'll be back in Rock Point in no time."

Finian saw it then, why this man was here—why he kept coming back. "You need Rock Point to remind you that you still have a life."

The comment seemed to catch Colin off guard. "Funny, that's what I tell myself, too." He raised his glass again. "You're a wise man, Father Fin."

Father Fin. He would have to put a stop to that before it took hold.

His chowder arrived, steaming, thick with clams and potatoes. He tasted it. It was truly excellent. A good bourbon. Good chowder. New friends. Life in Rock Point was getting better.

"How do you navigate between what you can do and what you shouldn't do but know would help?" Finian asked.

Colin shrugged. "There's always a way."

His matter-of-fact response didn't match the serious look in his eyes. He stood apart from his friends and his hometown, Finian thought, but Colin Donovan needed Rock Point.

As I do.

As he'd said to Detective Garda, he now said to Special Agent Donovan. "Be careful, my friend."

Colin grinned at him. "Careful is for accountants, Fin. I just get the job done."

Alone, back at the rectory, Finian sat with a stack of files Father Callaghan had left for him in the living room to help him understand his small parish. Finian remembered the older priest that March evening at the O'Byrne House Hotel in Declan's Cross.

"Sometimes you're the first one to know something. Sometimes you're the last one to know. Sometimes you're the only one to know."

He'd been thinking he was the only one who knew Becan Kennedy had talked to him about his misgivings about what he was involved with.

What if he was wrong?

What if Becan's criminal associates—these smugglers—also knew? What if they'd been watching Becan, waiting to see if he'd betrayed their trust?

Finian leaped to his feet, his heart racing. The smugglers could easily figure out he and Sean Murphy were friends, although they wouldn't necessarily know Sean was investigating *them*...

"Now they do," Finian said aloud, his jaw clenched with tension.

He could see it all. Becan meeting him at the old distillery shed. Finian giving Becan the card with Sean's number.

Becan's associates finding out he and Finian had met.

Then following Finian to see what he would do. Those had been the men at the airport in Shannon. Smugglers.

Becan Kennedy was in extreme danger, and so was Sean Murphy.

"They're walking into a trap."

Finian raked a hand through this hair and forced himself to settle down. Becan knew what sort he was dealing with. So did Sean, who was an experienced detective with a capable team behind him.

What had can-do Colin Donovan said?

"There's always a way."

Still on his feet, Finian phoned Sean, but again got his voice mail. He left a message: "The men who followed me in Shannon know our friend contacted you. They're after him—and they're after you, Sean. Be careful."

Seven

Finian was still awake at eleven when Becan Kennedy called. It was four in the morning in Ireland. Becan's voice was ragged, hoarse. "They're going to kill me, Father. They know I've talked to the guards."

Finian switched on a side-table lamp. "Where are you now, Becan?"

"The shed behind Bracken Distillers. Where we met the other day. It's dark. We were supposed to meet for a drop, but there's not a soul here but me. They're coming to kill me. I know they are."

"Get out of there, Becan. Now. At once. There's a Garda station—"

Becan cut him off. "I'm scared to death, Father. I'm caught in the middle. The guards will arrest me, and my friends will be mad at me."

"Your friends won't just be mad at you, lad. You said it yourself—they'll kill you." Finian got out of bed, standing on a threadbare rug in the milky light of the simple bedroom. "I can't help you from Maine."

"They're here," Becan said, his voice lowered, hushed with terror. "Father…"

Finian could hear cursing in the background, but Becan disconnected without another word.

Wide awake, Finian rang Sean, who picked up immediately. "Fin, I'm at the distillery. I know your friend is Becan Kennedy. Where is he?"

"He's there, in the back field, by an old shed. His smuggling friends set him up. You, too. Sean, I don't know what to believe—"

"You don't have to know. Go back to bed, Fin. Don't call your brother or anyone else in Ireland. I'll be in touch."

"Are you alone? God in heaven, Sean—"

The connection was lost, or Sean had disconnected. Finian tossed his phone aside. He put on jeans and a sweatshirt and went downstairs.

He made coffee in his strange American kitchen. He knew he wouldn't sleep until he knew Becan's fate. Becan was a dead man if the smugglers got to him before Sean could. Finian had no question in his mind.

And if Sean did reach Becan first? Did he have backup?

What if the criminals he was after had outwitted him?

"Not possible," Finian said aloud, smelling the coffee as it brewed. "Just not possible."

It was hours before he heard.

Kitty O'Byrne Doyle rang him from Declan's Cross and gave him the news. "Sean's alive, thank God," she said, her voice hollow, her strain evident. "But he's in bits, Fin. Broken ribs, punctured lung, torn shoulder, cuts, bruises. They say it was an ambush."

"Any other deaths or injuries?"

"Not that I've heard. It's still an active investigation. They've broken up a smuggling ring. A nasty lot. A dozen arrested already." Her voice steadied. "The reports don't mention Sean by name, of course, but I know he was involved—I know that's how he was hurt."

"Will you go to see him?"

"No. I won't. I can't. Fin…"

"How did you find out?"

"His uncle—Paddy told me. I doubt he has the whole story, either."

Kitty wouldn't say it, but Fin knew: given the nature of Sean's work, it was unlikely any of them would ever know the whole story.

She added, "Paddy didn't want to be the one to phone you, but he said Sean told him to make sure you knew."

"I'll say a prayer for him, Kitty."

"You do that. Say one for his body to heal and another for him to get some blasted sense."

"You think this was his doing, then?"

"One way or the other, it was. I know it, Fin, and so do you. Sean's always thought he was invincible." Kitty sighed. "Maybe so did the rest of us."

Finian attempted words of comfort, but Kitty bounced back, suggested the best source for further updates would be Paddy or Sean himself.

He walked down to Hurley's, bustling although the sun wasn't yet up. He ran into lobstermen and fishermen carrying out coffees and doughnuts fresh from the kitchen, getting up from plates of eggs and bacon. One of them muttered he was having an egg-white omelet next time, and his friends roared with laughter.

Finian was suddenly starving. He sat alone at the back table in front of the harbor windows. He'd brought one of the folders of parish background materials that Father Callaghan had left behind in the rectory. It felt secret.

Finian would have to make sure no one looked over his shoulder when he opened it.

Worried, impatient, he ordered coffee and a cider doughnut. Just as they arrived, Sean phoned him from his hospital bed. "I'm in bits, Fin."

"That's what Kitty said."

"Kitty…ah, Kitty. Did she sound scared?"

"Annoyed. She says it's your fault you're hurt."

"That's my Kitty. Did I say 'my' Kitty? Blast, Fin. It's the drugs. I'm on morphine. I haven't gone completely mad." Sean paused, whether to picture pretty Kitty O'Byrne Doyle or merely to take a moment to cope with his pain, Fin didn't know. "Things didn't go as smoothly as I'd hoped, but all's well that ends well, right, Fin?"

"Becan Kennedy?"

"It is his real name, in fact. He didn't handle his end well, but he'd been on a razor wire for weeks—since he'd sought you out in March. He got cold feet when he talked to me. He thought he could extricate himself without our help."

"Had you been investigating these smugglers?"

"For a while, but we had nothing. What Becan told me in March pointed us in the right direction."

"Sean…the distillery…Declan…"

"In the clear. Not involved with the smuggling network. It was Becan's idea to use the back field a couple times in February and early March, but they moved on to other sites. It had nothing to do with Bracken Distillers."

"Thank God for that. The drop the other night—that was a ruse?"

"Yeah, Fin. A ruse. More like an ambush. They wanted Becan, and they wanted me."

"How did you get hurt?"

"The bastards grabbed Becan, and I got good thrashing saving him, but the worst, Fin—the worst of it came when I ducked a gunshot and fell in your blasted health club."

His health club. Finian could almost see Sean's devil-may-care smile, but he heard a grown of pain and suspected his friend's attempt at humor—this call—had cost him.

"I'll let you get some rest," Finian said. "I'm glad you're alive."

"It'll take another day or two before I'm glad of it."

A long recovery lay ahead. "Will you go to Declan's Cross to recuperate?"

"It would be a chance to further annoy Kitty," Sean said, but his voice was weak, then the connection was lost.

Finian didn't know if someone else clicked off the phone for his garda friend. He settled back in his chair and watched the sun come up over Rock Point harbor, the sky glowing with pinks and purples, a glorious June day ahead. He wondered where Colin Donovan was right now.

Not at a desk in Washington, for certain.

Finian opened the folder Father Callaghan had left him. Inside, right on top, was a newspaper clipping from the first week in June—just before Finian's arrival in Rock Point. He scanned the article, which featured the arrest of a notorious arms trafficker, a wealthy Russian, Viktor Bulgov, at the auction of a Picasso painting in Los Angeles.

"Sources say Bulgov leaves behind a trail of bodies…"

Finian flipped to the next page in the folder. This time it was a printout of a news article on the internet, with a photograph of Viktor Bulgov at a hotel in Los Angeles. He was a handsome middle-aged man in a well-tailored suit. The report hinted that an intensive federal undercover operation had led to Bulgov's arrest at the art auction. He was now in FBI custody.

Finian closed the folder and ordered another doughnut. So this was what his new American friend's work was. Colin Donovan was an undercover FBI agent.

Undoubtedly he'd dived back into his undercover role to tie up loose ends with the Russian's colleagues.

Despite his lack of sleep and his night of waiting and pacing, he felt surprisingly energized. Colin Donovan and Sean Murphy were very different men but both had tough, dangerous jobs—and Finian could see that part of his role as a priest was to be their spiritual advisor, but, most of all, he was their friend.

His doughnut arrived warm from the oven, sprinkled with cinnamon sugar. Pure heaven, he thought with a smile, ready to begin his first full day serving the people of Rock Point, Maine.

He looked out at the harbor, as lobster boats puttered out into the sunrise, and he knew that whatever trials and doubts lay ahead, he was where he was meant to be.

* * * * *